CRITICS RAVE ABOUT
L. H. MAYNARD AND M. P. N. SIMS!

"Maynard and Sims write with a voice that is both uniquely entertaining and profoundly disturbing. Their fiction reflects classic old-school style themes told with a decidedly modern perspective."

—Brian Keene, author of *Dead Sea*

"Maynard and Sims make readers accept terrible denizens from nightmare as casual fact."

—*Cemetery Dance*

"Maynard and Sims write with a fluid graceful style and know how to involve the reader in their story."

—Masters of Terror

"Reminiscent of the work of Ramsey Campbell."

—Gothic Net

"Maynard and Sims know what makes a horror story tick."

—*Shivers*

"WHAT'S HAPPENING," SHE SAID, HER VOICE TREMULOUS.

He ignored her as he continued to prepare his body for what was to come. Eventually he was ready. He stretched out a hand and ran it down the length of her body, feeling the goose bumps as they rose up on her skin. The hand paused for a moment on one of Anna's breasts, letting the nipple harden slightly under its touch, then moved on, stroking between her thighs, easing her legs apart.

"Let me see you," Anna said, feeling her body responding to the touch. "Please, let me see you."

There was the throaty chuckle of someone enjoying a huge joke at her expense. It was a horrible sound, barely human and she immediately regretted her request. Suddenly she didn't want to see who was in the room with her. And as she felt a sharp fingernail lift the edge of the tape covering her eyes she jerked her head back. But there was nowhere for it to go, and with a sudden, sharp tug the tape was peeled away from her eyes.

For a moment there was stillness and silence in the room. She had her eyes tightly closed, too frightened to open them.

Finally, she took a deep breath and opened her eyes wide, and for a second, just a second, thought she was alone in the room. Then she focused on the figure towering over the end of the bed, her eyes drinking in every detail, relaying the image to a brain that could barely comprehend what her eyes were seeing. Then the figure at the end of the bed moved toward her and she started to scream....

Other *Leisure* books by L. H. Maynard
and M. P. N. Sims:

SHELTER

DEMON EYES

L. H. MAYNARD
&
M. P. N. SIMS

LEISURE BOOKS   NEW YORK CITY

To Clare and Emily, with love.
And to Iain, Shara, Chris and Mum, with love.

A LEISURE BOOK®

December 2007

Published by

Dorchester Publishing Co., Inc.
200 Madison Avenue
New York, NY 10016

ISBN 10: 0-8439-5972-X
ISBN 13: 978-0-8439-5972-7

The name "Leisure Books" and the stylized "L" with design are trademarks of Dorchester Publishing Co., Inc.

Printed in the United States of America.

10 9 8 7 6 5 4 3 2 1

Visit us on the web at www.dorchesterpub.com.

ACKNOWLEDGEMENTS

Several people have helped us over the years and we would like to acknowledge them with this, our second Leisure novel. Hugh Lamb has been a constant source of support, and we are grateful to him. Steve Jones has been of immense help with advice and career planning. Without him the writing of novels would still be on the "to do" pile. Don D'Auria has shown huge faith in us. When we met him in Chicago at WHC in 2002 we were short story writers. The confidence he has given us, and which continues, means we are now novel writers and proud of it. Sean Wallace of Prime Books actually told us to take *Shelter* to Don rather than offer it to him, so thanks for that. William P. Simmons has been a friend of our writing for many years. Robert Morgan of Sarob Press gave us a good grounding with our story collections. Clare has been an unswerving and loyal wife and friend for twenty years and without her Mick would have given up many times. Emily gives Mick a reason to carry on and to make her as proud of him as he is of her. Len would like to thank Chris, Iain and Shara for their love and their boundless enthusiasm for his writing, and thanks to his mum. Thanks to all the team at Leisure who produce such fine books. Finally thanks to the readers and reviewers who took the trouble to let us know what they thought of the first novel, *Shelter*. Good comments and less favorable all help to make us better writers. Meeting so many people in Toronto for WHC 2007 was a great thrill and for those who said "let's keep in touch," let's do that....

DEMON EYES

CHAPTER 1

Nathan Wisecroft woke suddenly from a dream-filled sleep and stifled the scream that for the last five minutes had been working its way stealthily toward his lips. He took a moment to get his bearings, his eyes drinking in the details of the hotel room: the expensive furniture, the watercolor pictures decorating the walls, the state-of-the-art digital television that squatted in the corner of the room, shiny and new, waiting to trap the unwary and tempt them into spending their money on exclusive films, world-class sport and soft porn. His eyes finally settled on the woman in the bed next to him. She was still asleep; breathing deeply, snoring softly, her flame-red hair spread across the pillow and over her shoulders. He sighed deeply, disappointed with himself as usual.

The room smelled of stale cigarette smoke and sex. The floor was littered with empty beer bottles and clothes, stripped off in haste and left to lie where they fell. He slid his rangy body from the bed, went across to the window and pushed it open, breathing in the biting morning air and letting the sounds of traffic from the road below seep into the room. Slipping on his robe, he walked softly through to the en suite, his reflection in the bathroom mirror confirming how he was feeling. He looked terrible: gaunt, almost skeletal features, capped with a covering of short, curly gray hair. The ebony skin seemed stretched across the bones of his skull and his eyes had sunken into their sockets. They remained bloodshot no matter how much sleep he got or how many times he bathed them. Stubble covered his chin, graying like the hair of his head. He looked like a very old man, despite the fact that he had yet to see his fiftieth birthday. "You've let yourself go, man," he muttered to his reflection, even though he knew the truth went deeper than that and was far more serious, far more deadly.

He closed the bathroom door and pulled open a drawer of the vanity unit. His fingers closed around the clippers. He plugged them in, then stood in front of the mirror again and ran them over his head, watching the hair fall and gather in a silver pile in the sink. When he'd finished shaving his head he turned his attention to his face, letting the teeth of the clippers chew through the stubble. Finally he set the clippers down and picked up a cup of shaving soap and a badger-hair brush. He worked the soap into a creamy lather with the brush, then smoothed it over his chin and head. With a straight razor he took off the remaining bristles, then ran water into his cupped hands, washing away the white traces of foam and working the water into his eyes with his fingertips, washing away the sleep.

The reflection that stared back at him when he'd finished was an improvement. Not perfect, not the Nathan Wisecroft of old, but he no longer looked so ancient, so wasted.

The woman was stirring when he walked back into the bedroom. She rolled onto her back and stared up at him through bleary, sleep-dulled eyes. "Hi," she said dreamily.

"Hi back," Nathan said gruffly. "Coffee?"

The woman propped herself up on one elbow, reached across for the packet of cigarettes on the table beside the bed and lit one, blowing smoke up at the ceiling. "Yeah," she said. "Coffee's good. Then come back to bed and fuck me."

Nathan looked at her steadily. He wanted her to leave. He should have never brought her back here in the first place, but he'd been drunk and it had been a few weeks since he'd enjoyed a woman.

"You've shaved your head," she said, finally focusing on him. She was in her forties, running slightly to fat, her flaming red hair fading to a dirty gray at the roots. With her makeup slightly smeared, the pallor of sleep still coloring her face, she looked ten years older than she'd appeared the night before. Nathan wondered how he could have ever found her attractive. Then he remembered.

"Coffee, lover," she said, jerking him out of his inertia. He picked up the kettle and went back to the bathroom to fill it.

The coffee burned its way down his throat, the caffeine surging through his bloodstream, giving him a shot of energy. The woman hadn't moved from the bed, but was sitting up, leaning back against the headboard, her pendulous breasts exposed. There were teeth marks around the nipples. His. He felt a surge of self-disgust. "Get dressed," he said, flopping down on a chair opposite the bed, cupping the coffee mug with both hands.

"Aren't you coming back to bed?"

He shook his head.

She threw back the covers, exposing her bush of pubic hair. "It's juiced up and waiting for you," she said, opening her legs slightly in a gesture she imagined was seductive, but the sight of her plump white thighs only succeeded in repulsing him further.

He leaned forward and scooped up her clothes from the floor and threw them onto the bed. "I said get dressed."

She gave him a little girl pout and reached for her bra.

When she left ten minutes later there was no kiss good-bye, no arrangements made to see each other again. They'd met, got what they wanted from each other and parted; an almost businesslike arrangement that they both tacitly acknowledged. He shut the door behind her and sighed with relief.

He took one step toward the sitting room, then cried out and sank to his knees, clutching his head. The pain was excruciating; red-hot wires threading through his brain, searing his thoughts. Tears sprang to his eyes and poured down his cheeks, running into his mouth, salty and bitter. "Leave me alone," he said through gritted teeth. "Leave . . . me . . . alone!" But it was no use; the agony continued. In a few seconds the pain would recede and vanish as if it had never existed, and he would be left with a vision, a scene playing out in his mind. There had been many such visions recently, far too many to count; each one more vivid than the last; each one a part of a whole. He nearly had the full picture now, but the cost in pain was almost too much to bear. As each new vision increased in clarity, so the pain in his head intensified proportionately. He was not sure he could take much more of it.

As the pain ebbed away he closed his eyes, channeling his mind, straining his senses to see and hear the scenario playing out in his head.

Finally it was over and he fell back against the wall, pressing his fists to his eyes. It was worse than he could have imagined, and for the first time in many years he felt fear pressing at the perimeters of his mind, and the fear stirred memories of long ago.

A corrugated iron shack in a shantytown just outside Kingston, a woman shrieking in agony as a man, white, hard and muscular, rode the woman's body, forcing himself deeper and deeper into her. A small boy watching through a crack in the rusting iron wall, fist balled and stuffed into his mouth to stop himself from screaming as he watched his mother being raped. But this was no ordinary rape; not the animal need for sex being relieved forcibly. This was something more.

When it was over the woman, his mother, would be dead.

The boy tore his gaze away from the horrific scene being enacted within the shack and ran to another hut several yards away. Inside an old woman sat, her bony fingers clutching an ancient, leather-covered bible tightly to her chest, while her withered lips incanted a prayer of salvation. The boy ran to her, tugging at the hem of her dress, shouting at her to do something, anything to help his mother, her daughter. But the old woman remained resolutely immobile; her eyes tightly closed, shutting him out of her mind while she concentrated on her prayers.

Finally he gave up and ran back to the shack, pressing his face to the corrugated iron, finding the crack again. But the man had gone and his mother was dead, lying on her back on the cot, eyes wide open, staring blindly at the small cloud of flies that were already beginning to circle around her body.

Fat tears welled up in his eyes and ran down his face. He pulled himself away from the spy hole and walked on bare feet to the rough plywood door, pulling it open, and stepped into the cool, shadowed interior. He crouched down beside his mother's body, stretched out a tentative

*hand and used his fingertips to gently close her eyes. But
not before he'd stared into them and seen the look of horror there.*

*It was a look that he would never forget. It would live
with him forever, pressing at his thoughts during the day-
light hours, and inhabiting his dreams during the many
long nights that stretched ahead of him. It would inform
his life, giving him direction and a sense of purpose. But
more than that. It would feed the hatred that was beginning to burn inside him; stoking it into an unquenchable
fire that would infuse his daily life and never let him forget the moment of his mother's death. One day, he knew,
he would avenge her. He would find the man responsible for taking her life and he would kill him. A life for a
life, the Bible said. That would be his mantra from that
day on.*

Nathan Wisecroft pushed himself to his feet and stumbled through to the bedroom, falling facedown onto
the bed. Within seconds he was asleep.

When he awoke it was dark and the noise from the
street below was less frenetic, different. Commuter traffic had given way to those bringing their cars into the
city for pleasure. Somewhere there was music playing, a
thumping dance track, heavy on the bass. Seconds later
it was gone as the car stereo producing it passed by.

He hauled himself from the bed and picked up the
cup of cold coffee from earlier, swallowing the dark,
bitter liquid as he walked to the wardrobe and took out
a clean suit. He laid it on the bed, then went to shower.

Thirty minutes later he was dressed and ready to go
out. He picked up his credit cards from the small desk
under the window and slid them into his wallet; then he
pulled a drawer open in the dressing table and took out
what he needed. A clean handkerchief, his reading
glasses, a small but powerful spotlight, a leather pouch

containing a handful of salt, and a small Bible that he slipped into the pocket of his suit jacket. He never went anywhere without it these days, though he doubted it offered much protection—his faith wasn't strong enough for that—but it was a minor comfort and, like the salt, there was always the chance that he was underestimating its power.

He made a final check around the room to see if he'd left anything vital behind, but there was nothing immediately apparent. Trusting that he had everything he needed, he walked from the room, closing and locking the door behind him, and hurried down the short corridor to the elevator down to the basement car park.

"What have you got for me?"

The thin, rat-faced man shifted on the park bench. He was dressed in a suit, shiny at the elbows and knees, and stained at the lapels with the remnants of his lunch. He ran spindly fingers through his lank, greasy hair and licked his lips. "Money first," he said. "I could lose my job over this."

"Spare me the cliché." Nathan reached into the pocket of his jacket and produced a small brown envelope stuffed with ten-pound notes. He handed it across. The thin man took it, lifted the flap and peered inside.

"Count it if you like, but it's all there," Nathan said.

The thin man hesitated, fingers twitching. Finally he closed the flap and stowed the envelope away in the scuffed leather attaché case lying on the bench next to him. From the case he took another envelope, larger than the one he'd just been given, and handed it across to Nathan.

"Thank you," Nathan said, then stood and, without a backward glance, walked from the park and back to his car. He dropped the envelope onto the passenger seat and climbed in after it. With an impatience he'd concealed from the thin man he ripped the seal from the envelope and tipped the contents onto the seat.

There were a dozen or more ten-by-eight inch monochrome photographs, a list of names and dates, and two large pieces of paper, folded into quarters that he opened out to reveal the floor plans of a house. On the second sheet were more plans, but of a much smaller property. With a grunt of satisfaction he flicked through the photographs. The photographs weren't brilliant— obviously passport-sized photos overenlarged. They were grainy, but they would suffice. Finally his eyes ran down the list of names. He smiled to himself. All the usual suspects. He reached the bottom of the list and read the final name. He'd fully expected to see it there, but just reading it made his guts twist and squirm, and produced a hot flush of anger that threatened to engulf him. His fist closed around the paper and he crushed it into a tight ball, holding it tightly, waiting for the anger to subside.

Finally it faded, leaving him tired, more tired than he had ever been before. He slumped forward, head on the steering wheel. His head swam as the photographs he'd just looked at played like a slide show in his mind.

It would soon be over. One way or another, the nightmare he had endured for the past forty years would come to an end. He lifted his head from the wheel, pulled his cell phone from his pocket and punched in a number. The phone on the other end of the line rang twice then a voice said, "Hello?"

"It's begun. Be ready."

He ended the call and slipped the phone back into his pocket, then slid the key into the ignition and started the engine. There was nothing to do now but go home and wait for the call he knew would eventually come.

CHAPTER 2

"So, Emma, do you feel you're fulfilling your potential here at Keltner Industries?" Mark Lawrenson said, leaning back in his seat and fixing her with an inquisitorial gaze from his pale blue eyes.

Emma Porter shifted in her seat slightly and looked around the office, avoiding Lawrenson's eyes, trying to come up with a suitable response. The office was one of the smaller ones in the Keltner Complex, but still comfortably furnished. Lawrenson's desk was large and modern with a glass-inlayed top. The desk chair was black leather with a state-of-the-art ergonomic design. A low-slung couch sat against a wall lined with framed prints of modern artists, seemingly picked so they would settle unobtrusively into the scheme of the decor rather than for their artistic merit.

After a few moments she found her response. "I'd like to think so, yes."

Which was the truth. In four years she'd worked her way up from the typing pool to become PA to Jeff Williams, the company's marketing director. It hadn't been an easy climb. Many late nights, and the occasional Saturday; showing willing by putting in extra unpaid hours; appearing at all the company's numerous social events, and honing her interpersonal relationship skills with people from every level of the company's fiercely hierarchical structure. She was conscientious about her appearance, having her shoulder-length blond hair trimmed regularly to keep it neat, and always aware that the names on the labels of her clothes said a lot to others about who she was, and mattered almost as much as her secretarial abilities. She'd ticked all the boxes, dotted the Is, crossed the Ts, and so far it was working in her favor.

Lawrenson tapped his teeth with the end of his pen, finally sitting forward and scribbling a note on the white pad lying on the desk in front of him.

Once his gaze was switched off she felt herself relax slightly. She craned her neck, trying to see what he was writing, but it was impossible from where she sat. Office protocol dictated that her seat was lower than Lawrenson's, giving him the psychological advantage. He finished and turned the pad facedown, then came round and perched on the edge of the desk, no more than a few feet from where she sat. She noticed his paunch stretching the fabric of his shirt, bulging slightly over the top of his trousers. He thought of himself as something of a lothario, but Emma couldn't see that he had much to offer. Tall, but overweight, thinning, sandy colored hair receding at the temples, and a deep pink complexion that owed more to alcohol than it did to healthy living. But she knew that his position of Director of Human Resources gave him considerable power in the company and, for some, that power was an aphrodisiac. There were a host of female employees ready and willing to lay on their backs with their legs open in the hope that their compliance would advance their position in the firm.

Emma Porter wasn't one of them. Mark Lawrenson left her cold.

"I'll come to the point, Emma," he said, placing the pen down on the desk and aligning it neatly next to the pad. "Alex is looking for a new PA, and you've been short-listed. Actually, he added your name to the list himself."

Alex Keltner was Managing Director, but much more than that. Since the retirement of Louis Keltner, his father, and founder of the company, Alex was the major shareholder and the engine that drove it forward. He was a dynamic leader and a charismatic CEO, who enjoyed close friendships with several ministers of the government. Also invited to his table were a number of influential journalists, and Alex Keltner's instinctive grasp of public relations and his ability to provide headline-grabbing sound bites ensured that Keltner Industries was never far from the media spotlight.

He also had an efficient and formidable PA in Monica Patterson, a woman whose presence in the firm engendered admiration and fear in equal measure.

"I didn't know there was a vacancy," Emma said. "Is Monica leaving?"

A smile flicked across Lawrenson's lips; so brief it was barely noticeable. "Monica left last Friday. She won't be back."

Emma waited for a fuller explanation but none was forthcoming. "I see," she said at last.

"It's a great opportunity, should you be interested."

"Yes," she said. "Yes, I can see that. Can I ask you something though?"

"Of course."

"Why isn't Alex conducting this interview?"

Lawrenson seemed to consider this for a moment before replying. He walked across to the cooler in the corner and poured himself a paper cup full of water. "Can I get you one?"

Emma shook her head. "I'm fine, thanks."

He was sipping the drink as he came back and resumed his seat behind the desk, putting the conversation back onto more formal terms. "You see, this isn't really an interview. Alex asked me to sound out the names on his list as a preliminary step. If you're not interested in the position then there's really no need to take it any further. It would only be a waste of his time . . . and you know how valuable Alex's time is these days. Look, I'm not demanding an answer straightaway. Go home tonight and think about it. If you decide you'd be interested in working for Alex, then you can let me know in the morning and we can move on to the second stage of the process."

"Which is?"

Lawrenson chuckled. "Eager. Good, I like that. First things first, though. Think about what I've said, the possibilities, and give me your answer tomorrow."

She nodded her head decisively. "Okay. I will."

On the train home she was wedged nose to back with fellow commuters, all swaying in unison as the carriage rocked and rolled along the track. By Royston she found an empty seat and sat in relative comfort for the rest of the journey to Cambridge, thinking about Lawrenson's proposal and what it could mean to her life. Promotion meant more money, but it also meant more responsibility. Working for someone as dynamic as Alex Keltner would not be a cakewalk. Monica Patterson had a huge reputation in the firm. Some said that Alex would not be in the position of power he now enjoyed without her significant contribution. And it was no secret that a lot of the more mundane but important decisions in the company came from the desk of Monica Patterson, and not Alex himself. They were huge shoes to fill, and while she was flattered to even be considered for the job, she wasn't sure her feet were big enough.

She wrestled with the problem for the remainder of the journey home.

"Hi, hon, I'm home," she called as she pushed open the front door of her small mews cottage.

"In here."

Emma wandered through to the kitchen.

Helen Carver, Emma's partner for the last three years, was sitting at the kitchen table, fingers tapping away at a calculator, a stack of bills in front of her. Emma wrapped her arms around her and kissed the back of your neck. "Missed you," she said.

"Missed you too," Helen said, taking hold of Emma's hand and brushing it with her lips. "I don't suppose you have a spare grand or two in your pocket?" she said.

Emma eyed the bills. "Things looking bad?"

"They've been worse, I'm sure . . . but I really can't remember when."

Emma sat down at the table, picked up a credit card bill, looked at it and grimaced. "We spend too much," she said.

"Evidently," Helen said, a sardonic smile spreading across her face.

"We're hopeless."

"Again, evidently." Helen rummaged through the pile of paperwork and found her checkbook. "So what shall we pay? The electric or the gas?"

"How about both."

"Uh-uh," she said, shaking her head. "One or the other."

"If they cut off the electric supply we won't have television, stereo or the Internet. If they cut off the gas we won't be able to cook."

"You see my dilemma."

"We can always eat out or get takeaways. But imagine a life without music, or the soaps."

"And how could we survive without e-mail?"

"Electric. Pay the electric."

Helen reached for her pen. "Where would I be without your sage advice?"

"Richer, probably. Fancy a G and T?"

"I could murder one, but we're out of tonic."

"Vodka and Coke?"

"No vodka."

"Times are indeed hard," Emma said. She went through to the lounge and crouched down in front of the small drinks cabinet in the corner. "Tia Maria?" she called back to the kitchen.

"With Coke! Genius!" Helen called back.

Emma came back to the kitchen holding two glasses filled with the sweet coffee-flavored liquid. She put them down on the kitchen work top and opened the freezer to get some ice. "I had some news today."

Helen pushed the rest of the bills away from her in disgust and went across to get her drink. "Good or bad?"

"Good . . . I think. But I need to talk it over with you. It could be the answer to our prayers . . . at least as far as they're concerned." She pointed at the stack of bills on the table.

Helen sipped her drink, looking at Emma over the top of her glass. "Okay, I'm intrigued. Tell me more."

"Bath first," she said. "I need to unwind."

"Okay. I'll go and light the candles, and put some music on."

"Something soft and soothing."

"Motorhead it is, then," Helen said with a grin, and left the kitchen.

"So, what do you think?" Emma was laying facedown and seminaked on the bed while Helen massaged her back, concentrating on the spine, using strong thumbs to work out the knots that had formed during the day. The bath had helped a little, until Helen stripped off and climbed in with her, then all thoughts of relaxation had flown out the window.

"It's your call," Helen said, her face serious. She was three years older than Emma, and just about as different from her as it was possible to be. While Emma was tall and blond, Helen was small and dark. She kept her hair cut short, giving her a tomboy look, accentuated by her preference for jeans over dresses and skirts, and the fact that her tiny breasts barely made an impression on the T-shirts she habitually wore. Her ears were pierced several times, her nose just once, and she wore a small tattoo of a Celtic cross at the small of her back. "Do you think you're ready for that kind of promotion?" she said as she kneaded the flesh just above Emma's buttocks with her thumbs, making her groan with pain and pleasure.

"I'd like to think I am . . . but . . ." She groaned again and fell silent.

"Don't you dare fall asleep!" Helen said, slapping her bottom and rolling her over onto her back. "You promised to take me to dinner, remember?"

Emma looked up at her with half-open eyes. "Home delivery? Pizza? A nice Merlot? It'd be cheaper."

Helen grinned. "Nice try. But no." She climbed from the bed and tossed a towel in Emma's direction. "Get showered and dressed. We're going out."

Emma opened her eyes a fraction more. "Bugger!" she said, and rolled off the bed.

* * *

"So what's Alex Keltner like?" Helen said. They were sitting at a table at their favorite restaurant, Baggy's, in Mill Lane. The restaurant was light on atmosphere, but the food was superb, leaning toward Italian cuisine, but with rogue French dishes dropped into the menu at random. Over the past few years they'd become friendly with the owner and his wife, and often stayed on after the restaurant had closed, drinking and putting the world to rights. The restaurant was surprisingly crowded for a Tuesday—the refrain of "Happy Birthday" coming from a large table in the corner going some way to explaining the crush—but Giuseppe, the owner, had found them a table in a secluded corner.

"I don't really know him. I don't think anyone really does . . . except Monica, perhaps. After all, she was jetting off here, there and everywhere with him."

Panic flared in Helen's tourmaline green eyes. "You didn't tell me about *that* part of the job," she said, twisting her napkin into a knot and drumming it nervously on the edge of the table.

As soon as the words left her lips Emma realized she'd said the wrong thing. She flushed and she tried to backtrack. "I exaggerate, you know that. Once, twice a year, perhaps. Three times, tops. I wonder what happened to Monica," she said, trying to steer them off the subject. "Whatever it was, Mark Lawrenson found it rather amusing. He could barely contain his glee. But then they never liked each other." She cut a small piece from her pizza and popped it into her mouth, closing her eyes in pleasure as the combined flavors of tuna, prawn and anchovy rolled over her tongue. "Mmm, that's *so* good."

Helen dropped the twisted napkin onto the table next to her plate. "Perhaps she left because she got sick of the traveling," she said.

"Don't spoil it," Emma said. "If it becomes a problem I can always quit and go back to what I was doing before."

Helen shrugged and shook her head. "I couldn't work in an office," she said. "The politics would do my head in. All that bitching and backbiting. Give me my horses any day. You feed them, muck them out, ride them and love them, and for the most part they behave themselves . . . and they don't talk about you behind your back!"

"As far as you know," Emma said smiling, but secretly she envied her partner's lifestyle. Helen ran a livery stable in Cherry Hinton, a large chunk of real estate on the edge of Cambridge with two paddocks, an indoor school, and stabling for thirty horses. It was where they first met. Helen offered riding lessons, and Emma was one of her pupils.

It was a blazing hot Saturday in June. Helen took the class out for a hack across the fields surrounding the stables. It was the first time Emma had been allowed out of the stable to join them. She was nervous, and maybe her mount picked up on it. The horse was skittish and willful, tossing its head and making itself all but impossible to control.

Thirty minutes into the hack, a plastic carrier bag trapped in the branches of a hawthorn tree rustled in the breeze, making a loud, crackling sound that spooked Emma's mount. The horse bucked wildly and threw her. Emma landed flat on her back on the hard, sunbaked ground and lay there winded and embarrassed. Helen cantered back from her place at the front of the class and jumped from her horse. She crouched down beside her. "Are you okay?"

Emma groaned. "Nothing hurt but my pride . . . I think," she said, easing herself up onto her elbows. A few of the students had trotted back to see what all the fuss was about and were now circling them, watching.

Emma took off her riding hat and wiped the sweat

from her forehead with the sleeve of her shirt. A stray lock of hair escaped from her ponytail and flopped down over her eyes. Helen Carver reached out and tucked it back behind Emma's ear. It was a curiously intimate gesture that sent tingles through Emma's body. She looked up into the other girl's eyes and something passed between them. She'd fancied Helen for months, but had never made it obvious, fearing that any overt approach might be rebuffed. And while she was fairly sure that Helen felt the same way about her, she wasn't certain, and that uncertainty prevented her from showing her true feelings. But the moment Helen's fingers touched her skin and brushed the hair away from her eyes, Emma knew that she and Helen were going to become lovers.

There was a quality in Helen that she'd never found in any of her past loves, male or female; an honesty and openness that was at once disarming and slightly alarming. In that one touch a bond formed between them; a powerful alchemy that seemed to grow in strength the longer they were together.

"Well?" Helen said, jerking her back to the present.

"I'm going for it," she said.

Helen raised her eyebrows, scared now, although she didn't quite know why. "Are you sure? You don't want to sleep on it?"

"No, I'm sure. If I don't take this job, I'll be kicking myself forever."

Helen sipped her wine, took a breath and looked at her steadily. "As I said earlier, your call. Three times, tops, right?"

"Promise."

"I'll hold you to it."

CHAPTER 3

Lawrenson stepped into the elevator and hit the button to close the doors, then took a key from his pocket and unlocked the silver control panel in the wall. Emma watched, fascinated, as the panel swung open to reveal a mass of circuitry and another black button. Lawrenson punched it and the elevator began to travel upward.

"Your first visit to the eleventh floor?" he asked.

Emma swallowed, trying to get her salivary glands working. Her mouth was dry and her tongue was stuck to the roof of her mouth. Christ, why was she so nervous? She felt like a schoolgirl on her way to visit the headmistress. She nodded her head, not trusting her voice enough to speak.

"You get the gig and you get a key like this one." He held up the key he'd used to open the panel. "It's one of the perks. One of many."

The car reached the top floor and the doors slid open with the softest of hisses. Emma stood rigid, waiting for Lawrenson to make the first move. She looked out through the open doors onto a hallway painted a rich ochre, with a deep-piled maroon carpet. There were pictures on the wall: framed monochrome photographs, skyscapes, seascapes and landscapes, beautifully lit and composed. Set into the same wall was a door covered in studded ochre leather.

Lawrenson put his hand on the small of her back and gently steered her through the open elevator doors. "Go on. Nothing to be nervous about. Through that door there. Don't knock. You're expected."

Emma looked round at him apprehensively. "You're not coming with me?" Despite her mild dislike of Mark Lawrenson she would have found it more comforting to have him there for moral support.

He shook his head. "You don't need me. Just be yourself and you'll be fine."

Emma glanced round once more as she stepped out into the hallway and the elevator doors hissed shut behind her. Through the closing gap she saw Lawrenson give her a reassuring wink. He was smiling.

Right, get your head together, she told herself. *You've met Alex Keltner before. He's not an ogre.* Instantly the image of Shrek dressed in a sharp Versace suit popped unbidden into her mind. She smiled and felt herself relax slightly. Moving forward, she rested her hand on the leather-studded door, hesitating, listening. She could hear nothing. Despite Lawrenson's instructions she knocked, the sound muffled by the leather, then wrapped her perspiring hand around the brass door handle and turned it.

The room in which she found herself was empty—there was no sign of Alex Keltner—and it wasn't at all what she had been expecting. This had none of the trappings of an office but looked more like an apartment. There was no desk or filing cabinet, no computer or fax machine, but there was a beige leather couch and two matching chairs surrounding a glass-topped coffee table strewn with magazines and books. On one wall was a large plasma screen television tuned to the Bloomberg money channel, but with the sound turned down. A rack of hi-fi separates occupied another corner of the room, but she couldn't locate the speakers through which the voice of Norah Jones was wafting gently. *Come away with me . . .* Was it an invitation? Her mind immediately flashed back to Helen and how she had left her this morning, curled up asleep in the bed they shared, her cropped hair tousled and spiky, her thumb hovering by her lips, ready to suck. She wished now she were back in the bed with her. This was a mistake. She wasn't ready to take on a job like this. It was out of her league.

She was about to turn and retrace her steps to the elevator when a door opened and Alex Keltner padded into the room on bare feet, dressed only in a navy bathrobe, rubbing at his wet hair with a white towel. He spotted Emma and grinned, walking across to her, hand extended. "Sorry, Emma," he said. "Running late. Let me get you a coffee while I throw some clothes on."

She couldn't imagine he'd ever *thrown* clothes on in his entire life. She shook the extended hand and tried a smile. Her lips twisted and almost found the shape, but she knew she'd just pulled the most ridiculous face at him by the slight quizzical narrowing of his eyes.

"Nervous?"

She nodded, still mute.

"Don't be. I don't bite . . . unless badly provoked, and even then it's more of a nibble, really. Let me get that coffee. Take a seat. How do you like it?"

"What?"

"The coffee."

"Oh. White. No sugar."

"Grab a magazine while I make it. It's boring scientific

and aeronautical stuff mainly, but if you rummage
through you might find a copy of *Hello* or *Cosmo*."

The thought of Alex Keltner settling down in one of
the plush leather chairs flicking through *Cosmopolitan*
brought a proper smile to her lips, but she did as she
was instructed and watched as he disappeared again
into the rear of the apartment.

True to his word there was a copy of *Hello* buried
among the dry, academic stuff, but she'd read all she
ever wanted to about Elton John and David Furnish, so
opted for a magazine with a cover depicting a Lear jet
crossing an azure sky.

She'd barely had time to open it when Keltner returned with her coffee and set it down on the table in
front of her. As he leaned forward the robe gaped slightly,
revealing a well-muscled, hairless chest and the hint of
a six-pack. The smell of his aftershave was heady, but
traditional, dependable and very masculine, much like
the man himself, she thought. She could understand
why an awful lot of women found him attractive, and
why he was listed in the top ten of the most eligible
bachelors in the country. With his shock of curly brown
hair, chiseled bone structure and penetrating blue eyes
that matched the sky on the cover of the magazine she'd
been reading, he was a beautiful man, and she could
appreciate beauty. It was like looking at Michelangelo's
David, or a Hockney painting of Peter Schlesinger. It
was an aesthetic appreciation. Nothing more.

He straightened up and for an instant stared into her
eyes.

It was the emotional equivalent of being hit with a
cattle prod. As she looked into the clear blue eyes, she
physically jolted in her seat and her heart rate doubled,
leaving her breathless.

"Back in a moment," he said, smiling easily, seemingly oblivious to the effect he'd just had on her.

She sank back into the leather chair, sipping her coffee, and forced her mind back to Helen and the love they shared. But no matter how hard she tried she couldn't remember what Helen looked like.

Helen Carver soaked a hay net under the freezing water of the standpipe, running a damp hand through her hair, spiking it up. The day was hot and humid and the cold water on her scalp was a welcome relief.

"They're restless today," Sid Whelan said as he made his way, pitchfork in hand, to the muck heap. She seemed to have known Sid Whelan all her life, but she had only employed him since the livery stable opened five years ago. He wasn't a dynamic worker, more steady and methodical, but he was totally reliable. She couldn't remember him ever taking a day off sick in all the time he'd worked for her. He was in his fifties but looked ten years older, his skin weatherworn and leathery. The hair that peeped out beneath the denim cap he wore to hide his baldness was snowy, as was the stubble on his permanently unshaven chin, but he had the eyes of a teenager, sparkling with constant mirth and mischief. To Helen he was a surrogate father, so much more constant than the drink-sodden wretch who'd sired her, and she cared about him deeply. Also there was little he didn't know about horses and their welfare, and she depended on his advice and wisdom a lot more than she cared to admit, even to herself.

"Probably the weather," she said in reply to his passing remark. "I can feel a storm brewing. They can too."

Whelan squinted his eyes to shut out the smoke eddying up from the roll-up between his lips. "Could be right. It's certainly close enough for it," he said.

"Sid, I *am* right," she said with a smile, and hauled the hay net across to Nelson's stall. "Look at those clouds," she called back over her shoulder and pointed out to the eastern sky where black thunderheads were roiling and rolling above the landscape.

Nelson, a seventeen-hand chestnut hunter, flopped his head over the bottom half of the stable door and nuzzled her Puffa jacket, sniffing out the mints she habitually carried in her pocket. Helen slapped his nose gently. "Later," she said, then reached over the door and slid back the bolt.

She hung the hay net from a hook on one of the wooden beams that supported the roof, smiling as Nelson ambled across to it, started to pull out strands and chew them contentedly. Then she reached up and took a grooming kit from a high shelf at the back of the stall and slipped a currycomb over her hand, stroking Nelson's hindquarters. The horse backed away from the hay net and tossed its head, whinnying, clearly agitated.

Helen stopped combing and ran her hand along the horse's back. Nelson usually loved his morning groom, but today he seemed nervous, skittish. "It's okay, boy," she said soothingly. "You like this." But the horse responded by swinging its head round and knocking the currycomb from her hand.

"Nelson! Stop that!" she snapped, and bent to retrieve the comb. The horse moved to the side, catching her with its flank and almost pushing her to the ground. Helen backed away and looked the horse in the eye. "Nelson," she said, a warning in her voice. She tried again to pick up the comb, but the horse took a couple of steps forward, tossing its head, snorting, ears flat against its skull.

The first threads of alarm started to insinuate their way into her mind. The horse was usually docile, a great placid beast and one of her favorites. It could be, as she'd said to Sid Whelan, that the approaching storm was unsettling him, but there was something in his eyes that she'd never seen before. He looked hostile, angry, and the look bothered her.

She glanced toward the door, but there was no way she could reach it. Nelson had positioned himself to block her exit, and started to beat a tattoo on the floor of the stall with his hooves, kicking up straw. Helen pressed her back to the wooden wall and started to edge her way around the stall. There were few more dangerous places to be than trapped in a confined space with an agitated horse. It could kick out at any time and the iron shoes, razor sharp from their constant honing on the concrete floor, were lethal weapons.

Nelson started to back into her, pinning her where she stood. The kick, when it came, was so fast she barely had time to move. The hoof crashed into the wooden wall, sending splinters flying into the air. The second kick was even faster, and this time it caught her on the thigh, the shoe slicing through the denim of her jeans and through her skin, carving a four-inch gash into her flesh. Pain swept up through her body from the wound, so intense she thought she was going to pass out. Her head swam as she clamped a hand over the wound and lurched forward, desperate to reach the door, but the horse moved again, trapping her.

"Sid! Sid!" she yelled. There was panic in her voice and she cursed herself. It would only excite the horse more.

Nelson was breathing heavily, snorting air out through his nostrils. There was a wild, half-mad look in his eyes now, and white foam was beginning to fleck his lips.

"It's all right, boy. Just calm down," Helen said, but the horse wasn't hearing her. She managed to avoid the third kick by throwing herself to the side, her hand reaching out to clutch at a loose board in the stable wall, trying desperately to keep her feet. If she fell the horse would trample her. "Sid!" she called again.

The door was thrown open and Sid Whelan rushed into the stall, brandishing his pitchfork.

Helen watched with frightened eyes as he compelled the horse to back away, jabbing at the chestnut rump with the fork, edging the horse around the stall, out through the door and into the yard. "Go on, you bastard, get out of here," Whelan said, pushing his cap back on his head and wiping the sweat of exertion out of his eyes with a handkerchief.

Helen leaned back against the wall in relief, trying to get her breath back. A fresh spasm from her leg washed over her and she squeezed her eyes shut, trying to control both the pain and an increasing feeling of nausea that was threatening to overwhelm her.

Something thudded into her chest and she opened her eyes in surprise. She tried to move away from the wall but couldn't. Sid was standing in front of her, a blank expression on his face, the hand-rolled cigarette hanging from the bottom lip of his slacked-jawed mouth. Her gaze traveled downward and she realized why she couldn't move. The handle of the pitchfork was protruding from her chest, the tines piercing her body and pinning her to the wooden wall behind.

She looked up incredulously at Sid's expressionless face, opened her mouth to say something, anything, but blood gushed out, spattering the front of the man's waxed jacket. The last thing she saw was the blank look on Sid's face disappear to be replaced by one of shock and horror as the realization of what he'd done dawned on him. Her head dropped forward and with a small sigh of confusion and resignation Helen Carver died.

In the lane outside the livery stable the driver of a silver Mercedes started the engine, glanced back through the double five-bar gate at Sid Whelan staggering out from the stable. Smiling to himself, the man slipped on a pair of wraparound sunglasses, let in the clutch and moved away. Job done.

CHAPTER 4

When he came back into the room Alex Keltner was dressed in fawn slacks and a green cashmere sweater. He looked relaxed, in direct contrast to Emma, who was perched on the edge of her leather seat, drinking her coffee with nervous sips. He was carrying a manila folder that he dropped onto the coffee table, then sat down in the chair opposite her, adjusting his slacks to stop them bagging at the knees.

"That's your file," he said, gesturing to the folder. "Want to take a look?"

She smiled uncertainly. "Would I like what's in there?"

"Probably. I've read it through. Twice. That's one of the reasons you're sitting here." He leaned forward and slid the file across the table to her.

She flicked it open and scanned the first page. Her CV. It was a long time since she'd read it, but she remembered the details. Her schools, her qualifications, her previous jobs. Next were a bundle of her annual reports; comments by Marie Colvin who ran the typing pool with almost military precision—strange how it was still referred to as the typing pool, when everyone now used computers and Microsoft programs to deal with the vast administrative output of the company. She speed-read a note attached to her third-year report by Jeff Williams: a glowing testament to her skills and abilities. Nothing negative; nothing negative at all. She closed the file and handed it back to him.

He took it from her with a smile. "You see. You're well regarded."

"I'm flattered."

"Don't be. You've earned the plaudits." He dropped the file on the seat next to him, then leaned back and crossed his legs, again adjusting his slacks fastidiously. "So, you know why you're here. I'm sure Mark spelled out everything in detail for you."

"Well, not really . . ."

"Odd. I told him to put you in the picture," Keltner said, his smooth, tanned brow creasing into a frown.

"Oh, he did . . ." Emma said quickly, rushing to Lawrenson's defense, though she wasn't quite sure why. "Broadly, anyway."

The frown slipped away and the smile was back in place once more. "Well then, I'd better ask you formally. Would you be interested in becoming my personal assistant?"

Emma swallowed. This was it. The big question. The one that had turned her knees to mush and sent butterflies spiraling in a dervish dance inside her stomach. She'd rehearsed the answer over and over again: in the bathroom mirror, on the train coming into work, in the loo before she stepped into the elevator to come up here. She took a breath. "Yes," she said.

"Good," Keltner said with a smile. "That's settled then."

That threw her. "Pardon?"

"The job's yours. I'll leave Mark to sort out the finer details with you—salary, holiday entitlement, that sort of thing. He deals with that stuff much better that I do."

"But . . ."

"Yes?"

"I thought there was a short list; that this was just a preliminary interview."

"Whatever gave you that idea? I decided I wanted you a few weeks ago. It may surprise you to know that I've watched your career path with interest since you first joined the company. I would have had Mark approach you sooner, but I had to wait until . . ." His voice trailed off and he stared at his hands, lost in thought. Suddenly he snapped out of it. "What was I saying? Oh yes . . . a few weeks ago. It was just a case of going over your file to see if you were suitable, and then sounding you out to see if you were interested in taking me on."

"Taking *you* on?"

"Well, I agree it's a two-way street, but it's important that you're as happy with me as I am with you, otherwise it will never work."

"Is that the way it was with Monica?" Emma said.

"Very much so. She wore my skin. In so many ways she *was* me. That's what I'm talking about."

Emma took a breath and asked the question that had been niggling away in her mind. "Why *did* Monica leave?"

"Family reasons," Keltner answered without missing a beat. "I'm afraid my demands on her time became too much for her."

Panic flared momentarily within her. She thought of Helen. *Three times, tops.* She'd understand if that stretched a bit, wouldn't she? After all, this was the opportunity of a lifetime. She'd be an idiot to get this far and then blow it.

"You look pensive, Emma," Keltner said.

She shook herself. "No, I'm fine, really."

"Good. I thought I might have scared you. Monica's commitments at home increased and I think she just got tired of performing the juggling act." He stood and fished in his pocket. After a few seconds he produced a key and held it out to her. "You'll need this," he said. "The key to the elevator's control panel. It gives you access to this floor. Don't lose it," he added with a smile.

She took it, feeling the warm metal in her hand. It weighed little, but was heavy with responsibility. She clenched her fist around it tightly.

"So," he said, walking her to the door, "I'll see you Monday morning."

"Monday?" Again he'd surprised her. "What about Jeff? I thought I'd have to spend some time getting my replacement settled in."

"Jeff's a big boy. He can handle the job without you. I can't. Monday, nine o'clock."

"Right," Emma said.

"See you then," Keltner said with a smile, and closed the door behind her.

Back in her own office she sat down at the desk and retrieved her bag from beneath her seat. She felt breathless, like she'd run for a train and missed it, and her body trembled slightly. It had all happened so fast; and it was certainly the most bizarre interview she'd ever had. It wasn't even *a real* interview. Keltner had decided to give her the job even before she'd set foot in his office. She took out her cell phone. One message. She hit a button. Helen. She tapped the button again.

HI HON. GOOD LUCK 2DAY. PIZZA AND WINE 2NITE. LOL. H. BIG HUGS. XXX.

Emma smiled and checked the time of the message. 8:10. Just before Helen left for the stables. She hit speed dial and listened while the phone on the other end of the line rang . . . and rang. "Shit!" Emma muttered after fifteen rings. Helen had probably gone out on a ride and left her phone back at the stables. She was always forgetting her phone; it was one of the few things about her Emma would change. She sent her a text instead.

HI BACK. STUFF THE WINE. CHAMPAGNE 2NITE. I GOT THE JOB. C U LATER. CNT WAIT! HUGS BACK. LUV E. XXX.

She read the message, hit the send button, then dropped the phone back into her bag. God, they were going to celebrate tonight!

Julie Hansen, Mark Lawrenson's PA, popped her head around the door. "Just passing," she said. "I hear congratulations are in order."

"Christ, that was quick! The bush telegraph's working overtime today."

Julie laughed. "You know what this place is like. The drums never stop. Actually, Mark told me. He wants to see you, *ASAP*. Okay?"

Emma nodded. "Okay." She liked Julie Hansen. She was one of the very few people at the company she *did* like, but her tendency to use terms like *ASAP* irritated the hell out of her. "Tell him I'll be along shortly," she said.

The smile slipped from Julie's face. "I don't think *shortly* is an option. Sorry."

Emma stared at the pile of paperwork on her desk and frowned. It was only ten o'clock. With all she had to do today Helen would be in bed by the time she finally got home . . . not that the thought of that was so unappealing. Pushing herself out of her seat with a sigh, she followed Julie down the hall to meet with Lawrenson. As she passed the door to Jeff Williams's office, she looked in and smiled. Jeff looked up and held her gaze for a moment, but didn't smile back. Then he turned his attention back to his desk and shuffled some papers meaningfully.

He's pissed off with me, she thought, but it did nothing to dampen her spirits.

* * *

Her eyebrows climbed up to her hairline as she read the figures on the page next to the word *Salary*. Holiday entitlement: 50 percent more than she got now. Health insurance, entry to the company pension scheme, annual bonus projections. It was almost too much to take in.

"Well?" Lawrenson said. "Any complaints?"

He has to be kidding. "No. No complaints at all," she said.

"Good."

"Has Jeff said anything to you?" she said.

"Jeff's said a lot of things lately. Be specific."

"About me going to work for Alex."

Lawrenson smiled. It was almost reptilian. "Oh yes, Jeff's had a lot to say about that."

"So he's not happy."

Lawrenson spread his hands in a gesture of innocence. "I'm sure I don't know what you mean. Jeff's a team player, and whatever's good for the company he goes along with. Happiness doesn't come into it."

"Mark, you know it's not as simple as that."

"Do I?"

Emma shook her head. This was getting her nowhere. She'd confront Jeff herself. It was the only way she would get things straightened out with him.

After her meeting with Lawrenson she walked back down the corridor, stopped outside Jeff Williams's office and rapped on the open door.

"You don't need to knock, Emma," he said, without looking up from the paper he was working on.

She walked into the office and stood facing him across the desk. "I think we need to talk," she said.

He didn't sigh, but it was there in his movements as he lifted his head to look at her. "Okay," he said. "We'll talk. You want to know if I'm angry that you've taken Alex's job, right?"

She nodded.

"Well, for the record, yes I am. Bloody angry. We made a great team, you and I, and I thought you liked working with me as well. I tried to involve you in all the decision making . . . well, as much as I was at liberty to, and I gave you more autonomy than you should have had. But I suppose the lure of working for the big boss was too strong for you. You should remember that without me you wouldn't even be working here."

"That's unkind, Jeff, and unfair," she said with more asperity than she'd intended, but she wasn't going to roll over and play dead just to soothe his ego. Because that was what this was all about. His ego. It was bruised because she decided to take the opportunity to move up in the company and work for his superior. "What would you have done in my position?"

He ran his hands through his sandy hair, looking at her steadily. "Exactly the same, probably," he said, and seemed to relax slightly. "I said I was bloody angry with you. I didn't say I blamed you for taking the decision." He moved forward in his seat. "Close the door," he said, softly.

Emma did as she was told. He gestured to the chair. She sat.

"I've got some advice for you," he said, keeping his voice low. "Please take it to heart, because it's very, very important."

Emma leaned toward him, to hear him better, and because there was something in his manner that suggested he was about to commit a terrible indiscretion, and she didn't want anybody to overhear what he had to say. "Go on," she said, equally softly.

"Alex Keltner isn't all that he seems," he said. "Tread very carefully around him. Plus, and this is the most important part, once you work for him, he owns you, body and soul. Just remember that."

"Sounds awfully like sour grapes, Jeff." Emma said.

He frowned, then shrugged, leaning back in his seat and staring hard at her. "You believe what you want to believe. But one day you'll remember this conversation, and you'll wish you'd taken more notice of it."

"Then explain what you mean. What do mean, *Alex isn't all that he seems*? Why should I have to *tread carefully*, as you put it?"

He shook his head; it was a small dismissive gesture, barely perceptible. "I've said enough. You'll find out once you work for him." He picked up a document lying on the desk in front of him and swiveled around in his chair, pretending to read it.

"So that's it then?" Emma said.

Williams said nothing.

"Jeff!" she said, her exasperation finally boiling over.

He glanced round at her. "Good luck," he said.

"Thanks," she said. "Thanks a lot." She walked from the office, slamming the door behind her as she went.

The journey home was one of the usual stops and starts, with faulty signals cursing the train's progress. Delays all along the line meant that her train didn't pull into Cambridge until well after eight, over an hour later than it should have.

She opened the front door of the small mews cottage she shared with Helen and called out, "I'm home."

The cottage was silent. There were no lights on, which struck her as unusual because Helen was a light junkie and Emma was forever going around the house, switching off the lights in the rooms Helen had vacated. She walked into the lounge and flipped the switch. "Helen!" she called again, and wandered through to the kitchen. She checked the fridge where a dozen or more scraps of paper were attached to the white metal door with novelty magnets. This was their bulletin and message board. Along with shopping lists and reminders for bills that had to be paid, they posted notes to each other on the door. It was one of their ways of keeping in touch.

There was a note in Helen's hand with today's date scribbled across the top in Biro. FACIAL/MASSAGE. 1:15. LORRAINE, but there was no note to say where she was now.

Emma filled the kettle and set it to boil, a vague unease worming its way into her mind. Helen was always there when she came home from work. Always. And if she'd been called away somewhere, she would have left a note saying where she'd gone.

She took a mug from the hook on the dresser and threw in a tea bag. She was spooning in the sugar when the doorbell rang, startling her and making her spill sugar over the worktop. She swore and went to open the door.

"Did you forget your key?" she said, then stopped as she realized it wasn't Helen standing there. "Tony?"

Tony Carver, Helen's older brother, stood on the threshold, and she could see from his face, and from the redness of his eyes, that something was wrong. Something was *very* wrong.

"Tony," she said again, her voice apprehensive.

He reached out for her and wrapped her in his arms. "Emma, I'm sorry . . . I'm so sorry."

She writhed in his arms, struggling to free herself. "What?" she said, pushing him away, staring at him hotly. "What?"

"An accident . . . at the stable . . . Helen . . . she's . . ."

No! Don't say it! her mind screamed. *If you say it you'll make it true!*

"I'm so sorry, Emma," he said softly, in little more than a whisper. "There was nothing anyone could do. She was already dead when the ambulance got there."

"Oh my God!" A wave of cold nausea swept through her. She felt her knees buckle, and she sagged into his arms, sobbing. "How?" she said through the tears, her voice so small it barely escaped her lips. "Why?"

CHAPTER 5

Emma wrapped her hands around the mug of scalding tea, embracing the heat, wanting it to burn her; wanting to feel something other than this paralyzing numbness. It was slowly starting to sink in that she was now completely alone. Helen had not only been her partner, she'd been her family. Three years ago Helen had supported her during the aftermath of the horrific car crash that had claimed the lives of Emma's parents. At the age of twenty-six she had become an orphan. She had no siblings with whom to share the grief, only Helen. And Helen had been her strength: soothing her when the tears had come in the early hours of the morning; forcing her to reject the negative aspects of what had happened and to focus on the positive. Dragging her out of the hell of mourning into a brighter, lighter world, where the sun was allowed to shine once more and where there was no place for sorrow and tears. Rediscovering laughter and joy were the gifts Helen gave her, but now that had all been snatched away once more and she felt desolate and completely alone.

Tony took the cup from her and set it down on the table. She looked at him, as if seeing him for the first time.

"Is there anything you need?" he said.

God, he looked so much like his sister. The same spiky black hair, the emerald eyes, even the bone structure. Had he not been six inches taller than Helen and thirty pounds heavier Emma could have been looking at her lover.

"Will the police charge him? With murder I mean. Will they charge Sid with Helen's murder?"

"It was an accident, Emma," Tony said gently. "Sid Whelan would never have deliberately hurt Helen. He loved her like a daughter. He was still there at the stable when I arrived. He looked like a little old man, shrunken, used up. It was horrible to see him like that." He sat down on the couch next to her and took Emma's hands in his. They were still hot from the mug of tea. "One of the horses went crazy and pinned Helen in the stall. Sid was using his pitchfork to fend the animal off. Helen simply got in the way. In the wrong place at the wrong time. A tragic accident, nothing more."

A tear rolled down her cheek. She wiped it away impatiently with the sleeve of her blouse. "We were going to celebrate tonight," she said. "My new job. Break open the champagne. Fuck!"

He pulled her close. There was nothing more to say.

Alex Keltner tapped his driver on the shoulder. "Pull in over there, behind those hearses."

The driver checked his mirror and did as instructed. He killed the engine of the Bentley and climbed out to open the door for his employer.

Why are these places always so damned cold? Alex thought as he stepped out onto the graveled parking area of the crematorium. An icy wind was blowing in from the east that cut through the thick tweed of his overcoat. He adjusted his black leather gloves and leaned against the car, watching the people as they filed out of the chapel. He spotted her after a few seconds, walking alone, distanced from the rest of the mourners. No one was speaking to her, or she to them, as they walked along the row of floral tributes, checking the names on the cards.

Emma took a breath as she reached the wreath she'd ordered for today. White lilies set on a bed of soft green ferns. Elegant and simple. Helen's favorite flowers. Tony Carver came up behind her. "Are you coming back to the house?" he whispered in her ear.

Emma glanced around at Helen's mother, somberly dressed in a black cotton suit, her blond hair pulled tightly away from her face and gathered in a severe bun at the back of her head. The woman hadn't spoken a word to her today, and when Emma had tried to approach her, she'd turned her back in a stiff, formal rejection. Elizabeth Carver had never accepted her daughter's lifestyle, or choice of partner, preferring to think of Helen's sexuality as a phase that she would one day grow out of. Now there was no time for Helen to grow out of anything.

"I don't think I'd be very welcome, do you?"

Tony Carver looked across at his mother. He could almost feel the chill emanating from her. "She tries hard," he said. "But I think Mother always imagined Helen would marry a doctor, or lawyer or something, and populate the world with grandchildren. She took it badly when Helen told her she was gay. It was yet another disappointment in her life and one she refused to accept. I'm afraid she blames you for turning her gay, even though Helen was at pains to tell her about her previous partners, and gave her chapter and verse on all of them. But I think Mother recognized the relationship with you was something different, more serious.

Permanent. And I think she hates you for giving Helen something she'd never been able to give her herself. Unconditional love. It's really something quite special."

"You don't have to apologize for her, you know. Helen warned me what she was like, and why. That's why we never went to visit her."

"Very wise." He shuffled his feet slightly. "Look," he said. "This is all a bit embarrassing, but she's arranged for me to take the Maxwells back to the house in my car. I won't be able to give you a lift home."

Emma shrugged. "No problem," she said. "It was very good of you to bring me. I thought you'd probably want to come here in one of the hearses."

"Good God, no. Those bloody things make you feel you're dead already . . ." His voice trailed off, and he shook his head slightly. "It still hasn't sunk in, you know?"

"I know," Emma said, and took his hand. "One day we'll get back to something approaching normal. We'll paper over this . . . this chasm she's left in our lives."

"And hopefully we'll only occasionally fall into it," he said.

"As long as one of us is there to help the other out, I think we'll survive, don't you?"

"I'd like to think so," he said.

"Don't worry about the lift. I'll call a cab."

"If you're sure. I could always come back here once I've dropped the Maxwells off at the house."

"Really, it's no trouble. Besides, I think I want to stay here for a while . . . if you see what I mean?"

He squeezed her hand. "Yes," he said. "I think I do." He started to move back to the main group.

"Tony."

He looked back at her.

"Don't be a stranger, okay?"

He smiled. "I won't. Don't worry. I'll call you in a day or so. We'll do lunch."

"Yes, I'd like that."

She watched him meander his way back to his car, stopping occasionally to exchange words with various mourners, then turned her attention back to the flowers.

Someone had sent a wreath, the flowers fashioned in the shape of a horse. It was misshapen and looked more like a donkey. Emma smiled. Helen would have found it hysterically funny. That was what she'd miss most about her: her irrepressible sense of humor; the ability to see the funny side of any situation. A tear dribbled from her eye and ran down her cheek. She wiped it away with a gloved hand. Christ, would the tears never stop?

Away in the parking area people were climbing into cars, engines were being started, vehicles were moving away out through the ornate, wrought iron gates. A liveried undertaker was holding the door open of the leading hearse for Elizabeth Carver to enter. The woman took one look back at the crematorium, met Emma's eyes for an instant, and in that instant her own blazed in open hostility. Then she slipped on a pair of dark glasses to hide the hatred and stepped into the air-conditioned warmth of the car.

As the hearse pulled out of the car park Emma noticed the fawn Bentley parked just behind it, and recognized the figure leaning against the hood of the car. For a moment she was thrown. What the hell was Alex Keltner doing here?

He saw her looking and raised his hand slightly to acknowledge her, then beckoned her across.

"Alex?"

"Are you okay?"

"Yes. No." She shook her head. "Why are you here? You didn't know Helen, did you?" It was a stupid question. Of course he didn't know Helen!

"I came to offer moral support," he said, and surveyed the now empty car park. "And apparently to offer you a lift."

"You're very kind."

"Well, can I?"

"Can you what?"

"Offer you a lift."

She hesitated, reluctant to leave. Helen was still here. Behind her she heard the deep rumble of the crematorium's furnaces as they burst into life. She shivered violently. "Yes," she said. "Get me out of here."

"I'm sorry I've not been at work," she said as she settled into the leather seat of the Bentley.

"That's not a problem. No one expected you."

"No one expects the Spanish Inquisition."

"Pardon?"

"Sorry. Helen used to say that all the time. She was a huge Monty Python fa . . ." It was then her reserve crumbled and the tears she had been fighting back all day started to pour unchecked from her eyes.

As she sobbed Keltner pushed a button on his armrest and a glass partition slid into place, separating them from the driver. Then he slid his arm around Emma's heaving shoulders and pulled her close.

By the time the Bentley drew up outside her cottage Emma had managed to gather herself and was sitting in embarrassed silence. "Would you like to come in for a drink?" she said.

"Yes, I think I would."

"What about . . ." She gestured toward the driver.

"Perkins doesn't drink when he's driving. He'll be fine here."

She let them into the cottage and showed Keltner through to the lounge. "Can you give me a minute? I need to change out of these clothes."

"Take all the time you need. I'll be fine."

She ran up the stairs, taking off her jacket as she went. A few minutes later she'd changed into jeans and a T-shirt. When she returned to the lounge Keltner was sitting on the couch, a large glass of whiskey in his hand, flicking though a book on Italian architecture.

"I helped myself," he said, raising the glass to her. "Hope you don't mind."

Emma was instantly flustered. What was it about this man that made her feel about ten years old? "No, not at all. I should have offered before I went upstairs. I guess I'm not thinking straight at the moment."

"And who can blame you? I poured you one, by the way. There on the table."

She sat down on the chair opposite the couch and reached for the drink he'd poured. Vodka and slimline tonic. She raised her glass. "To Helen . . . wherever she may be."

"*Slainth*," he said, and sipped his whiskey. He was looking about the room and focused on the mantelpiece above the fireplace. There were dozens of framed photographs perched there, jostling for space with a vase of wilted flowers and a china statue of a horse.

She noticed where his gaze had settled. "Sorry," she said. "I haven't got round to putting things away yet."

"Please stop saying sorry," he said. "It's as if you're apologizing for being in love with her."

"Part of me is," she said.

"Explain."

She shook her head. "I can't. At least not in any rational way. My head tells me one thing, my heart something else. It's all very confusing." She took a long pull on her drink. "Helen's mother hates me, you know."

"It's not important now."

"No, I don't suppose it is." She stared down into the bottom of her glass. She wished the alcohol would hurry up and take effect. She wanted to recapture the numbness she'd felt when she first heard the news about Helen. Since then she'd been an open nerve: raw, flinching at the slightest stimulus. She craved oblivion.

"I think I should be straight with you," Alex Keltner said after a long silence. "My reasons for being here are not completely altruistic."

She was jerked back to reality. "What do you mean?"

"There was a more selfish reason for coming today. I need to ask you a huge favor. Feel free to refuse; I'll totally understand. But I should say that I think my proposal will benefit you too. If I didn't believe that then I wouldn't be here. I couldn't be that crass."

"What is it?"

He put his glass down on the coffee table and leaned forward, resting his elbows on his knees. "I have a house in the New Forest and this weekend I've got a few people coming to stay for a few days. It's a social event, not business . . . at least not formal business. There *will* be the odd deal discussed over the port and cigars—at least if things go the way I envisage—but nothing on the official agenda. I would really like you to come along."

"Why?"

"A fair question. Try this: Although you haven't officially started yet, you *are* my PA. Monica's replacement. And being my escort for this type of function is what Monica excelled at. I'm quite adrift without her."

"Rather large shoes to fill," Emma said.

"You knew that when you took the job. Look, all I'm asking you to do is to come to the New Forest, charm my guests, look good on my arm as we go in for dinner, and laugh at my jokes at the table. The last part is an absolute necessity." He smiled. "Think you're up to the job?"

Three times, tops, Emma thought. "I'm not sure," she said. "It's too soon. I'm not sure I'd be brilliant company at the moment."

"I understand that. But one day you're going to have to move on. I'm sure Helen wouldn't approve of you putting your life on hold just because she's gone."

Anger flared behind her eyes. How the hell did he know what Helen would or wouldn't have approved of? He didn't know her! The thought had reached her lips but she clamped them together tightly to hold it back. He was only trying to help. And he was right. Helen always moved forward and never looked back.

She steadied herself. "I'll come," she said.

"That's great. All I ask is that you're there at mealtimes. You'll have most of the day to yourself. You can explore the forest, go shopping, whatever you want. You don't drive, do you?"

"I can, but I never took my test. Helen was always nagging me about it."

"It's not a problem. A car and driver will be at your disposal, as and when you need it. We dress for dinner. You have evening wear?"

Emma grimaced. "Some, but I'm not sure I have enough to last more than two nights."

He shook his head. "No, you'll need more than that. We'll be there at least twice that long, possibly longer if everyone's enjoying themselves ... and they usually do." He reached into his jacket pocket and produced a credit card. He handed it to her. "Spend the next couple of days kitting yourself out. Charge it to the company."

She took the card and stared at it. "That's very generous."

He waved it away. "Investment. And let's face it, I've rather sprung this on you. It's only fair. Try not to exceed two thousand, though, or I'll have the Financial Director chewing my ear off."

Two thousand! She could dress herself for a year on that!

He stood. "I'd better be going," he said. "You'll be all right on your own?"

"Yes," she said. "I'll be fine. It's something I've got to get used to."

"Okay, then. I'll have a car pick you up Friday afternoon to take you down there. Is two o'clock okay?"

"Yes, of course."

"That's settled then. And I don't expect to see you at the office in the meantime. Go out, buy clothes, get yourself back on track . . . and practice laughing at awful jokes. That last part is an order."

She walked him to the door. On impulse she kissed his cheek. "Thanks," she said.

He took her hands in his. "Just remember that however you're feeling right now, and I know this is a terrible time for you, you're not alone. Not anymore."

She waited until the Bentley slid smoothly away from the curb, then she shut the door and listened to the silence of the house. "Oh, Helen," she said softly, and started to cry again.

When she went to bed that night a thousand thoughts crowded into her head, blocking out sleep, even though she was bone-achingly tired. After an hour of tossing and turning in frustration she went to the bathroom and rummaged in the cabinet until she found Helen's supply of sleeping pills. Her partner had been a chronic insomniac and took pills to help her sleep almost every night. She read the instructions on the bottle and took two, washed down with a handful of water from the tap on the hand basin, then padded back to bed and pulled the covers up to her chin, waiting for sleep to claim her. The thoughts still whirled in her mind, memories of times spent with Helen, the things they did together, the people they'd met, the places they'd been. But gradually the thoughts grew cloudy and less focused. She thought of Alex Keltner and his invitation for the weekend. Two thousand pounds to spend on clothes! Crazy!

Her last thought before the drug-induced sleep claimed her was, *How the hell did he know where I keep the drinks? And, how did he know I drink vodka and tonic?*

CHAPTER 6

Trevor Sorbie's salon in Covent Garden was thrumming with activity. Hair was being washed in back basins, stylists moved around their clients with brisk efficiency, scissors flashing, their inane conversation at odds with the fierce concentration in their eyes. Emma struggled through the door with her bags from Harvey Nichols and Prada, anxious not to be late for her three o'clock appointment.

Within ten minutes her hair had been washed and she was sitting with a coffee, waiting for Jo, her favorite stylist, to put the finishing touches to a cut she was working on three chairs away.

"Hi, Emma," Jo said, finally coming over to her. "Sorry to keep you. I'm a bit behind today." She ran her fingers through Emma's wet hair, checking for split ends and finding none. "Just a trim?"

Emma shook her head. "No. I want something different." She reached into her bag and produced a photograph of Helen from the summer before. A head and shoulders shot taken at a friend's wedding. It was

Emma's favorite photograph of her; she couldn't remember her ever looking more radiant, more beautiful.

She handed the picture to the stylist. "I want that."

Jo stared at the photo of Helen, at the short, pixie cut. "Radical," she said. "Are you sure?"

Emma stared at herself in the mirror. Yes, she was sure. She'd been thinking about doing this for days. It was to be her small tribute to Helen; something she knew her lover would have approved of, and would have found irresistibly sexy. Cutting her hair was something Helen had been trying to persuade her to do from almost the moment they met, and something Emma had always resisted. *Well, my love, this is for you. I hope you like it.*

She met Jo's eyes in the mirror. "Yes," she said. "I'm sure. Crop it."

At two o'clock sharp Friday afternoon the doorbell rang. Emma was ready. She'd followed Keltner's instructions and bought clothes—not only evening wear, but some smart casuals for the daytime. She had blown the budget, and raided her savings to supplement the money provided by the company. She checked herself in the mirror in the hallway before answering the door, still getting a shock from her cropped hair. It made her look so different: younger, less severe . . . less businesslike. She hoped Alex Keltner would approve, not that there was anything she could do about it now!

Standing on the step was a tall man of indeterminate age. He was wearing a smart black suit, his jet-black hair was swept back from his face, and he wore wraparound sunglasses to hide his eyes. He introduced himself as Erik, her driver for the trip down to Hampshire. She looked beyond him to the silver Mercedes parked on the street, went to pick up her suitcase but was relieved of it by Erik, who lifted the heavy bag as if it were filled with feathers and strode off back to the car where he stowed it in the boot. He then held open the back door for her to enter, only closing it again when he'd made sure she was comfortable and that her seat belt was attached. *A man of few words*, she thought as he settled into the driver's seat, adjusted the mirror and pulled away.

On the seat next to her there was a green folder with her name on it. Alex Keltner had phoned her earlier to check if she was still coming.

"Of course I'm still coming," she said. "I've followed your instructions and blown the budget you gave me. My suitcase is heaving."

"Good," Alex said, laughing. "I knew you wouldn't let me down. Now, listen. When the car arrives you'll find a folder on the backseat. Inside are dossiers on all our guests. Read them, get to know them. You'll find it help-ful when you get here. Don't worry—they're not too de-tailed, but the papers should give you all you need to know for the introductions. It will save a lot of unneces-sary fumbling for small talk."

"Thanks, I appreciate that. I must admit, the butter-flies are beginning to swarm in my stomach."

"You'll be fine. Don't worry. If it's any consolation, I find these types of gathering a bit nerve-racking."

She doubted that very much but said nothing.

"Just read the file. It'll make the journey go quicker," he said.

And that was just what she intended to do. Erik, the driver, was certainly no conversationalist, and she wasn't going to spend several hours sitting there staring at the back of his head. So she relaxed back in her seat, flicked on the car's interior light, and settled down to read.

By the time they reached the M3 she'd familiarized herself with the contents of the file. There were thumbnail sketches of each of the guests expected, and some added margin notes on each of them, some of the notes not very complimentary, which begged the question as to why they had been invited in the first place. Keltner had also thoughtfully added a local map and a few pieces of paper, flyers for local beauty spots she could visit. He'd thought of everything. She wondered if this was the standard form with Keltner; whether Monica Patterson had been given such a generous wardrobe budget and whether her briefing had been so comprehensive. Or was it because she was so new to the game that she was being given special treatment? In a way it was quite intimidating. She felt she had an awful lot to live up to, and hoped she would be able to cope with the job. She would hate to disappoint Alex Keltner, now that he'd shown so much faith in her.

They reached a town called Lyndhurst. During the entire journey Erik had said nothing. He had classical music playing softly as he drove, and whistled along with it occasionally, but there had been no contact with her since he'd picked her up from the cottage. Now he glanced back at her and said gruffly, "Almost there."

Emma had been dozing for the last few miles. At the sound of his voice she jerked herself awake, took a compact out of her bag to check her hair and makeup, and stifled a yawn. It would never do to arrive at such an important function half-asleep. She could almost feel Helen's presence in the car with her, bolstering her confidence, giving her the moral support she badly needed. It was comforting. "Wish me luck, babe," she said softly.

The town gave way to trees and more trees as the car headed into the forest once more. New Forest ponies grazed at the side of the road, munching idly at the grass, disinterested in the passing traffic, and occasionally she spied deer through the gaps in the trees. There was something wonderfully refreshing about seeing animals in their natural habitat, unaffected by civilization bustling around them.

Soon the road narrowed and Erik slowed the car to compensate, almost bringing it to a standstill as a tractor appeared from around a bend, trundling toward them, wheels thick with mud. It squeezed past the Mercedes with inches to spare, the driver smiling widely, used to the near misses on this stretch of the road.

Erik drummed his fingertips on the steering wheel as he waited for the tractor to pass them, his impatience bunching the muscles in his shoulders. Finally it was behind them and the driver sounded his horn by way of thanks. "Prick!" Erik muttered under his breath, then gunned the gas pedal viciously. The car lurched forward and Emma was thrown back in her seat, the back of her skull bouncing off the headrest.

"Careful!" she said. She stared at the dark glasses reflected in the rearview mirror, but as she couldn't see his eyes she had no idea whether Erik had heard her, or was even looking at her. She glared at him anyway.

Half a mile later they turned into a gateway: unmarked, anonymous, partially hidden by a thick hawthorn hedge. The trees gave way to a wide expanse of grass bisected by a narrow asphalt track and she could see the house in the distance, its clean Regency lines marred by a cage of scaffolding that all but covered it.

Gravel crunched under the wheels as Erik swung them onto the drive and pulled up outside the doors to the house. He opened the car door for her and waited until she climbed out, then he went round to the boot and fetched her suitcase.

"This way," he said. Though it was early evening and the sun had long since disappeared behind a layer of cloud, he still wore the sunglasses. *Perhaps he has an aversion to light,* she thought as she followed him up the crumbling stone steps. *Perhaps he's just a pretentious asshole!* She waited while he opened the door, staring back at the drive and the surrounding woodland. She couldn't begin to imagine how much this place had set Alex Keltner back. With its elegant architecture and grand setting, it had all the trappings of a stately home. Even the air of decay that hung around the place was appropriate and suited the place perfectly.

Once inside he closed the door behind them and put her case down on the flagstoned floor. "Wait here. Someone will be along presently." He smiled at her for the first time. It was like looking at the face of a leopard that had just smelled the whiff of prey on the air.

Without another word he walked through a pair of double doors at the end of the hallway and closed them behind him.

She checked her watch. Two minutes later she checked it again. Then she heard voices coming from behind the doors and waited expectantly. Seconds later they opened and a woman emerged. She was in her fifties, with a kind, motherly face and gray hair that curled attractively about her plump cheeks. "You must be Emma," she said brightly. "I'm Florence Dowling. It's my job to keep this place running smoothly . . . and believe me, it isn't easy."

"I can imagine," Emma said, warming to the woman immediately.

"I'll take you up to your room," she said. "No doubt you'd like to freshen up before you start."

Start what? Emma thought, but said nothing and followed Florence back through the doors and up a wide wooden staircase to a carpeted landing.

What struck her first was how bare the walls were. They were painted a dull cream, and there were dusty squares and rectangles marring the paintwork where pictures had once hung. Florence noticed her interest. "It's all in storage while the restoration work is going on. Believe me, I know what some of the pictures are worth, and you really wouldn't want anything to happen to them. Mr. Keltner is a very cautious man . . . and very wise."

"Is he here?"

"Oh Lord, yes. He arrived at the crack of dawn. Been working ever since. I really don't know how he does it. Barely eats, never seems to sleep, but he's fitter than you or me. A workaholic, I think."

"He's the same in London. He has something of a reputation in the company."

"Here we are," Florence said as they reached an open doorway. "This will be your room whenever you come down here, so please treat it like a home away from home. The next time you come you can bring some things with you to pretty it up, to make it your own. You'll have your own key, so privacy is assured. Of course, there *is* a master key, but I hold that, and it's only given to the maid when she comes to clean the room, and then it comes straight back to me. So there's nothing to worry about on that score."

"I wasn't worried, really," Emma said with a smile.

"Maybe not, but it safeguards my staff and me. There was an unpleasant incident last year when one of Mr. Keltner's guests claimed some papers had been taken from his room. Of course, they hadn't. He'd simply left them in a briefcase in his car, but for a few hours it caused quite a stir, and a lot of bad feeling. Now we take no chances. Anyway, enough of me prattling on. I'll leave you to freshen up. Mr. Keltner wishes to see you at six."

"Right," Emma said. "Where will I find him?"

Florence Dowling laughed, making her plump

cheeks wobble. "You won't. Not in this maze of a place. Twenty-five bedrooms, ten bathrooms, two kitchens, and God knows how many reception rooms. No, I'll come and fetch you at five to six, and take you to his apartment. That way you'll not spend the evening walking around in circles. I'll see you later."

When she'd gone, Emma lifted her suitcase onto the bed and started to unpack. The room could best be described as *tired*, but someone had worked hard to make it as comfortable as possible. There was an old black-painted iron bedstead, topped with polished brass finials, but the mattress was new and felt comfortable to the touch. The impression of tiredness came from the decor that was circa 1950: busy, but faded, floral wallpaper, and yellowing paint that bubbled in places on the woodwork. Some of the bubbles had burst to reveal the dark wood beneath. The carpet was pale green and seemed to be comprised of several smaller pieces, probably from other rooms, brought together to make a whole. There was an oak chest of drawers and matching wardrobe which smelled of mothballs, a fifties-style walnut veneered dressing table with a triptych mirror, and an easy chair fitted with a loose chintz cover. It reminded Emma of a hotel room she and Helen had stayed in Derbyshire during their courting days. It had been truly awful, but the excitement of being away together for the first time had been compensation enough, and afterward they'd agreed that despite all its shortcomings the hotel had been as near perfect as they could have wished.

The room had a small, en suite bathroom, a recent addition judging from the ultramodern fittings and the Jacuzzi bath. No expense had been spared, but the room seemed at odds and out of character with the rest of the house. She decided to explore the house tomorrow and see what other anomalies she could turn up.

But she didn't have to wait that long.

She'd finished unpacking and was lying on the bed with mixed feelings of apprehension and excitement, watching the hands on the clock on the bedside table crawl around the dial. At 5:45 she heard voices. They seemed to be coming from directly outside her window. Swinging her legs from the bed she padded barefoot across the carpet. She looked out through the glass but could see only the grounds of the house, which seemed to spread out forever, meeting the trees of the forest and merging as one with them.

The catch on the window was tight and stiff, and by the time she managed to slide it to one side and push the window open her fingers felt raw. Now the voices were louder, but the words were still indistinct. A man and a woman talking and, from the tone of their voices, arguing. Resting her fists on the dusty concrete sill she leaned out and looked down and along the side of the house. Several yards away she saw the now familiar figure of Erik engaged in conversation with someone who was hidden from view by a mass of ivy that covered the wall to her left. The only indication that there was someone there was a telltale stream of blue-gray smoke eddying up from a cigarette. Moments later a slender hand appeared, an index finger tapping ash from the end of the cigarette onto the path. The hand moved expressively and the female voice was rising.

Emma edged forward, conscious that there was nothing to stop her overbalancing and falling to the concrete below and, although she still couldn't see the owner of the voice, she recognized it at once. Strident, slightly nasal and very familiar.

"If you won't do it, I will!"

The words floated up at her.

"You'll do as you're told," Erik said.

"Who the hell do you think you are? It's not your place to tell me what to do."

Emma moved a little farther out, craning her neck to hear more. And the corner of the windowsill crumbled under her weight. She lost her balance and with a small cry of panic she pitched forward. Instinctively she flung her hand back to grab hold of the window frame, giving a sob of relief as her fingers closed around the frame. She landed hard, the cold concrete of the sill thumping into her stomach. Winded, she balanced there, gasping for breath, the nerve endings throughout her body tingling with adrenaline, making her feel nauseous.

The falling masonry and Emma's cry had attracted Erik's attention, and when she looked down again he was standing on the path below her window, staring up at her, his face a blank, expressionless mask.

Then he took off the dark glasses.

The eyes were pale, almost colorless, and they stared up at her with an intensity she could feel right down to her toes. In a panic she struggled to pull herself back inside, but the eyes held her, drawing her forward. They seemed to be sucking her out of the room. She tightened her grip on the window frame, trying to resist, but the pull of those pallid, lifeless eyes seemed too strong. They were drawing her toward them. Another few inches and her center of gravity would shift and there would be nothing to stop her plummeting to the ground below.

Desperately she tried to tear her gaze away from his, but it held her, like some incredibly powerful magnet, making her mind cloud over, her thoughts becoming woolly, confused and erratic. Suddenly she wanted to hurl herself from the window, to feel the cold concrete below. She let go of the window frame and inched forward.

"Erik!"

The voice jerked her back to reality. She looked down to see the woman emerge from behind the ivy.

Erik slipped his sunglasses on and turned away as the woman stepped out of sight again. Emma hauled herself back into the room and closed the window with trembling hands. She sat down on the bed, breathing deeply, trying to calm herself, and trying to figure out what had just happened. She'd nearly killed herself, but more than that, for a few seconds she had *wanted* to kill herself, and that frightened her badly. But there was another question burning in her mind: *What on earth is Monica Patterson doing here?*

CHAPTER 7

A few moments later there was a knock at the door.

"All ready?" Florence Dowling said as Emma opened the door.

"Yes . . . yes, of course."

Florence looked at her closely. "Are you all right, dear? You look a little pale."

Emma forced a smile. "I'm fine. A bit nervous, that's all," she said, brushing concrete dust from the front of her skirt.

Florence clicked her tongue. "Silly girl. There's nothing to be nervous about," she said. "Come along. You don't want to keep him waiting."

Legs still trembling, Emma grabbed the folder from the bed and followed the older woman out of the room.

She let herself be led down corridor after corridor, up one flight of stairs, down another, understanding now what Florence meant about the house being like a maze. She could never have hoped to find Alex's apartment without help.

Finally they entered another long corridor and Florence said, "Here we are," and stopped outside a door much like all the others they'd passed. She knocked once, sharply. Without waiting for a response she turned the handle and pushed the door open.

Alex Keltner was sitting behind a large mahogany desk, leaning back in his seat, a cordless phone cradled under his chin. "Yes, but call me when you hear. It's very important." He looked up at Emma and his eyes widened in surprise. "Listen, Raymond, I've got to go . . . Yes, okay, I'll call you." He dropped the phone back onto the desk. "Have a seat, Emma," he said, pointing to a chair. Emma glanced back at Florence, but the woman had already left the room and closed the door.

Emma sat, nervously fingering the short soft hairs at the nape of her neck. The haircut was making her feel self-conscious, not helped by the fact that Keltner couldn't take his eyes off it.

"What made you do it?" he said.

"What," she said, feigning ignorance.

"The hair. What made you cut your hair?"

"Is it a problem?"

He frowned and said nothing.

"I needed a change," she said, becoming more uncomfortable by the second.

He stood and walked around the desk. He walked around *her*. When he was behind her she could almost feel his eyes burning into the back of her head.

"Is it a problem?" she said again.

He sat back down behind the desk. There was a long pause while he considered the question. "No," he said at last. "It should be fine."

Which she thought was an odd thing to say, but she didn't pursue it. She had other, more important matters she wished to raise. Her haircut was a distraction she didn't need. "I have something to ask you," she said.

"Fire away . . . you know it makes you look a lot younger."

Stop going on about my hair! she thought, but said instead, "I need to know if you're being straight with me."

"I'm sorry, I don't think I understand what you mean."

"Monica Patterson's here."

He said nothing, but the skin around his eyes tightened slightly.

"Do you trust me to do this job or not?" she said.

"This sounds like a case of paranoia to me. Or first-night nerves," he said. "Of course I trust you. I appointed you as my personal assistant. I wouldn't have done that if I didn't have absolute faith in your abilities."

"So why is Monica here?"

"She has a house nearby. She rang me this morning to tell me she was down here for the weekend, and that she still had some papers of mine she thought I'd like back. She was just here to drop them off."

"I see," Emma said, unconvinced.

"You don't believe me?"

His face was a picture of wide-eyed innocence, but there was something going on behind his eyes, and she couldn't begin to decipher what it was. "I'm sorry," she said after a moment. "I must have misread the situation."

"Easily done," he said. "Right, let's get down to it, shall we? I see you have the dossiers. Have you read through them?"

"Twice," she said. "It was a long drive down."

"Good," Keltner said.

For the next thirty minutes they went over the contents of the folder, discussing the idiosyncrasies of the invited guests, and planning a rough timetable of events.

"Lars Petersen is already here, as are Keichi Yamada and the Steiners. The Bronsteins arrived at Heathrow two hours ago and are making their way down here by taxi. It'll cost them a fortune, but they can afford it.

Nicci and Massimo Bellini are flying in by Lear. Erik's picking them up from the local airfield and bringing them back here. And there will be one extra guest not listed there. I've had dealings with Nicci and Massimo before and I know they never go anywhere without Mario Bernardi, their bodyguard, so expect to see him too. You can't miss him; he's built like a chieftain tank."

"Isn't that a bit extreme, bringing him along for a social gathering?"

"Not really. They haven't got where they are in business without pissing off a lot of people, so they take no chances. And remember the people coming this weekend are high-profile personalities in their own countries. They're always in the public eye, and they have a powerful hold over many people's lives. It makes them all targets, to a greater or lesser degree, for any psycho with a grudge or an ax to grind. Mario Bernardi is one of the best security men in the business. I think everyone will feel safer knowing he's here. He was assigned to me once, and I know how thorough he is.

"Anyway, we'll hold a champagne reception at eight and expect to sit down to dinner at nine. I've had a word with Didier, and he says he'll be ready to start serving at nine sharp, so I'll be relying on you to keep a watch during the reception and start shepherding people along to the dining room no later than eight fifty. I don't want them filing in when the first course is being served. Have you met Didier yet? Incredibly temperamental, but a superb chef. Trained under Marco Pierre White and worked at the Dorchester for a while. I was very lucky to get him."

"I haven't really met anyone yet, except Florence . . . and Erik, of course."

"Ah yes, Erik. A man of few words," he said, echoing Emma's initial thoughts about him.

"Has he worked for you long?"

"For as long as I can remember." He looked at her

quizzically, narrowing his eyes. "Do you have a problem with him?" he said.

Christ, he was astute! She shook her head. "No . . . no problem," she lied.

"Well, he obviously seems to have made an impression on you."

"Yes, he has," she said. *For all the wrong reasons*, she added silently.

"He'll be pleased. I'll tell him."

"That's really not necessary."

"Oh, but it is. A lot of people have a problem with Erik. He can be . . . well, his manner can sometimes be seen as prickly. I know it upsets him when people take against him. But I can honestly say that, once you get to know him, and he you, you'll get along fine."

I won't be holding my breath, she thought sarcastically, but said, "I'll look forward to it."

"Right," he said, glancing at his watch. "We're all done here. You'll need some time to get yourself ready for the reception. Would you like me to show you back to your room?"

"No, that's all right. I'm sure I'll manage."

"Fine. I'll see you downstairs in about an hour, and we'll greet our guests." He rose from the desk and walked her to the door. "Going back to Erik for a moment," he said as he opened the door. "I hope you two hit it off. It's quite important that you do, because there really is no one in the organization I trust and rely on more."

"I see," she said.

Florence Dowling was waiting for her when she walked out of Keltner's study.

"All finished?" she said brightly. "I'll show you back to your room."

Emma felt slightly embarrassed. "Really, you shouldn't have waited. I would have found my way."

Florence looked at her skeptically. "I'm sure you

would," she said. "But we'll take no chances. Not on your first day here."

"Thank you," Emma said.

"So have you worked for the company long?" Florence said as they walked back down the labyrinth of corridors.

"Just over four years. You?"

"Oh, much longer," Florence said glibly. "I worked for Alex's father for a number of years, doing much the same type of thing. Then, of course, he retired and went to live abroad, and Alex took me on. It was very kind of him. He was under no obligation to do so, but then, that's the measure of the man. He looks after his staff very well. I've known him since he was a teenager and he's never changed. Kind, considerate and perfectly charming. Much like his father, of course. Louis Keltner was some man . . . still is, by all accounts."

"You obviously care about Alex a great deal."

"I do," Florence said. "I suppose he's a bit like a son to me. I can't say the same for his brother, though," she added candidly.

"His brother? I didn't know Alex had a brother."

"Well you should. You've met him."

"I wasn't aware I had."

"Who do you think brought you down here?"

"Erik? Erik is Alex's brother?"

"Older by three years and nothing like him. Chalk and cheese. Personally—and I really shouldn't be telling you this—I haven't got much time for him. He's a very difficult character, but Alex loves him, and won't hear a word against him. As I understand it, when they were growing up Erik saw himself as Alex's protector. Boys who tried to bully him at school had Erik to answer to, and word spread quickly. I think they soon learned to leave Alex alone; better that than face Erik. And, quite honestly, I think it's been that way ever since. In fact I don't think Alex would have got where he is, been so successful, if he hadn't had Erik there to watch his back. He once told me that his brother is his company's greatest asset, which I find hard to believe. But, if it's true, then it's just as well, because I know him, almost as well as I know Alex, and I really wouldn't want him as an enemy."

It was there in her voice, the unspoken warning.

"I'd better get on," she said as they reached Emma's room

"Of course," Emma said. "And thanks for escorting me. I don't think I would have found my way by myself."

"Of course you would . . . eventually," Florence said with a smile.

It was there in the bone structure if you were really looking for it, and in their coloring. But the eyes! The eyes were so different. Alex's were warm and caring, full of humor. Erik's eyes . . . She shuddered, remembering the cold, pale, dead eyes that had been urging her to throw herself from the window. Was she being hysterical, or just fanciful? How could someone force another person to do something against their will, just by looking at them? But she was certain that as Erik was looking up at her from the ground below she could hear his voice in her head. *Go on, jump. You know you want to. What have you got to live for now your lover's dead?* A wheedling, pernicious voice, repeating its refrain over and over again.

She undressed and went into the bathroom, turning on the taps and letting hot steaming water fill the tub. There were various bottles of bath crystals on the shelf above the basin. She chose one, scented with lavender, and poured a generous amount into the water. Instantly the small room was filled with the soothing aroma, conjuring up memories of her childhood, and of long summer holidays spent with her grandparents in Cliftonville, down on the Kent coast. Lavender was her grandmother's favorite scent and she'd keep small, silk bags of the herb in all the drawers in the bedrooms, letting the smell permeate clothes and bedding. It was ever-present and all-embracing.

She turned off the taps and slipped into the water, sinking down underneath the water, letting it soak her hair, enjoying the womblike warmth. Then she resurfaced, laid back and closed her eyes, letting her mind drift back to those carefree, innocent days, when all that was really important in her life was whether the sun would shine the next day and whether it would be fine enough to go down to the beach and gather more seashells to add to her already ridiculously large collection.

Her grandparents would huddle down in deck chairs, protected from the slightest breeze by a striped canvas windbreak, watching her as she played, ready to rescue her should she get out of her depth in the sea or should she fall while clambering over the rocks at the water's edge. It was a reassuring place to be, protected by their love. She missed them still, even though they'd both been dead for over a decade.

She yawned sleepily, folding a face flannel into a makeshift pillow and resting her head on it. She could allow herself a fifteen-minute soak, but no longer. She didn't want to be late for the reception, and she still had her makeup and hair to do, although the hair no longer took half an hour to blow dry and straighten. A quick rub with a towel, a fingerful of gel and it was done. Five minutes, no longer. *I should have cut it years ago*, she thought, her mind drifting, vaguely calculating all the time she could have saved herself had she done so.

There was a breeze playing on her cheek, cool and refreshing. A window must be open somewhere. A seagull called, away in the distance, and she could hear another sound, gently rising in volume. Waves, lapping over a stony beach, washing over rocks, leaving small pools in the sand, where crabs scurried through wet fronds of seaweed in search of food.

"*Don't slip on those rocks, Emma. They're treacherous.*"

"*I won't slip, Grandpa.*"

"*Listen to your grandfather, Emma.*"

"*I won't slip, Nan. Promise.*"

She clambered over the wet, slippery rocks. Yesterday when she was here she'd seen a whole family of crabs. A mother and father, and twenty or thirty babies. She thought she could remember which pool they were in, but now that she was down here among the rocks again all the pools looked the same. In one hand she clutched the handle of a brightly painted metal bucket filled with water; in the other, a small net attached to the end of a yard-long cane, just the thing for scooping up unsuspecting crabs, and any other sea life she came across.

Her foot slipped on a patch of seaweed, and she struggled to keep her balance, furtively glancing back at her grandparents to see if they had noticed. As she progressed over the weed-slick rocks she stared down at her feet, concentrating fiercely, determined not to slip again. Farther on something caught her eye; something that glimmered and sparkled at the bottom of a shallow pool. Crouching down she plunged her hand into the cool crystal water and her fingers closed around something cold and metallic. She gripped it tightly, not wanting to drop it, but also not wanting to even look at it until she was out of sight of Nan and Grandpa.

She found a dry spot of sand in the lee of a mussel-encrusted breakwater and squatted on her haunches, holding out her clenched fist in front of her and letting her fingers open like the petals of a flower.

It was a large gold brooch, set with dark, port-red stones; garnets, she guessed. They covered the face of the jewel, closely set side by side so that only the tips of the metal claws holding them in place were visible. She turned the brooch in her hand, revealing a long gold pin and a small frame set into the back of the jewel. There was glass in the frame, and behind the glass what looked like fair hair woven into an elaborate pattern. Around the edge of the frame an inscription was engraved into the gold. She tried to read it, but the sun was glinting off the metal, making it impossible, and if she shaded it with her hand the letters became illegible. She would wait until she got it home, then examine it through the large magnifying glass that her grandfather used when he looked at his stamps.

As she pushed the brooch down into the pocket of her shorts, the shiny point of the gold pin slid into the ball of her thumb, making her cry out in pain. She rammed her thumb into her mouth, sucking at the blood, trying to suck the pain away.

"Are you all right, Emma?" she heard her grandmother call out. "Where are you? We can't see you."

It was only a pinprick but the pain was intense, like nothing she'd ever felt before. It was making her feel sick and giddy, as if her brain were following the ebb and flow of the waves on the beach. She reached out her hand to steady herself on the breakwater, but the wood was wet and slimy and her hand slipped. She pitched forward onto the sand, and lay there, breathing heavily while the pain from her thumb spread through her entire hand, making it throb in hot, burning pulses.

Her thoughts were getting cloudy, confused, and her vision was blurring. She stared up at the bright blue sky and a ring of faces stared back down at her, black forms, no more than shapes, silhouetted by the sun.

"Can she hear us?"

"Probably. But it doesn't matter."

"She won't remember a thing."

"She's cut her hair. We didn't agree to that."

"Does it matter?"

"Do you think he'll mind?"
"Probably not."
"Seen enough?"
"We're satisfied. She's more than adequate."
"Good."

CHAPTER 8

Emma awoke suddenly, sat up in the bed and looked about the room in total confusion. The last thing she remembered was climbing into the bath. How did she get from there to here? Her head was throbbing, a sick headache pounding behind her eyes. It felt like a hangover, but she knew she hadn't been drinking. She lay down and closed her eyes again, waiting for the pain to stop. Threading her hands through her hair, she pressed her skull, hoping the pressure would ease the throbbing. It didn't, but she noticed her hair was dry.

How long have I been asleep? The question drifted through her mind. She tried to focus. For some reason the question was important, but her cotton-wool brain refused to assimilate it. A clock ticked away the seconds on the table by her bed. With a groan she turned onto her side and opened one eye to look at it. 7:45.

Shit!

She lurched upright. The reception! She was going to be late for the reception!

'Fuck it!" she said angrily and rolled off the bed, running across the room to fetch her clothes.

Her head was still aching as she raced down the stairs. She had dressed, done her makeup and hair in fifteen minutes flat, but she was still late. It would make a terrible impression, and she had so wanted this evening to run smoothly; if only to prove to herself that she was capable of taking over Monica Patterson's job. Well, she'd blown it. She didn't even know in which room the reception was being held. She pulled up sharply on the stairs, straining her ears, hoping to hear the sound of laughter or conversation; something, anything she could use as a guide.

Nothing.

She reached the bottom of the stairs and stood in the large flagstoned entrance hall, turning in a circle as she tried to decide which door to take. Ultimately it didn't matter. One of them would lead her to the reception. She ran to the door on her right. An empty room, dark, a few white shapes of furniture covered by dust sheets.

The second door she tried was a cupboard, crammed full with papers, books and box files.

And then she remembered the double doors through which Florence had emerged earlier. She ran to them and pulled them open.

At last.

Noise.

The double doors led onto a wide corridor, lined with yet more doors. The corridor was quite dark but she could see a strip of light coming from under the door at the far end. She ran to it and pulled it open.

She'd found the reception.

There were a dozen or more people in the room, some forming tight groups and talking animatedly, others in pairs, sipping drinks and holding quiet conversations. Alex Keltner was standing by a huge fireplace, talking to a small Japanese man with close-cropped hair and a thin mustache. Along one side of the room a small table had been set up and six champagne bottles rested in individual silver ice buckets, watched over by a young man in a waiter's outfit. In the far corner Florence Dowling stood alone, overseeing the proceedings with a professional eye, noticing when glasses were empty and signaling the waiter to provide top-ups. She looked across at Emma as she slipped into the room and beckoned her over. She wasn't smiling.

Emma tried to catch Keltner's eye. She was desperate to apologize for her lateness, but he had his back to her and his attention firmly fixed on the Japanese man.

"You're late," Florence said, the irritation evident in her voice. "I'm doing your job for you."

"Oh Christ, I'm so sorry. I don't know what happened. I dozed off. Did Alex notice?"

Florence frowned. "Alex notices everything. He's not amused."

Emma felt her heart sink. Mentally she was kicking herself. "How can I make amends?" she said.

"Mingle," Florence said. "Charm them. Make sure their glasses are full."

"Right. Okay."

"I'll leave you to it," Florence said, moving away. "I've got more important things to attend to."

As she moved something caught Emma's eye. Florence Dowling was wearing a straight gray skirt with a cream, high-collared blouse, fastened at the neck with a garnet brooch. It was the brooch Emma noticed as the other woman walked away. For some reason the piece of jewelry was familiar to her. She recognized it, but she couldn't think from where.

She pushed the thought from her mind. *Mingle*, she thought. *Christ, where do I start?*

It was then she noticed Jeff Williams, standing on the opposite side of the room, talking to a rather beautiful woman, her perfect face framed by curtains of coal-black hair. Almost as if he could feel Emma's eyes on him Jeff turned and met her gaze. He raised his glass to her and smiled, but the smile on his lips was not mirrored in his eyes.

Emma turned away, went across to the drinks table and helped herself to a glass of champagne, checked no one was looking and downed it in one long swallow, hoping it might steady her nerves. She couldn't understand what Jeff was doing here if, as Keltner had said, this was a social event. It was bound to cause friction throughout the weekend, and she silently cursed Alex Keltner for not telling her and allowing her the time to prepare herself for meeting him again.

"You must be Emma," a voice said behind her.

Emma spun round and found herself face-to-face with the woman Jeff had been speaking to. From a distance she was beautiful. Close up she was breathtaking. Flawless, sun-kissed skin, deep brown, almond-shaped eyes, hair the color and iridescence of a raven's wing. She held out a slim, elegant hand. "Nicci Bellini," she said, the Italian accent lilting in her voice.

"Emma, Emma Porter," Emma said, taking her hand.

Nicci Bellini frowned. "Your hand is cold, Emma. Frozen. Come, stand by the fire."

Emma looked across anxiously at the fireplace, but Alex Keltner had moved on and was now on the other side of the room, talking to a large, fair-headed man. Lars Petersen, she guessed.

Still holding her hand Nicci Bellini led her across the room to the fireplace. Burning logs were roaring and spitting in the grate, spilling their heat into the room.

"I want you to meet my brother, Massimo," Nicci said, turning and scanning the room with her almond eyes, spotting him in the doorway, standing alone, sipping from his champagne glass. "Massimo!" she called loudly, seemingly unaware that all eyes in the room had turned to look at her. "Massimo, come and meet Emma, Alex's new friend."

"I hardly think . . ." The words petered out as Emma realized that everyone was now looking at *her*, including Keltner, who was smiling slightly, as if he found the whole thing amusing.

Massimo Bellini was slim, dark and as handsome as his sister was beautiful. He sauntered across the room toward her. Emma had never actually seen someone saunter before, but that was the only way she could describe how he moved. He gave the impression of total self-possession, as if he owned the room.

He held out a hand as he drew near. "Emma," he said. "Delighted to meet you." Like his sister his English was flawless, but the slight accent gave it color, summoning up images in her mind of gondolas moving as serenely as swans along the canals of Venice. As Emma stretched out her hand to his he took it and kissed it. There was nothing courtly or old-fashioned in the gesture. The lips barely brushed the skin, but where they touched they produced a tingle of excitement. The gesture was pure seduction.

"Alex told me he had acquired a new assistant, but he didn't tell me he had managed to find such a beautiful one. I'm sure your predecessor was very good at her job, but lacking somewhat in social grace."

"Massimo!" Nicci said reprovingly. "That's an awful thing to say. We all loved Monica, and she was Alex's right arm, as she proved time and time again." She turned to Emma. "Forgive me, but I speak the truth. I'm sure that we will grow to love you in the same way."

Emma smiled graciously. "It's okay. I know I have a lot to live up to. Besides, she's here, you know?"

Nicci Bellini's eyes widened slightly. "Monica, here? Alex never said." She turned and found Alex Keltner with her eyes. "When he's finished with that bore Peterson I will have words with him. If Monica is here then she should be at this reception."

"Please," Emma said quickly. "Don't make an issue of it. I'm not sure I'm meant to know that she's here."

"There, Nicci, don't go making waves so soon after arriving," her brother said to her. "You wouldn't want to get Emma into trouble." He turned to Emma and took her hand again. "Perhaps you will accompany me to dinner tonight?"

Nicci Bellini gave a short laugh and said something to her brother in Italian. His smile faltered a little.

She slid her arm around Emma's shoulders and whispered in her ear. "I told him to save his charm for someone who might be receptive to it."

"Sorry?" Emma said.

Nicci Bellini's face grew serious. "Alex told me about the terrible loss you suffered recently. It is always so difficult to lose someone you love so much."

Emma flushed. She had no idea her personal life was under such scrutiny, and it bothered her. "He shouldn't have told you," she said.

Nicci Bellini slid her arm down from Emma's shoulders to her waist, pulling her closer. "It's all right. It's nothing to be ashamed of," she said, her voice still little more than a whisper.

"But I'm not ashamed," Emma said, feeling her temper rising to her cheeks, making them hot. She pulled away from her.

Massimo Bellini's eyes sparkled with amusement; then he said something in his sister's ear.

For a moment anger flared in her eyes, but it quickly subsided. "You're impossible," she hissed at him.

"The offer stands, Emma," he said. "Accompany me to

dinner. A man is judged by the beauty of the woman on his arm and I think I would be judged well."

"Perhaps," Emma said, making an effort to smile again. "But I think Alex might have other plans for me."

"Then I will get him to change them," Massimo said, and peeled away from them, spying Alex Keltner by the champagne table and sauntering across to him. "Alex, a word please," he said for all the room to hear.

"I can tell I've upset you," Nicci said to Emma. "I'm sorry. That wasn't my intention."

Emma relaxed a little, took a breath. "No, I'm the one who's sorry. I'm just a little raw, that's all. Oversensitive, I suppose."

Nicci slipped her arm back around Emma's waist. "You've every right to be. Come," she said. "Let's get a drink and we can start over."

Emma nodded. "Okay."

By the time dinner was served Emma was feeling a little better. She had managed to speak to several more of the guests and shepherded everyone into the dining room by 8:50 as instructed, including Massimo Bellini.

"You were right; Alex wants you for himself tonight. He's promised to let me escort you tomorrow evening, if you have no objection."

"No, none at all."

Finally there was only herself and Keltner left in the reception room.

"I'm sorry I was late," she said as he took her arm.

"You made up for it so don't apologize. I was watching you with the guests. I think I made the right choice when I picked you for the job. You're a natural. The Bellinis seem very taken with you, especially Massimo."

"He knows I'm gay."

Keltner laughed. "I shouldn't think a mere technicality like that will deter him. I know him only too well."

"Then he'll be disappointed." She hesitated at the

doorway. "To be honest with you, Alex, I feel a little out of my depth," she said. "For most of the time when I was talking to people I felt terrified. I was worried they were going to ask me impossible questions, about you, about the company."

"You underestimate my guests, Emma. They all know your situation; they're aware of your inexperience, but none of them are crass enough to capitalize on it. You may have been terrified, but you certainly didn't show it, and that's all the counts. I'm very pleased with the way you handled yourself. Shall we?" he said, and steered her toward the door.

CHAPTER 9

Halfway through the meal she started feeling sick. It had nothing to do with the food, which was delicious, but there was another large fireplace in the room piled high with burning logs which made it feel oppressively hot, and the heat was starting to affect her. She looked around the table but apparently nobody else was bothered by it. The dress she was wearing seemed to be shrinking, tightening around her breasts, restricting her breathing and adding to the feeling of nausea. She took a sip of wine and fanned herself with her napkin, the cool breeze giving her some respite from the suffocating warmth.

Nicci Bellini was sitting to her left, Jeff to her right, giving her the feeling of being hemmed in. Jeff leaned over and whispered in her ear. "Are you feeling all right?"

She shook her head slightly, not trusting herself to open her mouth to speak.

"Perhaps some air?" he said.

"Mmm."

He stood up and helped her to her feet. The room had started to spin alarmingly and she leaned into him for support. No one at the table seemed to be looking at them, all of them deep in conversation with their neighbors.

As they moved toward the French doors which led onto the terrace Emma glanced back at the room, but the picture was the same. They could have been invisible.

The cold night air hit her like a frozen hand and she immediately began to shiver. Jeff took off his dinner jacket and draped it over her shoulders. "You'll feel better in a moment or two; just breathe deeply."

She doubted he was right. All she wanted to do was to escape to her bed, pull the covers up to her chin and sink into a deep, deep sleep. She felt so tired her whole body was aching. Even the roots of her hair seemed to be crying out in agony. But she followed his advice and took a lungful of air, slowly followed by another.

Jeff had taken two steps away from her and was lighting a cigarette. She watched him as he blew a thin cloud of smoke up at the night sky. She had worked for him for a year and they had got along well. He had always been considerate and kind to her and now, standing out here in the chilly night, she felt guilty that she had left him to work for Alex Keltner.

"I'm sorry," she said.

"For what?"

"Everything, I suppose." She ran a hand through her hair. He'd been right; the feeling of nausea was dissipating with each breath of fresh air she took. "Leaving you in the lurch at work. And now this, dragging you away from the table."

"You don't have to apologize for that. I could see you were suffering. Besides, I was grateful to have an excuse to come out here and smoke. Alex hates smoking and never allows it in the house."

"You've been here before, then?"

"Many times."

From the terrace she had a clear view across the garden. The gazebo she could see from her room stood in the middle of a wide expanse of lawn, crumbling into disrepair, the iron framework rusting and weather-worn, many of the windows cracked and broken. Lit by the moonlight it stood, an old, decaying remnant of a distant past, its former glory long since consigned to history.

"It's a rather sad house," she said. "Don't you think?"

"Probably. I've never given it much thought."

"It's so vast, yet so empty. It needs people to bring it to life."

"It has people tonight."

"Yes, but the wrong kind," she said. "A house like this needs to be lived in, needs to feed off the energy of those within it. Houses are like batteries; they store that energy. You can feel it as you walk into a place. You can tell whether the house has stored positive or negative energy. It tells you something about the people who live, or who lived, there. This place is cold and sad. I felt it when I first entered, and it will take more than a few dinner parties to redress the balance and swing the energy level around again."

"Why do you care?"

She shrugged. "I don't know that I do."

"Then why the speech?"

'I'm . . .' Her voice caught in her throat as she tried to speak. She coughed to clear it. "I'm missing Helen very much tonight. Energy was her thing. She loved crystals, pyramids and all that kind of stuff. Very into it. She used to say that we were untouchable because of all the positive energy we gave off. She was wrong. We weren't untouchable at all. We were just as vulnerable as everyone else. Just gliding blithely along, unaware that life was just waiting to smack us in the face. Serves us right for being so smug." She felt a tear slide down her cheek, realized she was crying and swore silently for letting her emotions get the better of her.

"You shouldn't have come here," Jeff said. He moved close to her and slipped an arm around her shoulder. "You shouldn't have taken Alex's job."

"Not now, Jeff. I can't discuss work now."

"This isn't about work. You shouldn't have come here."

"I know. You said."

"Leave," he said. "Promise me you'll leave in the morning. I'll drive you into town. You can catch a train back to London."

"I live in Cambridge," she said, starting to feel slightly irritated by his obliqueness.

"I know, but . . ."

She slid out from under his arm, turning to face him. "I can't leave. You know that. And why should I? Just because I've got a fit of the blues tonight? Don't worry, I'll be as right as ninepence tomorrow. Fighting fit and ready to go, and insufferably good-humored. Besides, Alex needs me."

"More than you know," Jeff said.

"Meaning?" She looked into his eyes. They were troubled; she could almost see through them to the turmoil in his mind.

"There's something you have to know. The reason for you being here. It's not what it seems. Not what it seems at all."

He kept doing this: dropping heavy hints about something but refusing to elaborate. She almost wanted to take him by the shoulders and shake the explanation from his lips. "Then tell me," she said.

His eyes were flitting from side to side, afraid to meet her own. Finally they came to rest, and she saw the anguish in them. "I must tell you . . ."

There was a small cough, a clearing of the throat behind them, and Erik was there on the terrace, not two
yards from where they stood, almost as if he'd material-
ized out of thin air. "Alex would like you to go back inside now," he said. "Dessert is about to be served."

Emma looked from him back to Jeff, who had taken a
step away from her and was staring at Erik with something like fear etched into the lines of his face. "Of
course," he said. He took Emma's arm. "Come," he said.

Emma shrugged him off. "Hold on. Wait a minute."
She turned to Erik. "I was feeling unwell. I needed
some air."

Erik's face was impassive, all expression lost behind
his dark glasses. "You're better now," he said, a slight
smile twisting his lizard lips.

Jeff took her arm again, gripping it so tightly she
could feel his fingers bruising her bicep. "Alex is waiting," he said urgently.

She stopped resisting. "Okay," she said. "Okay." And
she let herself be led through the French doors and
back into the house.

"Are you feeling better now?" Nicci Bellini said as
Emma slid back into her seat beside her.

"Yes, I am, thank you."

"Good. We were getting worried about you."

Emma looked around at the faces at the table. Everyone was staring at her. She hid her embarrassment by
taking a long pull from her wine glass. It had been re-
plenished in her absence. "Thank you all for your concern," she said, looking up to meet the faces. "I'm fine
now. Really."

Jeff had also resumed his seat and was staring down
at the plate of food in front of him as if it were a plate of
poison that he was expected to eat.

"Glad you're feeling better, Emma," Alex Keltner said
from the head of the table, spooning a mound of straw-

berry pavlova into his mouth. He swallowed and wiped his lips with his napkin. "Lars was just telling us an interesting story about a merger he conducted last year." He turned to the Swede. "Continue, Lars."

The man's words washed over her as she ate her dessert. She kept stealing sideways glances at Jeff. He wasn't touching his food, and there was a distant look in his eyes. When everyone had finished he folded his napkin, rose, and with a mumbled, "Excuse me," left the table, and the room.

"Are you sure you're all right now," Nicci Bellini said quietly, leaning in so her head was almost touching Emma's. Emma could smell her perfume: an exotic, heady aroma that stopped just short of being overpowering. "I was worried about you. You looked so pale when you left the table."

"I didn't think anyone had noticed. Now it seems that everybody did. I feel a complete fool."

"There's no need. I think everyone was concerned, that's all." She slid her hand over Emma's, squeezing reassuringly.

"I'm just having a rough time at the moment. Losing Helen . . . well . . . it's been difficult."

"You loved her very much?"

Emma slid her hand out from underneath Nicci's. "I'd rather not talk about it, if you don't mind," she said, as diplomatically as she could, resenting the question but not wanting to cause offense. She'd made so many mistakes already that she was beginning to feel wretched, humiliated and completely out of her depth. *Oh, Monica, why did you have to leave?*

As coffee and liqueurs were served, the old-fashioned ritual of leaving the men to their port and cigars was observed. Emma could scarcely believe the formality of the evening. It was like taking in dinner at a grand country house with the incumbent lord as the host.

As Emma, Marta Steiner, Sylvia Bronstein and Nicci Bellini left the room, Nicci threaded her arm through hers. "Come," she said, pulling back from the others. "Let's skip the coffee. I have something much more stimulating in my bag."

As the other two women went on ahead, Nicci steered Emma into a darkened room to the left of the dining room. With a schoolgirl giggle she flicked on the light and closed the door. Emma heard the click of the key turning in the lock.

"I should be with the others," Emma said anxiously.

Nicci pulled a face. "What, and be bored to death by their stories of the menopause? God help us. I'd rather rip off my ears than suffer that."

The room Nicci Bellini had chosen was the library, every wall lined with leather-bound volumes. They all looked unreadable and probably were; a rich man's collection, designed to show off his erudition but only serving to prove his illiteracy.

There was a large oak table in the center of the room. Nicci had set her bag down and was going through it, searching for something. Finally she swore savagely and turned to Emma. "They're gone. Fuck it, they're gone!"

Emma looked at her uncomprehendingly.

"That bastard Massimo. He's always interfering in my life. He must have taken them."

"Taken what?" Emma said.

"Fuck him, fuck him!" Nicci said, still searching her bag. "I will not be treated as a child!"

"Does it matter?" Emma said.

Nicci Bellini wheeled on her. "What, that he treats me like a child? Or that he's taken the one thing from me that would have made this weekend bearable? Of course it matters." Her accent was getting stronger the angrier she grew, until she left English behind completely and drifted into a stream of Italian invective.

Emma was relieved she didn't understand the language, but the violence of the cadences and inflections left nothing to the imagination.

"We should go back and join the others," Emma said, trying to calm her.

Nicci ran her hand through her raven hair and stared at her, anger simmering in her eyes. "Not you too," she said, coming back to English once more. 'When I first met you I thought you were different from the others. I thought you had . . . fire. Now you want me to become part of that whining cartel of old hags. You're just like him, like Massimo. 'Behave, Nicci. Act your age, Nicci.' Well, I'm sorry to disappoint you, Emma, but this is me. This is how I am." She took two steps forward, grabbed Emma by the shoulders and kissed her on the lips.

It wasn't the kiss that shocked her as much as her own reaction to it. She found herself kissing back, with a passion that matched anything she had shared with Helen. With a gasp she pulled back and stared at the other woman, confusion clouding her eyes.

Nicci Bellini was smiling darkly. "Perhaps these next few days will be interesting after all."

"No," Emma said, trying to force determination into her voice. She failed and her voice sounded weak, pathetic. "No," she said again.

"You think it's too soon. Too soon after . . ."

"Too soon after Helen. Yes, I do. I'm sorry."

Nicci pulled her close again, kissed her again, more softly this time, but just as passionately. Her hand curled around Emma's neck, pulling her deeper into the kiss. Again Emma responded, her fingers weaving their way through Nicci's hair, forcing their lips together. Waves of pleasure rippled through her body as their tongues entwined. She felt Nicci's hand close on her breast, her thumb flicking softly over her hardened nipple, sending shock waves of arousal through her body.

The kiss ended but neither of them pulled back. Emma stared into Nicci's eyes, trying to fathom what was going on behind them. Was she toying with her, using her for amusement? Or was there something deeper there? She couldn't tell. And at that moment she didn't care. "My room," she said breathlessly.

Nicci Bellini inclined her head slightly and smiled.

CHAPTER 10

Emma lay on the bed, watching Nicci put her clothes back on. She slid effortlessly into the skin-tight black dress, adjusted the straps of her bra, and ran her hands through her hair, smoothing out the tangles. Standing in front of the dressing table mirror she put her earrings back on, then produced a small bottle of perfume from her bag and sprayed her wrists, rubbing them together. She gave herself a satisfied smile, then walked across to the bed, bent forward and kissed Emma softly on the lips. "See you at breakfast," she said, then went to the door and let herself out. Emma rolled over onto her stomach and buried her face in the pillow.

Nicci Bellini closed the door behind her.

"Well?" Massimo was leaning languidly against the wall outside Emma's room.

"You bastard, you could have ruined everything," she said.

Massimo smiled. "I don't think so. Let's walk."

"Where is it?"

Her brother patted the breast pocket of his jacket.

"When? It was there when I went down to dinner. I checked."

"Just after I saw you drug her wine."

"Oh, you're good. I never saw *you*. You could make a living on the streets of Napoli with skills like that."

"So could you with skills like yours."

She smiled and punched his arm, but the blow was playful. She found it impossible to stay angry with her brother for long. "Why did you take it?"

"It was necessary. You don't need cocaine. You lose control when you're on it. And it wasn't safe for the girl to take it either. She was high enough." He stopped walking and grabbed her arm, turning her around to face him. "You know he'll probably kill you if he finds out what you've done."

"But he won't find out, will he?"

"Hopefully not. I kept the men talking over their port for as long as I could. The two old crones could be a problem, though."

"I doubt it. They were both drunk. They didn't even notice us slip away."

"The English have an expression for this," Massimo said. "'Sailing close to the wind,' I think they say."

"Is that what we're doing, then?"

"It's what *you're* doing. You could be like everyone else here and observe the proper protocols. You know what he wants her for."

"And where's the adventure in that? Where's the risk? Besides, how do we know we can trust Alex?"

"We don't. But I also know it would be very unwise to cross him." He stroked her cheek with the back of his hand. "Dear Nicci, always looking to push the boundaries. One day I fear you'll push them too far."

She took his hand away from her cheek and kissed his fingers. "And you, dear brother, do you really want a safe life—dull, mundane, predictable? I don't think so. We don't belong with these dried-up old husks. How did they lose their fire, their passion? Protocol! It was never about protocol. It's just a game; a great game, an adventure. The problem is they've sucked the life out of it and turned it into some thing dead and desiccated."

"We don't make the rules," Massimo said.

"No, but they expect us to live by them. Well fuck them. We make up our own rules. We do what suits us." Nicci Bellini was smiling, her eyes glittering with excitement.

"To hell with it." Massimo yawned. "I'm going to bed. I think tomorrow could be interesting and I want to be awake enough to enjoy it. You?"

"No," Nicci said. "I've never seen these grounds at night before. I'd like to take a walk before I turn in."

"Then take Mario with you."

"No. I'd like some time on my own."

"And I think it would be safer if you took Mario."

She laughed. "What do you think is likely to happen to me? I'm a big girl now. I can look after myself."

"I'm sure you can. But indulge me, this once. Take Mario."

"Very well. I'll indulge you. But you worry too much."

"Someone has to."

She kissed Massimo on the cheek. "Sleep well, brother."

With a finger he brushed a small strand of hair away from her eyes. "You too, little sister. Dream well," he said.

"Oh, I will," she said. "Believe me, I will."

Emma stared up at the ceiling, listening to the clock ticking away the night. *What just happened? Why did it happen?* She didn't understand her motives, her feelings. She felt she had just betrayed Helen and negated all the years they had spent together in love.

She threw off the sheets and went across to the window, opening it wide and sucking the night air into her lungs, but it did little to ease her confusion. A pale moon was hanging in the sky, casting its milky light over the garden. A breeze ruffled the heads of the flowers, making the stalks sway and the leaves rustle, creating a susurration of sounds that played as an undercurrent to the hooting of owls in the trees of the forest.

Two figures came into view to her left, walking slowly along the tree line. She pulled back from the window, not wishing to be seen, but keeping them in her sight. As they drew nearer she recognized Nicci, and felt her pulse start to race. She was walking with a man, but he was on the far side of her and she couldn't see his face. Another few steps and they turned sharply right and disappeared into the trees. Emma watched and waited for them to reappear. Minutes passed but Nicci didn't reemerge from the forest. With a sigh of disappointment she reached up to close the window, then froze as something broke from the cover of the trees and raced across the grass toward the house.

A small deer dashed across the lawn, its pale fur glinting silver in the moonlight. For a second Emma was captivated as she watched the creature running, but then a darker realization struck her. The deer was running for its life.

As it ran it kept throwing frantic glances behind, looking back at the trees. She could see the steam of exertion gushing from its nostrils as it fled in panic from something unseen. Emma's eyes searched the tree line but saw nothing that could have made the deer react in such a way. Unless Nicci and her companion . . . She pulled herself up short. Now she was just being ridiculous.

The creature had almost reached the center of the lawn when it stumbled and somersaulted, rolling over and over on the grass, coming to a stop yards away from the gazebo, where it lay panting.

She watched it for a few moments, waiting for it to move again, debating whether or not to go down and help it. But then what could *she* do to help? She had no veterinary skills, unlike Helen who seemed to be able to mend a bird's broken wing with nothing more than kind words and a gentle touch. Feeling useless and inadequate, she closed the window, drew the curtains to shut out the animal's plight, and went back to bed.

It was then that Erik Keltner stepped from the gazebo where he'd been watching the nocturnal events occurring on the grounds. From the cover of the gazebo he watched Nicci Bellini and her companion walking by the tree line and listened to their conversation, storing up what he'd overheard for use later.

He heard Emma's window open, and for a while he watched her as she stared out into the night, imagining what he'd like to do to her. If it weren't for Alex he would give full reign to his fantasies. Instead he had to be content just watching her, with his hand thrust down the front of his trousers, massaging himself, bringing himself to the point of release.

And then the deer burst from the trees. It was an unwelcome distraction. He spun round and glared at the animal as it ran, focusing all his anger and pent-up frustration on the hapless animal, then watched with satisfaction as it stumbled and fell. But then he heard Emma's window sliding shut. He glanced back at the house. She'd retreated inside, pulling the drapes closed behind her. He swore savagely and walked across to the fallen deer. He prodded it with the toe of his shoe, then bent forward, picked it up by its scruff and did something horrible to its neck.

Mouth bloody, deer flesh and fur hanging from his lips, Erik turned and walked back to the house, the dead deer draped over his shoulder, blood dripping from its mutilated throat.

* * *

The night stretched into forever. She couldn't sleep, the events of the evening playing over and over in her head. Her eyes kept drifting across to the hands of the clock but they seemed static, moving at a snail's pace, belying the frantic ticking which was beginning to drive her mad. Images whirled in her head: Nicci, naked, crouched over her body, kissing her breasts; the frightened eyes of Jeff Williams as he looked at Erik Keltner on the terrace; the pathetic form of the fallen deer. These and so many more, jostling for space in her sleep-deprived mind.

At one o'clock she went to the bathroom and poured herself a glass of water. She stood at the sink, staring at herself in the mirror of the bathroom cabinet. The pale, almost translucent skin and the dark circles under her red-rimmed eyes told their own story. The hair, which she thought took years off her, looked flat and dull and only served to underline the gauntness of her features. "You're falling apart," she said to her reflection.

Sleep came just before three, but it was uneasy and fitful, filled with lurid dreams and punctuated by short sharp periods of wakefulness that found her staring into space, a space that was occupied by Nicci Bellini's face. She was dreading seeing her at breakfast, and, at the same time, could barely contain her excitement at the prospect of their next meeting.

But the excitement was quelled at the breakfast table the next morning. She arrived downstairs early and helped herself to a bowl of muesli from the long sideboard that stood against one wall. Taking the seat she'd had at dinner, she took sparrow pecks of the cereal while she waited for the others to arrive. Nicci Bellini was one of the last to enter the dining room and ignored the seat Emma had saved for her, positioning herself instead at the farthest end of the table and entering into an intense conversation with Keichi Yamada, the dapper little Japanese man.

Emma kept glancing in her direction but her attentions were ignored. Even when she choked on a piece of toast stuck in her throat Nicci Bellini remained resolutely oblivious to her.

Across the table Rolf Steiner, a large jowly man in his late fifties, was having a loud, angry-sounding conversation in German with his wife, Marta, who was as thin as he was fat. As the maid poured coffee into her cup, she spilled a drop in the saucer. Marta Steiner caught the girl's arm roughly. "Stupid girl, look at the mess you're making!"

The maid, a Polish émigré called Anna, started visibly and slopped more coffee over the tablecloth. She pulled her arm away from Marta Steiner's grasp, mumbled an apology and moved on along the table, dispensing the coffee from a silver jug.

She finally reached Emma's seat. "Coffee, madam?" she said, but as she spoke she kept stealing nervous glances back at Steiner's wife.

"Thank you, Anna. Yes, please," Emma said with a smile.

The girl was pretty, with high cheekbones, dark chocolate-brown eyes and a mouth almost, but not quite, too large for her features. Her prettiness was kept in check by the starched black and white uniform she wore, and by the fact that her hair was pulled severely back from her face and fastened in a bun at the back of her head. As she leaned forward to pour Emma whispered, "Take no notice of her. She probably got out of bed on the wrong side."

The girl managed a tight smile, and moved on.

Emma glared at Marta Steiner, but the woman was now engaged in a conversation with Sylvia Bronstein and didn't notice. Her husband did, however, and shrugged his broad shoulders expansively at her, as if to apologize for his wife's boorish behavior.

It was only when Emma was on her third cup of coffee that she noticed Jeff Williams's absence. He hadn't come down for breakfast. She put down her napkin and rose from the table, walking to the head where Alex Keltner sat, pulling the meat from the bones of a kipper with practiced strokes of his fork.

She leaned into him. "Jeff hasn't come down this morning. Is he all right?" She remembered the queasy look on his face when he had resumed his place at the dinner table the night before. Perhaps he was sick.

Keltner dabbed at his lips with a napkin. "He had to go back to London," he said. "Left first thing. Erik drove him to the station."

"But didn't you need him here?"

He shrugged expansively and looked at her closely. "Did you sleep well last night?" he said.

She fingered the dark circles beneath her eyes self-consciously. "No, not *well*, not really. Strange bed. Do I really look that bad?"

"After breakfast find Florence and ask her for something to cover up the bags under your eyes. I don't want you walking around looking as if you're about to fall asleep." He spoke quietly so the others could not hear, but there was an edge to his voice.

"Yes," she said. "Yes, I will. Sorry." She returned to her seat and finished her coffee, feeling chastened and humiliated. She wasn't sure how much more of this she could take. She'd heard of Keltner's reputation as a hard taskmaster—some said slave driver—but this weekend was the first time she'd experienced it. And she had only herself to blame.

She was aware of eyes upon her and she looked across the table to find Massimo Bellini staring at her, a smile playing on his slightly parted lips. Christ, did he know? Had Nicci told him? She swallowed the last of her coffee and left the dining room, rushing back to her room. She forgot about trying to find Florence; she didn't think she could face the older woman's disapproval again this morning. Sitting down at the dressing table she opened her makeup bag and set about repairing the damage to her sleep-deprived face.

Staring at her reflection in the mirror she found that she barely recognized herself. Behind her the unmade bed stood as a testimony to what had happened the previous night, the crumpled sheets mocking her as she tried to put the incident to the back of her mind. She must have been drunk, but she couldn't remember having that much to drink. She'd never seen herself as promiscuous, but as soon as she'd felt Nicci Bellini's lips on hers she'd known that she wanted her. And the desire had been stronger than any she had ever experienced, even with Helen. That in itself was enough to fan the flames of guilt within her. It was betrayal, an insult to Helen's memory.

Maybe if there had been something more there, other than lust, she may have been able to justify it. But as it was it nestled in her thoughts like a leaking bottle of poison, seeping into her thoughts and twisting them; making it impossible to think about anything else.

She had to see Nicci, to talk it through with her; to try to make some sense of her behavior. The fact that Nicci had ignored her at breakfast bothered her more than she cared to admit. She hated to think that what had happened between them was nothing more than a one-night stand, a pleasant diversion, a gratifying of mutual lust. It made her feel cheap, and it diminished the significance of her relationship with Helen.

Checking in the mirror that she looked halfway presentable she let herself out of the room and went to find Nicci.

CHAPTER 11

Tony Carver pulled up outside the eighteenth-century farmhouse Sid Whelan shared with his wife of twenty years, Rosemary. Little had changed since he'd last been here, although the window frames had been given a coat of paint and the front door had been re-hung so that it no longer slouched to one side, looking in imminent danger of falling off. He climbed out of his car and took a long breath, filling his lungs with the crisp morning air. Around him he could hear the sound of the crows who had taken up residence in an oak tree to the left of the property, and the occasional deep-throated bark of Ed, the Whelan's lurcher, who was obviously engaged in a game in the garden at the rear. He walked up to the front door and pressed the doorbell, hearing it ring somewhere at the back of the house.

Rosemary Whelan's face broke into a wide smile as she opened the door and recognized their visitor. "Tony!" she said, and stepped forward, wrapping him in her arms and kissing him on the cheek. "It's been ages."

"Too long, Ro. I've missed you."

She stepped back, holding him at arm's length and staring up at his face. "Let me look at you. You've put on a bit of weight. Good, it suits you. You look well." Her face clouded over and the smile slipped. "About the funeral. You realize how sorry I was not to come . . . but in the circumstances . . ."

He put a finger to her lips. "No apology necessary, Ro, you know that. I totally understand."

The smile returned, but not as bright as before, as memories of recent events flooded through her mind. "Come in, come in. I was just making tea."

"I must have smelled it," he said, and followed her into the house.

The house, as usual, was immaculate. Decorated sympathetically and furnished with period pieces bought at the local auction. It looked as it had always looked when he had come to play here as a child. It even smelled the same: the fresh, slightly astringent aroma of beeswax furniture polish.

"Sid's in the greenhouse, potting his cuttings. Shall I call him in?" she said as she fussed in the kitchen, spooning leaf tea into a huge brown pot and pouring in steaming water from the freshly boiled kettle. "Just let that brew for a while," she said, almost to herself, then turned to him. "I can't believe you're here. I worried that I might never see you again after . . ."

He put a hand up to stop her. "It was an accident, Ro. A tragic accident. I don't hold Sid responsible."

"He'll be so relieved. When we heard nothing from you we feared the worst. Although I totally understand why you didn't get in touch."

"The police advised me not to," Tony said. "Though I'm not sure of their logic."

"I'm sure they had their reasons. But, in all fairness to them, they've been very kind. They could see how distraught Sid was . . . still is, in fact. He's been dreadful since it happened. A different man really. The old spark's gone. It's as if he's retreated into himself and closed down the shutters. He still goes to the stables every morning to tend the horses, but then comes back here and hides himself away in the greenhouse, looking after his begonias. I hardly ever see him, and when I do he doesn't speak much . . . not that he ever did, but now there's this awful remoteness in him, as if all his thoughts are turned inward. He thought of you two as his own, you know. When you were little and used to come and play in the barn it would light up his life. It was compensation for him for being married to a woman as barren as the Sahara." She took two mugs from the dresser and poured in some milk from a jug on the table. "Still two sugars?"

Tony nodded.

She grinned. "Still the sweet tooth."

"I miss your meringues, Ro . . . and the cavities they used to give me."

"Get away with you. You only had yourself to blame for rotting your teeth. Your appetite for them . . . and my scones were insatiable. I've never known a child eat so much and not put on any weight. Both you and your sister were as thin as twigs." She paused, staring off into the distance, lost in the much happier past. She shivered, as if she had seen something that chilled her. "I could knock you up a batch of meringues if you like. Only take a couple of hours . . . if you're staying," she added hopefully.

He glanced at his watch. "Tempting, but I'm afraid I can't stay that long. I've come to see Sid; to talk to him."

A slight frown creased her slightly pink and plump forehead.

"Nothing to worry about, Ro. I just want to touch base. Reassure him that we're still friends."

"As I said before, he'll appreciate that," she said, and

poured scalding tea into the mugs. "Sit first and tell me what you've been doing since I saw you last. Do you have any plans for the stables?"

He pulled up a chair at the kitchen table and sat down, picking up the mug and sipping the sweet, dark-brown liquid. No one made tea like Rosemary Whelan, and just tasting it again brought back memories of summer days, grazed knees and fishing for sticklebacks in the stream that ran at the back of the Whelan's house. This was Helen's and his playground as children. Their parents owned a house a few hundred yards up the lane, but they were busy people without time to care for two boisterous, excitable children, except in strictly practical matters. They were fed, housed and educated by Ronald and Elizabeth Carver, but that's where their involvement ended. They had more important things to occupy their lives, she with her endless round of coffee mornings and exuberant social climbing; he with his daily meetings with Jack Daniel's and Johnnie Walker.

Sid and Rosemary Whelan, however, were the exact opposite. Robbed of the ability to have children of their own by a cruelty of nature, they had embraced the childish antics of him and his sister with something close to passion and, for all those formative years, acted as surrogate parents to them, allowing them to run free over their property, encouraging them in their unsophisticated enthusiasms, listening to their problems, guiding and steering them through those early days with kindness and a rough, earthy wisdom.

When Tony decided to invest his money in the stables, it was more than just allowing Helen to fulfill a childhood dream. He made it a stipulation that she take Sid Whelan on as her second in command. The man had recently lost his job, looking after the dray horses at the local brewery, and was having no luck finding another position.

Throwing Sid a lifeline had gone some way to repaying the debt Tony felt he and his sister owed the Whelans. Some way, but in no way did he consider the account settled.

"Have you seen anything of Emma?" Rosemary said, joining him at the table.

"Not since the funeral, but I think she's been rather busy. When I last saw her she told me she'd just been promoted at work, so I expect she's got a lot to keep her occupied."

"Probably just as well," Rosemary said. "Sid and I thought she was a lovely girl. When they last came to see me you could tell how much they were in love just by the way they looked at each other. There was a spark there. It reminded me of how Sid and I were when we first met."

"It's just a pity that Mother could never see how happy Helen was. She was determined to close her eyes to it; pretend it wasn't happening. She didn't say a word to Emma at the funeral, which I thought was incredibly rude and totally unforgivable."

"I know it's not my place to say this, Tony, but I always thought Elizabeth was a rather silly woman. More interested in appearances than reality. I shouldn't waste too much time worrying about it. I doubt that Emma was fazed by it. She struck me as quite a tough young lady. Adorable, but very grounded, and very sure of her place in the world. And let's face it, your sister was no pushover either, and she didn't suffer fools, gladly or otherwise, so I think they were well matched. I'm sure Emma will be fine."

The back door opened and Sid Whelan stepped into the kitchen, rubbing his earth-streaked hands on the legs of his trousers. He saw Tony sitting at the table and turned as if to leave.

"Sid," Rosemary said, before he had a chance to escape. "Tony's come to see you. That's nice, isn't it?"

Whelan hovered on the threshold, caught in two minds. Finally he came to a decision, and with a deep sigh closed the back door and approached the table. "Tony," he said, extending a hand.

Tony Carver got to his feet and took the man's outstretched hand, shaking it warmly. "Sid. It's good to see you."

"And you," Whelan said with a curt nod of his head, and then turned to his wife. "Any more tea in that pot?"

"I'll get you a mug," she said.

Whelan sat down at the table and pulled a silver tin from his pocket, flipped it open and began to fashion a cigarette from its contents. Then he stuck the roll-up between his lips and lit it with a Zippo lighter.

A waft of petrol fumes reached Tony's nostrils. Another familiar smell, another raft of memories.

"So, how are you keeping?" Whelan said.

"Good, Sid. I'm good."

Whelan pulled an ashtray toward him and rolled off a tube of gray ash. "So you've come to see me. What you doing, closing the stables? Have you come to give me my notice?"

Tony shook his head. He could see that Sid Whelan was growing more and more uncomfortable by the minute. At any moment he might leave the table and retreat back to the sanctuary of his greenhouse. "Quite the reverse, Sid. I've no intention of closing it down. Actually I came to ask you whether or not you'd consider running it for me. I've thought about it long and hard and I can't think of anyone more suitable for the job."

Rosemary clapped her hands excitedly. "But that's wonderful, Tony. Sid, isn't that wonderful news? What an opportunity."

Whelan squinted as the smoke from his roll-up irritated his eyes. Then he got to his feet. "No disrespect, Tony, but I think I've accepted enough of your charity over the years. Excuse me." He walked to the back door and pulled it open.

"Sid!" Rosemary called, but the door slammed in its frame and from the kitchen window she could see her husband stalking back to the greenhouse.

She turned to Tony. "I'm so sorry, Tony. He's not himself."

Tony sipped his tea. "I'll give him a moment, then I'll go out and see him. He's had a rough time of it. I think I know how he feels. But it's not charity, believe me, Ro. The livery stables are thriving. Helen built it up into a very profitable business, and if all her hard work was to be for nothing it would be a crime. Besides, I meant what I said. Sid's the right man for the job. I didn't mean for the offer to be seen as a handout. If I'd known he was going to react like that then I would have dressed it up differently. My fault, not his."

CHAPTER 12

Sid Whelan eased the begonia cutting from the four-inch pot and, holding it by the leaves, placed it carefully in a pot a good two inches larger. Then he dribbled in compost from the palm of his hand and tamped it down, firming the plant. "Grow away, my beauty," he said softly, almost lovingly. Begonias were his biggest passion after his wife and the horses he tended, and he'd won many prizes at local flower shows with his displays. It never ceased to fill him with a sense of wonder when he planted the unpromising, withered corm at the beginning of the season, only to watch the leaves start to develop under his tender care; and the reward of a head of incredibly beautiful flowers sometimes took his breath away.

He picked up another pot and studied the cutting it contained. Then a shadow closed over his face and he hurled the pot to the floor, smashing it into fragments. What the hell was Tony Carver doing here? Was this never going to end? He stared down at the cutting lying forlornly in a splash of compost and bent to pick it up.

"Accident?" Tony said from the doorway of the greenhouse.

"They happen," Whelan said, not looking up.

"Yes, they do," Tony said. "And it's important to remember that."

Whelan straightened. "Why did you come here?"

Tony stepped into the greenhouse, wincing at the humidity. He loosened his tie. "I think we need to talk."

"We talked. In there." Whelan pointed back at the house. "I've made my decision. There's nothing more to say."

"Fair enough," Tony said. "I won't twist your arm. Just remember that every decision you make affects Rosemary too. Wouldn't it have been better to talk things over with her first before deciding to reject the offer?"

Whelan looked at him steadily. "Just go," he said.

"If you want me to, I will. But one day you're going to have to face up to what happened to Helen, and you *will* need to talk about it. When you do, give me a call."

The two men stared at each other, eyes locked. There was a wealth of history hanging in the space between them; so many memories it was almost overwhelming.

A sob broke in Sid Whelan's throat and he turned away, grinding his knuckles into the splintering surface of the potting table. "I don't remember," he said in almost a whisper.

"What do you mean?" Tony said gently.

Whelan turned to look at him. There were tears in his eyes. He shook his head slowly. "I've been through it in my mind, over and over again, but I can't remember what happened. I don't know how Helen died." With shaking hands he pulled the silver tin from the pocket of his trousers and started to roll a cigarette.

"Would it help to talk it through?"

"I talked it through, with the police. I went over it time and time again. Eventually they pieced it all together and that became the statement I signed . . . but I'm not sure it's what actually happened."

"I see," Tony said, his mind trying frantically to assimilate this piece of information. The reason he had been able to treat Helen's death so stoically was because he believed it was simply an accident. What Sid Whelan was saying now cast doubt onto that belief, and Tony felt the grief and anger come crashing in on him. He cleared his throat, trying to keep his voice neutral. "Perhaps you should go through it again, now, with me."

Whelan lit the cigarette and blew smoke out through his nose. "There's no point," he said. "Won't make any difference."

"Maybe not. But I'd like to hear it as you remember it." He could feel the anger creeping into his voice and checked himself. "Sid, I think you owe me that."

Whelan regarded him steadily. Finally he nodded his head. "Let's walk," he said, and pushed past Tony Carver, out of the greenhouse and into the garden.

"Just start from the moment you arrived at the stables that morning," Tony said as he followed Whelan along a path between two rows of peas, long since gone to seed.

"I got there at seven as usual. I like to give myself a couple of hours before everything kicks off. I get a chance to talk to the horses, set them up for the day. It's important, little things like that. I learned that at the brewery. The horses respond to it, see? Makes them feel special."

"Did you talk to Nelson?"

"Of course."

"Did he seem any different to you? Strung out? Nervous?"

Sid Whelan snorted. "A lot of them seemed a bit tense that morning. We put it down to a storm coming. But Nelson? No. He didn't seem affected by it. Gentle as a lamb that one. Placid as hell. And that's how he was that morning. Anyway, I went through my usual routines, mucking out, filling the water troughs. No different from any other day. Helen arrived, we had a bit of a chat; then she went to sort Nelson out. I remember the bloody Mercedes was in the lane again, and the driver was standing by the fence, looking in. I was just about to go and tell him to sling his hook when I heard Nelson kicking out and Helen calling for me. I grabbed the pitchfork and ran over there. He had her pinned against the wall, kicking out at her. Well, I just charged in there and started prodding at him, trying to get him out into the yard, away from Helen. She was hurt; he'd kicked her in the leg, drawn blood. I got him outside, then . . ." Sid Whelan stopped walking. They'd reached the end of the vegetable garden and drawn up alongside a hawthorn hedge.

"Then what, Sid?"

"Fucked if I know. One minute I was outside with Nelson, the next I was standing in front of Helen, and she was pinned to the wall on the end of my pitchfork. The look on her face . . . Jesus, *the look on her face!*" His voice rose to a wail of despair and his shoulders heaved. He began to sob, fat tears dribbling down his weatherworn face.

Tony put a hand on his shoulder. "So Nelson was out of the stall when Helen was . . . got injured."

Whelan nodded.

"So the accident didn't happen as you were trying to force him out."

"I told the police just as I've told it to you. They said that I must have got confused in the excitement of it all. But I wasn't confused. I just don't remember." He wiped his face impatiently with the sleeve of his shirt. "All I know for certain is, I wouldn't have hurt a hair on that girl's head. Ro and I, we loved both of you, like our own. I would have rather cut off my hands than hurt her."

"I believe you, Sid," Tony said. And he did. The older man's regret and remorse was almost painful to watch. It had aged him a good ten years, and robbed him of the spirit that had been a source of inspiration to Tony Carver for much of his life. It was exactly as he'd told Emma all those days ago: Sid Whelan was a broken man, and it was heartbreaking to witness it.

"You mentioned a Mercedes. The driver looking at you over the fence?"

"Don't see that's got anything to do with anything. We get them from time to time. *Noseys*, Ro calls them. Horse lovers some of them, but most of them just pull up in the lane to have a good look at what we're doing. I don't like to encourage them. There are some strange people out there. Ever see that film *Equus*? Richard Burton. All that stuff about blinding horses. It happens. Happened at the brewery once. Not blinded, but maimed. Lovely old dray; big old girl, stood eighteen hands. Someone broke in one night and cut off her tail. Lucky she didn't bleed to death. But it finished her off. Broke her spirit. She was never the same after that. Since then I've been very wary of strangers poking their noses in where they don't belong."

"Had you seen the man before?"

"Oh yes. He'd been there a few times in the days before. Just standing there, staring over the fence. But as I say, I don't see that it has anything to do with what happened."

"No, probably not," Tony said thoughtfully.

On the drive home Tony Carver mulled over everything Sid Whelan had told him. None of it made much sense. It had been just another day at the stables, no different to any other, nothing happening to signal the tragic events that were about to take place. The only thing that seemed out of place was the watcher in the Mercedes, but that could be something or nothing. He'd gone to see Sid Whelan in the hope that he would finally understand what happened the day of his sister's death, and to get something approaching closure. Instead he was left with a conundrum, a mystery, and the mystery would eat away at him until he finally solved it.

He punched in a number on his cell phone.

The phone on the other end of the line rang three times before a familiar voice said, "Hello."

"Emma, it's Tony."

There was a long pause.

"Emma?"

"Tony, hi. How are you?"

She sounded strange, distracted. Tony Carver frowned. "Sorry, am I interrupting something?"

"Sorry, no, I was miles away. How are you?"

"Not bad. I was just wondering if we could meet up for a chat. Perhaps do lunch? Baggy's?"

"Oh, Tony, I'd love to. But I'm not in Cambridge at the moment. I'm down in the New Forest."

"What on earth are you doing down there?" The question was instinctive, and it was only after he had asked it that it occurred to him that it was none of his damned business. "Sorry," he said quickly. "That was very rude of me. Don't feel obliged to answer."

She laughed. "It's okay. It's no great secret. I'm working. My boss is hosting a social event down here . . . he has a house . . . I'm helping out, doing the meet and greet thing."

"So I picked a bad time to call."

"No, not at all. It's just a shame that I'm down here and you're up there. It would be lovely to meet up and talk."

"Is all your time taken up, or do you get some free?"

"Apparently I get the afternoons off. I was just looking through some brochures of local beauty spots and planning how I was going to spend the time."

"I could drive down. Perhaps we could meet up. I know a few towns around there from my student days. Whereabouts are you?"

"I think Lyndhurst is the nearest town."

"Yes, I know Lyndhurst."

"It's an awfully long way to come just for a chat. Can it wait until I get back?"

"How long are you going to be down there?"

"To be quite honest, I'm not really sure. I think I should be back by Wednesday or Thursday, but don't hold me to it."

He drummed his fingers on the steering wheel as he drove, thinking hard. He couldn't wait that long to speak with her, even though he wasn't sure why it was so important to see Emma again. But in this he was being led by his instincts, and his instincts were telling him that it was.

"I can be there by three. Would that suit you? There used to be a cafe in the High Street, the Copper Kettle. Do you know if it's still there?"

She thought for a moment, retracing the journey through the town, trying to picture the streets in her mind. "The Copper Kettle . . . wait a minute . . . yes. I passed a sign. Blue sign with an old-fashioned kettle on it."

"That's the one," he said. "Shall we say three o'clock then?"

"Okay."

He switched off the phone and turned off the main road. Minutes later he was heading back the way he'd come.

CHAPTER 13

Emma listened to the phone go dead and slipped it back into her bag. The last thing she needed right now was a visit from Tony Carver. But, like his sister, he was never easily dissuaded from a course of action, once his mind was set on it. Guilt was pressing heavily on her mind, and she was certain the story of last night's indiscretion was etched into the lines of her sleep-deprived face; an open book for Tony to read should he so choose.

Her attempt to see Nicci and talk things through with her had been fruitless. She'd found her room by asking directions from one of the maids, but there had been no answer to her persistent knocking. Frustrated and depressed, she walked back through the house, but couldn't face the prospect of sitting in her room stewing. The morning was bright, the sun burning in a cloudless sky, taking the chill from the crisp autumnal air. She made her way downstairs and slipped out of the house through the back door.

When she took Tony's phone call she was out in the grounds, just north of the gazebo, walking toward the point in the forest from where the deer had emerged the night before, and where she had last seen Nicci. She wondered who her companion had been. Not her brother; the figure was too tall for Massimo, and also his gait was wrong. This man didn't saunter, he strode. She had it in her mind that it might have been Alex Keltner, but it could just have easily been his brother. Again it may have been neither of them. Nicci's companion for her midnight stroll seemed too big, too broad to be either of the Keltners. Ahead of her was the gap in the trees where they had veered off into the forest. She headed toward it.

Once the thick canopies of the trees closed above her head she shivered. It was much cooler in the forest, and the lack of sunlight gave the place a hooded, almost sinister atmosphere. The dense foliage above her head also deadened some sounds and amplified others. The always present but distant hum of the main road quietened to nothing, while the noise of her feet crackling through the lush carpet of dried leaves and bracken seemed almost deafening. There were other sounds as well, coming from all around her: the soft rustling of the undergrowth as an unfelt breeze moved through it; the occasional call of a bird high in the treetops; the steady beating of her heart. She was apprehensive and nervous, though she didn't know why.

There was a path of sorts—ferns flattened and broken—that led deeper into the forest. She took her cell phone from her bag again and checked the strength of the signal, just in case she got lost and needed to call assistance. The signal was faint, but steady. She slipped the phone into the pocket of her jeans and set off along the path.

Nicci Bellini was lying on the bed, reliving and relishing the events of the night before. It had been fun; a challenge met, a conquest. But now the foolish girl was knocking on her bedroom door and calling out to her. She picked up a book from the bedside table and opened it, letting her eyes drift over the words as the knocking persisted. She was almost tempted to open the door and tell her to go away, but decided that ignoring her was more prudent. Confronting her would only cause a scene and that was one thing she wanted to avoid at all costs. Breakfast had been difficult, studiously ignoring her despite being aware that Emma's eyes were on her for the best part of the meal. Dinner tonight could be awkward, but if she continued to rebuff all her advances, eventually she'd get the message. It was important that nobody realized what had happened between them, or there would be some difficult questions to answer. But then the risk was a large part of the game, and without risk the whole seduction would have been unsatisfying, if not pointless.

Eventually the knocking stopped and silence filled the room, only to be broken seconds later by the shrill ringing of the telephone on the bedside table. She sighed deeply and reached out a hand to pick up the receiver. "Yes," she said.

"It's Alex. Could you come along to my office please? We need to talk."

"Now? I'm sleepy."

"Now, Nicci. This can't wait."

Five minutes later she pushed open the door to Alex Keltner's office. "I should say now, Alex, that it doesn't amuse me to be summoned like a member of your staff."

Keltner looked up from his desk. "I wasn't trying to amuse you, Nicci."

She took a chair facing him, took a packet of cigarettes from her bag and lit one, knowing it would infuriate him.

He glared at the smoke eddying up to the ceiling but said nothing. Instead he reached into the desk drawer and produced a brass ashtray that he slid across to her. "I want to show you something," he said.

She took a long pull on the cigarette, letting the smoke trickle from her nose. "Really?" she said. "I'm intrigued."

He stood. "Follow me," he said, and walked across to a door set in the far wall. "And leave that thing in the ashtray."

"So masterful, Alex. You'll make someone a wonderful husband one day. Some little hausfrau who likes a man to boss her about. Emma, perhaps . . . oh no, I forgot, you have other plans for her."

He ignored her and opened the door. "Through here."

He led her down a long corridor. At the end of it was another door. He took a key from his pocket and opened it. She followed him inside.

The room was sparsely furnished—a computer table, a chair, nothing more. On the table were a screen, a keyboard and a mouse. Cables snaked away from the screen to be swallowed by a hole in the wall. The keyboard and mouse worked on infrared signals.

"Sit," he said.

She did as he instructed. Despite herself she was beginning to feel apprehensive. She had never seen Alex Keltner this serious or, yes, this angry.

He leaned across her and clicked the left-hand button of the mouse. She could smell his aftershave, an old familiar smell that sent a raft of pleasant memories drifting through her mind.

She was brought back to the present with a start as the first image flashed up on the screen. A black and white shot of her, naked, straddling Emma Porter's thighs, her head bowed, hair draped across the girl's face as Nicci kissed her breasts. More images followed, all showing Nicci and Emma in various stages of passion.

She turned round in the chair to face Keltner, eyes blazing. "What is this? You've been spying on me?"

"Nicci, I spy on everyone," Keltner said in a bored voice, unconcerned by her anger. "Perhaps you'd like to tell me what the hell you think you were doing last night? Or would you like me to run the whole thing for you, just to jog your memory?"

"What do you mean?" she said, a hint of uncertainty and apprehension in her voice.

He gestured to the screen. "These are just some of the stills I selected; some snapshots, if you like—edited highlights. But I have a digital recording from the moment you and Emma entered her bedroom to where you kissed her good night—very touching. I watched the whole thing from beginning to end this morning. Interesting. Which drug did you use?"

"What makes you think I needed to drug her?" she said.

"Her dilated pupils, for one. You can see it quite plainly in some of the close-ups. And the fact that I know how you two operate."

The anger in her eyes faded. She smiled slightly and sighed in resignation. "Very well. It's something Massimo has made up for him by a chemist in Milan; very effective at removing inhibitions, and at the same time leaves the senses quite sharp. The only aftereffect is a slight headache. Would you like me to ask my brother to get you some?"

He slapped her across the face. The blow was fierce, rocking her head to the side and splitting her lip.

She wiped the blood away with the back of her hand and sat for a second looking down at the red smear. "Bastard!" she hissed.

"You know the rules, Nicci, and you broke them. The question is, what am I going to do about it?"

"Do what you like."

Keltner smiled. "Now, you don't really mean that, do

you? If I go to the others and tell them . . . well, you know that your position here with Massimo would become untenable."

"You wouldn't," Nicci said, fear flashing in her eyes.

"I should. You know damned well I should. But . . ."

The fear was replaced by hope.

"There's my position in all this to consider," Keltner said. "After all, the transgression happened under my roof. I might be deemed responsible. And that would never do."

"It won't happen again," Nicci Bellini said.

"Oh, I'm sure it won't. I was watching you at breakfast, desperately trying to avoid making eye contact with Emma, in case she blurted something out." He reached across her again and closed the picture on the screen. "Okay. For now this stays between you and me."

The sigh she gave this time was one of relief. "Thank you," she said, her voice barely a whisper.

"But there is a condition."

She managed a smile. "I thought there might be," she said. "And what would that condition be?"

He reached out and snaked his fingers through her hair, pulling her roughly from the chair. He then kissed her, deeply, his tongue plunging into her mouth. She struggled, trying to pull away from him, but the grip on her hair was too fierce. Instead he pulled her closer, pressing his body against hers. In desperation she bit down hard on his tongue. He gave a strangled cry and pushed her away, then swung his arm and hit her with the back of his hand, knocking her to the floor.

"Bitch!" he said viciously, then brought his foot back and kicked her in the stomach.

She curled herself into a ball, gasping for air. He moved behind her and kicked her in the kidneys. Then he backed away from her, swallowing the blood that was filling his mouth, smiling slightly. He licked his lips. "I can still taste her," he said.

She rolled onto her back, staring up at him, tears of pain and rage pouring down her cheeks. "Then why don't you fuck the little whore instead of trying to fuck me?"

"Because I want to fuck you. And I will." He stared down at her. She looked like a frightened animal, eyes darting from side to side, looking for a means of escape.

"Please," she said. "It's too dangerous."

"But I thought you liked danger, Nicci. I thought you liked taking risks."

She shook her head. "I do, but not this. You'll destroy me."

"Yes. I may do. But then again I may not. It's my choice. Don't you trust me?"

Tears were pricking at her eyes, but she was determined not to cry; not to show any weakness. If she did he'd lose any vestige of respect he had left for her. She raised her chin defiantly. "What do you think?"

He smiled. "It will be interesting to see how far you've come down this particular path. You may be strong enough to survive it. After all, it's been a long time since I made you what you are."

"At what cost, Alex? At what cost?" She pushed herself up onto her elbows, the pain in her kidneys abating a little. "Are you so arrogant that you think I wanted things to turn out like this? Living this half-life; this wretched existence?"

"I gave you a great gift, Nicci. You could have been like all the others. I could have destroyed you. But I saw something different in you. The hunger was there. You wanted this life, Nicci. You begged me to make you what you are."

She opened her mouth to protest.

"Don't deny it, Nicci. You'll just make yourself look

even more pathetic. I gave you what you asked for. It's sad you're so ungrateful now, but not *so* unexpected." He started to unbuckle his belt.

She looked away from him, shaking her head slowly, then stretched out on the floor, opened her legs and closed her eyes tightly. "Just do it, then," she said. "Do it and get it over with."

He looked down at her and something shifted in his eyes. It had been good once. Their relationship had meant more to him than anything else in the world. That time had passed, but the memories were still vivid in his mind. He turned away from her.

"Just do it!" she yelled at him.

"Get up," he said without turning around. "Get up and get out."

She hesitated for a moment, then struggled to her feet, wiping away the blood that had trickled down her chin. "Alex . . ."

"Don't speak. Just get out before I change my mind."

She hurried to the door, stepped through and pulled it shut behind her. From inside the room there came a howl, an animal cry of rage and frustration. Without looking back she ran from the office and back along the maze of corridors to her room.

Emma pressed on farther into the forest. The path was still fairly clear. It was obvious that it had been well trodden in the past few days. But where was it leading?

Her question was answered a few moments later when she pushed past a stand of elms and found herself looking at a small thatched cottage standing in a grassy clearing. The cottage was surrounded by a white picket fence, with a gate that hung open.

She took two steps toward the gate and the cell phone in her pocket shrilled. Spinning on her heels, she ran back to the cover of the trees, yanking the phone from her jeans and switching it off. She pressed her back against the wide trunk of a horse chestnut and stood there cursing modern technology, her breath coming in panicky gasps.

A few seconds later she stole a look back at the cottage. The front door was open and the bulky form of Rolf Steiner stood on the gravel path just outside the cottage, his eyes scanning the trees. He was naked to the waist, his overweight torso covered in a thick mat of body hair, overcompensating for the lack of hair on his balding head.

From inside the cottage a female voice sounded, but the words were muffled and unclear. Steiner glanced behind him. "I thought I heard something," he called back inside, his German accent thick, sounding drink slurred. He stared out at the trees again, almost looking directly at Emma, who pulled her head back at the last moment.

She heard Steiner mutter darkly in German and then the sound of the door slamming. When she looked again he'd gone back inside. She was still clutching her cell phone. She switched it on again. One missed call. One voice message. She hit the dial button and listened.

"Hi, Em, it's Tony. Just heard a traffic report and, surprise, surprise, there's a snarl up on the M25 by Heathrow. Listen, I may be a little later than planned. But have your phone with you, and I'll call you when I reach Lyndhurst. Bye for now."

She turned the phone off again and slid it back into her pocket, then slipped out from behind the cover of the tree and crept silently toward the cottage. Ducking low she entered the front garden and ran to the side of the cottage, pressing herself against the cold brick wall. She edged her way cautiously toward the window; then, taking a deep breath, she peeked through.

She found herself looking at an empty kitchen. She

cursed softly. There was another window a few yards away. With more confidence now she approached it and after the slightest hesitation glanced inside.

Rolf Steiner was sprawled on a leather sofa, his chest still bare, but his trousers now around his ankles. Emma's initial worry that she might be seen peering in was quickly dismissed. Rolf Steiner was too preoccupied with the young, naked girl straddling his fat thighs to notice anything else. The girl moved sinuously and sensually, riding him as if he were a thoroughbred stallion. Her hands were planted in his chest hair, while Steiner's chubby fingers kneaded her breasts.

The girl was obviously reaching her climax. She threw her head back and moaned so loudly Emma could hear it through the closed window. And as she threw her head back Emma recognized her. Anna, the maid who had served her coffee this morning, looking so very different out of her starched black and white uniform, with her hair hanging loose and wild.

She'd seen enough . . . too much. The sight of Rolf Steiner's naked body turned her stomach, and the thought of an attractive young woman like Anna pleasuring an obese old man like him was almost too much to bear. She ran out through the gate and back into the forest.

CHAPTER 14

She needed to talk to someone, to tell them what she'd just witnessed. She wished Jeff Williams hadn't left. It was obvious he had issues with the setup Keltner had here. Maybe he knew that the place was being used as nothing more than a glorified brothel. Maybe that was what he was trying to warn her about.

She couldn't believe that Alex Keltner wasn't aware of what was going on, but she wasn't prepared to tackle him on it just yet; not without some solid evidence. The other difficulty was that she didn't feel able to take the moral high ground. Not after her liaison with Nicci Bellini the night before. Now, more than ever, she was regretting it and was wishing it had never happened.

If breakfast had been difficult, lunch would be even more difficult still. How could she ever look Rolf Steiner in the eye again? Worse still, how could she engage his wife Marta in small talk knowing what she did about her husband?

She felt adrift. If Helen were here she'd know what to do, how to behave. She tried to put herself inside her lover's mind, but it was impossible. Every time she tried to focus on Helen's face the image folded and faded, and transmuted into the face of Nicci Bellini, smiling at her lasciviously, dark eyes gleaming with lust and ridicule.

She changed out of her jeans and sweatshirt and put on a slim black dress, bought with the money Alex had given her, then stood staring at herself in the full-length mirror of her wardrobe. The dress looked superb, simple yet sexy, elegant yet slightly wanton. And as she stood there an awful thought insinuated its way into her mind.

Was this the reason Alex had wanted her to come down here; to whore for him?

Anger made her fingers fumble with the zipper as she struggled to take off the dress. Finally it released and she let the dress slide to the floor, stepping out of it and crossing to the wardrobe. She found something more demure: a cream linen trouser suit and a white blouse with a high collar. She checked herself in the mirror again. There was nothing remotely sexy about the outfit. It was smart and businesslike. Satisfied, she went down to have her meal.

Lunch was served in the dining room, and again Anna was on duty. Emma gave her a searching look as she poured apple juice into a glass for her, but the Polish girl was not making eye contact this afternoon. She looked tired, washed out, with dark half-moons shading the skin under her eyes. But after her excesses of the morning Emma found that hardly surprising.

What she *did* find surprising was that Marta Steiner's attitude had completely changed toward the girl. She took Anna's arm again as the girl passed her, but instead of a rebuke, issued a half-whispered apology for her behavior at breakfast. Anna mumbled something in response, but from where she sat Emma couldn't hear what she said.

Rolf Steiner was patently ignoring the girl and had to be prompted by his wife to respond to Anna's inquiry as to whether or not he wanted apple juice with his meal.

Nicci Bellini wasn't at the table at all, but her brother was tucking into a plate of cold meats with the fervor of a condemned man savoring his final meal.

Emma turned her attention to the Bronsteins who, apart from a small altercation with each other at the dinner table the night before, had so far been fairly anonymous. Sylvia Bronstein had once been a very beautiful woman. Still tall and elegant, she carried herself like a catwalk model. But time had caught up with her complexion, and the once taut skin sagged now, hanging in folds, the wrinkles partially obscuring her still very bright blue eyes. Her hair was gray and cut into a simple, elegant bob, but her hands were claws, emphasized by long, red-painted fingernails that she had a habit of drumming on the table as she spoke.

Her husband, Theo, was smaller, more wizened and far more ugly than his wife. He had never been handsome, or even vaguely good-looking. Everything about him was sharp. The angles of his face, his nose; even his bones seemed to press against his clothes, making them seem stretched, ready to split. The wig he wore was yellow and ancient and barely a disguise for his baldness, especially as the sparse hairs that poked out from beneath it were silvery white. Despite his skinny body he seemed to possess the appetite of a football team, spearing slices of ham and turkey on his plate and forcing them into his mouth with a speed that Emma found not only disgusting, but also a little unsettling.

An odd couple, she thought, and wondered how on earth they had ever got together in the first place. She also wondered how they fitted into Alex Keltner's social circle. Theo Bronstein had once been a prominent industrialist, his wife, something in the cosmetics industry. But they were both now retired. From the way she'd observed Keltner act toward them, there was nothing to suggest they were close friends. In fact, the previous evening Keltner had made a barbed comment to Theo Bronstein that suggested he couldn't stand the man, and could barely tolerate the wife. There had been nothing in the dossier she'd read about them to help her slot them into this scenario; but the fact was they were here and enjoying Alex Keltner's generous hospitality.

Emma ducked out of her reverie to find Sylvia Bronstein staring at her. There was nothing hostile in the look; more a flat indifference. But as their gaze met something moved in the woman's eyes and Emma felt a sharp pain spear her under her navel. She gasped, clamped her hand against her abdomen, looked again at the woman, but Sylvia Bronstein had fixed her attention elsewhere and was now talking to the Japanese man, Yamada, about perfume. Almost as instantly as it had come the pain vanished, leaving in its place a numbing coldness.

"Emma?" Alex Keltner said.

She looked along the table at him. "Yes?"

"Were you planning to go into Lyndhurst today?"

"Yes, Alex, I was." She almost added that she was going to meet a friend there, but bit back the words at the last minute. Somehow she felt that wouldn't meet with Alex Keltner's approval.

"Only there's something I'd like you to pick up for me in town, if you have the time."

"Of course," she said. "No problem."

Keltner beamed at her. "Excellent. I'll organize a car to take you in. Shall we say thirty minutes?"

She checked her watch. 1:45. "That'll be fine," she said, praying that it wouldn't be Erik driving her. She couldn't bear the idea of spending more time alone with him. She stood from the table. "I'd better go and get myself ready," she said. "I'll call into your office before I go."

As she pushed open the dining room door she nearly collided with a giant of a man who was about to enter. It was the first time she had seen Mario Bernardi, but knew who he was immediately from his photo in the file, although the photograph had done nothing to convey the sheer size of the man. It wasn't so much his height, though he must have been a few inches over six feet, but more the fact that he seemed to be almost as wide as he was tall. The beautiful fabric of his Italian-cut suit was stretched tautly across his heavily muscled chest, seams straining, and the collar of his shirt looked as tight as a garrote around a neck roughly the diameter of a small tree. His head was shaved down to the bone, his nose flattened, suggesting that he might once have been a boxer, and his hands were so large that it was easy to imagine that when closed into fists they would resemble sledgehammers. He looked hard, tough and extremely menacing.

The voice, when it came, was remarkably gentle. "Excuse, please, *bella*," he said in fractured English, and stood to one side.

"Thank you," she said with a smile, and squeezed past him. She turned and watched him as he strode into the room, and realized suddenly that Bernardi had been Nicci's companion on her walk in the grounds the night before. There was no mistaking the way he moved.

With that small mystery at least resolved, she went back up to her room to change back into her jeans.

CHAPTER 15

Tony Carver found a parking space in a side street in Lyndhurst and leaned back in his seat, stretching, trying to straighten out the kinks in his back that only a long drive can produce. Despite the murderous traffic on the motorways he'd managed to get to the town with ten minutes to spare before he was due to meet Emma. But the drive had tired him, and he climbed out of the car wearily.

The Copper Kettle was packed with locals and late-in-the-season holidaymakers taking a respite from their sightseeing duties. He looked around but couldn't see Emma at first. It was only when she pushed herself to her feet and waved that he recognized her. She was sitting at a small table at the far end of the room. He waved back, drawing curious glances from the customers sitting at nearby tables, then threaded his way through to her.

"I barely recognized you," he said. "The hair; it makes you look so different."

"It's good to see you," she said, wrapping her arms around him and kissing his cheek.

"You too," he said. "Though I'm amazed I made it in time. But once I got off the motorway it was plain sailing."

They ordered two pots of tea—English Breakfast for him, Earl Gray for her—and two pieces of a succulent-looking carrot cake.

"So, how have you been?" Tony said.

"Busy," she said, not really knowing how to answer the question. Since Helen's death she'd been on an emotional roller coaster, with her moods changing from day to day, sometimes hour by hour. There was no pat answer, nothing she could say that wouldn't either trivialize or overdramatize how she was feeling.

"Busy's good," he said. "It's how I'm coping with it too."

She let out a breath. He understood.

Their waitress appeared and set down a tray on the table.

"So, why the haircut?"

Emma poured the tea. "I needed a change, and having it all chopped off seemed like an instant fix."

"Well it was certainly that. It makes you look . . . different. I think Helen would have approved."

"You think so?"

"I know so . . . and so do you," he said.

She smiled. "Yes, I suppose I do."

"I went to see Sid Whelan this morning," Tony said, changing the subject abruptly.

She stopped pouring. "Why?"

He shook his head. "I'm not really sure. Ever since it happened I've been scrabbling around looking for answers. For reasons why she died."

She opened her mouth to say something but he cut across her.

"I know, I know, it was an *accident*. I should come to

terms with it and let it go. But for some reason I can't. She was so vibrant, so full of life. For that life to end in such a way seems completely senseless to me; absolutely pointless. And if her death was pointless, then it follows that her life was pointless, and I refuse to accept that."

"I understand how you feel," she said. "But I don't see how going to see Sid would help. Surely you're just keeping the wound open."

He nodded. "I accept that. Perhaps I feel the wound's not ready to heal just yet. That's why I had to come and see you."

She finished pouring the tea and pushed his cup and saucer toward him. "But, Tony, I've told you everything I know. There's nothing more to add. When I left for work that morning she was still asleep. I never even got to say good-bye to her." Tears sprung to her eyes. She blinked them away.

"I just need to talk it through with someone and, as you and Helen were so close, it has to be you. I'm sorry, I know it's painful for both of us, but I need to do this."

Emma shook her head in resignation. "You're just like her; a dog with a bone, forever worrying it. When Helen got an idea in her head, she never let it go. Okay, talk," she said.

She sipped her tea, took a mouthful of cake then laid her fork down on her plate. The cake, she was sure, was delicious, but at that precise moment it tasted like sawdust.

Tony talked through his morning and she listened without interruption. When he'd finished she said, "So Sid remembers nothing at all about the accident?"

"That's what he says."

"I find that hard to believe."

"Well after speaking to him and seeing how he is, I believe it. But . . ."

"But?"

He sipped his tea. "I'm beginning to think that it wasn't an accident."

"You've just said you believe Sid's explanation. You can't have it both ways."

"Yes, I know. The thing that jars is the horse. Why was he so unsettled that morning? Sid himself said that his behavior was totally out of character. If he hadn't kicked out, none of this would have happened. According to Sid, once the accident happened, Nelson quietened down and allowed himself to be led away to another stall, and since then he's been his usual placid self."

"So what happened that morning to upset him?" Emma said.

"That's what I've been thinking about all the way down here."

"And your conclusion?"

"I think he might have been drugged."

"Drugged?" She stared at him incredulously.

"It's the most plausible explanation."

"But why would anyone want to drug Nelson. He's not exactly a Derby prospect, is he? He's just a hack."

"Yes, but a hack owned by one of our richest owners. Had he damaged himself that morning, Cyril Buckland, Nelson's owner, would have been demanding Helen's head on a plate."

Emma leaned back in her chair. This was getting more implausible and more bizarre by the minute. "And had that happened, who would have benefited?"

"You know the area. In Cambridge there are more livery stables than you can shake a stick at, and competition is fierce between them. Cyril Buckland is a very influential character. He has six horses at our stable, one for himself and his wife and one for each of his daughters. If he suddenly decided that we were no longer suitable and pulled his horses out, I can think of at least five more owners who would follow suit, and go with him to the next livery stable he decided to grace with his presence. When you tot it all up that's one hell of a lot of money. Losing Buckland and the others would be the kiss of death for us. And, at the same time, gaining Buckland and his cronies would mean a serious increase in annual income for another stable. Someone may have thought that drugging the horse was worth the risk." Finally Tony Carver picked up his fork and dug into the carrot cake. He took one mouthful and pushed the plate away from him. "I keep going back to that character watching the stables from the lane."

"What character?" Emma said, nonplussed.

"Didn't I mention him?"

Emma shook her head.

"Sid told me about him just before I left. It seems the stable had been under scrutiny for a few days. This guy in a Merc, just watching from the lane to see what was going on there. I'm starting to think it might have been our saboteur."

"Rather a jump in logic, isn't it? He might just be someone with a passion for horses. Besides, what evidence do you have that Nelson *was* drugged?"

Tony shifted uncomfortably in his seat and avoided her eyes. She was right; all this was pure speculation. But the pieces fitted into the scenario, and at least it gave him an avenue to explore. Anything was better than taking the facts at face value and accepting that his sister had died as a result of a freak accident. If it hadn't been for him and his financial injection, she would never have opened the livery stable, and if she hadn't then she would still be alive today. Indulging his little sister and giving her exactly what she wanted had cost her her life. That thought was almost too much to bear. "I have no evidence," he said. "Just a feeling."

"A *feeling* wouldn't stand up in a court of law," Emma said.

"I know. But this isn't about the law, or justice, or any of that. I just need to know."

She reached out and rested her hand on his. "Stop beating yourself up, Tony. None of this was your fault."

"If I hadn't interfered in her life . . ."

"Stop it!" Emma said sharply. "Helen loved the stables. Working with horses had been her dream. You gave her that dream. I don't know any brother who could have done more for a sister than you did for Helen. And she loved you for it. Take comfort from the fact that for the last few years of her life she was happier than she had ever been."

Tony Carver looked at her bleakly.

"I mean it, Tony. She would hate to know you were torturing yourself in this way. Just let it go."

He shook his head. "I know you mean well, Em, and you're probably right. But I've got to go on with this. At least until I find out who the person in the lane was and what he wanted."

Emma gave a sigh of resignation. There would be no turning him from this course of self-flagellation. "Describe him to me. It might be someone I've seen when I've been at the stables."

"I doubt it. Sid didn't recognize him."

"Try me."

"Okay. He was tall, over six feet. Dark hair, longish, swept away from his face. And he was driving a silver Mercedes saloon."

"Is that it? It's not much to go on."

"He was wearing sunglasses, even when Sid saw him in the evening. Never took them off. Anyone you recognize?"

She suddenly felt cold, as if she'd been plunged into a bath full of ice. "No," she said. "No not at all." She glanced at her watch. "Sorry, Tony, I've got to dash. I still have an errand to run for my boss."

"Oh. Right," he said, looking at her curiously. "I'll get the bill."

Outside the shop she kissed Tony Carver on the cheek. "Keep in touch," she said. "And let me know if there's any more developments."

"I will," he said.

With a small wave of her hand she hurried off down the street. Her mind was racing, her heart beating like a trip-hammer in her chest. It was the sunglasses that had triggered it, and the fact that the man wearing them never took them off. Put that fact together with the details given by Sid Whelan and suddenly the shadowy figure watching the stables from the lane had form, had a name. Tony had just described Erik Keltner.

CHAPTER 16

Tony Carver watched Emma disappear into the crowd of afternoon shoppers, shrugged and headed back to his car. He turned the key in the ignition, then paused and switched off the engine.

Her reactions were all wrong. When he'd described the watcher in the lane something had changed in her eyes. They'd become evasive, and suddenly she needed to leave. Had she recognized the stranger from his description? Was that it?

Christ! He was becoming obsessed, jumping at shadows. No. He'd always been good at reading people, and he was sure he was reading Emma correctly. She was hiding something. He climbed from the car and headed back into town.

The Three Crowns stood on the high street, sandwiched between a bookmakers and a dry cleaners. The Victorian frontage was festooned with hanging baskets filled with late-flowering pansies, and screwed to the wall by the door was a chalkboard advertising food, real ale and rooms. Inside was a solitary drinker seated at a table in the corner of the pub, nursing a half-drunk pint of beer while his eyes flicked over the racing results at the back of a newspaper. Behind the bar stood a large man with dark curly hair and a ruddy complexion, hand clutching a pen, jotting down answers to a crossword. He looked up as Tony approached and laid down his pen. "What'll it be, sir?" he said with a smile.

"A pint of Abbot, and I'd like a room if you have one."

"No problem," the landlord said. "How long would you be needing it for?"

"A couple of days. Maybe three."

The landlord ducked his head around a doorway at the back of the bar and bellowed. "Hazel!" Seconds later a young woman emerged, wiping her dripping wet hands on a towel.

"Gentleman needs a room."

"I haven't cleaned it," Hazel said, a hint of surliness in her voice.

The landlord smiled. "That's why I called you. Would you like to go and do it, then?"

The young woman looked from the landlord to Tony and back again. "I suppose," she said.

The landlord beamed at her. "Off you go then," he said, then turned to Tony. "If you'd like to sit and drink your pint, the room will be ready for you by the time you finish. Hazel's a good little grafter. She may complain, but she'll have it done in a flash."

"I didn't mean to put you to any trouble," Tony said.

The landlord laughed. "It's no trouble. We wouldn't advertise rooms if it was any trouble. Now, have you eaten? I can fix you a sandwich. Chef's on his break and doesn't start cooking again until five. But I've got some lovely turkey, and some fantastic granary bread, baked locally. How about it?"

Tony thought about if for a few seconds. He hadn't

eaten since breakfast, apart from a mouthful of cake at the tearoom. "Yes," he said. "Sounds good."

"Excellent," the landlord said, and leaned across the bar, hand outstretched. "Jim Davies," he said.

Tony Carver shook the man's hand and introduced himself.

"Well, Tony, I'll go and make that sandwich. You take a seat. Oh, before you do, though, I'll trouble you for a swipe of your credit card. Looking at you I'd say you'd be an unlikely candidate to do a moonlight flit, but you can't be too careful these days." He laughed again to show he was only joking, but he still took the credit card when Tony offered it, and swiped it through the PDQ machine.

Tony found a table by the window and took a long draft of his beer. He couldn't sit for long. He'd come completely unprepared for a stay away from home. Once he'd had his sandwich he'd go shopping for clothes, underwear and, most importantly, a toothbrush. He'd also fetch his car and leave it in the pub car park. All that could wait, though. Jim Davies placed the turkey sandwich on his table and all thoughts disappeared apart from eating.

Wiping his lips on a napkin he called across to Davies, who was stacking mixers on the shelves behind the bar. "Can I book a meal here tonight?"

"Liked the turkey then," Davies said with a smile.

"Possibly the best I've ever tasted."

"No *possibly* about it. What time? Eight suit you?"

Tony nodded. "Fine."

Emma walked around the town, her mind in a daze. Of course it was possible that the stranger keeping a watch on the livery stable wasn't Alex Keltner's brother, but there was a small insistent voice wheedling away in her mind telling her that of course it was. But why? Why had Helen been the object of such scrutiny?

She'd been walking aimlessly for thirty minutes or so before she remembered she had promised to pick something up for Alex Keltner. She pulled a street map from her bag, located Roydon Street and took a left down the next road she came to.

The photographer's shop was set in the middle of a newly built arcade. In the window, smiling just-marrieds stared out from their photographs; eyes fixed firmly on an idyllic future, undimmed by a harsher, more cynical reality. She pushed open the door and a bell rang somewhere in the back of the shop.

Seconds later a small, overweight man appeared from behind a beaded curtain, brushing away ripples of perspiration from his brow with a grubby handkerchief. His eyes were enlarged by the thick lenses of his spectacles, giving him the look of a grubby owl. He smiled obsequiously. "Can I help you?"

"Yes, I've come to pick up a package for Alex Keltner."

The smile faltered a little and the eyes narrowed slightly. "You're new," he said, the voice no less oily.

"Yes."

He stood for a moment more, staring at her, then pushed back through the beaded curtain. When he returned he was clutching a bulky manila envelope. "I should see some identification," he said.

"Should you?"

"I'm sorry, but in this day and age . . ."

Emma rummaged in her purse and produced a credit card. "Will this do?"

He took it from her with a nod of thanks and retreated again behind the curtain.

She drummed her fingers on the counter while she waited for him to return.

Finally the beaded curtain parted again and the man

handed her the envelope. "Sorry about that, but in this . . ."

". . . day and age . . . yes, I understand." She held out her hand. "My card?"

"Ah yes. No doubt I'll be seeing you again, Miss . . ." He looked her up and down, then glanced at the credit card. "Miss Porter."

She took the card from him, tucked the envelope into her bag and left the shop without another word.

Once out on the pavement and walking again she allowed herself a shudder. There had been something almost obscene about the way the photographer had looked at her. As if he'd been able to see through her clothes and was appraising her body. She took the envelope from her bag and turned it over in her hands. There was a label giving the address of the shop, a Bulgarian stamp and a postmark dated a week ago. The envelope was well padded and no amount of kneading with her fingers could tell her what was inside. Frustrated, she shoved the envelope back into her bag and carried on walking.

A few hundred yards later she found herself at the gates of a small public garden. Following a path through the autumn-withered beds she found herself on the grassy bank of a duck pond, with wooden benches set out at regular intervals. There were a few people occupying the benches, some sitting, feeding the ducks, others just watching the world go by, but she found an empty bench on the far side and sat, opening her bag and taking out her cell phone.

She was thinking again about Jeff and his sudden departure from Bexton Hall. The more she thought about it the more wrong it seemed. Last night he'd wanted to tell her something, something important, yet he'd been frightened into silence by Erik's sudden appearance on the terrace. And for the rest of the meal he'd looked like a condemned man.

Erik again. Everything seemed to be coming back to Erik Keltner.

She needed to speak with Jeff, needed to find out what he was going to tell her last night. There was no point in phoning the office. They only employed a skeleton staff at the weekends, and he would not be one of them. She scrolled down through her address book but she didn't have his home number. She was about to give up when she remembered the text message in-box. She was sure he'd sent her a text last week, and she couldn't remember deleting it. Pressing the button to open the in-box she scanned through the messages. Because she didn't have his number on her cell she had to open each message where there was no caller ID. Eventually she found it; sent the previous Monday. The message was unimportant, but another press of a button gave her the number of Jeff Williams's cell phone. She called it and listened to the phone on the other end of the line ring repeatedly.

"Answer the phone, damn it!" she said, but there was no reply. Finally a mechanical voice told her that the cell phone she was calling was not being answered (obviously) and if she wanted to leave a message she could do so after the tone.

"Jeff, it's Emma. I need to speak with you. Call me back when you get this message."

She dropped the phone back into her bag and sat for a few more minutes, watching a duck with a brood of ducklings move slowly across the oily water of the pond.

Jeff's assertion that Alex Keltner was not what he seemed extended to the others staying at the house. In fact *nothing* was what it seemed. When she'd woken this morning her initial reaction was to follow his advice and get out of there. The incident with Nicci Bellini was her cue to leave. Now, with most of the day behind her, she found it hard to accept she'd behaved in such a way. She'd never been promiscuous, even though there had been plenty of opportunities for it in the past. In her late teens and early twenties the crowd she hung around with changed sexual partners on a whim. But she'd never indulged. There had been the occasional fling, but most of those liaisons had left her feeling sullied and cheap, and she'd decided, at the age of twenty-three, that she was a monogamist. One partner, one lover. It was more satisfying and more secure. When Helen had entered her life she was still licking her wounds after being dumped by her previous long-term lover, Hermione, who had met someone else and fallen hopelessly in love with them. The wound-licking period had lasted almost two years, and even in that time she hadn't been tempted to ease the pain she was feeling with random and casual sex. She just didn't do it, which made last night's incident seem so strange and out of character.

As she watched the ducks, she tried to put it together in her mind. The dinner, the conversation on the terrace with Jeff, and Erik Keltner's ill-timed (or perfectly timed, depending on your point of view) interruption, Nicci Bellini's solicitous attention. She'd felt no obvious attraction for the woman, despite the fact that Nicci was incredibly beautiful. But then, in the library, all that had changed. She wanted her; desperately wanted her. And what was more shocking to her was that, sitting here in the prosaic setting of the manicured public garden with the ducks swimming on the pond and the chill autumn breeze ruffling her hair, she knew that she still did, and if the opportunity to make love with her again arose she'd grab the chance. It was as if her libido had its own agenda, detached from her rational thought processes, detached from common sense.

Something had happened to her in the last twenty-four hours that had left her feeling confused and vulnerable. More than ever she needed Helen. Helen had been her rock; her oasis of calm. She'd been able to talk to Helen about everything. Her deepest, darkest secrets were shared, all her doubts and insecurities exposed, examined and, finally, expunged. Helen would have an instinctive insight into what was driving Emma sexually at the moment, and without her counsel, her plain-speaking good advice, she felt lost and adrift.

Tony Carver turning up had done nothing but muddy the waters further. She could no longer think about the ramifications of what he'd told her. If she thought about it more then she'd have to *do* something about it, and all she really wanted to do at the moment was to sit here, watch the ducks and let the world float away.

CHAPTER 17

The streets of Lyndhurst were still quite busy despite the fact the shops were soon to close. Tony Carver picked up what he needed, and a holdall to carry it in, retrieved his car and headed back to the pub.

Jim Davies showed him up a narrow stairway to a room on the first floor. "Not exactly four-star accommodation, but at least it's clean, and the bed's comfortable."

Tony looked around the room. Surprisingly it was decorated in a very feminine style. Laura Ashley wallpaper, the chintz cushions of the chairs matching the curtains and bedspread. On the large oak chest of drawers in the corner was an assortment of china ornaments, dogs and cats mostly, but in the center was the figure of a clown, complete with floppy china hat and an expression that could only be described as mawkish. Davies noticed his interest. "Don't be put off by the fancy stuff. That's Hazel. Gets a bit carried away sometimes." he said. "In my last pub Kathy, my wife, did the set dressing. Good at it she was."

"Past tense?"

"Cancer. Thirty-two. No fucking age," Davies said gruffly, but Tony could see the emotions were still very close to the surface.

"Sorry. I didn't mean to . . ."

"You get used to it. Them not being here, I mean. It's a bugger of an adjustment to make, though."

"I know what you mean. My sister . . ." He stopped himself as he felt a lump forming in his throat and tears prickling in his eyes.

Jim Davies put a hand on his arm. "Recent?"

"Very."

"Life can be very cruel," Davies said. "Come on down and I'll fix you a whiskey. On the house."

Tony looked around the room again, seeing it now through different, better-informed eyes, then dropped his bag on the bed and said, "Good idea."

Three whiskies in and he was starting to feel the effects; his head was starting to swim and there was a slight ache behind his eyes. He wasn't a drinker but here in the convivial surroundings of the Three Crowns he let go of his usual reserve. The place was starting to fill up now, with early evening drinkers and a few families having their dinner in quiet secluded groups. Jim Davies was still working the bar, along with a young barman called Wayne who wore his long hair in a ponytail and had sleeves of tattoos covering his arms. Despite his rather daunting appearance Wayne was good-natured, with a line in humor that bordered on the sarcastic but never slipped over into offensiveness.

"Get you another?" Wayne said to him.

"No thanks," Tony said. "I've reached my limit. Any more and I'll be falling off the stool. Actually, I think I'm going to go for a walk. Try to clear my head a bit before the hangover kicks in."

"Lightweight," Wayne said with a smile.

"Featherweight, actually," Tony responded.

As he left the pub and set off down the high street he increasingly started to regret drinking so much. The evening was chilly and the cold air exacerbated the effects of the alcohol, making him feel even more light-headed. He checked his watch. Just after six and twilight was stealing in. He yawned. At this rate he'd be curled up in bed and asleep by nine.

He walked through the gates of the municipal garden and down the path to the small pond. There were few people about, the town having pretty much cleared once the shops shut. There was a young woman sitting on one of the benches. She seemed to be sleeping. As he drew closer he realized it was Emma.

He slid onto the bench beside her and put his hand on her shoulder. She awoke with a start, a look of panic dashing across her face. As her eyes focused she recognized him. "Tony! What the hell are you doing here?"

"I could ask you the same question. It's a bit late in the day to take a siesta."

She looked confused for a moment. "What time is it?"

"Just after six."

She pushed herself to her feet. "I've got to get back. I had no idea . . . I didn't mean to fall asle . . . Oh, shit!" She reached into her bag for her phone and dialed the house, arranging her ride back. She dropped the phone back into her bag. "Ten minutes," she said, looking at her own watch, squinting her eyes to check she was reading it correctly. "I should have gone back ages ago," she said.

"Well, if you've got ten minutes you might as well sit down again." He patted the seat next to him.

"You still haven't explained what you're still doing here. When I left you earlier I thought you were driving straight back to Cambridge."

"Change of plan. I owed myself a few days' holiday

and I just thought that as I was down here I might as well take them and spend the time exploring the area. It's been years since I was down this way."

She accepted the lie at face value. "Have you been drinking?"

He grinned. "I'm staying at the pub. The landlord there is a very hospitable host."

"But you don't drink. Helen always said that you were wrecked after two glasses of wine."

"And so I am. But I've been drinking whiskey. Apparently I can drink three of them and still remain coherent."

She looked at him doubtfully. "Well, you're a big boy. I'm sure you know what you're doing."

"Why don't you cancel your ride and let me drive you back."

"After three whiskies? I don't think so."

"Point taken. Where is it you're staying anyway?"

"It's only a few miles away. Bexton Hall."

"Sounds very grand."

"I'm sure it was once, and will be again, but at the moment it rather resembles a building site. Alex Keltner owns it and he's having it refurbished."

"Just how rich is Alex Keltner?" Tony said.

"No one actually knows. I don't think he's in the same league as Bill Gates, but he might rival Branson."

"You rarely read anything about him."

"He prefers it that way." She glanced back at the street, wishing her car would arrive. She didn't know why Tony had decided to stay down here, but it was the last thing she needed right now, and this inquisition was doing nothing to change her mind about that. She just wanted to be left alone, to work things out in her own way.

"How did he make his fortune?" Tony pressed on.

"He didn't. His grandfather did. Sugar. He owned several plantations in the West Indies. I'm not saying that Alex hasn't added to it, though."

A silver Mercedes drew to a halt outside the gates of the garden.

"Looks like your ride's arrived," Tony said, pointing toward the gate. The driver was getting out.

Her relief at the arrival of the car was short-lived. "Shit!" Emma said. "It's Erik."

"Erik?"

"Erik Keltner, Alex's brother. I hate him. He makes my skin crawl."

Tony looked beyond her to the man standing at the side of the Mercedes. "Tough luck. Could I come and visit you at Bexton Hall?"

Emma hesitated. "I'm not sure."

"Where's the harm? I'd really like to see the place. I love exploring old buildings," Tony said and, even to him, it sounded like a weak excuse. "I'll call you tomorrow."

"Okay," Emma said uncertainly, and began to move toward the gate. Toward Erik Keltner, who stood, relaxed, arms at his side, sunglasses in place, despite the fact that the light was rapidly fading from the sky.

Tony fished in his pocket for his phone. "A photo before you go," he called after her.

She turned with a wan smile.

He aimed the lens of the phone and took the picture, shooting past Emma to capture a perfect likeness of Erik Keltner.

"Who's your friend?" Erik said as he opened the door of the Mercedes.

"No one important. Just someone I met in the garden," she lied, and slid onto the backseat.

Erik closed the door behind her and took his place behind the steering wheel. "Dangerous," he said to her. "Talking to strange men could lead you into all sorts of trouble." His voice was slightly mocking.

She ignored him.

He put the car into drive and eased away from the

curb, his eyes fixed on Tony, who was still standing on the path, phone in hand. "And I'll remember you too, my friend," Erik said under his breath, and put his foot down.

Tony Carver watched the car pull away, then checked the picture on the screen of his phone. Sid Whelan didn't possess a cell phone; in fact, he hated them, thinking them a gross invasion of privacy. But Rosemary embraced modern technology. A room upstairs at their house was a testament to that, with a state-of-the-art computer and all the peripherals. And surfing the Internet was her passion. She also had the latest Nokia cell phone. Tony pressed a few buttons and sent her the photo he'd taken, with a message: "Show this to Sid. Is this the man in the lane?" Then he slipped the phone back into his pocket and headed back to the pub.

"Erik Keltner?" Jim Davies said. "Yes, I know him. Or I should say, I've had dealings with him."

"Dealings? Sounds ominous."

Davies laughed. "Everything about that one is ominous. Not the type of person you'd want to get on the wrong side of. What's he to you?"

Tony explained about Emma's job and her connection with the Keltners.

"I haven't got a problem with his brother," Davies said, pulling on a beer pump and filling a glass. "Met him once or twice and he seems okay, a bit smarmy maybe, but okay. Erik though . . . he's a different kettle of fish. Hard to believe they're related."

The ringing of Tony's phone interrupted the conversation. "Excuse me," he said. "I have to take this." He fished the phone out of his pocket and walked to the door, stepping out into the fresh evening air.

"Hello, Tony, it's Ro. Sid would like a word with you."

There was a muffled exchange, then Sid's voice blasted into his ear.

"You don't have to shout," Rosemary said in the background.

"Hi, Sid," Tony said.

"Tony, it's him." The voice was quieter now, but still loud enough for Tony to have to move the phone away from his ear.

"You're sure?"

"'Course I'm sure. I saw enough of him that week. I'm certain. How did you get his photo?"

"Just by chance."

"Any way you can come over?" Sid Whelan said. "I'd like to talk about this."

"Not right now," Tony said. "I'm in Hampshire, the New Forest."

"So when did you take the photo?"

"About half an hour ago."

"There?"

"Here."

"Bugger me! He gets around a bit then."

"Evidently."

"Who is he?" Whelan said. "I thought he'd be a local."

"His name is Erik Keltner."

"Means nothing."

"No, it wouldn't. Look, when I get back I'll call round and give you all the details."

"So is he trouble then, this Keltner?"

"Apparently, yes. But I still haven't been able to work out the connection between him and what happened to Helen." And as soon as the words left his lips he realized he'd been missing it. It was staring him in the face, but he'd been approaching it from the wrong angle. He'd been so absorbed with the idea of a rival trying to put the livery stable out of business that he'd missed the most obvious connection of all.

"Sid, I'll see you when I get back. Okay?"

"Okay, lad. And take care."

Tony walked back into the pub, ordered a pint from the bar and found an empty table in the corner. Of course, *Emma* was the connection. She was about to be employed as Alex Keltner's PA. And Keltner had obviously sent his brother to Cambridge to check on her background, including her relationship with Helen. It still didn't explain why he'd spent so much time watching the stables, but at last Tony had a starting point; a crack in the seam of things that he could get his fingernails under. Perhaps now he could start peeling back the layers of the mystery.

Jim Davies sat down heavily next to him. He was a big man who seemed even bigger now he was round this side of the bar. He rested his muscular forearms on the table. "About what we were talking about earlier . . . the Keltners."

"Yes?"

"Well, they're not too popular around here. Since Alex Keltner bought Bexton Hall there have been murmurings."

"Murmurings?"

"Local tittle-tattle. A bit of resentment. They don't employ any local people on their staff you see. Seems they ship them in from abroad. Eastern Europe mainly. Maids, cleaners, I think even the gardener's Hungarian. Well that kind of thing gets into people's bellies, stirs them up. I'm not racist or anything like that. Christ, I was in the army, served in Bosnia. I grew to love those poor people, so I haven't got an issue with them. But some folks around here aren't so tolerant. They see it as taking the bread from the mouths of the unemployed in the area. It caused a bit of a stink in here a few months ago."

Tony leaned forward in his seat. "Why?"

"It was a Sunday, a fairly quiet night usually. But on that occasion Erik Keltner came in with a couple of workers from the Hall. They ordered a meal and went and sat quietly, just over there." He pointed to a round table on the other side of the pub. "It all seemed perfectly normal, apart from the fact that Keltner was wearing his sunglasses. I mean, even during the day that part of the pub is fairly dark. It's tucked away from the windows and never gets the sun. Anyway, if he chooses to wear dark glasses what's it to me? So long as people put their money over the bar they could be dressed in a monkey suit for all I care. I don't have a problem with it. But that night Billy Farrier was in with a few of his mates. Farrier's the local tearaway. Not a bad lad really, but not particularly good either, and a bit of a loud-mouth. They spot Keltner and his cronies in the corner, and start taking the piss, making comments about Russian spies, the KGB, James Bond."

"I get the picture."

"Well Billy's a big lad. Six-three and about eighteen stone, most of it muscle. He must have fancied his chances with Keltner because he went across to him, snatched the sunglasses off his face, and put them on, parading up and down the pub. 'Look at me. I'm Bloefeld,' and all that kind of stuff. To give him his due, apparently Keltner just sat there and took it, and when one his friends started to get out of his seat, he pulled him back down and had a quiet word with him.

"I had to go out to the kitchen to sort some food out, but told Wayne to keep an eye on things. A few minutes later someone comes rushing through and tells me we've got a bit of a situation brewing. Of course I race out there, but by the time I arrive it's all over. There's Billy Farrier lying in the corner, blood all over his face, his mates crowding round him. Erik Keltner and his friends have gone."

"So what happened?"

"Well, that's the damnedest thing. No one really knows. I asked everyone who was there that night and couldn't get a straight answer out of any of them. Most of them had wildly different accounts about what went down, but three of them seemed to agree in the general details. They said that one minute Farrier was strutting around the pub, the next he'd picked up a pint glass and smashed it into his own face, and kept stabbing himself with it until two of his mates managed to subdue him, by which time he'd put out an eye and his face resembled chopped liver. We got him to hospital as soon as we could, and they patched him up, but he's going to need plastic surgery. He was a mess."

"And what was Keltner doing while all this was going on?"

"The short answer to that is nothing. He was just sitting watching Farrier as he mutilated himself. Smiling, someone said, but then someone else said his eyes were glowing, but then I figured they'd been watching too many horror films. Mind you, it was pretty horrific. I don't think anyone here that night will forget it for a long time. I know I won't, and I saw some sights during my time in Bosnia."

So that was twice that Erik Keltner was on the scene when something tragic had happened. It could be a coincidence, but Tony Carver didn't believe in coincidences.

"Where does he live, this Billy Farrier?" he said.

"Over on the Brookman's estate. Lives with his father, a rough bugger called Charlie. He came to the pub a couple of days after it happened and things got a little bit nasty. He was shouting the odds, blaming me for letting his son get hurt. I'm afraid I had to deck him in the end and he hasn't been back. Why do you want to know?"

"I might go and see him."

"Who, Billy? I wouldn't waste your time. From what I hear he's turned into a bit of a hermit. Never goes out and doesn't let anybody see him. Not even his mates. He was pretty scarred up. Before the glassing he was something of a ladies' man, but that's well in the past for him now."

Tony finished his pint.

"Another?"

"No, I'm going to turn in," he said. "It's been a long day."

The ride back to Bexton Hall was tense but mercifully brief. Emma got out of the Mercedes and hurried up to her room. She stripped, showered and wrapped herself in a towel. It was only when she was sitting in front of the dressing table mirror, running a comb through her wet hair that she remembered the package she'd picked up earlier. She checked her bag and breathed a sigh of relief that it was still there. The way her mind had been butterflying around this afternoon she could have left it anywhere. That she remembered to pick it up from the photographer's was in itself a minor miracle.

Well, Alex Keltner had waited a week for whatever it was. He could wait a few more minutes while she dressed and dried her hair. She dropped the package onto the bed and picked up the hair dryer.

A little later, walking along one of Bexton Hall's seemingly endless number of corridors, she had to admit she was hopelessly lost. All the corridors looked the same to her. It was only by chance that, twenty minutes later, she turned at the bottom of yet another corridor and found herself standing outside Alex Keltner's office. She only recognized it because the door was open and she could see his desk.

The room was empty. She stepped inside. There was an open door behind the desk, leading to another room. "Alex?" she called, and listened, but there was no reply. She crossed to the door, her footsteps muffled by the deep-piled carpet, and peered into the room beyond. Like the office it was empty. There was just a small desk, a chair and a large, flat, computer screen,

black and lifeless, but there was no sign of Alex Keltner.

It was too good an opportunity to pass up. She sat
down in front of the screen and moved the mouse. Instantly the screen blossomed into life to reveal an image of a naked back and wild hair. The image filled the
screen and it took her a few seconds more to realize
that the hair was moving as if caught in a breeze. She
moved the mouse forward and the image enlarged, the
lens of the camera filming the scene, zooming in until
the screen was just a mass of hair. She pulled the mouse
back toward her and the image widened out, and she
was confronted with a very familiar scene; similar to
the one she'd witnessed earlier at the cottage, but this
time the copulation was being performed on a four-
poster bed in an opulently appointed bedroom. And, as
before, the naked back and wild hair belonged to
Anna, the maid, but when she leaned forward sharply
Emma could plainly see that she had a different sexual
partner. This time it was Keichi Yamada, sprawled on
the bed, a beatific look on his face as Anna writhed on
top of him.

This was sick. What on earth was happening here? It
was obvious now that Alex Keltner was running some
kind of brothel. But for whose pleasure? Was it for the
benefit of his guests, or was he getting some perverse
voyeuristic kick, sitting here alone in this spartan room,
watching the performance?

She didn't want to see any more. With a click of the
mouse the image minimized, shrinking down to a small
icon at the bottom of the screen. In place of the image
was a menu. *Bedroom 1, Bedroom 2, Bedroom 3* . . . She
scrolled down. *Bedroom 4* was highlighted and obviously the movie file playing at the moment. She revealed a long line of folders, each one named, and was
stunned to see a folder labeled *Emma, Cambridge*. She

clicked on it and opened a submenu. *Lounge, Dining Room, Bedroom 1, Bedroom 2* . . . The ramifications of what she was reading on the screen began to sink in, but before she could open any of the files she heard voices: Alex Keltner and Florence Dowling, their footsteps sounding on the parquet floor as they came along the corridor toward the office.

Quickly she clicked on the icon at the bottom of the screen and opened the movie once more, anxious to leave the computer as she had found it. Things had moved on. Anna was now on her knees, her face buried between Yamada's legs. His hands were on her shoulders, gripping her fiercely. But something didn't look right. It appeared that Yamada's fingers were disappearing into her flesh, the fingertips buried to the first knuckle.

Emma stared at the image, trying to make sense of what she was witnessing, but then she had to tear her attention away from the screen. The voices were getting louder, but the footsteps had fallen silent, which could only mean Keltner and Florence Dowling had entered the outer office. She was trapped.

She just had time to hide behind the door as Florence said, "And what time did you say they're arriving?" The woman's voice sounded so close she could have been standing next to her.

"Their flight gets in at four. Erik's arranged to meet them at the airport at five, which should give them enough time to get through passport control and pick up their bags. They should be here by seven."

Emma could feel the sweat prickling her palms. She clenched her fists, taking shallow breaths in case they heard her breathing.

"I've prepared the yellow room for them. I'd like you to check it, just to see that everything is satisfactory."

"There's no need. I trust you implicitly, Florence."

"Nevertheless, I'd still like you to take a look. This is a very special occasion, after all, and I don't want anything to detract from it."

Emma heard Alex sigh. "Very well, Florence. I'll check it out."

"Now?" Florence said.

Yes, Emma thought. *Go and check it now.*

"Later," Alex said. "I'll be along later."

"There's only thirty minutes to dinner," Florence said, her voice edged with impatience. "When later?"

"I'll be along in a few minutes."

"Very well," Florence said. A few seconds later Emma heard the woman's feet clicking busily back down the corridor.

Emma pressed herself against the wall as Alex Keltner strode into the room. He sat down in front of the screen and clicked the mouse. Instantly the room was filled with the soundtrack to the film, Yamada's muffled grunting and Anna's disgusting sucking noises. Using the sound as cover Emma slipped from behind the door and ran on tiptoe across the outer office. She opened the door silently and stepped through into the corridor, closing the door behind her. It was only then she realized she was still holding the package.

Taking a breath she knocked on the door and waited. A few seconds later she knocked again.

"Come in."

Keltner was seated behind his desk, phone in one hand, pen in another. The door behind the desk was closed and there were no sounds coming from behind it.

She held out the package in front of her. "Your parcel," she said, trying to keep her voice expressionless.

Keltner looked up at her. "Thank you. I hope it wasn't too much of an imposition, picking it up. Anderton's a bit of a reptile."

"Anderton?"

"The photographer. Cyril Anderton."

"Oh, him," Emma said, reliving the revulsion of watching his eyes undress her. "Yes," she said. "Not a very pleasant man."

"No," Alex Keltner said. "But very good at what he does. And as you know, I only employ the best." He smiled.

There was something in the tone of his voice that made her feel he was mocking her.

"Well," she said. "If there's nothing else I'll go and change for dinner."

He was still smiling. "No, nothing else."

She turned away from the desk.

"You know it's quite all right if you want to meet up with friends while you're down here," he said as she reached the door.

She froze.

"Whatever you do in your free time is your business."

She turned slowly to face him. She didn't need to ask him how he knew she'd met Tony. Erik would have told him minutes after arriving back at the house. What troubled her was the fact the Erik hadn't bought her story. She wondered if they knew who Tony was.

"Thank you," she said.

Keltner said nothing more but held her gaze.

After seconds that felt like minutes she tore her eyes away from his and left the office. As she walked back to her room she marked her route, making landmarks of the pictures that hung from the walls and the ornaments that inhabited small alcoves in the walls. The next time she visited Alex Keltner's office she wanted to have no trouble finding it. And she wanted to visit his office again soon. There were things on his computer she needed to see.

CHAPTER 18

Dinner was an ordeal.

There were so many thoughts spinning through her head that she feared it might burst. Alex had insisted she sit to his right at the table and was talking to her incessantly, asking her questions about her childhood, forcing her to find answers as she tried to keep up the polite pretense.

Nicci Bellini was seated at the far end of the table. She seemed subdued and withdrawn. Emma caught her glancing along the table toward Alex from time to time, but she couldn't read the expression in her eyes. Everyone else seemed in high spirits, even Lars Petersen who, up until now, had presented himself as a rather dour, serious type. Tonight he was animated and a wealth of funny stories were told in a self-deprecating manner.

There was no sign of Anna this evening. Instead there was a waiter: young, good-looking, his olive skin contrasting sharply with the white shirt he wore. His English was fractured but his teeth-dazzling smile more than made up for any conversational inadequacies, as did his body, which, despite being camouflaged in the standard waiter's uniform of shirt, black slacks and maroon waistcoat, was lithe and obviously toned to perfection. It was obvious that the two older ladies at the table were smitten with him, and he played the game, giving them extra attention while serving their food and pouring their drinks.

Even the men seemed to be paying him more than the usual cursory attention.

Only Nicci Bellini seemed immune to the boy's charms, staring at him frostily and answering his polite inquires with curt, monosyllabic answers.

Over coffee Alex Keltner leaned over to Emma and said, "Two more guests will be arriving tomorrow."

"Right," she said.

"I thought you'd better know, because these guests are very special."

"I see."

Abruptly he got to his feet and tapped the side of his wineglass with the edge of his spoon. "Ladies and gentlemen." he said formally, then smiled. "Friends. I have a rather special announcement to make."

The table quietened, a hush of anticipation. All eyes turned to Keltner, except for Marta Steiner, who was watching the waiter pour Massimo Bellini's coffee with rapt attention.

"As you all know, my father arrives in the country tomorrow and will be joining us tomorrow evening. As you also probably know, not long after he arrived in Johannesburg ten years ago, my mother sadly passed away. But what you don't know is that recently my father met another woman, fell in love and married her last month."

This raised a ripple of conversation at the table. Then a round of spontaneous applause broke out, started by

Massimo Bellini and picked up by the others. When the applause died away Alex Keltner continued.

"The reason I'm telling you this now is that this afternoon I received a fax from my father, and I'm delighted to say that not only is he on his way to England, but he's bringing his new bride with him for you all to meet."

"When will they arrive?" Sylvia Bronstein said, her voice almost quivering with excitement. "I can't wait to see him again." She looked across at Emma and in a stage whisper said, "I love that man. And to think he's married again. It's so exciting."

"I'm afraid you'll have to be patient a little longer, Sylvia, but, if all goes according to plan, my father and Maria—that's her name by the way—will arrive here the day after tomorrow."

"The old dog. Married!" Theo Bronstein said. "I knew he wouldn't be on his own forever. I could tell you stories . . ."

"I'm sure you could, dear," Sylvia said, cutting across him. "But I'm equally sure they're not for the ears of polite company."

Laughter rose and fell around the table. Nicci Bellini didn't join in. She was staring down into the bottom of her coffee cup, a frown creasing her forehead. Suddenly she got to her feet. "Please excuse me," she said. "I have a terrible headache. I have to go to lie down."

"Of course, Nicci," Alex Keltner said. "Is there anything you need? Aspirin?"

"No thank you, Alex, I have some already," she said. "But sleep is really all I need."

"Of course."

Keltner watched her as she left the room, a slight smile hovering on his lips. In turn Emma was watching him, trying to work out what had gone on between him and Nicci Bellini today. There was something, that was certain, but she couldn't begin to think what it was.

And it bothered her into the early hours of the morning. She'd drunk too much wine and her head was pounding. She checked her bag for painkillers and found none. There were no analgesics in the bathroom cabinet either. She knew from past experience, when she had got drunk with Helen, that if she didn't take an aspirin or a paracetamol before she went to bed, she would be awake all night, and that was the last thing she needed. She had plans for tomorrow, and she needed to be sharp-witted and alert, not hungover and half-asleep.

She threw on a robe and left her room. She was beginning to get her bearings in the house now and was pretty sure she could find her way to Nicci's room. As she'd revealed at dinner, Nicci had a supply of aspirin, and Emma was sure she wouldn't mind sharing them.

Besides, it was an excuse to see her alone again.

As she turned the corner into the corridor where Nicci and Massimo had their rooms she froze, then ducked back out of sight. Standing outside Nicci's room was Mario Bernardi, his bulky form taking up a lot of space in the corridor. He wasn't alone. Wrapped in his arms, lips affixed to his in a passionate kiss, was someone who shouldn't have been here at all. Monica Patterson was running her hands up and down the Italian's broad back. They were too engrossed with each other to have noticed her. The kiss ended and Monica spoke breathlessly. "It's been so long," she said. "I was beginning to wonder if you would ever come back."

"I promised, *bella*," Bernardi murmured. "I always keep my word."

"Can you get away from them tomorrow to come and see me?"

"They're horse riding in the morning. I'll have time then."

"They've grown so powerful, Mario. If they ever found out about us they'd kill us."

"They're vermin, parasites, nothing more. Them and their kind. I could crush them without a second thought."

"Careful what you say, Mario. We need these freaks as much as they need us."

"Cocksuckers! They don't own me."

"But they do, Mario. And that's the problem. They do. You and me both, body and soul." Monica reached up with her mouth and found his lips again.

Emma turned and hurried back to her room, headache forgotten.

CHAPTER 19

In a darkened basement room of Bexton Hall, Anna, the maid, lay spread-eagled on an iron-framed bed. Her ankles and wrists were bound with silk ropes so as not to chafe the skin. She was naked and she'd been shaved of all her body hair. She remembered the shaving vaguely, soft foam being spread over her skin, the whispering razors slowly denuding her. She had an idea that there was more than one person doing the shaving, but the tape across her eyes blinded her and she was reliant on her other senses. An impression, nothing more, but she was sure she'd felt the touch of more than one razor working at once.

Some time ago she'd given up on the thought of calling out. Her lips were taped as securely as her eyes and apart from a muffled murmuring she could make no sound. She tried to think back to the last time she was conscious, but her mind was fuzzy with the drug they'd given her in a cup of sweet hot chocolate, so sweet it masked the taste of the narcotic. It had worked quickly; just two sips and she'd slumped unconscious onto the hard stone kitchen floor. And now she was awake but still under the drug's influence. She felt no alarm, no panic, just a soft resignation to her fate, whatever it should be. She just wished they'd remove the tape so she could see where she was. Her grandmother had lost her sight in her seventies and the fear of blindness had lived with Anna from that day. She could remember clearly the old woman moving around the apartment in Warsaw, bumping into furniture, burning herself on the cooker, once falling down an entire flight of stairs and breaking her hip.

Now she was blind herself and it was the only part of her current situation that caused her anxiety.

A door opened and closed and she heard the distant sound of voices, but they were indistinct, unclear.

In the small flagstoned hallway outside the basement room Florence Dowling and Monica Patterson sat at a table drinking tea.

"She was good," Florence said. "Steiner, Yamada and Massimo. Not many can take three."

"She comes from good stock," Monica said. "I went over her file with Alex and recommended her. I knew she'd be value for money."

A door at the end of the hallway opened.

Monica glanced at her watch. "Here he comes. As regular as clockwork."

"Nothing if not reliable."

Erik Keltner strode the length of the hallway and stood by the women's table. "Is she prepared?"

"Of course," Monica said. "Ready and waiting."

"Will she last? The one before her died before I'd barely started."

"Her heart was weak," Florence said. "Congenital. No one could have predicted that. She'll last, this one. She's strong."

Keltner sniffed, as if unconvinced. "We'll see," he said, and pulled open the door to the room.

Anna heard the door open and close, and could hear the breathing of someone in the room with her; someone male this time. She wasn't sure how she knew this because whoever had entered the room hadn't spoken, but the presence *felt* masculine. Very masculine.

Keltner walked to the bed and looked down at her, lifted the corner of the strip of tape gagging her and ripped it off. The action made the girl buck on the bed, not so much with the pain of it, which was brief, but more the surprise. Erik Keltner smiled as he watched the girl's tongue flick across her dehydrated lips.

"Drink," she said in a voice that was little more than a croak.

There was a jug of water and a glass on the small table beside the bed. He poured the water into the glass, lifted Anna's head and held it to her lips. She sipped at the water furiously, like a bird drinking, and laid her head back on the bed. "Thank you," she said.

Keltner took a step away from the bed and started to undress, peeling off his clothes and dropping them to the floor where he stood. Finally he took off his dark glasses that he laid down carefully on a small table at the side of the bed.

He then took a few moments to prepare himself.

Anna twisted her head, listening to what was happening beside her. She heard the soft rustle of the clothes as they hit the floor but wasn't sure what she was listening to. There then came another noise, a creaking and snapping that sounded to her like bones being broken. The sound was insidious and strangely alien, and she felt herself shiver. "What's happening?" she said, her voice tremulous.

Erik Keltner ignored her as he continued to prepare

his body for what was to come. Eventually he was ready. He stretched out a hand and ran it down the length of her body, feeling the goose bumps as they rose up on her skin. The hand paused for a moment on one of Anna's breasts, letting the nipple harden slightly under its touch, then moved on, stroking between her thighs, easing her legs apart.

"Let me see you," Anna said, feeling her body responding to the touch. "Please, let me see you."

There was the throaty chuckle of someone enjoying a huge joke at her expense. It was a horrible sound, barely human, and she immediately regretted her request. Suddenly she didn't want to see who was in the room with her. And as she felt a sharp fingernail lift the edge of the tape covering her eyes she jerked her head back. But there was nowhere for it to go, and with a sudden, sharp tug the tape was peeled away from her eyes.

For a moment there was stillness and silence in the room. She had her eyes tightly closed, too frightened to open them. The stillness and silence continued, and she was almost convinced that whoever had been in the room with her had gone. She concentrated, listening for the slightest movement, the barest sound. When she heard nothing, not even breathing, she lifted her eyelids slightly, letting through the smallest crack of light. She could see nothing. She opened her eyes further and saw the ceiling above her, rough plaster crisscrossed with wooden beams; dusty and cobwebbed. A spider scuttled across the white plaster from one beam to another. She shivered again. She hated spiders.

Finally she took a deep breath and opened her eyes wide, and for a second, just a second, thought she was alone in the room. Then she focused on the figure towering over the end of the bed, her eyes drinking in every detail, relaying the image to a brain that could barely comprehend what her eyes were seeing. Then the figure at the end of the bed moved toward her and she started to scream, the sound starting deep within her and bursting through her lips, grating through her vocal chords. She screamed, and kept screaming for twenty minutes until finally she was silent.

At the table in the hallway Florence Dowling and Monica Patterson turned as one as the door to the basement room opened and Erik Keltner stepped out of the room. He closed the door behind him. He looked at them, arrogance and contempt in his eyes. "Fodder," he said dismissively. "Clean it up." Then he stalked back down the hallway and left through the door at the end.

Florence looked at Monica. "Some people are never satisfied," she said.

"Erik was, is and forever will be a pig," Monica said.

"Come on," Florence said, getting to her feet. "Let's clear up the mess he made."

With a sigh of long-suffering resignation Monica stood up and walked across to the door. She paused before turning the handle. She hated this part, and no matter how many times she did it, and there had been many, had never got used to it.

Florence rested a hand on her shoulder. "Would you like me to go in first?"

Monica nodded.

"Very well." Florence moved her gently to one side and pushed open the door.

The combined smell of animal lust and death hit her like a physical blow. She turned back to Monica, who hovered in the doorway. "I've seen worse," she said.

"I'm sure," Monica said. "I'm sure." And followed the older woman into the room.

CHAPTER 20

The door to the room where Alex Keltner kept his computer was locked. Emma twisted the door handle and swore. She had a small window of opportunity to do this and was aware that there was no time to waste. She'd watched the others leave the house earlier in a small convoy of cars, led by Erik driving the Mercedes, on their way to the local riding school and golf club where activities were planned for the day. She'd declined Alex's offer to join them, citing the fact that she didn't play golf, and that horse riding would bring back too many memories of Helen. She felt guilty about using that particular excuse, even though there was a large element of truth in it.

She gave up on the door and pulled open a drawer in Alex's desk, carefully lifting papers and files, looking for keys. The first drawer proved fruitless. The second one she opened was more interesting. Tucked inside was the package she had picked up from the photographer's the day before. It had been torn open. Inside were three CD-ROMs, each labeled in black marker pen. Hungary,

Romania, Bulgaria. Other than that there were no clues to what the discs contained.

The third drawer down held the keys. A small anonymous bunch, sitting in the corner of the drawer beside a stapler and hole-punch.

It took a few moments to find the right key to fit the door, but within seconds she heard a satisfying click and the door opened as she turned the handle.

The computer screen was blank. She sat down in front of it and jiggled the mouse. Instantly the screen sprung to life and she was startled to find herself staring at a picture of herself. But what shocked her even more was the fact that she was naked, about to step into the bath at her cottage in Cambridge.

"What the fu . . ." she muttered under her breath.

Her hair was still long and tied up in a ponytail and she tried to work out when the photo could have been taken. It could have been any time in the last few months. But how? She pushed the thought to one side for a moment.

At the side of the screen were a series of icons. The first one she clicked on was labeled *Bulgaria*. Seconds later the screen was filled with a series of thumbnail photos of young men and women. She clicked on a thumbnail of a girl at random and a file opened showing a larger photograph. A sidebar gave various details of the girl in the photo. Name, age, weight, color of hair, eyes, the list went on. She scrolled down. Underneath the photo was a short background history of the girl, and a brief commentary about her current status. Apparently she was twenty-three, single and was currently employed as a cleaner at Bourgas airport. At the end of the report was an italicized comment. *Immediate availability.*

She opened two more files and was presented with similar dossiers, but closed them again quickly. These were not what she had come here to see.

A few more clicks of the mouse and she found the menu she'd been looking at the day before. She scrolled down the screen until she found the folder marked *Emma, Cambridge* and clicked on it. The second menu that filled the screen gave her a series of options. She opened the one that said *Lounge* and sat back, openmouthed, as an image of the lounge at the cottage filled the screen. Again by manipulating the mouse she could sweep around the room, closing in on various parts of it, pulling back to see it in its entirety. She zoomed in on the clock standing on the mantelpiece above the fire. The hand pointed to ten o'clock. She checked it against her watch. Accurate to the minute. This was a live feed! Somehow Alex Keltner had broken into the cottage and installed surveillance cameras throughout.

She felt sickened, violated. How long had they been there? Why had she never spotted them? How much had they seen? How much had *he* seen? *No wonder he knew where I kept the drink*, she thought bitterly.

She went back to the first menu and clicked on the file that said *Lodge*. With everybody out either horse riding or playing golf, she didn't expect the Lodge to be occupied, but she looked anyway. The downstairs rooms were as empty as she expected them to be. The sofa in the lounge where Steiner and Anna had performed their sexual gymnastics looked tidy, cushions plumped and in place. She switched her attentions to upstairs.

The bathroom was basic, as were two of the bedrooms. Simply furnished and plain decor. She was about to move on to another file but decided to check the last bedroom before she did so.

The room was occupied. There was a small divan in the center of the room and a man was lying, fully clothed, on top of the covers. There was something about his posture that bothered her. It looked awkward, twisted. And then she realized that whoever it was lying there was actually bound with rope, his wrists tied behind him and attached to bonds around the ankles, making his body arch like a bow. She used the mouse to zoom the camera in and focused on the battered and bloody face of Jeff Williams. "Oh my Christ!" she said softly.

CHAPTER 21

The Brookman's Estate hung just to the left of Lyndhurst, nestled between a sprawling industrial area and
a business park. The houses had gone up in the eighties
when the housing boom was at its height and every
spare piece of land in the area had suddenly mush-
roomed with new builds.

Tony Carver pulled the car over to one side of the
road and checked the piece of paper on which Jim
Davies had scribbled down Billy Farrier's address. On
reflection he should have asked for more specific directions because all the roads in this area looked the same
and he was beginning to feel he was driving around in
circles and getting nowhere.

On the other side of the street an elderly woman was
dragging an equally elderly and hugely obese black
Labrador behind her as she walked briskly along. He
wound down the window.

"Excuse me. I'm looking for Ellesmore Avenue."

The woman stopped walking and looked at him suspiciously. The black Labrador stopped too and sat

down heavily, staring at Tony with something like gratitude in its tired eyes.

"Ellesmore you say?" the woman said.

Tony nodded, smiling.

"It's on the other side of the estate."

"Ah," Tony said. "Could you direct me?"

The woman looked down at her dog. "What do you think, Percy. Shall we tell the man where it is?"

Percy the Labrador showed his interest by stretching full out on the pavement and closing his eyes.

The woman rolled her eyes, dropped the lead and crossed the road. "He's getting on," she said. "Not much longer for this world, I suspect." The last was delivered in a conspiratorial stage whisper. The dog flicked open a watery, world-weary eye and looked at her balefully.

"Ellesmore . . . now let me think. What's the easiest way to get there?"

Five minutes later, thanks to the old woman, Tony pulled into Ellesmore Avenue. The Farrier's house was one of the more run-down looking properties in the street. The small front garden was a neglected weed patch, and on the crumbling concrete drive a VW camper van was ending its days in rusty depression. More weeds pushed their way through the cracks in the crazy-paved path that led to a front door with peeling blue paint and a drunkenly askew letter box.

Tony knocked on the door. A few seconds later it was yanked open. Charlie Farrier was in his late forties. He wore stained gray sweatpants, a faded Def Leppard tee shirt and three days, stubble on his chin. His hair was lank and greasy, turning gray at the temples, and framed a face covered in broken veins, with a hooked nose, a small, tight mouth and rheumy, belligerent eyes. "What?" he said in a voice that was three parts aggression and one part drink. Tony took an involuntary step backward as the stale and sour whiskey fumes wafted over him.

"Is Billy home?"

Charlie Farrier looked him up and down, trying to assess who Tony was simply by his appearance. "What's it to you?" he said.

"I'd like a word with him, that's all."

"And what word would that be? He owe you money?"

"No, nothing like that."

Charlie Farrier rubbed the stubble on his chin, his eyes narrowing shiftily. "He's out," he said, and made to shut the door.

"I was told that Billy doesn't go out anymore," Tony Carver said quickly before the door could close. "Not since his trouble at the Three Crowns."

The look of belligerence in Farrier's eyes deepened to one of fury. He reached out and grabbed the front of Tony's jacket, pulling him forward, within range of the sour whiskey breath. "What's that got to do with you?" he said, his voice dropping to a menacing whisper.

"Only that I think we have a common adversary," Tony said, keeping his voice neutral. He'd been told that Charlie Farrier was a man given to sudden and unpredictable violence, and he really didn't want to get into a fight with him.

Farrier's eyes narrowed. "What do you mean?" he said, relaxing his grip on Tony's jacket.

Tony stepped away from him, if only to get away from the alcohol fumes. "Well, as I understand it, your Billy's troubles started with a run-in with Erik Keltner, right?"

"That scum," Farrier said, his face twisting into a look of disgust. "Go on."

"Well I have reason to suspect that the same man played a significant part in a tragedy in my family."

"So why do you want to see Billy?"

"I need to find out what really happened that night. Why he took a glass to his own face."

Surprisingly, tears welled up in the big man's face. He

pulled a dirty handkerchief from the pocket of his sweatpants and blew his nose. "He's out the back, with his pigeons. That's all he seems to do these days. Either that or he's sitting upstairs on his bloody computer. It's not right for a lad of his age." He stood to one side. "Come through," he said.

Even from the back door Tony could hear the cooing of pigeons coming from a large timber-built shed at the end of a cluttered garden. There was no path to reach it, just a muddy track across a threadbare lawn. Charlie Farrier led the way, Tony following a few steps behind. At the door to the shed Farrier knocked on the door. "Billy! Someone to see you."

"Tell them to piss off," came the response from inside the shed.

"Not this time, Billy," Farrier senior said, his voice reasonable, even gentle. "He wants to talk to you about that bastard Keltner. Seems he's had problems with him too."

There was a muffled curse from inside and the sound of a bolt being drawn back. The door swung open.

Charlie Farrier stood to one side to allow Tony to pass. "He'll see you now," he said with all the manners of a secretary.

Tony moved into the gloom of the shed. The walls were lined with small cubicles with wire mesh doors in which lean racing pigeons sat contentedly. The smell wasn't as bad as he'd imagined, just a soft mustiness pressing at the edges of his sinuses. Billy Farrier was standing at the end of the shed, cradling a pigeon in his hands. He had his back to Tony.

"This is Persephone," he said, raising his cupped hands. "She's a champion. My favorite."

"Persephone's an unusual name for a pigeon," Tony said.

"Greek goddess," Billy said. "They're all named after

Greek gods and goddesses. The one on your right is Demeter, on your left is Adonis."

Tony stole a look to his left and saw a rather plump bird with ruffled plumage. They were obviously named arbitrarily.

"You know Keltner?" Billy said.

"Not personally."

"What did you want to talk about, then?"

Tony took a breath and explained about Helen, about Sid Whelan's loss of memory. All the while he spoke Billy Farrier kept his face turned away, while his thumb stroked the back of the bird in his hands. It cooed softly under his touch.

When he'd finished speaking there was silence. Finally Billy Farrier moved slightly and put Persephone back in her cubicle. As he moved Tony caught a glimpse of the damage to the young man's face, but then his back was turned to him again and Billy spoke. "So what do you want to know?"

"The night your . . . accident happened, what do you remember about it?'

"We were larking about. Nothing heavy, just having a laugh. Taking the piss really. I nicked Keltner's glasses and put them on. Then apparently I picked up a glass and rammed it into my face half a dozen times. Simple as that really." The bitterness was heavy in his voice.

"Only it wasn't as simple as that, was it? You said *apparently*. 'Apparently I picked up a glass.' *Why* did you pick up the glass, Billy? What led you to mutilate yourself? Or is it that you really don't remember, just as Sid Whelan doesn't remember killing my sister?" He watched Billy Farrier's shoulders rising and falling as he breathed heavily.

"This Sid Whelan," he said finally. "Did he say anything to you about hearing voices?"

"Voices?" Tony said. "What do you mean?"

"Voices! In his head. Or rather, *one* voice."

"He didn't say."

"Didn't or wouldn't?"

"That I don't know."

"Well he wouldn't would he? Start saying to people that you hear voices telling you to do things and suddenly it's time for the men in the white coats."

"So what are you telling me here, Billy?"

"What I'm telling you is that he told me to pick up the glass. Told me to smash it into my own face." Billy Farrier's voice was flat, emotionless, then he laughed. "Told me it wouldn't hurt!"

"Erik Keltner told you to?"

"Yes, but like I'm saying, not with his voice. I could just hear him, in here!" He tapped the side of his head. "I could hear his voice, niggling away at me, over and over again, telling me to pick up the glass . . . to smash it . . . to . . ." His voice ended in a sob. Slowly he turned to face Tony.

A single tear dribbled from his one good eye, trickling down a cheek that was a livid lattice of red scar tissue. The other eye had gone, just an empty socket remaining. Part of the nose had been sliced off, and scars tugged at the corners of his mouth, pulling the lips up in a permanent sneer. The damage was far worse than Tony had imagined, and it took all his willpower not to avert his eyes. He concentrated and focused on the single tear as it meandered down the ravaged face.

"Not a pretty sight, is it?"

Tony said nothing.

"I used to be quite something with the girls round here, you know. Used to have to beat them off with a stick. Not now though. Fucking Quasimodo now, aren't I?"

"Plastic surgery can do . . ."

Billy held up a hand. "Please . . . don't. I've looked into it and I can't afford it. And I'm not going to one of those National Health butchers."

"They can do good work," Tony said.

"You'd better go."

"But I . . ."

"Just fuck off and leave me alone. I've nothing more to say."

Tony faced him for a moment, then shrugged and walked out of the shed.

"He's not a bad lad, you know." Charlie Farrier was waiting outside the door. He walked Tony back to the house. "He was very bright at school. Got his mother's brains. University material, or so his teachers said. Unfortunately his mother pissed off with the insurance man and Billy never got over it. Sent him off the rails. He might have her brains but everything else he gets from me, more's the pity. Sorry to hear about your sister."

"You heard?"

Farrier shrugged. "How old was she?"

"Twenty-eight."

"That's no age. Billy's been through the wars, but at least I've still got him."

They stood by the front door. "The story he told me, about hearing Erik Keltner's voice in his head, is that what he told you, told the police?"

"Told me, didn't tell them. Like he said, he didn't want them to think he was mad."

"Do you believe him?"

"Billy's twenty-two years old. In all that time I've never known him lie to me, so yes, I believe him. Do you?"

"Yes, I think I do. But I also think there's a lot more he's not telling anyone."

Charlie Farrier nodded. "I can vouch for that. You should see his room. Crammed full with computers and files. I snuck a peek in there one day. He's become obsessed with the Keltners, got stacks of stuff about them. I don't know what he plans to do with it, but if I was him I'd be trying to nail Erik Keltner's bollocks to the wall. And as I said, he's got a lot of me in him."

"I'd like to talk to him again sometime, perhaps when he's not feeling so angry," Tony said. "Could you have a word with him, try to persuade him to meet with me again? I'm staying at the Three Crowns. You can reach me there."

Charlie Farrier pulled a packet of cigarettes from the pocket of his sweatpants and lit one. "I'll make you no promises," he said. "But I'll see what I can do. I warn you now though, he can be a stubborn little git when he wants to be. If he makes up his mind he doesn't want to see you again, no amount of nagging by me is going to make him change his mind."

"Just do what you can. I'd really appreciate it." Tony walked back to the car.

"He'll get him," Charlie Farrier called after him.

Tony looked back. "Pardon?"

"That bastard Keltner. Billy will get him in the end, one way or another."

Tony gave a tight smile and drove away.

CHAPTER 22

Her heart thumped in her chest as she ran through the forest. She lost her way twice and had to stop to get her bearings, all the while fighting down the panic that was bubbling like lava in her stomach. What the hell had they done to him? And why?

But she knew the answer to the second question.

Erik had overhead them talking on the terrace and knew Jeff had been about to tell her something about Alex Keltner and the setup here. Now Jeff had been taken out of the equation. Silenced.

Guilt mingled with the panic. If she hadn't accepted Alex's offer of a job then none of this would have happened.

She took the path around the side of the cottage and peered in through the window. The place still appeared to be empty. She reached the back door and gave the handle a tug but it was locked. She'd expected nothing else. Farther on she came to a small window with frosted glass. A cloakroom perhaps. The window was badly seated in its frame and there was a gap large enough to get her fingers in. She squeezed her fingers through the gap and pulled sharply. The window opened with a loud creak.

She leaned forward and looked in. As she'd suspected it was a cloakroom, with a white porcelain toilet bowl, a matching sink and not much else. The sink was under the window and her trainers left a muddy skid mark as she climbed through. She stopped to wash it away, running her hand around the smooth porcelain, anxious to get rid of any clue that could reveal her presence. Although there didn't appear to be anyone else here, she was taking no chances.

She moved to the door, opened it an inch and looked out. There was a small carpeted hallway and a couple of doors leading off from it. One led to the lounge where Steiner and Anna had . . . She blocked off the thought with a shiver of revulsion. The other must lead to the kitchen. At the end of the hall was a flight of stairs.

She slipped out of the cloakroom and padded along the carpet and crept up the stairs. Once at the top she found herself on a landing with four closed doors to choose from.

The first one she opened was a linen cupboard, shelved out and filled with bedding and towels. The door next to it gave onto a small bedroom. There was a bed, a chair and a whitewood wardrobe. The bed was unmade, sheets and blankets folded neatly and stacked at the end of the naked mattress, but there was nothing else in the room; no Jeff.

The next room she tried was similar, but this one had its bed made up, the blankets covered by a chintz quilt, but still no sign that anyone was using it.

She approached the door of the last bedroom, wrapped her hand around the handle. Just as she was about to turn it, she heard a sound from below and froze, her heart leaping to her throat. Downstairs the front door opened, closely followed by heavy footsteps sounding on the stairs.

Close to panic she ran back to the room she'd just left and ducked inside just as the footsteps reached the top of the stairs, then cursed silently as she realized the footsteps were heading in her direction.

She glanced about the room looking for a hiding place. There was only one, and without further thought she slid her body under the bed.

The footsteps stopped outside her room, then moved on. She heard the door to the next room open and for a moment there was silence. Then the footsteps started again, heavier this time. And then the door to her room opened.

She looked out from under the bed and saw a pair of denim-clad legs. She held her breath, watching as the legs moved across her line of sight. Above her head the mattress sagged as something heavy was dropped on it. Then the legs moved back to the door and out onto the landing. The door closed and Emma let the air in her lungs escape in a long, low exhalation.

From outside the room she could still hear the sound of movement. Another door opened and closed, followed by silence, but she stayed where she was in case the denim legs came back to her room.

Eventually she heard the heavy footsteps sound on the stairs and the front door slam shut. Whoever it was had gone.

She crawled out from underneath the bed and stood up, brushing her clothes down with her hands to get rid of the dust bunnies clinging to them, then turned to see what had been dropped onto the bed.

A cry broke in her throat as she looked down on the beaten, bound and unconscious body of Jeff Williams lying on the bed.

His face was a mess. Livid purple bruising covered one side of it; his nose looked broken, little more than a yellowing, misshapen blob of flesh in the middle of his face; the lips were swollen and split. He was breathing, but it was a painful, ragged sound, as if his ribs had been broken and pushed into his lungs. His arms were tied behind him, attached by rope to his ankles, which were bound by thick duct tape. He was lying at an awkward angle, legs twisted, having been unceremoniously dumped on the bed with no regard for his comfort.

She knelt down beside him and touched his face tentatively, brushing his hair away from his brow. "Oh, Jeff, who did this to you?" she said, even though she knew the answer before the words had even left her lips.

He stirred slightly and his eyelids fluttered open. He looked up at her, trying to focus, then he tried to smile, but the effort was too much.

"Can you move? Roll over and I'll try to untie you."

His eyes flickered and he looked at her bleakly, shaking his head slightly. Then he looked beyond her and his eyes widened in alarm. She saw the look and glanced behind her, just in time to see Erik Keltner's arm arcing down. His fist connected with the side of her head and she was plunged into blackness.

"You idiot! I told you not to mark her," Alex Keltner said.

Erik shrugged. There was a bruise on the side of Emma's face where his fist had landed, but that was just too bad. Alex should never have let it get this far. But Alex liked playing games. *Too much*, Erik thought.

He'd laid Emma on the bed next to Jeff; now he and his brother stood at the side of the bed, staring down at them.

"You should have let me get rid of him when I wanted to," Erik said.

"That's not our decision to make."

"You're weak."

Alex said nothing, but closed his eyes.

A second later Erik clasped his hands to his temples, cried out in pain, and sank to his knees by the side of the bed. "Stop it!" he wailed. "Stop it!"

Alex Keltner snapped open his eyes and the pain in Erik's head vanished. He slumped forward on the bed, breathing raggedly.

"Physically you may be stronger than me, Erik, but that's the only way you are. Never forget that." He reached down and ran a finger over the bruise on Emma's face. "Tie her up and put her in the other room. I'll deal with her later."

Erik nodded meekly. "And him?"

"Leave him here. He's going nowhere." With that he turned and left the room.

Erik watched him go, something like hate simmering in his eyes. All those years ago, when they were children, *he* was the strong one, Alex's protector. Over the years he'd watched his little brother grow and evolve, developing his mental abilities, toning and training them like an athlete trains his body, to a point where he was now immensely powerful; more powerful than Erik could begin to imagine. It was Alex who was the protector now, and Erik was nothing more than a subordinate, a lackey. It hurt him and humiliated him deeply, and he was beginning to hate Alex for it.

CHAPTER 23

"So how did it go?" Jim Davies said as he pulled a pint of bitter. "Did you see Billy?"

"I saw him," Tony said, and pulled up a stool at the bar. "And it went almost exactly as you said it would."

"He's a bit of a mess, isn't he?"

Tony nodded and took the pint Jim offered him. He shouldn't really be drinking this early in the day, but the beer tasted good and his throat was parched. "He knows more than he's telling."

"Do you know that for a fact?"

"More a feeling really. A hunch."

"Good things, hunches. Unless you're Quasimodo that is."

Tony smiled. "Funny you should mention him. That was how Billy described himself."

"Poor bugger. I used to know a guy, a staff sergeant who caught the fag end of a land mine. It blew half his face off. He never recovered from it. Couldn't bear to look in the mirror, avoided walking past shops with plate glass windows in case he caught sight of his reflection. Ended up blowing his brains out. Then there was another guy, same regiment, whose face was ninety percent scar tissue. Met a beautiful woman, married her and had two wonderful kids. Some people cope with that kind of thing better than others."

"Well I don't think Billy Farrier's coping that well at all. Even though his father seems very supportive."

"Charlie Farrier, supportive? Now you *have* shocked me." Jim looked longingly at the pint in Tony's hand. "I think I'll join you."

Tony took out his phone. "I'm going to call my friend at Bexton Hall, see if I can pay her a visit."

"Is that wise? It's a bit like entering the lion's den."

"I'll take my chances. I'd like to take a look at Erik Keltner close up."

Jim Davies raised his eyebrows, sipped his beer and ambled off to the other end of the bar so Tony could phone in private.

Erik Keltner carried Emma through to the next room and had just finished tying the silk rope around her ankles when the cell phone in her pocket began to ring. He slid it out of her jeans and flipped it open. The caller ID read *Tony Carver*. Erik frowned, hit the speak button, closed his eyes and concentrated.

"Hello? Emma? Hello? Are you there?"

Keltner could feel the heat building inside his mind. He visualized it as a small, white-hot ball, centered in the middle of his forehead. At the same time his mind's eye built a mental picture of Tony Carver, where he'd last seen him, standing in the municipal gardens, phone in hand after taking a photo of him. He aimed the white-hot ball at him, to the phone in his hand, let it go and felt the heat surge from his body and travel through the phone network.

*   *   *

Tony Carver sat at the bar, cell phone pressed to his ear, listening to the silence at the other end of the line. No, not silence. If he concentrated he could hear someone breathing.

"Hello? Emma? Hello? Are you there?" But even as he spoke the words he knew that it wasn't Emma who had answered the phone, and a sick feeling of dread dropped to the bottom of his stomach like a brick.

The heat, when it came, was instant and intense. It was as if the phone had suddenly caught fire, although there were no flames, no smoke. He jerked it away from his ear, swearing, but something made him hold on to it, if anything gripping it tighter. He stared down at it, feeling the heat searing his flesh, but the more he wanted to hurl it away, to relieve the pain, the more his fingers tightened around the plastic, feeling it grow soft and pliable in his hand. Tears pricked at his eyes and his breath was coming in ragged gasps as the pain pulsed through his body. He closed his eyes and tried to slow his breathing, getting it back under control. He tried to focus, concentrating fiercely on the heat, pushing it back.

Inch by inch he felt it recede, traveling back down his arm toward the phone in his hand. Sweat beaded on his forehead and trickled down his face, but he was controlling the heat now, forcing it back into the phone, feeling it subside, the phone becoming cool again.

Keltner gave a grunt of pain as the phone he was holding started to melt. He dropped it to the floor, kicking it away from him as it burst into flames, then he stared at his hand. Red wheals, blistered at the edges, striped his palm and fingers. With a curse he stomped out the flames and rushed to the bathroom, turning on the tap and letting the cold water gush over the burns. When the pain had abated he wrapped his hand in a towel and went back to the bedroom, nudging the charred remains of the phone with his foot.

This was an interesting development. He'd never experienced anything like it before, although he knew it was possible. He'd learned a long time ago that there were people resistant to his powers, not many, but certainly a few. And Helen Carver was one of the few. So it wasn't too much of a surprise that her brother had the same resistance. However, this was the first time he'd encountered anyone who could actually channel the power back and use it against him. And he felt a small thrill of fear at the thought of it. But at the same time he also experienced a burgeoning sense of excitement.

By rights he should tell Alex about Carver, about the threat he posed, but almost instantly decided he wouldn't. This was something he wanted to handle on his own. He wanted to play this out to its logical conclusion and see where it led him. It was dangerous, and he knew he was jeopardizing Alex's carefully laid out plans. But he didn't care. He needed to face Carver one-on-one, and he was beginning to relish the challenge.

Tony leaned forward and rested his head on the bar, the phone slipping from his fingers and clattering to the floor. He felt exhausted, as if he'd just run a marathon.

"You all right?" Jim Davies was at his shoulder.

Tony pushed himself upright again. "Yeah, fine."

"Well you don't look it." Jim reached down and scooped up the phone, turning it over in his hand, staring at it. "How the hell did it get in this state?"

Tony took it and laid it on the bar in front of him. The plastic casing was indented where his fingers had gripped it. He told the landlord what had happened.

Jim listened intently, his eyes narrowing slightly, and when Tony had finished said, "Weird."

"Yes, I know. And I also know it wasn't Emma on the

other end of the line. I could sense someone there, but it wasn't her. Which means that someone else has her phone. Of course there could be a perfectly innocent explanation for it . . . but then again . . ."

"You think she's in some kind of trouble?"

"I don't know. She could be. She certainly didn't seem herself when I saw her."

"Then I suppose we ought to work out a way to get her out of there," Jim Davies said matter-of-factly.

"We?"

Jim picked up his pint again and looked at Tony over the top of the glass. "Well, I suppose you could try to do something on your own, but I doubt you'd be very successful. I, on the other hand, have experience. Years of training in surveillance and covert operations. I could help."

"You miss the army, don't you?"

"Every bloody day. But this isn't about me trying to re-capture past glories. It's about helping a friend."

"I appreciate the sentiment, Jim, but twenty-four hours ago you didn't know me from Adam. Besides, we don't know what we're up against here."

"We know that in some way Keltner has an influence on people's minds and has the power to make them do terrible things to themselves and others."

"Do we actually know that? Or are we fabricating some kind of supernatural scenario just to make a set of unusual circumstances fit together?"

"And the phone?" His fingers traced the indentations on the plastic casing.

"Now that I can't explain. It's outside the parameters of my understanding."

"But not mine," Jim said.

Tony looked at him askance. "Explain."

Jim Davies drummed his fingers on the bar, hesitating, as if uncertain whether to continue. "I get feelings," he said at last. "Clairvoyance, precognition . . . I rarely talk about it. I learned that lesson the hard way when I was in the army. Start showing that you're different from the herd and it leaves you wide open for people to take the piss. And I also think it scares them a little. People can't really handle those they perceive as different from themselves. All I know is that I've been like it since I was a kid. When I was in my teens I looked into it more closely. Read a lot, did the whole third-eye bit, all the Eastern mysticism. Most of it was fanciful bollocks, but I learned a bit and realized that the kinds of things I was experiencing were quite well-documented phenomena. So I stopped thinking of myself as some kind of freak and started to accept that I was just different from most people.

"During that time, though, I met a man called Nathan Wisecroft. He lived in a squat in Kings Cross. Someone told me that he was experienced in this kind of thing and that he would, as they said, *help me down the road to understanding*."

"And did he?" Tony said.

"No. He just scared the shit out of me. As I said, I was only young, and I'd gone there with a girl I was seeing at the time. She was as mad as a box of frogs, but that's another story for another time. Anyway, she'd been banging on about this guru she'd found called Nathan. Apparently all her friends were seeing him. He could do magic, she said. Not conjuring tricks but the real deal. I suppose curiosity got the better of me so I went along with her one evening. As I said, it was a squat, just off the Kings Cross Road, but you've never seen a squat like this one. Carpets on the floor, flock wallpaper, silk drapes, the works. I've see tattier apartments in Park Lane. It was the name that threw me, I think. *Nathan Wisecroft*. For some reason I was expecting a gray-haired old man, perhaps dressed in a kaftan, sitting on a silk cushion pontificating on the meaning of life."

"And he wasn't quite what you expected?"

Jim Davies shook his head. "I left the girl I was with at the door and got shown through to a small room at the back of the house, for a private audience with the great man himself. I remember opening the door and almost choking on clouds of ganja smoke that poured out of the room. Nathan Wisecroft turned out to be this huge West Indian. Six-foot-five and at least two hundred and eighty pounds, dreadlocks, beard, the lot.

"He was sitting in a large leather armchair, feet up on a matching footstool surrounded by four beautiful young women who seemed to be hanging on his every word. In one hand he had a brandy snifter almost filled to the brim, in the other the biggest spliff I've ever seen in my life. As he saw me walk into the room he smiled and nearly blinded me. Every tooth in his mouth was gold, some of them studded with diamonds. What a character! And what a teacher!

"I stayed with him for a month. For some reason he was rather taken with me. He knew I was slightly psychic and it just seemed to strike a chord with him. He saw himself as my teacher and set himself the task of developing my abilities."

"And did he?"

"Did he hell! I left the squat four weeks later just as useless and unfocused as the day I arrived there. But he did do something for me. He took me on a journey, a guided tour if you like, of the occult. I said he scared the shit out of me and that's true. He'd spent some time in Haiti and learned from a *Houngan*—a sort of voodoo holy man who'd shown him many of their rituals. He'd explored western witchcraft and demonology, and had a working knowledge of curses and spells. He showed me things, terrifying things, stuff I'd rather not revisit. And he seemed to have the power to bend people to his will, to get them to do things that in other circumstances they'd think twice about."

"Like Erik Keltner."

"Yes, but Nathan was benevolent. He'd use it as a confidence-building tool. It was all to do with empowering the individual. Which was why so many people flocked to him. When I was there there were at least another twenty sharing the squat. We were like his children, if that doesn't sound too weird."

"It does."

"Then I'm not doing him justice. He cared about us, looked after us; tried to make us better people. That was his aim, I think."

"So what happened to him?"

Jim Davies smiled. "Went into private practice. Left the squat, bought a big house in Maida Vale and became guru to the stars."

"You're kidding."

"On my honor. You see, despite all the frightening things he was capable of, he was extremely charming. Well-read, intelligent, and he had about him a magnetism that just drew others to him. He ended up a very rich man."

"Are you still in contact with him?"

"We send each other Christmas cards."

Tony studied his face to see if he was joking.

"I'm serious," Jim said. "The guru to the stars shtick lasted into the early nineties, then he sold up and disappeared for a while. I heard he'd moved to France, but it was all very vague. I wasn't sure where he was. Then about six years ago I ran into him in Putney. I was manager of a pub there, on the river. The Golden Fleece. I'd not long married Kathy and we were running the pub together. We had a couple of spare rooms upstairs and Kathy had just started the bed-and-breakfast lark.

"It was a Friday night and I'd just rung last orders

when the door opened and in walked Nathan Wise-croft. I barely recognized him. It was as if he'd shrunk. He'd shed a lot of weight and it didn't suit him. His clothes hung on his bones. He looked ill, wasted. He came up to the bar and said hello and smiled. The teeth were the same. They looked like a walking advert for Cartier.

"He never said why he was back in London, just something vague about business, but he stayed with us for about a week. He and Kathy hit it off immediately and quite often I'd walk in on them talking about the type of things he'd once discussed with me. When he left he took me to one side and said . . . well whispered, really . . . 'Cherish the time you have left with her,' meaning Kathy of course. And this was a good two years before her cancer was diagnosed. I think he knew, even then, that she was going to die.

"So you see, I'm quite open-minded to these kind of things. I realized through meeting Nathan Wisecroft that there is another world out there that we barely know about, let alone understand."

Tony Carver nodded. "That's as maybe, but I can't expect you to put yourself in a potentially dangerous situation on my say-so. Besides, I could be blowing the whole thing up out of all proportion. Emma may be perfectly okay. I'm raw, Jim. Losing Helen has left me emotionally fragile. I recognize that much. I may be creating scenarios here; jumping at shadows."

"No," Jim Davies said. "You're not."

"What makes you so sure?"

"Because you're here. And because I was told to expect you."

"By whom?"

"By Nathan Wisecroft."

CHAPTER 24

Emma opened her eyes and found she couldn't move. She was lying on her side on a bed, her arms tied behind her, her legs bound at the ankles. The side of her face throbbed painfully and the memory of being hit by Erik Keltner rushed at her, making her gasp and sending a shiver of fear fluttering through her body. She rolled over onto her back and looked about the room. It was the one she had explored earlier, bare except for a wardrobe and chair. The drapes had been drawn tightly across the window but soft sunlight filtered through the thin floral fabric, bathing the room in a diffused orange light.

She lay like that for a few minutes before the weight of her body pressing down on her tied wrists became unbearable and she moved back onto her side. A hundred thoughts were jostling for space in her mind; too many for her to focus on a single one clearly, but she remembered Jeff Williams bruised and beaten, tied, like herself, and left in the other room. She wanted to call out to him, but was scared the sound of her voice might bring unwanted attention from someone else.

What did they mean to do with her? The question spun slowly in her mind but she kept pushing the possible answers away, not really wanting to face the reality of her situation. Her mouth was dry, and she desperately wanted a drink of water. She swallowed once or twice, trying to get her salivary glands working. She had no idea what time it was or how long she'd been lying here. How could she have been so stupid? Playing out her Nancy Drew fantasies; imagining she could snoop around the place without being discovered. The people who had beaten Jeff to a pulp were serious players in a dangerous game, and she had naively blundered into it and in doing so had put her own life on the line.

She heard a noise outside the door, the sound of a key being turned. The door opened and Florence Dowling bustled into the room carrying a plastic bowl, a towel draped casually over her shoulder.

"Ah, you're awake. Good."

Emma said nothing but watched the older woman carefully as she nudged the door closed with her knee. She didn't lock it again. *The first chance I get . . .* she thought. But the woman wasn't going to give her any chances. She walked across to the bed and placed the bowl down on the floor.

"I must say I'm disappointed with you. I never imagined you as a busybody," Florence said, and rolled Emma roughly onto her back. She grabbed a handful of her hair and twisted her head from side to side, looking closely at the bruise on her cheek and tutting loudly. Then, still holding onto her hair, she reached down for something in the bowl. Her hand came back clutching an ice pack that she pressed against the bruise. "This should take the swelling down," she said.

"Why are you doing this to me?" Emma said, unable to keep silent any longer.

"Got to pretty you up," Florence said distractedly. "Can't have you looking like damaged goods. That would never do . . . never do at all."

The ice pack was beginning to burn her skin. Emma pulled her face away, but Florence kept a tight hold on her hair and put more pressure on the pack.

"I don't mean *this*," Emma said, jerking her head away again, wincing as she felt a cluster of hairs part company with her scalp. "Why are you keeping me prisoner? Why am I tied up?"

"It's for your own good," Florence said, her voice bland and uninformative. "Otherwise you might be tempted to leave us; go running off to that friend of yours who's staying at the Three Crowns. And then of course he'd kill you, and your friend too I shouldn't wonder."

"Who would kill me?" Emma said, her voice rising in panic. "Erik?"

Florence Dowling made a sound in her throat that was halfway between disdain and amusement. "Erik!" She almost spat the name out. "Erik doesn't even fart without his brother's permission. No, Alex would kill you, and wouldn't think twice about it. The only reason you're alive now is because he has plans for you, and has had from the start."

"Plans? What plans? And what do you mean, he's had them from the start?"

"Christ, you *are* naive! Monica said you were, but I thought you had more about you than that. When I first met you I rather liked you, which is unusual, because I don't warm to strangers generally. But I thought you were different." She took the ice pack away from Emma's cheek and examined her face closely. Then without warning she leaned forward and kissed her on the lips. Pinned to the pillow Emma couldn't pull away. Instead she opened her mouth slightly and bit down hard on Florence's bottom lip. With a yelp the older woman pulled away. "Bitch!" she said, and wiped away the blood that was trickling down her chin. She raised her hand as if to strike, then paused and seemed to gather herself. Slowly she lowered her hand again and a smile spread across her face. "You've got spirit, I'll give you that." Then she sucked at her lip, picked up the bowl and walked across to the door. She looked back at Emma, who was rolling on her side again to relax the pressure on her wrists. "He's going to enjoy you," she said, then walked out onto the landing, closing the door and locking it behind her.

Emma closed her eyes tightly, forcing back the tears. *This is madness*, she thought.

Billy Farrier glanced round as his father entered the shed. Gently he placed the pigeon he was holding back in its stall and reached for a bag of bird food from the shelf above his head.

"Go on, say it," he said.

Charlie Farrier shifted from foot to foot, uncomfortable as always in his son's company. He could barely bring himself to look at the boy's face. It had been a struggle ever since Sharon left him. The boy had always looked so much like her that often he was tempted to plunge his fist into Billy's face, feeling that in some way he would be striking out at her. He'd always managed to resist, but his son's presence in the house was a constant reminder of her betrayal, and their relationship had suffered because of it. Now, of course, since the *accident*, there were other reasons why he found looking at Billy difficult. A dozen of them, crisscrossing the boy's face in a livid spider's web.

"That bloke who was here . . ." Charlie began.

"Yes?"

"I was thinking: it could be useful to keep on the right side of him."

"How do you work that out?"

Charlie reached up to one of the pigeons and ran a gentle finger down its back, feeling the silky texture of the feathers.

"Leave her alone," Billy snapped at him. "Persephone doesn't need to be poked and prodded by you."

Charlie Farrier sharply drew his hand away from the bird. "Think about it," he said. "This Carver bloke, he has as much reason to hate the Keltners as we do. It would be good to have him on our side. You never know, he might have a way of getting back at them that we haven't thought of."

Billy Farrier smiled. "I doubt it. Besides, I'm working on a way to finish the Keltners off for good."

His father frowned, suddenly worried. Whenever Billy got that look in his eyes it invariably meant trouble. And trouble with people with the power and the wealth of the Keltners was to be avoided at all costs. "What have you got in mind?"

"You'll find out soon enough . . . and so will they."

"Just you tread carefully, that's all. Look what happened when you last went up against a Keltner."

"Yeah," Billy said, running a finger down one of the scars on his cheek. "But I was unprepared then. I didn't know what I was getting into."

"And you do now?"

"Oh yes. All that time on the computer, trawling the Internet, has paid off. I probably know more about the Keltners and what they are than anyone else on the planet. In fact I'm certain of it."

"And you're not going to tell your old man?"

"You wouldn't be able to handle it," Billy said cruelly.

"You'd dive into the nearest bottle and stay there for the rest of your life."

Charlie Farrier stared at the floor, hurt by his son's words. "I haven't been much of a father to you, have I?"

"No, and you weren't much of a husband either. That's why mum buggered off. But I'm still here, so that must say something."

Charlie looked up, hope flaring in his eyes. "Promise me you won't do anything stupid."

"Yeah, right."

"I mean it, Billy. I lost your mother, I'd hate to lose you as well."

Billy Farrier stared at the rumpled, pathetic man standing before him and wanted to feel something; some empathy, even some sympathy. Instead he felt only contempt. "Isn't there somewhere else you should be? Only I'm rather busy."

"Yes," Charlie Farrier said. "I can see that. I'll leave you to your birds. But think on what I said. That bloke Carver could be useful. He's staying at the Three Crowns."

"Yes. I know," Billy said, and reached for one of the pigeons, cupping it in his hands and lifting it out of its stall. Then he turned his back on his father and started whispering to it fondly.

Charlie Farrier stared at his son's broad shoulders, then shrugged and left the shed, closing the door behind him.

"Emma? Emma?"

Emma jerked awake. She'd been dozing fitfully for an hour. Her shoulders ached and the arm she was lying on was numb.

"Emma?" The voice came again.

"Jeff?"

"Thank God!" Even through the wall the relief was evident in Jeff Williams's voice, but the voice itself was weak and strained. 'You're okay?'

"Trussed up like a Christmas turkey, and aching from head to foot, but yes, I'm okay. What about you?"

A pause.

"Not so good. But as long as you're all right . . ." His voice faded away.

Emma called through the wall, "Jeff! Speak to me!"

"Okay." He sounded exhausted, as if their brief conversation had tired him beyond measure. "Florence has gone. We're here alone."

Emma rolled onto her other side, moving her dead arm, trying to restore the circulation. "What are they going to do with us?" she said. It was so difficult conversing through a brick wall, but it was better than nothing.

"I suspect they're going to kill me," Jeff said.

"And me?" She couldn't keep the desperation out of her voice.

He fell silent again. The drug Florence Dowling had injected him with to keep him sedated was powerful and it was taking all his strength to fight it.

"Jeff!"

A groan, then, "Sorry. Alex brought you down here for a reason."

"I know that much," Emma said. "But what's the reason?"

From the other side of the wall came the sound of coughing. A horrible liquid sound. And then silence.

"Jeff? Jeff!"

In the room next to Emma's, Jeff Williams lay on the bed, blood spattering his lips. Something was happening inside him. Something was broken. He tried to speak again but it was as if hot knives were being pushed into his lungs. He tried to move his body to alleviate the pain but he was too weak. He had totally underestimated Alex's power. The beating he'd suffered had been slow and methodical; a thorough demolition job. Ribs were broken, as were his arms. Organs were ruptured and he was now bleeding internally.

Fists and feet had rained down on him, Alex Keltner's rage taking on a physical form, and for a moment he thought it might be the end. But the beating stopped before he'd even lost consciousness, even though Alex could have killed him easily had he so desired. But he'd held back from delivering the final killing blow, sparing his life, though not from any sense of compassion. Alex stopped the beating for a reason. Tomorrow, Louis Keltner would be arriving at the house with his new bride. He had been left alive for the old man's benefit and it would be he who would decide his fate. That thought was terrifying and made him wish fervently that Alex had finished him off.

"Jeff?"

He heard Emma's voice faintly through the wall but the sedative was too strong to withstand any longer. He was too weak, too tired now to reply to her. His eyes fluttered closed and he drifted into a dark and dreamless sleep.

CHAPTER 25

Tony looked at Jim Davies steadily. "I think you'd better tell me everything, don't you?"

"Yes, I do. But not here. Come upstairs and we can talk in private."

Tony glanced around at the pub and realized that while they'd been speaking the place had started to fill up. Several tables were now occupied and Wayne and Hazel were dealing with a small queue of customers at the bar.

He followed Jim Davies up the stairs. "This way," Jim said. "It's not much, but it's home."

The lounge was a comfortable, but cluttered, room that reflected his bachelor/widower lifestyle. Magazines sat in piles on every flat surface; a huge flat-screen television dominated one corner, the floor around it littered with DVDs; a set of golf clubs occupied the opposite corner.

On top of a cheap dark-wood sideboard was a selection of spirits. "What can I get you? Scotch?"

"Fine."

Jim pointed to a large, leather-covered sofa, its cushions hidden by three-days' worth of newspapers. "Clear a space and sit down," he said as he poured equal measures of Famous Grouse into two cut-crystal glasses.

Tony pushed the newspapers to one side and sat as Jim handed him the glass. He took a mouthful of whiskey, letting it burn down his throat. He wanted to deaden the pain. The fury and despair that had been building in him all day. The fact that he was investigating his sister's death had, to a certain extent, made it easier to cope with the loss of her. But now it was obvious that Helen's death was no accident; that someone, namely Erik Keltner, was responsible. And that thought was like a burning ember in his mind, igniting the flames of anger. He wanted retribution. He wanted justice for his sister. But more than anything else, he wanted to know why Helen had been killed.

"Okay," he said. "Say I believe you. How could you, or this Wisecroft character for that matter, have known I was coming here. I only decided to stay in Lyndhurst today. It was a spur of the moment decision. When I woke up this morning I had no idea I'd even be in Hampshire."

"I think you've got to get your head around the fact that nothing ever happens by chance. You coming to Lyndhurst, and more importantly, coming to this pub, was foreseen. Let me take you back to when I last saw Nathan. It might make things a little clearer." He joined Tony on the sofa, leaning back into the plump upholstery and closing his eyes. He sipped his scotch.

"Nathan turned up at Kathy's funeral. We buried her. She hated the idea of her body being burned. It was a surprise to see him there because I hadn't been able to get in touch with him to tell him she'd died. The service had gone smoothly and there was quite a good turnout, considering most of Kathy's family had traveled down from Scotland. She was an Edinburgh girl, you see?

"Afterward most of the mourners came back to the pub for sandwiches and drinks. I suppose I was in a bit of a daze; realizing she'd gone, but not quite accepting it. I kept expecting to turn round and see her standing behind the bar. Just there the way she used to be. Smiling, always smiling, even when she knew she was dying . . ."

His voice petered out. Tony could see the memory-fed tears pushing at the edges of his eyes. He was silent for a moment, then seemed to shake himself and come back to the present.

"Anyway, it was late in the afternoon. Most of the guests had gone, just Kathy's parents and my folks left, and we were just sitting drinking, getting quietly hammered. I looked back at the bar, and like I said, I was half expecting to see Kathy, but instead I saw Nathan. He was just standing there, staring at us. I hadn't seen him come in, and I knew damned well he hadn't been there earlier in the day. He was too big to miss!" Jim laughed, but the sound was brittle and edgy.

"I opened my mouth to say something to him, but he put his fingers to his lips. I checked the table to see if anyone else had seen him, but they were too preoccupied with reminiscences to notice anything. When I looked back to the bar, he'd gone.

"I found him upstairs, in the kitchen, pouring water into the kettle. 'Coffee,' he said. 'Strong and black.' Just like that.

"When I saw him up close he looked very ill, worse than when I'd last seen him. He'd grown his hair and beard again; it was coming through gray. His eyes were bloodshot, as if he hadn't slept for days, and his hand was shaking, as if the effort of holding the kettle was too much for him. When I asked him what was wrong, he sidestepped the question and asked me one in return. 'How do you feel about moving to Hampshire?'"

Jim Davies took a final pull of his whiskey and set the empty glass down on the seat beside him. "Hell of a question," he said. "Came at me from left field, and I wasn't really sure how to respond to it. When I said nothing he told me he'd bought the Three Crowns, and wanted me to run it for him. I laughed. The thought of Nathan Wisecroft owning a pub seemed totally absurd. But then he explained why he'd bought it and why he wanted me down here. He said some very bad people had moved in to Bexton Hall, and he needed me here to be his eyes and ears. If anything strange or untoward happened I was to report back to him. He gave me a cell phone number and told me I was only to use it if I was reporting an unusual event concerning the Hall. Apart from that I was to carry on as normal a life as possible; run the pub, make it pay. He wanted nothing in return. No cut of the profits, no income whatsoever. To be frank, I thought he'd finally lost the plot. But the more he told me about the Keltners, I realized that he'd never been more rational or serious about anything in his life. So I agreed to do it."

"So what did he tell you?" Tony said.

"I'd rather let him tell you himself. He can explain it much better that I can."

"Fair enough," Tony said. "So was there much to report?"

"At first no. In fact for the first eighteen months I'd say, nothing happened at all. Like I said before, there were a few disgruntled people moaning about the foreign staff they employed there, but in general the Keltners got on with their business and left us pretty much alone. We saw very little of them. That changed with the Billy Farrier incident."

"And what did he make of that?"

"Well, to be quite honest, not a lot. I expected him to hare on down here, but he seemed quite laid back about him. Didn't say a lot, just told me to keep him posted if anything else developed. Of course, nothing else did. Life went back, more or less, to normal. And then, a couple of weeks ago, I got a call from him completely out of the blue. 'It's begun. Be ready.' That's all he said. I didn't have a clue what he was talking about. I thought about it for a while then rang him back. That's when he told me to expect you. Although he didn't mention you by name. He just said that someone would arrive, they would need help, and in some way it involved the Keltners. And then I was to call him."

"And have you?"

"No. I wanted to fill you in first."

"Thank you. I appreciate it," Tony said. "Call him now. I think I should meet him."

"Yes," Jim said. "I think you should." He went out to the hall and dialed a number.

The conversation was brief.

He came back to the lounge and flopped down on the sofa.

"Well, what did he say?"

"The message was very clear and very simple. We're to do nothing until he gets here."

Tony leaned back in his seat, steepled his fingers and blew across the top of them. "I'm taking a lot on trust," he said.

"Me too," Jim said. "Me too."

"When will he arrive?"

"He said to give him a few hours, but he'll be here before this evening."

There was a hesitant knock at the kitchen door and Hazel poked her head into the room. "Sorry to interrupt, but there's someone in the bar asking for Mr. Carver."

"Who is it?"

Hazel grimaced. "I can't be certain. He's got a scarf wrapped around his head, hiding his face, but I think . . . I think it's Billy Farrier."

CHAPTER 26

Shortly after Tony Carver left the Farrier house Billy finished feeding his birds and went back to the house. Thankfully his father had gone out; probably to the pub, but Billy didn't give the matter more than a second's thought. His room was at the front of the house, looking out onto the street, but Billy rarely opened the drapes these days, leaving the room in a state of perpetual gloom. He flicked on the electric light, sat down at one of his three computers and poked the keyboard with his index finger. The screen blossomed into life. A hundred more keystrokes and he had successfully hacked into the mainframe at Keltner Industries.

He'd been working for weeks to break protocols and passwords and three days ago he'd been successful. He'd stayed for barely a minute in case his presence was noticed, but the important thing was he now had access whenever he liked.

The virus he'd been working on for longer. It was a modification of the one he'd written while still at school. The idea then had been to hack into the school's computer system and bring it crashing down, but the plan had been thwarted by his computer science teacher, Mr. Reynolds, who'd realized that someone had been hacking in and had changed the access codes the day before Billy was to put the plan into operation.

This time he'd been careful not to announce his presence. He'd learned a lot since leaving school and the technical knowledge he'd gained allowed him to slip in under the net undetected.

He opened a drawer in his desk and took out a disk. The disk was in a case with a gaudy cover depicting a soldier in full combat fatigues, machine gun in one hand, grenade in another, storming an enemy position. Anyone seeing the cover would not have given the disk another look, thinking it just another computer war game; and, in a way, it was exactly that. He *was* at war with the Keltners, and this disk was his weapon of choice. He took the disk from the case and slid it into the drive. He estimated it would take about a minute to download it into the Keltner mainframe. Then all he had to do was to sit back and wait while the virus systematically corrupted every kilobyte of information stored there.

Of course the IT people at Keltner Industries would eventually identify the virus, fight it and destroy it. If they had any sense all the information contaminated would be backed up safely somewhere. It wouldn't be a disaster, but it would be a major inconvenience and would eat up many expensive man-hours. It would cost Keltner Industries dearly. And for the moment that would be enough for Billy. This was, after all, only meant to be the beginning of his campaign, his opening salvo. He had many more ways mapped out to screw the Keltners, and Erik in particular. Ahead of him was a lifetime of disfigurement and everything that brought with it: the difficulty getting a job, the sidelong looks of revulsion from people in the street, the lonely, celibate life of an outsider from society. And he fully intended to get his revenge for the suffering they'd inflicted upon him.

He hit the key to send the virus and the screen went blank. That shouldn't have happened. He frowned and sat back in his chair, trying to figure out what had gone wrong. The frown deepened when large letters suddenly appeared on the screen in front of him.

HELLO, BILLY.

He lurched forward in his seat, fingers scrabbling at the keyboard, but the keystrokes had no effect. He'd been locked out of his own computer.

VERY NAUGHTY, BILLY. YOU SHOULDN'T BE HERE.

How had they got onto him so soon? He hit the keys again, even though he knew it was useless. Sweat prickled on his skin, trails of it slithering down his back. Seconds, and then minutes, ticked by as he watched the screen, waiting for something else to appear. When it finally did, he gave a strangled cry and ran from the room.

PIGEON PIE FOR DINNER.

He burst from the back door and ran the length of the garden, throwing open the shed door. Inside he was met with a scene of carnage. Bird bodies ripped and torn, blood and entrails spattering the walls, the air full of feathers, dead pigeons littering the floor.

"Bastards!" he said quietly. "Bastards!"

The silence in the shed was absolute, as if death had thrown a heavy blanket over the building, muffling all sound. He was aware he could hear his own heartbeating underneath the thrumming rush of blood that coursed through his ears. And then hope, a small hope. The soft cooing of an uninjured bird.

He picked his way through the bodies on the floor to Persephone's stall. The bird was there, huddled right at the back, head buried in her chest, fear making her yellow eyes glitter. Gently he reached in his hand and scooped her up, lifting her clear of the stall and bringing his other hand up to cup her trembling body.

He stroked her head with his thumb, whispering words of reassurance. Her chest inflated and deflated quickly in panic and the cooing increased, signaling her distress.

"It's all right," he said softly. "I've got you. You're safe now." But no sooner had the words left his lips than the bird's trembling increased, becoming so violent he could barely hold her. Then, with a suddenness, that made him gasp, the plump avian body exploded, the chest ripping open, splattering him with blood and guts.

He stared down at the empty husk of his beloved Persephone and the tears started to flow, running in a crooked trail down his ruined cheeks. He sank to his knees and hung his head in absolute despair, the bird's remains dropping from his hands to join the other corpses on the floor.

"So what made you change your mind?" Tony said. He found them a table in the far corner of the pub—private enough for Billy Farrier to remove the scarf from his face. Tony looked at him. There was something different. The scars were the same, but the face looked softer, less aggressive, and the eyes looked red from crying.

"They killed Persephone," Billy said softly, avoiding eye contact.

"How?"

Billy ran through the sequence of events that had unfolded after Tony left earlier that morning. The computer, the virus, the carnage in the pigeon loft.

'How do you think they got on to you so soon?'

"I underestimated them. I was too cocky. I went storming in there like a fucking commando, all guns blazing. Not subtle, not subtle at all." There was anguish etched into the scars of the boy's face. "And now Perse-phone's dead and it's all my fault."

Tony thought Billy was going to cry again, but the boy bit back the tears and continued.

"They must have sussed me the moment I first hacked in. They've probably just been biding their time to see what kind of move I was going to make. Keltner killed your sister?" he said, switching tack suddenly.

"I believe Erik Keltner was responsible for it, yes. But I have no evidence, and if I went to the police with my suspicion I'd probably find myself in the asylum quicker than I could spit."

"So what are you going to do about it?"

"At the moment I don't know. There's something more urgent that needs attending to first." He quickly out-lined his fears for Emma.

"She was working for them. I say she deserves every-thing she gets," Billy said.

"Not if she didn't know what she was getting herself into," Jim Davies said. He'd come out from behind the bar and sat down at the table with them. Billy Farrier watched him suspiciously.

"It's okay," Tony said quickly. "Jim's on our side."

"He flattened my father."

"Yes, I did," Jim said. "But he deserved it."

Billy Farrier thought for a moment, then gave a twisted smile. "Yeah, he probably did. Right, so there's the three of us. What are we going to do?"

"For the moment, nothing," Jim said. "And it's four, not three." He told Billy about Nathan Wisecroft, painting his character in bold, slightly sensational, strokes.

"So we're just going to sit here twiddling our thumbs and wait for this freak," Billy said with a slight sneer.

"Yes," said Jim, slightly annoyed by the tone of the boy's voice.

"No," Tony said.

Jim looked at him sharply. "You agreed to wait until Nathan got here."

"And I stand by that. Though I have to say I'm still pretty skeptical about him. But yes, we'll wait. But there's no reason why we should be idle."

Jim Davies's eyes narrowed. "What have you got in mind?"

Tony Carver turned to Billy. "You said that the only reason they discovered you'd hacked into their computer was that you'd been careless. If you had another chance, do you think you could do it without being discovered?"

Billy nodded his head slowly. "I could, but not from my computer. They've locked me out."

"What do you need, equipment-wise?"

"Another computer with broadband capabilities. Nothing else."

"I have my laptop in the car. Would that do? It's only a couple of months old, and it's pretty high spec. Bluetooth."

"Should do the job, then. But why do you want me to hack in again?"

"I was going to ask the same thing," Jim said.

"We need to gather as much information about them as possible. Something that will give us an edge. Bexton Hall, for instance. From what you've told me about the place, it's undergoing extensive renovation. There might be a floor plan in a file somewhere."

Jim snorted with laughter. "You don't need to hack into their computer to get that."

"Why not?"

"Because the plans for the renovation work are available for public inspection at the town hall. For all his money and clout Keltner still has to abide by local planning regulations, and would have had to obtain planning permission before the first brick was touched."

"Could we go and see them, then?"

"I'll make a phone call."

"And would it be all right for Billy to set up in my room?"

"No. There's no telephone point. I'll set him up in the lounge upstairs. I've got broadband there," Jim said.

Tony Carver turned to Billy. "Are you happy with that?"

Billy shrugged. "Why the hell not?" he said. "I'll have to go home first though. There's some other stuff I need."

"Stuff?"

"Disks."

"You're not to try the virus again," Tony said firmly. "That could have been what gave you away last time. This is just information gathering. Nothing more, nothing less."

Billy Farrier sat back in his seat, a sullen expression on his face. Finally he nodded his head sharply. "Okay, but I'll still need the disks. I've been researching Keltner Industries for weeks and I've got a stack of intel about them and some of the nasty little scams they're into."

"Such as?"

"Human trafficking for starters."

Jim and Tony exchanged skeptical looks. Jim Davies gave an almost imperceptible shake of his head.

"It's true!" Billy said vehemently. "I've seen the files. They're bringing illegals in from the Eastern bloc for a price."

"But why?" Tony said. "Why would Alex Keltner be involved in something as risky as that? It's not as if he needs the money."

"That's the thing about the very rich." Jim said. "They always need more money. It's like a drug to them."

"That's a bit sweeping, Jim," Tony said.

"Put it down to my working-class roots. I'm just speaking from my experience of them."

"All right," Tony said. "We'll accept that, for whatever reason, Keltner Industries is running a sideline in white slavery. How does that help us?"

"It doesn't," Jim Davies said flatly.

"Ammunition," Billy Farrier said. "My plan was to gather as much information about it as possible, then blow it to the press. I daresay a story like that, no matter how much it's refuted, would put a dent in their share price." He got to his feet and wrapped the scarf around his face. "I'll be back soon."

"Bring everything you have," Tony said.

"Don't worry. I will."

As Billy Farrier walked out of the pub, Tony Carver's cell phone rang.

"Tony, it's Emma."

"Emma! But I thought . . ."

"Thought what?"

"Doesn't matter. Are you okay?"

"Fine, Tony. I'm fine."

"Good," he said. "It's all right if I come over to Bexton Hall to see you, then?"

"Why on earth would you want to do that?"

"I told you yesterday, remember?"

There was a pause. "Yes," she said vaguely. "I remember now. But I'd rather you didn't. I'm very busy."

"I see. What can I do for you, then?"

"Do?"

"You phoned me."

"Oh, yes. Stupid. Of course I did. I just wanted to tell you that I'm going away for a while."

"Away?"

"Yes. To America. Alex has promoted me, but the post he's got for me is in Boston."

"I see," Tony said. "And when are you going?"

"Tomorrow."

"Tomorrow? That's a bit sudden, isn't it?"

"Yes, I know, but there's a bit of a crisis out there, and I've got to go and help sort it out."

"When will you be back?"

"I can't say at the moment, but I could be away for a while. I'll write once I get there. Look, Tony, sorry, but I've got tons to do. I'm sure you understand. I'll be in touch soon. Bye."

The phone went dead. He stared at it, shaking his head.

In Alex Keltner's office Monica Patterson put down the phone and smiled at her boss.

"Did he buy it?" Alex Keltner said.

"Oh, yes, I think so," Monica said, patting the small gray box to which the telephone was connected. "This piece of equipment is almost foolproof. It uses her actual voiceprint as a template. Although you hear me speaking normally, whoever's on the other end of the line hears Emma, or whichever voiceprint I use. It's been very useful in the past."

He walked across and squeezed her shoulder. "Whatever would I do without you?" he said.

"A boss is only as good as his PA," she said.

"Oh, how true," Alex Keltner agreed. "How true."

CHAPTER 27

Nicci Bellini stepped from the shower, wrapped a towel around her waist and walked through to the bedroom. Her brother had let himself into the room and was lounging on the bed. She looked at him and frowned but made no effort to cover herself up. Instead she sat down at the dressing table and started to brush her wet hair.

Massimo propped himself up on the pillow and stared at her, noticing the livid bruise just above her kidneys. "What happened to you?" he said.

"Alex happened to me."

In the mirror she saw anger flare in Massimo's eyes. "Why?"

"Not here," she said. "I'll get dressed. I could use some air. Come for a walk with me."

He was about to argue but saw something in his sister's face that silenced him. "Okay." He pushed himself up from the bed. "Call me when you're ready."

When he'd left the room she picked up the hair dryer and dried her hair. She couldn't stay here. Not now. The bruising was painful, tender to the touch, but her emotions were more so. She'd always loved Alex Keltner and, in a way, still did, despite the beating he'd inflicted upon her.

She'd loved him from the moment they first met, before she knew what he was. But even when he revealed the truth about himself, her love for him was undiminished. Which was why she had begged and pleaded with him to make her as he was. She couldn't bear the thought that they would ever part and she was prepared to make any sacrifice to keep him at her side.

But his love for her had eventually faded, as she'd always feared it would. No one woman could hope to keep Alex Keltner forever. He'd grown bored and restless, moody and irritable. That last summer in London had been a trial. An endless string of conquests; a feeding frenzy. She knew enough about him by then to make the decision to leave him and go back to Italy.

She stood and let the towel drop to the floor. Turning slightly she examined the bruise in the dressing table mirror. Black and purple, yellowing at the edges. She winced as her fingertips traced its outline. It wasn't the first time he had beaten her, but it would certainly be the last. And this time she would make sure he paid a heavy price for his violent temper.

She threw on her clothes and went to meet her brother.

"The whole house is wired," she said. "Cameras and microphones in every room. He sees and hears everything."

Massimo leaned against a tree and closed his eyes. "So he saw you and Emma?"

"He has a digital recording of it."

"Shit! Why didn't you tell me this before?"

"I was too shaken. I couldn't decide what to do."

"You realize if he shows that recording to the others, to Louis, we're fucked."

"I know, I know. I'm beginning to wish we'd never come here."

He opened his eyes and glared at her. "I'm only here because you wanted to see Louis again. I suppose the news that he'd remarried came as a bit of a bombshell?"

"Shut up."

"But surely that was your agenda. Dumped by the son, so move on to the father. Do you think I'm really so stupid that I couldn't see what game you were playing? What sweet revenge it would be for you."

"Louis and I were always very close. I think he looked upon me as a daughter. But no, I won't deny I thought there might be a possibility of something more developing."

"Christ, you're ambitious," Massimo said, shaking his head. "My little sister wanted to be queen. It's a pity you couldn't control your libido."

"Thanks for the support," she said sarcastically.

"Shit!" Massimo said again. "So what are we going to do now?"

"We're leaving."

"If we do we'll become outcasts."

"I am anyway. Alex may forgive what I've done, but he'll never forget it."

"So that's it. We just run away and hide for the rest of our lives."

"Something like that. But we can start again. New identities; a different country. We'll survive."

There was a fire in her eyes, and defiance, there in the set of her chin. Massimo knew the look of old. As children she was always the dominant one, the one ready to take on the world, and to take it on on her terms.

"But I'm not leaving here before I give Alex Keltner something to think about," she said. "Something that

will make him regret he ever met me. He's going to pay
for the bruises he's given me."

"What did you have in mind?" Massimo said.

"Come with me."

She led her brother through another stand of trees,
then stopped and put her finger to her lips. "Through
there," she whispered, pointing to a gap between two oaks.

"It's the Lodge," he said. "So what?"

"It's where they're keeping Emma." At that moment
the front door opened and a man stepped out of the
cottage. He was tall with cropped hair and a hard,
Slavic face. A beer belly hung over the belt holding up
his black corduroy trousers, and a hunting rifle was
slung loosely over his shoulder. He stood, staring into
the forest, then unzipped his fly and relieved himself in
one of the flower beds. Zipping himself up again he ambled back into the house.

"As you can see," Nicci said, "they're guarding her."

Massimo shook his head. "That was a guard? Marco
could snap him in half with one hand tied behind his
back. Hell, I could snap him in half!"

"Agreed, but probably not before he raised the alarm."

"What exactly are you planning?"

"All in good time. Go and find Monica Patterson and
bring her here to me."

"Why Monica?"

"Because she's Alex's pet, and she should be able to
get to the girl without arousing suspicion."

He looked at her steadily. "You're sure about this?"

"I never been so sure about anything," she said.

Nicci Bellini was standing in the cover of the trees, staring back at the Lodge as Monica Patterson approached,
followed closely by Massimo. There was apprehension
in the woman's eyes. "You wanted to see me?" she said.

Nicci turned slowly to face her. She was smiling.

"Good of you to come," she said, and turned to her brother. "Massimo, leave us for a moment. Women's talk."

Massimo held his sister's gaze for a moment, then turned on his heel and walked back through the trees, finding a fallen trunk a hundred yards away and perching on it.

"Look, Nicci, what's all this about? Only I'm very busy. Louis and his wife arrive in a few hours."

"Yes, of course they do, and I'm sure you have your hands full, now that Alex's personal assistant is . . . incapacitated. So I'll come straight to the point. Why have you been fucking Mario when you know he belongs to us?"

The color drained from Monica Patterson's face and cold nausea crept up from her stomach. She knew this day would eventually come; she and Mario couldn't have hoped to keep their affair a secret forever. "I love him," she said when she found her voice.

"How quaint," Nicci said. "At least you show me the courtesy of not denying it. And Mario, does he feel the same?"

Monica nodded.

"I see," Nicci said. "So what am I to do with you?"

Monica's instinct was to run, but she knew she'd never get away. Especially with Massimo so close. "Please don't kill me." The words sounded trite, pathetic, but she didn't know what else to say.

Nicci Bellini regarded her for a moment. "And why shouldn't I? Mario is our pet, as you are Alex's. What do you think Alex would do to you if he found out about this?"

Monica Patterson closed her eyes, her body trembling. "You're going to tell him?"

"I might, I might not. That really depends on you."

Monica saw the slender lifeline she was being tossed and grabbed it with both hands. "What do you want? Anything, I'll do anything."

"Yes, Monica," Nicci said. "I know you will."

* * *

"Get off the bed," Monica Patterson said.

"I thought you'd retired," Emma said.

"Don't be so bloody naive."

"Well, you fooled me. And everybody else at work. Poor Monica can't take the strain. Well, yes, probably I was naive."

"Get off the bed," Monica said again.

Emma regarded her bleakly. "How?" she said.

"Use your imagination."

"I'll imagine my arms and legs are untied then, shall I?"

Monica opened her mouth to say something, thought better of it and snapped her lips shut and left the room. She returned moments later with a long, dangerously sharp kitchen knife. She reached down and grabbed Emma's ankles. The blade sliced through the bonds as if they were made of toffee. She slit the bonds on her wrists and said, "Now get off the bed. And don't try anything silly. I'm watching your every move."

I'm sure you are, you cow, Emma thought as she stretched her legs out. Cramps attacked her instantly and she buried her face in the pillow to stop herself crying out. Gradually the pain receded and she rolled to the side of the bed, swinging her legs down onto the floor.

"Can you stand?"

"Yes, I think so."

"This way then." Monica grabbed Emma's arm and led her from the room. "In there." She pointed to the bathroom. "Do what you have to do. I don't want you pissing yourself."

"Such charm, Monica. You really are revealing hidden depths. I suppose that's what the gorilla loves about you. Your hidden depths."

The woman's eyes narrowed. "I don't know what you're talking about," she said, but Emma could tell the barb had hit its target.

She hobbled slightly as she entered the bathroom. "I don't suppose I could close the door?"

Monica Patterson smirked. "Not a chance."

It was only when she sat that Emma realized her bladder was full. The relief was exquisite.

She looked about the room, her eyes searching for a weapon, not that it would do her much good. Monica was watching her closely and still holding the knife. Without the element of surprise she hadn't a hope of overpowering her.

"Hurry up," Monica said.

"What's the rush?" Emma said, flushing the toilet.

"Someone's wants to see you."

"Who?"

"You'll see soon enough. Down the stairs. You first."

They reached the bottom of the stairs and the guard swung out of the lounge, rifle cocked. "What you do?" he said in fractured English.

"None of your business," Monica said sharply. "Move out of the way."

The guard didn't budge. "I have orders," he said.

"And I have instructions from Alex Keltner, your boss. Now *move out of the way, you fat pig!*"

Confusion clouded the guard's dull gray eyes, and he stepped to one side, reaching for the small two-way radio attached to the top pocket of his jacket.

Monica plucked it out of his grasp. "And that won't be necessary."

"But I should tell—" he said, making a grab for the radio.

As he closed in, Monica sidestepped and plunged the kitchen knife into his protruding belly. The guard's eyes widened in surprise and he sank to his knees, his hands clasped to the wound in his stomach, trying to staunch the blood flow. As he looked up at Monica she lashed out with the knife and slashed his throat, slicing through the windpipe. With a disgusting gurgling noise the guard toppled forward, dead.

"Now, come on," Monica said to Emma.

Emma was rigid, frozen where she stood by the sudden violence.

Monica grabbed her arm. "I said, come on!"

She pulled Emma through the house, out of the front door and down the path that bisected the garden.

"Why did you kill him?" Emma said, her gaze fixed on the blood-smeared knife.

"I'll do the same to you if you don't hurry yourself."

Monica dragged Emma into the forest. All thoughts of escape were behind her now she'd seen what Monica Patterson was capable of doing. She concentrated on trying to keep up with the older woman.

They passed a small thicket of rhododendrons and came to a small clearing.

"You took your time," Nicci Bellini said as they stepped from the trees.

"The guard was problematic," Monica said.

Nicci glanced down at the blood-smeared knife. "Not any more apparently. Hello, Emma. I've missed you."

"What do you want with me?" Emma said. "What does anyone want? I don't understand what's going on."

"And why should you?" Nicci said, stroking Emma's cheek with the back of her slender hand. "Poor kitten. So many dreadful things have happened to you. But I'm glad to say that it's all over now. You're free to go."

"Now hold on a moment," Monica said, rushing forward and grabbing Emma's arms from behind. "She's not going anywhere. You said you just wanted to talk to her."

Massimo moved toward them, but Nicci held up her hand. "It's all right, Massimo. I can handle this. Monica, dear, it's not only Emma who's being offered her freedom. You too are free to go. Go back to the house; pack your things, and tell Mario to pack his. You can take our

car. Go away and start a new life together, with our
blessing."

Monica Patterson stared at her as if she couldn't believe what she was hearing. "Just like that," she said.
"You'd let us go away together?"

Nicci smiled. "Mario has served us well over the
years. He, like all of us, deserves his chance of happiness. And if you make him happy . . ."

Monica let go of Emma's arms. "Why are you doing
this?" she said. "When Alex and Erik find out what
you've done they'll hunt you down and kill you. They
won't rest until they do. You know how important she is
to them."

"Why am I so important?" Emma said, becoming
more confused by the moment. "I'm just a bloody secretary. I'm not important to anybody."

Nicci ignored her outburst and spoke to Monica. "I
think, after all these years, I can handle Alex. After all, it
was my shoes you stepped into. And Erik . . . well, Erik
does exactly what his brother tells him. I can see no
problems. Come," she said, spreading her arms wide.
"With our blessing."

Monica took a hesitant step forward and Nicci embraced her. "Thank you," Monica said. "Thank you so
much."

As Emma watched, the two women kissed. And she
watched Nicci's right hand creep up Monica's back until it reached the back of her neck. She could see Monica struggling to end the kiss, but Nicci's fingers had
threaded their way through the woman's hair and were
holding her head so she couldn't pull away.

Monica's struggles became more violent, more desperate, but the kiss continued. Emma switched her attention to Nicci's other hand. The fingers appeared to
be lengthening, an inch, and then two. And as they
lengthened they became thinner, the fingernails be-

coming more pointed, like sharp little daggers. Suddenly Emma could no longer see them, and she realized they had penetrated Monica's clothes and were burying their way into the flesh of her back.

"No!" she shouted, and made to move forward, but this time it was Massimo pinning her arms and he was much stronger than Monica.

Wrist followed hand, followed fingers, until half the forearm was buried in Monica's back. Still the kiss continued. Monica's body was shaking, going into spasm. And then she made a small noise, halfway between a sigh and a groan, and Nicci withdrew her arm. Clutched in the fingers was something wet and red, which pulsed for a second or two, then stopped. The kiss ended too, and as Monica pulled away Emma caught a glimpse of an impossibly long, pink tongue sliding back into Nicci's mouth. More disturbing was the look in her eyes as she released Monica's body, letting it fall to the ground. Sated lust, and something more; something incredibly old and rotten.

"What are you?" Emma yelled at her.

Nicci blinked and her eyes were back to normal, and the smile was back on her lips. "Dearest, Emma. Time for you to run away."

"What?"

Massimo released her arms. "The road is that way," he said, pointing off to the north.

Panic finally got the better of her inertia and Emma started to run in the direction of Massimo Bellini's pointing finger. As she ran she heard Nicci laugh, but she didn't look back, and she didn't stop for breath until there were two hundred yards of trees between her and the carnage she'd left behind.

In the room behind Alex Keltner's office, Erik watched the guard at the Lodge sink to his knees. In a movement so swift his eye could barely follow it, Monica slashed the guard's throat and he toppled forward to the floor, dead. Erik ran to the door, almost colliding with Florence Dowling, who was dressed as if she were going to a dinner party.

She'd spent the afternoon getting ready for Louis Keltner's arrival and she was satisfied that the long black skirt and cream blouse, fastened at the neck by her garnet brooch, had hit the tone she was striving for. Elegant, slightly chic, but not mutton dressed as lamb. It was important to present a professional appearance to her former employer. He'd expect nothing less.

"Careful!" she said as Erik cannonballed out of the room.

"Find Alex. Tell him we have a problem."

"I was just coming to tell you that Alex has driven to the airport to pick up your father. He's saving you the trouble. What's the problem?"

Erik jerked his thumb back at the computer screen and ran from the office.

Florence went across to the screen. She could see the guard lying dead on the hall floor. She flicked to the camera in the room they were keeping Emma. The bed was empty. "The little bitch!" she said under her breath. And then, rather inelegantly, ran from the room.

CHAPTER 28

Tony didn't know if it was his imagination or not, but the lights of the bar seemed to dim slightly as Nathan Wisecroft walked into the pub. It was unmistakably him. Tall, black, bald, with a sense of power that seemed to ripple the air around him. From his seat at a table in the corner he watched Jim Davies come out from behind the bar, walk up to Wisecroft and hug him affectionately. It was a slightly bizarre image. Two well-built men, who looked as if they would be more than comfortable mixing it in an alley brawl, embracing like long-lost lovers. Finally they parted and Jim led Wisecroft over to Tony's table.

Wisecroft looked down at him and stuck out his hand. Tony shook it and Nathan Wisecroft sat.

"I'll get us some drinks. Tony, bitter?" Jim said. "And Nathan, your usual?"

The big man nodded. "And Jimmy, have one yourself." And then he laughed: a great booming bellow of a laugh that drew curious and slightly fearful glances from a family of holidaymakers enjoying a late lunch at a nearby table.

The laugh stopped and Nathan turned to Tony, his face serious. "Hear you've been having some trouble," he said.

Tony shrugged. "I'm not so sure now," he said, remembering Emma's voice telling him that everything was all right.

Nathan looked skeptical. "Really? Why don't you tell me about it anyway?"

Jim came back to the table carrying a tray of drinks: two bitters and a pint of Guinness. Nathan took the Guinness and downed half of it in one swallow, put the glass back down on the table and drew the back of his hand across his lips. "Jimmy, you still pull a mean pint. Your man here was about to tell me what's been going down. But he seems a little confused. Is there a problem here?"

Jim looked from Nathan to Tony and back again. "I think so, yes."

"But the phone call," Tony said. "Emma seemed fine; a little distant maybe, but she didn't sound as if someone were standing there holding a gun to her head, making her say the things she did."

"They don't need guns to make people do as they wish, or to say what they want them to say," Nathan said, lifting his glass again. "So, start at the beginning and tell me everything."

By the time he'd finished Nathan had downed his second pint of Guinness but Tony had barely touched his bitter. "Well? What do you think?"

Nathan Wisecroft regarded him steadily. "My friend, I think you definitely have a problem here." He turned to Jim Davies. "Jimmy, is there somewhere we can go that's a little more private. I can see ears flapping all around us."

"Good idea. Let's go up to the lounge."

"Shouldn't we wait for Billy?" Tony said.

As if on cue the door to the pub opened and Billy Farrier sidled in, head still swathed in a scarf. He spotted the three of them seated at the table and came quickly across. He was holding a plastic carrier bag stuffed full of papers and computer disks. Jim made the introductions.

"Good to meet you, Billy," Nathan said. "Now, let's all go upstairs."

In the lounge Billy Farrier and Tony sat on the couch, Jim Davies on one of the armchairs. Nathan Wisecroft pulled up a hard, straight-backed chair and set in it the center of them. "Billy, take off the scarf. I like to see who I'm speaking with."

Billy Farrier hesitated for a moment and glanced round at Tony, who nodded his head slightly. With great deliberation Billy unwrapped the scarf from his head and looked at Nathan challengingly.

To his credit Nathan Wisecroft didn't flinch at the sight of Billy's ravaged face. In fact his face showed no flicker of emotion whatsoever. He simply said, "Thank you," in his deep, mellifluous voice. Then he turned to Tony. "Are you sure it was actually Emma who phoned you?"

"It *was* her. Definitely. I recognized her voice."

"Or you thought you did. Maybe you heard someone who sounded very much like her."

"No it was her. I'd swear to it."

"Hold on a minute. Am I missing something here?" Billy said.

"Emma phoned Tony after you left," Jim said. "Told him she was fine and that Keltner was sending her to the U.S."

"Bullshit!" Billy said. "That's too bloody convenient."

"Nevertheless, Tony is convinced it was Emma on the phone. That's right, isn't it?" Nathan said.

Tony hesitated before answering. He was no longer sure. Nathan Wisecroft had planted the seed of doubt in his mind. It had certainly sounded like Emma's voice, but the way she spoke, that was all wrong. "Not convinced," he admitted.

Nathan smiled. "My friends, these are the deceivers. They can make you see things that are not there, do things it would be against your nature to do, and they can make you hear things that are not real. Billy, the night of your . . . accident. What did you experience? I suspect you heard voices in your head? Or maybe it was just one voice. Am I right?"

Billy nodded. "He told me to pick up the glass and smash it."

"Did he then tell you to ram it into your own face?"

Billy winced at the words. "No. *I* did that. I couldn't stop myself. I just wanted to do it."

"There was something else though, wasn't there, Billy?" Tony said, prompting him.

Billy stared down at the floor, feeling slightly foolish. "He said it wouldn't hurt," he mumbled.

"Sorry," Nathan said. "I didn't catch that."

"He said it wouldn't hurt!" Billy said, his voice rising. "But it did! It bloody did!"

"I'm sure, Billy," Nathan said. "And whose voice was it you heard?"

"Erik fucking Keltner," Billy said. "It was as if he was there in my head. His thoughts and mine fighting for space. I thought I was going mad."

"You were, Billy," Nathan said. "At that moment you weren't in control of yourself. You were Keltner's puppet, and he was jerking the strings." He turned to the others. "Gentlemen, it's what they do. At least, it's what some of them do. Not all of them are as accomplished at it as Alex and Erik Keltner, and some of them don't possess the gift at all."

"You're talking as if it's more than Erik and Alex Keltner we're up against here," Tony said.

"If only it were that easy," Nathan said with a sigh.

"You'd better tell them everything, Nathan," Jim said.

The big man looked at him bleakly. "I think you're right," he said. "What we're dealing with is a race of parasites. They aren't human, though they take human form out of sheer convenience. They feed by drawing the life force from their victims."

"Vampires?"

"What, bloodsucking Hammer Horrors? No. There are no such things. Agreed there are those who drink the blood of others, but they're mostly people suffering from a deep psychosis that make them think they will gain immortality if they do so. But blood is just blood. It has as much to do with the spiritual as sweat and spit. It's a bodily fluid, nothing more. And, of course, there are other types of vampires, ones who feed on the emotions of others, but again, there is nothing supernatural about them, and believe me, I know. I've met many of them in my life, as I'm sure you all have."

"Then what are they? *How* do they feed?" Tony said.

Nathan sat back in his chair and rested his hands in his lap, appraising the others, weighing them up. Were they ready for this? Were they strong enough to deal with what was ahead of them, and survive? Davies, he suspected, might. His army training had instilled in him a sense of discipline, and a resourcefulness that would stand him in good stead. Also his psychic powers were strong, if unfocused. Tony Carver had a natural resistance to the mind games that had driven the young boy sitting next to him to mutilate himself, so he too might be useful. The young boy though, Billy Farrier, was a problem. Susceptible to psychic trickery, and mentally immature. He was at once a loose cannon, and the weakest member of the trio.

He considered his options for a moment, then sat forward, resting his hands on his knees. "Tell me,

Jimmy, what is the most singular driving force of the human race?"

"Procreation," Jim said at once. "The need to reproduce."

"Indeed. And it's such a strong instinct that we dress it up with all sorts of social mores. Linking it to love, romance, marriage. But take away the social niceties and we are nothing more than animals, rutting in the dark, letting our libidos lead us in the constant quest to multiply, to ensure the survival of the species. The instinct is so strong that it constitutes much of what we call our life force, our very souls. That is what these creatures feed on. By acts of sex they can draw that powerful energy out of us, using it to strengthen themselves, to prolong their lives. As I said, they aren't human, but they use that basic human energy as a food source. These are the creatures that exist in legend. The creatures who gave birth to the stories of the incubi and succubi."

"Sexual vampires then," Billy Farrier said flatly.

"If you want to put it crudely, or to hang a convenient name on them, then yes. That one's as good as any other. Myself, I call them *soul fuckers*. I suppose it appeals to my West Indian roots." He smiled, briefly. "But understand, they're much much more than that. You," he looked squarely at Billy, "have felt their power at first-hand. As I said before, not that all of them have that kind of psychic gift. Much like us, there are those who have it and use it, and those who don't. But the ones who possess the gift are incredibly powerful, and very formidable."

"How do you know all this?" Tony said. He was struggling to get his head around everything Nathan Wisecroft was telling him. It was all too weird, too fantastic. Yet he had experienced something of it himself when his phone melted in his hand.

Nathan knew the question would be asked and he'd

prepared his response carefully, knowing that telling the story would mean reliving the moment that changed his life and set him on his present course. It would be painful to speak it, but he needed to share it with them. He could keep it inside no longer. He reached into his jacket pocket and produced a photograph, passing it to Jim. "Show them," he said.

CHAPTER 29

She ran until her breath felt like hot knives slashing at her lungs, and then stopped, leaned back against the trunk of a huge oak and tried to get her bearings. Hopelessly lost, she had no idea where the road was and, without the road, she hadn't a hope of finding the town and safety. She slid down the trunk until she was squatting at its base, the blood pounding in her ears, sucking in air in quick panicky gasps.

The forest was silent, and that brought relief. At least no one was following her. Her mind was still reeling at what she had witnessed at the clearing. Monica Patterson's death. She hadn't liked the woman, but to die in such a way . . . She shivered, remembering her nighttime liaison with Nicci Bellini. The woman wasn't human, despite her beauty, her wonderful, soft skin. She imagined she could still feel her hands on her body, slender fingers caressing her breasts, her nipples. Emma leaned forward and retched, the image of those attenuated fingers burying themselves into Monica's back bringing wave after wave of nausea. *It could have been me*, she thought. *It could have been me!*

Erik Keltner prodded Monica's body with the toe of his shoe. She was lying on her back, eyes open, not a mark on her, but obviously dead. He recognized the gray, waxy pallor of her face. Using his foot he turned her onto her stomach and revealed the puncture in her back: a deep wound to the right of her spine, with white splinters of broken rib mixed with the blood. On the ground next to the body was something red and wet, already drawing a cluster of black flies swarming in the air above it. Monica Patterson's heart had been plucked from her body and discarded like a piece of offal. He swung his foot at it, kicking it into the trees, then took off in the direction of the Lodge.

The girl had gone, the cut ends of bindings telling their own story. He picked up a length of the silk rope and held it to his nose. He could smell her perfume, impregnated in the cord. Angrily he stuffed the rope into his pocket and stormed out onto the landing. He kicked open the door to the room next door and stopped dead, surprised to see Jeff Williams still trussed and lying on the bed. He appeared to be unconscious. If it wasn't him, then who had released the girl? Erik Keltner walked across to the bed, grabbed him by the front of his shirt and slapped him hard across the face. Blood flew from Jeff's lips but he didn't wake, even when Erik shook him like a rag doll and said, "Where is she? Who killed Monica?"

Jeff's eyes fluttered for a moment but there was nothing more. In a kidney dish on the nightstand was a hypodermic needle. Jeff was still heavily sedated. Erik Keltner swore savagely. He was wasting his time.

He let him drop back onto the bed and went across

to the window. She could be anywhere by now, but he suspected she'd head for the town. And she didn't have too much of a start on him. There was a possibility he could catch up with her. He ran from the Lodge and sprinted into the forest.

She heard a car. Thank Christ! The sound came from behind her, the opposite direction to which she was traveling. She spun round and started to run, veering off the path and blundering through the trees.

She pushed her way through a dense clump of rhododendrons and found herself on the road. Almost sobbing with relief she started to walk, keeping to the side of the road, ready to dart back into cover should she need to. She realized suddenly she had no idea which way it was to town, but it didn't really matter; she was out of the bloody forest with all its dead-end paths and confusing geography. Eventually she would come to a road sign, and at least then she'd get some idea of where she was.

The road curved slightly. She heard the car before she saw it; somewhere ahead of her, coming her way. For a moment she hesitated, caught between jumping back into the cover of the trees and waving the car down to beg a ride. As a small green Volvo emerged from around the bend the decision was made for her. It was too late to hide. She stepped out into its path and waved her arms.

Instead of slowing down the car increased its speed, barreling toward her. At the last moment it swerved, missing her by inches, and carried on along the road. She caught a glimpse of the laughing faces of two teenage girls. "Thanks a lot," she muttered and carried on walking.

Almost immediately another car hit the bend in the road. A dark blue Audi with tinted windscreen. Again she waved her arms, praying they'd stop, and this time the car slowed, pulling into a lay by a hundred yards ahead. Emma ran toward it, words of thanks and explanation hovering on her lips. She had almost reached it when the door opened and the grateful words died before they could be uttered.

Florence Dowling stepped from the car.

Emma threw herself into the trees to her left, tripped on a root and nearly fell. She recovered and carried on running. She glanced over her shoulder and almost cried out when she saw Florence no more than a few paces behind her, moving with a speed that belied her age. The woman was smiling, keeping pace with her with seemingly no effort whatsoever. She looked almost comical, dressed in her elegant evening wear, skirt hitched up almost to her waist. But there was nothing funny about the look in her eyes. They were glittering triumphantly. Another fifty yards and the woman would overhaul her. Emma stopped running and spun round to face her. Her eyes darted from left to right, seeking some kind of weapon and finding it in a fallen branch. Three feet long and as thick as her forearm. She scrambled for it and held it out in front of her. *Right, you bitch. Bring it on!*

Florence Dowling had stopped running too and was standing just a few yards away, watching Emma cautiously.

"What do you want with me?" Emma shouted at her.

"Don't you think you're being a little hysterical?" Florence said. "Put the stick down and let's talk."

"Fuck off!" Emma said, waving the branch threateningly.

"Look, Emma, I know things haven't gone as you'd expected, but Alex has his reasons."

"I don't want to hear them."

"But you must." As Florence Dowling spoke she

edged nearer. "His father's due to arrive soon with his new bride. And you *must* be there. You don't realize how important it is. Louis Keltner chose you. You, Emma, out of the hundreds submitted to him. Don't you know what an honor that is?"

Emma was curious despite herself. "Chose me for what?"

Florence smiled. "He chose me once, you know? A long time ago. And I served him well for all those years. But Louis is still a young man. He needs more than I can provide these days. He needs a pet who's vibrant, alive, still full of all that youthful vigor. You're that person, Emma. You."

"Pet?" Emma said. "What are you talking about? And he's Alex's father. How the hell can he still be a young man?"

Florence ignored the questions and her voice took on a wistful tone. "When I'd reached the end of my time with him, he gave me a great gift. One that I cherish every day. You never know, if you perform well, please him, provide him with everything he needs, one day he might give the same gift to you."

"I'm not going to be anybody's whore," Emma said.

A frown creased Florence's face. "Is that what you think you'll be? Is that what you think *I* was?"

"It's what you're describing."

"Well, yes, sex is part of it, I agree. You will be expected to provide that, but only when there's no other alternative. But most of the time you'll just be there for companionship. As someone to talk with, to confide in. Louis told me so much in the time I was with him. So many fascinating stories. He's a wonderful man, you know? So interesting. And so sexy. Often I wished there were no alternatives to be had."

Emma blinked her eyes. She suddenly felt very tired and had an almost overwhelming urge to drop the branch and lay down on the ground to sleep. Florence's voice had a soothing quality about it. Listening to her words was like pulling down a veil over her consciousness.

"Louis was always very kind to me, always very considerate. A lovely man. I'm sure you two will get on like a house on fire," Florence continued, the words becoming fuzzy in Emma's brain. She was becoming lethargic. It was almost too much effort to hold on to the branch. Her eyelids fluttered, and she brought herself up sharp.

Concentrate!

"I know he has a new wife now, but there will still be plenty of time for you."

She concentrated on the woman's mouth. The bottom lip was slightly swollen where Emma had bitten it.

Good. Focus on that. Focus on the lip. Watch the mouth.

The tip of the branch she was holding was now resting on the ground. Florence Dowling continued to speak, but the words were muffled and sounded as if they were coming from the end of a very long tunnel. Emma swayed, her eyelids finally flickering shut.

And Florence Dowling pounced.

Emma was brought back to reality by the suddenness of the attack. The branch, her only weapon, had been knocked from her hand, and Florence's arms were around her waist, her face inches away from her own. *Christ, she is strong!* There was a manic look in the woman's eyes. Emma threw herself backward and they tumbled to the ground. The fall made Florence loosen her grip and Emma rolled away from her, but the older woman's arm snaked out and her hand grabbed Emma's hair, almost pulling it out by the roots. Emma yelled and swung her fist, catching the woman just under the rib cage. Florence's breath rushed out of her with a whoop and she drew her legs up, but her hand held tight to Emma's hair, pulling her head clear off the ground, then slamming it back down against the hard, compacted earth. Emma grunted in pain as red lights flashed in front of her eyes.

And then Florence was on top of her, straddling her midriff, strong hands pinning her shoulders.

"I don't want to hurt you, Emma," she said breathlessly.

Emma swung her fist again, but this time the woman caught her wrist easily, twisting her arm back over her head. Emma's other hand scrabbled at Florence's grinning face.

"You can't win you know. You *will* come back with me."

Emma was tiring. The woman was too powerful for her. And she was changing. Something was happening to Florence's body. She seemed to be stretching, becoming taller, thinner, her arms elongating, the fingers of her free hand flexing and lengthening, the tips becoming pointed, the fingernails drawing out into fine daggerlike points.

In desperation Emma clawed at the woman's neck, her hand closing around the garnet brooch at her throat. She was growing weaker. She felt a sharp pain in her side as Florence's fingers started to burrow under her skin. The look in her eyes had changed. The manic gleam had gone, to be replaced by something akin to ecstasy.

As the fingers burrowed deeper into her side, Emma made one final effort. She wrenched the brooch from the woman's blouse. The pin was long and sharp; it was her only weapon now. Emma thrust her hand forward and rammed the golden pin into Florence's eyeball.

For a moment time stood still; then, with a howl of rage and pain, Florence Dowling threw herself backward and hit the ground, writhing, her elongated fingers scrabbling at her face, trying and failing to get a grip on the brooch to pull it from her eye.

Emma scrambled to her feet and watched in horror as Florence's body changed still further. The fine clothes split and ripped as her body stretched. The skin was turning a leprous yellow, the hair falling from the head in clumps. Skin was pulled tightly over a shifting skull, splitting under the chin, allowing a thin gray liquid to dribble out onto the ground. Lips pulled back from blackened teeth in a rictus grin, then they too split. The split traveled up Florence's face, bisecting the nose and forehead until bare bone was showing. All the while the garnet brooch protruded from her eye, an emblem of something unholy.

When the skull exploded Emma backed away, tucking herself in behind a tree. She watched with morbid fascination as the body rotted and fell apart in front of her. Until finally there was nothing left to watch, just a pile of clothes lying in a pool of muddy, yellowish gray fluid, and even that was quickly evaporating, becoming a thin vapor that was caught by the breeze and wafted away.

When it was over she walked back to the pile of clothes, reached down and picked up the brooch, and in doing so broke the dream she'd had in the bath on the day of her arrival. She turned the brooch over in her hand and stared down at the inscription she knew would be there.

To Florence, in appreciation. Louis Keltner. June 1893.

There was something else. Pierced by the pin was a dark brown plastic contact lens. She slid it from the gold and cupped it in her hand. It was significant, but she didn't know why. She searched the ground around her feet. Another lens winked up at her; this one undamaged. She picked it up and slipped both the lenses and the brooch into her pocket. Questions could be answered later, but now she had to get out of there.

The keys were still in Florence's Audi. She slid in behind the wheel and started the engine. As she put the car into drive and pressed the gas pedal Erik Keltner burst from the trees twenty yards ahead of her.

She slammed the pedal down to the floor and the car shot forward. He made no attempt to get out of the way, but simply launched himself at the car, bouncing onto the hood and rolling over the roof. Emma kept her foot down, feeling her stomach lurch at the sickening sound of the collision. In the rearview mirror she saw Keltner lying on the road. She braked hard, skidding into the grass verge. She must have killed him. No one could take an impact like that and survive. She put the car into reverse and was about to back up to where he lay, when the wound in her side went into spasm, taking her breath away. She clamped her hand against it, waiting for the spasm to pass. When she took her hand away, her fingers were covered in blood. She checked the mirror again. Erik Keltner was still lying there. He hadn't moved. Then suddenly his body heaved. He pushed himself up from the ground and dusted down his clothes. He looked about him as if searching for something, then took two paces forward and picked up his sunglasses. He slipped them on, turned to face Emma and smiled, and then started walking toward her.

Fumbling with the shift lever, she slammed the car into drive and flattened the gas pedal, watching Erik Keltner in the mirror as he receded into the distance.

CHAPTER 30

Tony stared down at the photograph. It showed four men standing, posing for the camera, in front of a motley collection of huts and shacks, some of them fabricated out of wood, others constructed from corrugated iron. The men were dressed in safari suits and wide-brimmed hats. All of them wore dark glasses. The photograph was old, very old. The paper on which it was printed had browned with age and the edges of the print were starting to crumble.

"I'm sorry, I don't see the significance."

"Look harder," Nathan said. "See anybody you recognize?"

"Jim, do you have a magnifying glass?"

Jim Davies went across to the sideboard and pulled open a drawer. A few seconds of searching and swearing later he returned and handed Tony a large magnifying glass with a tortoiseshell handle. "Try that."

Tony studied the photograph again, then looked up at Nathan questioningly.

Nathan Wisecroft simply nodded. "Show it to the boy. See if he sees what you see."

Tony passed the photo and glass across to Billy, who was scowling at Nathan, irritated at being called *the boy*. He peered through the lens at the four men in the photograph. "That's Erik Keltner," he said, jabbing his finger at the figure on the left of the group.

"That's right, it *is* Erik. Next to him is Alex Keltner and next to him their father, Louis."

"But that's impossible," Tony said. "The photograph must be fifty years old."

"Older than that. It was taken in 1922."

Billy was still studying the photograph. "Who's the one on the other end?" he said.

"Erik and Alex's brother. Vincent."

"So where is he now?"

"He was reported dead in 1972."

"Who's the girl?" Billy said.

"Girl? I didn't see a girl." Tony took the photo and studied it again. "Yes, I see her now. In the background. Pretty little thing. Big eyes."

"Look at those eyes, Tony, and tell me what you see in them."

Tony drew the lens back, enlarging the picture still further. He frowned. It was plain to see now. "Fear," he said.

"Yes," Nathan said. "Fear. Abject terror to be precise." He reached out for the photograph. Tony handed it to him. "The girl in the picture is my grandmother, Hannah. She was terrified for most of her life. And the men you saw in the photograph were responsible for that terror."

"Your *grandmother*?" Billy said.

Nathan nodded his head. "Louis Keltner owned a sugar plantation a few miles away from St. Xaviour, the town where that photograph was taken, and where, gentlemen, I was born. Much of the plantation's work-force came from our town, but there was a heavy price to pay for their continuing employment. The Keltners also used the town as their larder, coming in every few weeks to feed."

"Every few weeks!" Tony said. "But surely that must have decimated the population."

"No, because they rarely killed their victims. They would just use their bodies, drain them to a certain point, and then withdraw, letting them live and recuperate. Then later, maybe months, maybe even years later, they'd come back and take them again. It was a living hell for those chosen by the Keltners. The ones picked by them to satisfy their hunger lived, but it was a pitiful existence. Even as a child I remember how the people not chosen by the Keltners would shun those who had been. They called them halflings—people with only half a life. The halflings would struggle to eke out an existence. They rarely worked. Employers would shy away from using them in case it drew unwanted attention from Louis Keltner and his sons; and because they were so weakened by the constant draining of their life force, they were not much good for any type of labor. The feeding process also aged them prematurely.

"I remember seeing an old woman hobbling around the town, begging for scraps of food, or anything else to make her life a little easier. It was only when I got close to her that I recognized her as my mother's best friend. They had been born just days apart and had grown up together. Two young girls laughing and playing under the beautiful Jamaican sun. But on this girl's eighteenth birthday her parents had given her to Louis Keltner. It was quite common for parents of large families to do this. They usually offered the Keltners the youngest child as a way of protecting their brothers and sisters.

"I was just seven years old when I saw this woman begging, but the image has stayed with me ever since.

She looked eighty; frail, skin wrinkled, hair white, but she, like my mother, was barely thirty."

Jim got to his feet. "I think I need a drink," he said.

"I'll join you," Tony said.

"Nathan, Billy?"

"Vodka," Billy said.

Nathan Wisecroft shook his head.

When they were all seated again Nathan continued. "My mother's friend died a year later. The Keltners were no longer feeding from her—she had nothing left to give them—but what they'd taken from her left her too weak to fight the mildest of illnesses. She caught a cold that developed into pneumonia, and within two weeks she was dead. My mother organized her funeral. A pathetic affair. Not one member of her family turned up to pay their respects. To them she died when the Keltners first started feeding from her. There was my grandmother, my mother and me, and two or three halflings who I think had come out of curiosity. And Louis Keltner."

"You're kidding!" Jim said. "The bastard went to the funeral of the woman he'd killed?"

"Oh yes. The Keltners always showed their victims that much respect. I think it amused them." Nathan fell silent for a moment, staring at the floor. Tony watched the big man's hands, balling into fists and slowly relaxing again. He was struggling to contain his emotions, his rage.

"At the funeral I stood on the other side of the grave from Louis Keltner. He was a handsome, charismatic man. He spoke a few words to the priest, turned to go, then stopped and looked back at my mother and me standing there. I'll never forget that look for as long as I live." Nathan shuddered at the memory. "I knew then that our days were numbered. A few weeks later he took my mother for the first time. She died two years later.

"After she died I was given to Vincent by Louis Keltner. A gift. I think it might have been his birthday. I was nine years old."

An uneasy silence fell over the room. There were so many questions to ask, but no one knew how to broach them. It was Billy who finally spoke. "So what happened to you? If you became one of these . . . half-people, how come you're sitting here now?"

"Because Vincent was different from his father and brothers. He was almost human. He only took what he needed to survive. But most of the time we'd just sit and talk. That was how I learned so much about them; about their ways, their needs.

"Vincent got me a job at the plantation. It was lowly work, but I earned money. And I saved every penny I could. By the time I was sixteen I had enough money to leave St. Xaviour and travel to Kingston. I won't bore you with how I survived once I got there. I'll just say that my time spent with Vincent had given me all the experience I needed. And I discovered something. The relationship with Vincent was in some way symbiotic. He had taken from me, but I in turn had taken from him. I started getting premonitions, precognition. Somehow I'd become psychic. The power was raw, unfocused. Like you, Jimmy, I had something special but didn't know how to use it. But I learned. Out of necessity I learned how to harness the power. I practiced. I exercised it. It's like a dormant muscle. It needs to be worked to make it strong. By the time I was twenty I was able to control it and in doing so found I could use it to make money. Again, I'll spare you the details. Nothing I did in those days was very palatable, and some of the things I did still haunt me now. But I survived."

"And then some," Billy said, clearly impressed.

"I survived, but I'm not proud about the way I did it," Nathan said to the boy. "What have you got in the bag?"

Billy was flustered for a moment by the sudden

change of tack. "Papers, disks," he said. "I've been hacking into the Keltner Industries mainframe."

Nathan frowned. "That was very foolish and very dangerous."

"Maybe," Tony said, coming to the boy's rescue. "But Billy discovered some interesting facts. Alex Keltner is up to his neck in human trafficking. Bringing in young people from Eastern Europe."

"I know," Nathan said.

"You know? How?"

"One of the benefits of having money is the ability to pay for certain information that would otherwise be unobtainable. I've had someone on the inside of Keltner Industries for some years. There's very little that Alex Keltner does that I don't know about. What else did you find out, Billy?"

Billy Farrier shifted uncomfortably in his seat. "Nothing. But I was going to try from here. Hack in again I mean. See what else I can find out."

"No," Nathan said. "You won't."

"Hold on a minute," Billy said, some of his old belligerence flaring up.

"I said you won't. I don't want to give them the slightest edge. Keltner Industries has one of the smartest anti-hacking teams in the world, probably only rivaled by MI6 and the CIA. They'll have you pinned down the moment you enter their system."

"I got in before."

"Only because they let you. They probably wanted to see what you were after. No, you'll stay away from their mainframe."

"If you knew about the human trafficking," Tony said, "why didn't you do something about it? You could have told the authorities."

"You're being naive, Tony," Nathan said. "Alex Keltner is very clever. He's covered his tracks well. Any official investigation would be a waste of time because they wouldn't find anything. The only thing it would achieve would be to put Keltner on his guard. He'd review his security and plug any leaks he found there. And I need that channel left open. Tell me, why do you think someone as rich as Alex Keltner would risk getting involved in such a venture? For him, the proceeds from human trafficking are paltry. They probably wouldn't even cover his annual laundry bill."

"I wondered about that."

"And you were right to wonder. As I said before, back in Jamaica Louis Keltner and his brood used our small town as their larder. Once they left Jamaica they began to spread their poison. You must open your mind to the fact that there are others out there just like the Keltners. The same needs, the same hunger."

"How many?" Billy said.

"Their numbers run into thousands."

"Shit!"

"It's global. In every country of the world they are ravaging the population in order to survive and thrive."

"But surely the authorities of these countries . . ."

"Spare me, Tony, please. People with immense wealth have their own ways of dealing with the authorities, and the Keltners are an immensely wealthy family. They are at the very top of the food chain."

"So is he the leader of these . . . these creatures?" Tony said.

"He certainly considers himself such. His family has the longest history, and he's pretty much deferred to. But there are others just as powerful as the Keltners. In fact some of them are gathered at Bexton Hall as we speak. There's Yamada from Japan. The Bellinis from Italy. Rolf and Marta Steiner run the German and Austrian group, while Theo and Sylvia Bronstein do much the same in the U.S. Lars Petersen controls things in

Scandinavia. And there are others, in the Antipodes, Asia and Africa. That's an awful lot of soul fuckers worldwide. And all of them have to feed, replenish themselves without drawing attention to their actions."

"So how do they do it?" Tony said.

"Brothels," Nathan said.

"Oh, come on," Billy said. "If this thing is as big as you say there'd be no prostitutes left in the world."

"These brothels are run for their exclusive use. Young girls and boys are shipped in from all over the world; many from Eastern Europe, but also from the Philippines, Thailand and India. I believe there's even a group in China now, but they tend to look after their own affairs.

"They bring in these illegal immigrants and set them up in the brothels. These people are invisible; they exist outside society, off the radar. If they're never seen again who's going to ask questions? You have to admit it's a very clever solution to an ongoing supply problem. But then the slave trade in the nineteen hundreds served the same purpose, so the idea isn't a new one."

"So the brothels are nothing more than feeding stations?" Tony said.

"They call them *restaurants*," Nathan said without humor.

Tony sat forward. "Then we're wasting our time," he said. "What the hell can we do against so many? We'd just be pissing in the wind."

"We're not here to fight them all," Nathan said. "Just the Keltners."

"So is this just a revenge trip? Are you looking to pay them back for what they did to you and your mother?" Tony said.

"No," Nathan said.

"Well it seems that way to me."

Nathan looked across at Jim Davies. "Is that what you think too, Jimmy?"

Jim avoided the big man's gaze. "I'm not sure," he said. "But I think if I'd known the full story I might not have been so ready to get involved in this."

Nathan sighed heavily and spun away from them. He walked across to the window and pressed his forehead against the glass. His head was beginning to throb, and it was taking a huge effort of will to keep the headache under control. "This isn't just about me," he said. "It's about what Erik did to Billy; it's about what they did to Tony's sister. It's about Emma, and all the other innocent souls they've taken and ruined." He turned round to face them again. There were tears in the big man's eyes. "The Keltners have become so arrogant, so power crazed; they think they can intrude into our world with impunity. They're out of control. We have to try to stop them."

"So what do we need?" Billy said. The big man's words had convinced him at least. It may not be revenge for Nathan Wisecroft, but it certainly was for him. He'd make that bastard Erik Keltner pay for what he did to his face. "Crosses? Garlic?" he said.

"Billy, forget the vampire thing. Confront one of them with a crucifix and they'll take it from you and shove it up your ass."

"Then how do we stop them?"

"Nature likes balance. Yes, they have immense power. They have longevity. They have the ability to rejuvenate. Shoot them and they heal, quickly. Cut them and the wound closes within minutes. But they do have a weakness, an Achilles' heel. Years of interbreeding have left them with a congenital defect. It give us a small chance to defeat them."

"So what is it?" Billy said.

Before Nathan could answer, a voice said, "Their eyes." They turned as one as Emma walked into the room.

CHAPTER 31

Mario Bernardi was lying on the bed reading a magazine when the door burst open and Erik Keltner walked into the room. "Where are they?"

Bernardi put down the magazine and rose from the bed. He stood a good six inches taller than Erik and wasn't at all intimidated by him. "Who are you looking for?"

"The Bellinis. I've checked everyone else. It has to be them, and the fact they're not around confirms it."

Bernardi looked down at Erik with ill-concealed contempt. "I don't know what you're talking about. Get out of here and leave me in peace."

Behind the dark glasses something shifted in Erik Keltner's eyes. Carefully and deliberately he took the glasses off and stared at Andretti. "I won't ask you again," he said.

Bernardi flinched slightly at the sight of Erik's dead-fish eyes; pale and liquid orbs in an otherwise good-looking face. "And I told you, I don't know what you're talking about. I'm not their keeper. They could be anywhere."

"I know what you are to them, so don't expect me to show you any respect. Tell me what you know. When did you last see them?"

"Go to hell!"

Erik Keltner shrugged. "Very well." He looked about the room. On the table by the bed was a plate containing a spiral of apple peel and a paring knife. It would do. He closed his eyes for a second and concentrated. When he opened them again Bernardi was sitting on the bed, the knife in his hand, a bemused expression on his face. With slow deliberation he raised the hand holding the knife and stabbed himself in the cheek. Blood poured into his mouth from the wound. Bernardi could feel the blade rolling over his tongue as he twisted the handle of the knife, opening the wound further. The pain was excruciating, but he couldn't stop himself. Beads of sweat had popped out on his forehead and were running in rivulets down his face, mingling with the blood.

The hand holding the knife began to make sawing motions, slicing through the flesh of his cheek.

"Stop," Erik Keltner said.

Bernardi stopped sawing and stared up at Keltner with frightened, pain-filled eyes. He couldn't believe he'd just stabbed himself in the face, but the evidence was there in the searing pain and the blood, filling his mouth and smothering his hand.

"Now, we'll try again. Where are Nicci and Massimo?"

Bernardi spat a gout of blood onto the bed covers. "I don't know. I haven't seen them since this morning."

"Then you won't know that they've taken the girl."

"Girl?"

"The girl, Emma. They killed the guard at the Lodge and set her free. When Monica Patterson tried to stop them, they killed her too."

The words washed over him like a cold wave. "They

killed Monica," he said thickly, dribbling blood down his chin.

Erik Keltner nodded.

"You're lying."

"Why should I lie?"

"To trick me. Monica can't be dead."

"Would you like me to take you and show you her body? You can see the wound for yourself. Her heart has been ripped out."

Mario Bernardi squeezed his eyes shut, trying unsuccessfully to force back the tears. They rolled down his cheeks, mingling with the blood, making pink rivers.

"What's it to you anyway?" Keltner said. "I wasn't aware you knew her that well."

Bernardi sniffed. The pain in his cheek was nothing compared to the pain in his heart. "I loved her," he said in almost a whisper. But it didn't matter now. There was no longer any need for secrecy. It didn't matter who knew. They could punish him, hurt him, kill him. Without Monica, without her love, he was dead anyway.

"I see," Erik Keltner said, mirth twinkling in his pale eyes. "Oh dear. So the Bellinis have pissed on you too. So much for loyalty." His cell phone rang. "Yes?"

"There's been a slight delay," Alex Keltner said. "The Lear was late taking off, but they should touch down in the next twenty minutes. Is everything prepared there?"

Erik Keltner hesitated for a second before answering.

"Erik?"

"There've been a few developments," Erik said.

"We can't afford developments."

"It's nothing I can't handle."

"Good. Make sure everything's in order by the time we arrive."

The line went dead. Erik slipped the phone back into his pocket and turned to Bernardi. "My father will deal with you when he gets here."

"What about Nicci and Massimo?"

"What about them?"

"What will happen to them?"

Erik Keltner shrugged. "They'll be dealt with too, eventually. They won't be able to hide from us forever."

He left Bernardi sitting on the bed and went down to his car. He had a couple of hours to restore order at Bexton Hall. And order *would* be restored, of that he was certain.

He took the silk rope from his pocket and raised it to his nose. He could still smell her perfume impregnated in the fibers. He breathed deeply, closed his eyes and concentrating, let images flood into his mind. He could see houses, shops. He was looking through her eyes, seeing what she was seeing. But the images were brief, mere snapshots. A deserted car park. A narrow back street. A pub. He rubbed his temples, forcing himself to concentrate harder. A pub sign. Crowns. Three Crowns. And then she was inside, and he could smell the malty aroma of draft ale. His eyes snapped open and he smiled as he started the engine of the car.

"You're hurt," Tony said.

"It's okay," Emma said.

Nathan Wisecroft joined them in the doorway. "Let me look at the wound. Lift up your shirt."

Emma looked at Tony uncertainly.

"He's on our side," he said.

Emma lifted her shirt, blushing slightly as Nathan crouched down and studied the wound. She winced as he took a folded handkerchief from his pocket and wiped away some of the blood. "Who did this?"

"Alex Keltner's housekeeper. Florence Dowling. I killed her," Emma said. And only then the enormity of what she'd done struck her.

As she was driving back to town, the need to escape

had been the only thing on her mind, pushing out all other thoughts, forcing her to concentrate.

She'd driven for twenty minutes before she saw a sign to Lyndhurst, and then it was pointing in the opposite direction to which she was traveling. She had to drive on another two miles before a gateway to a field gave her the opportunity to turn round. The pain in her side was like a physical presence, nagging away at her, catching her as she changed gear, making her draw in her breath sharply.

Eventually forest gave way to houses and she found herself on the outskirts of the town. Tony had told her he was staying at the Three Crowns in the high street, but she realized she couldn't just drive up to the door and park. If they were looking for her, and she was pretty sure they would be, then she would have to hide the car, get it off the road, and make her way to the pub on foot.

She reached the center of town, noted where the pub was situated and drove past it. At the next junction she turned right and then took a side road that took her parallel to the high street. There was nowhere obvious to leave the car and she was about to give up when she noticed a builders merchants, set back from the road. A sign fixed to the wall announced, CUSTOMER PARKING AT REAR. The place was closed, but there was no barrier to stop her driving down the narrow alleyway that ran along the side of the building. She edged the car down and found herself in a concrete quadrangle with parking bays for eight cars. She drove into the bay in the farthest corner and switched off the engine. This would do.

The pub was busy. Most of the tables were filled and there was a small queue at the bar. She waited, trying to catch the eye of the bar staff. Eventually it was her turn, and the young barman gave her smile. "What can I get for you?"

"Nothing," Emma said. "I'm looking for Tony Carver. I believe he's staying here."

"That's right, he is. Do you want me to find out where he is?"

"I'd appreciate it."

The barman disappeared into the back, only to return a few seconds later with a young woman. "Serve that lot down the end, Wayne," the woman said. "I'll deal with this."

Wayne nodded and strolled down to the other end of the bar to a small group of workers from the nearby bank.

The barmaid turned to Emma and switched on a professional smile. "Now, how can I help you, Miss . . . ?"

"Emma Porter. I'm looking for Tony Carver. I know he's staying here."

"Yes. Is he expecting you?"

"No, but I must see him. It's very important." At that point she gasped as another spasm of pain erupted in her side. She grasped the edge of the bar for support.

"Are you okay?" the barmaid said, the smile slipping, her expression softening.

"Just give me a moment," Emma said through gritted teeth. Gradually the pain ebbed away.

The barmaid lifted the flap at the side of the bar. "Come through," she said. "Up the stairs and along the landing. He's in the lounge with Jim, my boss, and a couple of others."

"Thank you," Emma said.

"I don't suppose you could tell me what's going on, could you? Only it's been a bit weird here ever since your friend arrived."

Emma stopped, her foot on the bottom stair. "You

don't want to know," she said to the barmaid. "You *really* don't want to know."

"She's barely penetrated you, but it's still nasty," Nathan said as he examined the wound more closely. "You were lucky. How did you get away from her?"

Emma told him.

"So that's how you knew about their eyes."

She nodded.

"Jimmy, do you have a first-aid kit?"

"I'll fetch it."

Nathan wrapped his arm around Emma's shoulders. "Come and sit down. I'll patch you up; then you can tell us everything."

It was then Emma noticed Billy Farrier. He averted his face quickly, but not before she'd seen the horrific scarring.

"This is Billy," Tony said quickly, sensing her uncertainty. "Another victim of the Keltners."

Emma sat down in the armchair. "Hello, Billy," she said.

Billy Farrier mumbled a response but didn't look at her.

Jim Davies returned moments later with a green plastic case containing the first-aid kit. Nathan took it from him and selected a dressing and a tube of antiseptic cream, then he crouched down beside Emma and lifted her shirt. "This might sting a little," he said, his voice gentle. There was something about his manner, about the way he looked at her, that she found strangely comforting. Despite everything she'd been through she was suddenly reassured, just by being in his presence. She was back to her childhood again, a little girl with grazed knees, crying on her mother's lap while her father gently bathed away the blood and dirt, making her feel better again. Nathan's fingers had the same soothing effect as they moved over her skin.

She only winced a little as he applied the dressing,

and within seconds the pain had receded and she sank back in the chair. "That's better," she said with relief.

"The cream will help," Nathan said. "It has a mild local anesthetic. But let me know the moment the pain comes back, also if you start feeling unwell. Dizzy, nauseous."

"Is that likely?" Emma said, staring deep into his eyes. There was something there, a curious recognition. She felt as if she had known Nathan Wisecroft all her life.

"It's possible," he said, and pushed himself to his feet. Eye contact was severed and the moment passed. "I've got to go back," she said.

"Back where?"

"To Bexton Hall."

The three men exchanged looks. "Why?" Tony said.

"Because they're still holding a friend of mine. I need to get him out of there, before they do something worse to him than they've done already. Will you help me?"

"Who is this friend of yours and why are they keeping him prisoner?" Tony asked. Emma's desire to go back to Bexton Hall had thrown him. He needed to speak with her, to tell her about Erik Keltner and how he had been responsible for Helen's death. But it was not something he wanted to broach in company. He suspected she might fall to pieces, and he knew her well enough to know that she would not appreciate an audience.

"His name's Jeff Williams, and he's my old boss," Emma said. "I worked for him up until a few weeks ago. I don't know for certain why they're keeping him prisoner, or why they beat him up so horribly, but I think it's because he was trying to warn me. He seemed to know a lot about the Keltners, and he was trying to persuade me to get away from there from the moment I arrived. I just can't leave him there with them. I'm certain they're going to kill him."

"It's a very bad idea to go back there," Tony said. "I think I should take you home."

"No," Emma said.

"Em, be sensible. With everything you've been through . . ."

"And she'll go through worse if you take her back to Cambridge," Nathan said. "They'll find her. It may not be today, or even tomorrow, but they *will* find her. While she's here with us she at least has some protection."

"Then what do you suggest?" Tony said, irritated by Nathan's interference.

"We do what I came here to do."

"Which is?" Emma said.

"Destroy the Keltners and everything they stand for."

"Look, Nathan, this isn't our fight," Tony said. "I appreciate that you've suffered greatly at their hands, but I think Emma's been through enough."

"Tony," Emma said. "I appreciate your concern, but I think I'm old enough to make up my own mind about this. I've seen things today . . . horrible things . . . that I wouldn't have believed possible had I not witnessed them firsthand. And today *I've* done a horrible thing. Tony, I *killed* someone today. And it was all their fault! Alex, Erik, even their father. I don't know what the Keltners are, but I know they're pure evil, and they have to be stopped. I'm with Mr. Wisecroft on this."

"And you two?" Tony said, turning to Jim and Billy.

Jim shrugged. "Sorry, Tony. I agree with Emma."

"Billy?"

"What do you think? I've got fuck all to lose."

"I'm not asking you to help, Tony," Nathan said. "You can pack your bags and walk out of that door now. No one would blame you. What we're getting into here is extremely dangerous. We might not survive, none of us. But think of the countless lives they've ruined or destroyed. Can you, in all conscience, do nothing when we have the opportunity and the means to stop them?"

Tony walked across to the window and looked down at the handful of people walking along Lyndhurst high street, unaware that there were creatures living among them, ready to pluck them out of their safe and secure existence and to use them for their own gratification. Still he found it hard to justify going after the Keltners with the express purpose of destroying them. It would be murder, premeditated, cold-blooded murder, and such a proposition weighed heavily on him.

Jim Davies got to his feet suddenly. "Something's wrong," he said.

Nathan was at his side instantly. "What?"

"I don't know. Listen."

Nathan cocked his head to one side. "I can't hear anything."

"Precisely. No jukebox, no fruit machines. No sounds of people talking, laughing, arguing. Sometimes it gets so bad for noise up here I have to have the volume on the TV blasting out or I can't hear anything. I'm going down."

"I'll come with you," Nathan said. "Tony?"

"Okay. Billy can stay here and look after Emma. Close the door behind us and don't let anyone in except for us."

Nathan fished in his pocket, produced a small leather pouch and handed it to Billy. "Use this if you need to," he said.

"What is it?" Billy said, untying the bag's drawstring.

"Salt. Aim for the eyes. It will blind them and give you a chance to get away."

Emma was on her feet. "I'm coming with you," she said, then winced as the wound in her side produced a fresh shaft of pain, and she slumped back down on the couch.

"You're in no condition," Nathan said. "We'll handle this, if indeed there's anything to handle. It could be nothing."

Jim looked at him sharply. "I know my own pub," he said. "And I know how it's suppose to sound."

The three men left the lounge and closed the door behind them.

Billy Farrier hefted the leather pouch in his hand. "Salt," he said, shaking his head. "Crazy."

With Jim Davies leading the way the men crept quietly down the stairs. Jim was right, the pub was unnaturally quiet. The silence made the atmosphere heavy, oppressive. They reached the doorway to the bar and stopped. Jim gripped the handle, turned it slowly and pushed the door open.

The pub was empty.

"What the . . ." Jim said as he stepped out from behind the bar. There was no one to be seen. Drinks stood half-drunk on the bar, meals left uneaten on the tables. In two of the ashtrays cigarettes had smoldered away to tubes of ash. In the corner a game of darts was halfway through, two darts in the board, the third lying on the floor where it had been dropped. It was as if there had been a mass exodus.

"It's like the *Marie* bloody *Celeste*," Jim said as he wandered through the tables. Coats still cluttered the coatrack, and women's handbags were left abandoned. One of them had been kicked over and had spilled its contents over the floor. Jim bent down and picked up a small silver tube of lipstick and set it down on the table, next to a rapidly congealing plate of lasagna. He turned back to the other two. "Any idea what's happened here?" he said, then saw something down the other end of the bar. "Fuck!" He started to run.

Hazel was wedged into a corner by the fruit machine. She was crouching, her arms wrapped around her knees, her eyes tightly closed. Jim Davies reached her and squatted down beside her. He reached out and touched her hair. "Hazel?"

Her eyes snapped open and she stared at him uncomprehendingly, then her mouth opened and the pub was filled by a keening, high-pitched scream. Her hands beat at the air in front of her, and Jim threw himself backward to avoid being hit.

"It's all right," he said. "No one's going to hurt you."

But the words fell on deaf ears and the scream continued.

Suddenly Nathan was at his side. He reached down and grabbed one of Hazel's wrists, yanking her brutally to her feet. His other hand swung back and slapped her across the face. The scream died instantly, but she was still struggling, still flailing. Nathan grabbed her by the shoulders and shook her, staring deep into her eyes. "Look at me," he commanded. "Concentrate on my face."

The struggles were getting weaker and Hazel began to whimper, tears dribbling down her cheeks. "Make . . . it . . . go . . . away," she said softly, almost inaudibly. And then she found her voice again. "MAKE IT GO AWAY!"

Nathan pulled her close, wrapping his arms around her, pinning her arms at her side. "Tell me what you see," he whispered in her ear.

"Can't . . . frightened."

"It's okay. It won't hurt you now. Tell me what you see."

She shook her head violently from side to side. "Horrible. So tall. Gray. That skin, those eyes. Those horrible dead eyes!" Her voice rose to a scream. Nathan held her tighter still.

"Hazel. It's gone now, and it won't be coming back."

She looked up him beseechingly.

He smiled at her. "It's true. It's gone."

"Upstairs," she whispered. "Before you came down, it went upstairs. Didn't you see it?"

"Jim!" Wisecroft pushed Hazel into Jim Davies's arms and ran back to the bar.

"What's wrong?" Tony called after him.

"It's upstairs!" Nathan called back as he disappeared through the doorway leading to the first floor.

With Tony following on his heels, Nathan took the stairs two at a time. He reached the landing. It wasn't good. The door to the lounge was wide open, and through the doorway, he could see Billy sitting on the floor, holding his head, blood running down his face. Of Emma there was no sign.

He ran into the lounge. "Where is she?" he said.

Billy Farrier looked up at him. "Don't know," he said. "She came at me from behind. Clouted me over the head with that." He pointed to the jagged fragments of a broken glass vase. "When I came to she'd gone."

Nathan rushed to the window, but the street was deserted. When he looked back Tony was helping Billy to his feet.

"I'm sorry," Billy said. "I was listening at the door. I had my back to her. I wasn't expecting . . ."

"It's not your fault," Tony said.

"They were controlling her," Nathan said. "Damn it! I should have expected something like this."

"Who was controlling her?" Billy said, thoroughly confused.

"The Keltners. One of them was here. Hazel described him."

"Hazel described a monster," Tony said.

Nathan looked at him bleakly. "Exactly."

CHAPTER 32

"How much farther?" Louis Keltner said from the back of the car as he watched the car's headlights bouncing off the hedgerow.

"We're almost there," Alex said, glancing in the rearview mirror at the figure sitting next to his father. Swathed in black, with an impenetrable black net covering her face, was Louis Keltner's new wife, Maria. So far he hadn't seen her face, nor heard her speak. His father had carried her down the steps of the Lear and settled her in the waiting wheelchair, then pushed her across the tarmac to Alex's car. He'd then lifted her from the wheelchair and eased her into the Mercedes, whispering soft endearments and getting no response.

So far he'd offered no explanation for Maria's obviously fragile condition, and Alex hadn't been tempted to ask what was wrong.

"Did your brother say what the problems were?"

"You know Erik. Never uses ten words when one will do."

"You shouldn't have left him in charge. He's not reliable. Why do you think I let you run the business and not him?"

Alex didn't respond. His father had always been quick to criticize. Yes, he'd let him run the business, but his interference was never more than a phone call away. It had gone on for years, but Alex was used to it now and rarely rose to the bait.

In the back of the car Louis leaned in toward Maria and whispered something in her ear. Whether or not he received a response Alex couldn't tell. The woman remained immobile, a black-shrouded wraith.

The turning for Bexton Hall was coming up on the right. "We're here," Alex said.

"About bloody time," Louis said, then turned to Maria. "We're here, my love."

She might have nodded her head in response, or it may just have been the motion of the car that gave the impression of movement; Alex couldn't tell for sure. Either way he'd be glad when the journey was over and she was out of the car. He found her presence unsettling. And there was very little these days that unsettled him.

Emma opened her eyes and realized she was in a car being driven along. She was lying on the backseat, her wrists bound behind her. How did she get here? The last thing she remembered was sitting on the couch in Jim Davies's lounge, watching Billy Farrier prowl around the room, stopping at the door every few seconds to listen for any sounds coming from downstairs. How she'd got from there to here was a blank.

She raised her head slightly and saw Erik Keltner, his face illuminated by the headlights of an oncoming vehicle, and a feeling of sick dread settled in her stomach.

She heard the clicking of the indicator as the car pulled into the drive at Bexton Hall, followed by the crunch of the tires over gravel. Erik stopped the car and glanced over his shoulder. She shut her eyes quickly, but not quickly enough. "So you're awake. Good. Saves me having to carry you."

It was the most he'd ever said to her. He got out of the car and opened the back door. "Come on, and don't try anything. You've caused me enough trouble today."

She wormed her way along the seat and slid her legs from the car. Erik grabbed her roughly by the arm and pulled her the rest of the way.

His mouth opened to say something else but stopped when he saw another car sweep up the drive. Emma watched the other car's lights reflected in Erik Keltner's dark glasses as it approached the house. It was a distraction. If she made a break for it now . . . But the idea died the instant the other car stopped and Alex Keltner stepped out from behind the wheel. The back door opened and another man got out. Tall, gray-haired with patrician features, and fiercely intelligent, brown— almost black—eyes, Louis Keltner regarded her curiously, then snapped. "Erik, untie her immediately."

"But . . ."

"I said immediately." He walked across to Emma and rested his hand on her shoulders, studying her features. "I'm sorry," he said. "I didn't recognize you immediately. The hair . . . it's shorter than I remember from your photograph." He raised his hand and traced the contour of the bruise on her cheek. "Who did this, my dear?" he said.

Emma said nothing, but looked across at Erik, who avoided her gaze and moved around behind her to untie her wrists.

"I see," Louis said. "Any other injuries?"

Emma nodded, sensing she might have an ally at last. "My side," she said. "I have a gash in my side."

"And did Erik do that too?"

"No, that was Florence."

Louis Keltner clicked his tongue in disappointment. "Then I'll have to have words with Florence."

"You're too late. She's dead. I killed her." The words came out before she could stop them, but she felt so dazed, so confused by recent events she could hardly think straight, let alone control what she was saying.

Louis continued to hold her shoulders but something shifted behind his eyes. "Then I see I shall have to watch you very carefully, dear girl," he said. "Right, let's get you inside, out of this cold night air. Alex, attend to Maria. Erik, gather all the staff and put them in the dining room. I don't care what you tell them, but make sure they are all there and lock them in. After that invite our guests down to the library. Tell them I'll be along to greet them in forty-five minutes. You and Alex I'll see in my office in half an hour." He wrapped an arm around Emma's shoulders and led her into the house.

Alex watched them disappear inside, then opened the boot of the car and took out a collapsible wheel-chair. He set it down on the gravel, unfolded it and then beckoned to Erik. "Seeing that you made such a mess of everything, you can give me a hand. Get her out of the car and into the chair."

"I got the girl back though, didn't I?" Erik said.

"Yes, you did, but how did she get away from you in the first place?"

"Ask your friend Nicci. She and her brother let her go. But not before they killed Monica. Ripped out her heart and tossed it away like so much garbage." Erik relished imparting that last piece of information, and equally relished the stunned looked on his brother's face.

"Monica's dead?"

Erik nodded and reached into the car, slid his arms under Maria's featherlight body and lifted her out. He placed her in the wheelchair.

Alex was staring into space. "Why?" he said.

"I would have thought you were in a better position to answer that than me," Erik said.

"I'll kill her," Alex said.

Erik smirked. "I always had my doubts about Nicci Bellini. Never knew what you saw in her."

"Shut up," Alex said.

Erik shrugged and pushed the wheelchair toward the house.

When Hazel had calmed a little Nathan sat her down on the couch in the lounge and started questioning her gently about recent events. Her answers were tearful and uninformative. She simply couldn't remember. Or wouldn't. She'd been badly frightened.

Finally she said, "I'm sorry, but I don't know what you want me to say. One minute I was standing at the bar pulling a pint, the next the pub was empty and you three were standing there."

"And something had scared you."

"I don't remember," she said, her voice rising. *"I don't fucking remember!"*

"Nathan leave it!" Jim said. "We've a pretty good idea what happened. There's no point putting Hazel through the wringer. She's been through enough."

Hazel looked up at her boss with gratitude in her eyes.

"Would you like me to run you home?" Jim said.

"Please. Jim, what happened to Wayne?"

"I haven't seen him."

"Only he . . ." Her voice trailed away and she stared down at her hands. They were still shaking.

"He what, Hazel?"

She couldn't meet his eyes. "He was fighting it. The monster, he was fighting it."

"I thought you couldn't remember," Nathan said, but Jim Davies shot him a warning *I'll handle this* look.

"Where was this?" Jim said.

"Everyone had gone. They stopped eating, stopped drinking and just walked out of the pub. I didn't know what was going on. I couldn't think straight. I wanted to go too. I felt I had to get out of there—if I didn't something awful would happen."

"But you stayed. Why?"

"You left me in charge," she said. "That was important. I remember thinking about the till. How, if I left, anyone could help themselves to the cash."

"So the pub was empty. You were still behind the bar. Where was Wayne?"

"Collecting glasses. We were running short, so he was out picking up the empties. And then *he* walked in. There were still people leaving but he just pushed them aside . . . and they let him."

"Who was it, Hazel?"

"Erik Keltner."

"So all our customers left the pub and Erik Keltner came in."

"At least I thought it was Erik, but as he walked up to the bar he started to change."

"Change? In what way?"

She shook her head and screwed her eyes tightly shut. Even so the tears squeezed out from between her lids and trickled down her face. Her entire body was trembling.

"I think he was trying to protect me," she said, her voice barely audible.

"Who? Wayne?"

"Mmm."

"What happened to him, Hazel?"

"I told you. I don't know." She was hugging herself, rocking backward and forward on the seat, salt tears falling freely. "I hid, Jim. Wayne was fighting that . . . that thing, and I just hid in the corner like a baby. I'm so ashamed."

Jim Davies put his arm around her, pulling her close. "It's okay," he said gently. "You did the right thing. You mustn't blame yourself."

"You'd better take her home, Jimmy," Nathan said.

"What about Wayne?"

"I'll go and check downstairs," Tony said. "Coming, Nathan?"

Nathan Wisecroft nodded and together they left the room.

"Where do we start?" Tony said as they reached the bar.

"Cellar."

"You think he's dead?"

"I think Keltner would have done what was necessary to stop him raising the alarm and warning us."

"So you think he's dead."

Nathan shrugged. "Probably."

The cellar was reached by a trapdoor in the floor behind the bar. Nathan pulled it open and peered down into the unlit space. "Check the light switches," he said to Tony, who flicked switches up and down until he found the one to the cellar.

There was a narrow wooden staircase leading down to a concrete floor. Along one wall was a row of metal beer kegs, linked to the pumps above by an arterial network of plastic pipes. Adjacent to the kegs were crates of bottled beers and mixers, and in the corner a huge chest freezer.

Nathan looked round at Tony, who had descended the steps and was standing at the bottom, staring at the freezer. "You're thinking what I'm thinking?" he said.

"Seems likely."

Nathan walked across to the freezer, lifted the lid, looked inside and then shut it again.

"Well?" Tony said.

"No."

"Perhaps he got away."

"The girl said he was fighting with Erik. There could be only one outcome."

"So where's the body?"

Nathan looked about the cellar one last time. "Well, not down here."

As they emerged from the trapdoor Jim Davies was pushing open the pub door. "Any luck?"

"No. Did you get her home okay?" Tony said.

"Yes, but I'm not happy about leaving her on her own. I'll go back in the morning and see that she's all right." He sniffed the air. "Smokey in here," he said, and went across to the fireplace, where the embers of a log fire were glowing. He picked up a poker from the hearth and prodded the glowing charcoal. The remainder of one log coughed and spluttered and spewed out a shower of sparks onto the carpet. Jim swore and stamped them out.

Nathan plucked the poker from his grasp and approached the fire. Shielding his face from the heat, he reached into the fireplace and jabbed the poker up the chimney. A shower of soot dropped down in a cloud, followed by a heavily tattooed arm, which hung down, swinging like a macabre pendulum. They'd found Wayne.

CHAPTER 33

"Right, so would one of you like to tell me what the hell's been going on here?" Louis Keltner said, pacing the rug in front of the fire in the study. "Florence dead, Monica dead. It's a bloody mess!"

Alex and Erik sat on a black leather chesterfield, arms folded defensively. "I think you'd be better directing that question at Erik," Alex said.

"I'm directing it at both of you. It's not just what happened today, is it? It's the way you've handled the whole affair. I gave you a simple task. Bring the girl to me. That's all I wanted you to do."

"That's what we've done," Alex said.

"Yes, but look at the state of her. I specifically told you she wasn't to be harmed in any way, yet she's damaged. Physically and emotionally."

"The physical damage is superficial."

"Oh, I agree, she'll heal, but that's hardly the point. I've been speaking to her. She says she's been treated like a prisoner."

"She was snooping around," Erik said.

"But why? If everything was under control here, then there should have been nothing to arouse her suspicions."

"Blame Williams. He was the one who unsettled her," Alex said.

"And he works for *you*," Erik added.

Louis glared at him. "Yes, well I'll deal with him later. Emma told me that Nicci Bellini killed Monica. Where is she?"

"Gone," Alex said. "Both she and her brother."

"And you don't know where?" Louis said. He crossed to the drinks cabinet in the corner, poured himself a large brandy, downed it in one, poured another and went to sit at the desk.

"No. But I *will* find them."

"Oh I'm sure you will . . . one day. I'm sure you've heard the expression about shutting the stable door. I told you at the time that it was a mistake to turn her. As a pet she was reliable. Turning her gave her ideas, aspirations she was not entitled to."

"You turned Florence," Alex said. "And in similar circumstances."

"What happened between Florence and myself is none of your damned business. But, I knew I could trust her. We had a history together. She'd been a loyal servant for years and she deserved the gift I gave her. You made the mistake of letting your dick rule your head. I knew from the moment Nicci turned her brother—her brother, for God's sake!—that we were going to have trouble with her."

"If you were that concerned, why did you give her control of Italy?" Alex said. "In fact I'd go so far as to say that you seemed very fond of her," he added, watching with satisfaction the barb hit home.

Louis picked up an agate-handled paper knife from the desk and tapped the blade against his teeth. "Yes," he said after a moment's thought. "A lapse in judgment on my behalf. I'll give you that. But I knew what a problem she might become, which was why I indulged her. Theo Bronstein gave me hell about it at the time. He knew she was a potential danger, but I was covering your ass, Alex. By throwing my weight behind you, and putting Nicci in a position of trust, I was showing them all that I approved of what you did. I took the heat away from you." He dropped the knife back onto the desktop and swilled the brandy in the glass. "I wish now I'd listened to Theo. It would have saved us all a lot of trouble." He finished his drink and set the glass down on the desk. "It's time to meet the others," he said. "But this doesn't end here. We'll speak of it again tomorrow." He got to his feet. "Erik, go and fetch Williams and bring him to the library. Alex, you come with me."

Emma lay on the bed, staring up at the ceiling. She was still frightened, but the presence of Louis Keltner in the house eased her fears slightly. He didn't seem to wish her any harm, and seemed angry with Erik and Alex for the way they'd behaved toward her. Perhaps Louis would let her go; would just let her walk out of here. She still didn't know what they really wanted with her, and she couldn't imagine that she could be in any way important in their lives.

She sat up at the sound of someone knocking at the door. "Come in."

The key turned in the lock and Louis and Alex Keltner entered the room.

Louis Keltner smiled at her. "Emma," he said. "Alex has come to apologize to you. I think there's been something of a misunderstanding."

"So can I go now?"

The smile widened. "Presently," Louis said. "But I was wondering if you would indulge me first. I've flown over from Switzerland to make a rather important announcement to my friends here, and you are rather integral to what I have to say to them."

"Me? How?"

"Just bear with me for a little while longer. I know I don't really have the right to ask for your patience after the appalling way you've been treated here, but if you could indulge me just a little while longer I would certainly appreciate it."

Emma looked at him uncertainly. "I think I'd rather just go," she said.

Louis sighed. "Yes," he said. "And I can't say I blame you." He turned to Alex. "Alex, make your apologies to Emma and arrange for her to be driven home." He walked to the door. "I'll make sure you're adequately compensated for what you've suffered here," he said to Emma.

He was halfway through the door when Emma said, "Wait."

He turned slowly.

"I want to know what all this has been about."

"Well, as I said, when I make my announcement to the others it will all become clear."

"Tell me now," she said.

"Impossible, I'm afraid. Sorry." He turned back to the door.

"How long will it take?"

"Thirty minutes. No longer."

"And then I can go?"

"If you still want to."

She hesitated for a moment. "All right, I'll listen to what you have to say."

He turned to her, smiling. "Splendid. I'll see you downstairs in the library a few minutes."

Alex followed him out of the room and closed the door behind them, the apology unuttered.

Emma lay down on the bed again, her thoughts jumbled. She couldn't understand at all why she'd agreed to stay when all she wanted to do was to get as far away from Bexton Hall as possible. But there was something softly insistent about the way Louis Keltner had spoken to her. An undercurrent hiding behind the actual words that seemed to rob her of her free will. Even now, alone in the room and with ample opportunity to get up and leave, she lay there, staring at the clock on the bedside table, watching the minute hand sweep around the dial with infinite slowness.

Wayne's body was laid out on one of the benches by the wall and covered with a blanket.

"What are we going to do with him?" Jim said.

"He's not a priority at the moment," Tony said. "We must go after Emma. Christ knows what they're planning to do to her."

"We can't just leave him there," Jim said angrily. "He's got family; a mother and sister. They need to be told."

Nathan stepped between them. "I agree with Tony. We can't do anything for Wayne now. But we *can* try to help Emma. I know what Louis Keltner has got planned for her, and we can't waste any more time."

"If you know," Tony said, "then why the hell haven't you said anything before now?"

"Because I needed to see how things played out. Nothing was definite, and when Emma turned up here I thought I may have misinterpreted what I'd been told, but now I know I didn't. By midnight Emma will be out of the country and then it will be too late to do anything."

"I would have thought the more important question was, *how* does he know?" Billy said from his seat in the corner. He was still holding a wad of tissues to his head, taking it away every so often to see if the bleeding had stopped.

"Billy's got a point, Nathan," Jim said. "How *do* you know?"

"I have contacts," Nathan said.

"You told us about your mole at Keltner Industries. You mean there's more?"

"I have someone at Bexton Hall," Nathan said. "Someone I know and trust, and who's going to help us tonight when we go to get Emma."

"One of *them*, you mean?" Billy said.

"It doesn't matter who he is. Just that he's willing to help."

"Any more contacts?" Tony said.

"Yes."

"Who?"

Nathan Wisecroft sat down at a table and picked up a half-drunk glass of beer. He took a swig and wiped his mouth with the back of his hand. "Vincent Keltner," he said.

Tony and Jim exchanged looks and sat down at the table opposite him.

"But you told us Vincent was dead," Tony said.

Nathan smiled. "And that's the part that takes some understanding. Vincent Keltner *is* dead."

The library was the largest of the downstairs rooms at Bexton Hall. Book-lined walls closed in the space but there was still room for four huge, leather-upholstered sofas, three tables and two desks. The lighting was subdued, table lamps glowing under amber art deco shades. The Steiners, Yamada and Petersen occupied one of the sofas; adjacent to them were Theo and Sylvia Bronstein. They sat in expectant silence. So far no one had mentioned the absence of Nicci and Massimo Bellini.

The door opened and Erik Keltner entered the library, pushing a wheelchair. The guests turned as one, studying the shrouded figure in the chair curiously. Seconds later Louis Keltner stepped into the room, followed by Alex, who was holding Emma by the hand.

Erik parked the wheelchair to the right of the huge Adam fireplace and left the room. As Alex and Emma sat on one of the vacant sofas Louis took up a position at the side of the wheelchair. He looked at them each in turn, a smile turning up the corners of his mouth.

"Friends," he said, and spread his arms wide.

Everyone started speaking at once.

"Louis, you old dog."

"Great to see you."

"How was the flight?"

Sylvia Bronstein rose from her seat and went across to him, kissing Louis on the cheek and wrapping him in her arms. "Louis, it's been too long, far too long."

"Good to see you, Sylvia," Louis said, returning her kiss and ushering her back to her seat. "If you could all be patient for just a little longer, until Erik returns. But I must say, it's good to see you all, and thank you for making the effort to be here. I sincerely appreciate it."

The door opened again and Erik pushed another wheelchair into the room, this one containing the bound and bloodied Jeff Williams. Jeff's eyes were open, but were unfocused. He stared straight ahead as his chair was wheeled past the others and set opposite the shrouded figure in the other chair.

"Please excuse the state of our final guest," Louis said as eyes turned questioningly from Jeff to him. "I will endeavor to explain how he came to be in such a . . . But first things first. Erik, can you see to it that all our friends have a drink?"

Erik's face creased into a frown but he did as he was instructed and soon all the guests were sitting with full glasses, expectant looks on their faces.

"Right," Louis said, walking to a spot in front of the

fireplace, effectively taking center stage. But that was how he'd planned it. This was *his* night. This was the night he'd anticipated for so long, and he wanted them all to realize how important it was. "Erik, you can sit."

Eric was hovering by Jeff Williams's wheelchair. "But . . ."

"I don't think Mr. Williams is going anywhere, do you?"

Erik grunted an assent and took a seat next to the Bronsteins.

"That's better," Louis said. "Right, let's start at the beginning."

CHAPTER 34

"Firstly I think I owe you all an apology," Louis Keltner said. "I'm afraid I've been guilty of a little subterfuge. And that apology extends to my sons as well, because even they were not in possession of all the facts. Alex, I know you thought you were recruiting Emma here to be my new companion, my new . . . pet—I hate that word by the way; so demeaning, for both them and us. Anyway, I digress. The truth is that I never intended Emma to fulfill that role."

"Then why have I gone to all this trouble?" Alex said, the anger evident in his voice. "I don't appreciate being duped, even by you."

"Alex," Louis said placatingly. "Calm down. Once you hear what I have to say, you'll understand why I had to keep you and everyone else in the dark. What I'm about to tell you here has implications for us all, and huge implications for our race as a whole."

"Well let's hear it, then," Theo Bronstein said. "Though I must admit, I sympathize with Alex. I'm your oldest friend, Louis. It saddens me to think you didn't fully trust that friendship."

Louis held up his hands. "Please, all of you. Hear me out before you judge me. I took a course of action that I saw as necessary. I think when I've finished you will see why." He looked around at the confused and concerned faces in the room and drew in a breath.

"This story starts over thirty years ago," he said. "We were living in the States at the time and controlling Keltner Industries from there. I'm sure all of you remember Vincent, my son who was tragically killed in a plane crash. You'll probably remember that Vincent traveled his own path. He was something of a rebel, rejecting many of our ways, our traditions. And although many of you despaired of him, I couldn't help admiring that independent streak. It set him apart, made him different.

"Don't misunderstand me, Vincent was also the bane of my life, and on many occasions I wished he'd turned out like Alex, a fine son of whom any father could be proud. But I suppose I had a certain empathy with Vincent because he reminded me so much of myself, or as I was at his age.

"But where he and I differed most was in our philosophy. And in 1970 he did something I would find unthinkable. He met and fell in love with a woman not of our race. An ordinary human. Of course he tried to keep the affair secret, and he was fairly successful in that. I found out about it, but I was complicit in keeping his secret. It was, after all, nothing I wanted to boast about, and I could only see disaster ahead for him. I tried to persuade him to end the relationship. Indeed, I offered him all kinds of inducements and, I'm ashamed to admit now, even resorted to crude threats. But he wouldn't be swayed. He was in love and nothing I could do or say would change the fact.

"A year after they met the girl fell pregnant . . ."

"Impossible!" Theo Bronstein was on his feet, his face red with anger, a purple vein throbbing at his temple.

Sylvia tugged at his sleeve. "Sit down, Theo. Hear him out."

"Damned if I will!" Bronstein said. "Louis, you are straining the boundaries of our friendship. What you are saying is preposterous. You know there can never be any progeny from our couplings with *them*. It's biologically impossible. You're telling us a fairy story, and I for one don't appreciate being taken for a fool."

His wife pulled at his sleeve again, but Theo Bronstein snatched it away and continued to glare angrily at Keltner.

"Theo has a point, Louis," she said. "You can't expect us to sit here meekly and listen to this . . . this fantasy."

"I'm sorry, Sylvia, but this is no fantasy. Believe me, I know how incredible this sounds. But the fact is my son, Vincent, got this human pregnant, and the pregnancy went to term and a child was born. A healthy, normal *human* child."

"And you did nothing about it?" This from Yamada, who looked as agitated at Bronstein. "The child should have been destroyed at birth."

"Yes," Louis Keltner said. "That was my thought at the time. But Vincent preempted any action I could take by taking the girl and the child away. They left America the day after the birth and it took me months to track them down. By then they were living in England under an assumed name. And by that time the baby had gone."

"Gone? What do you mean, gone?" Erik was on his feet now, pacing the carpet in front of his father, looking as if he might strike him at any moment.

"I wish everybody would just calm down. You're all guilty of reacting as shortsightedly as I did then. You are missing the bigger picture here. Well, perhaps not all of you." Louis looked across at Alex, who was sitting, relaxed, legs crossed, a slight smile playing on his lips. "You understand, don't you, Alex?"

"What about the child's eyes?" Alex said.

"As I said, perfectly healthy in every way."

"And I take it the need for sustenance is . . ."

"Very human," Louis Keltner said with a smile.

Erik stopped pacing and Theo Bronstein sat back down next to his wife, as the full importance of what Louis Keltner was telling them finally sunk in.

"As I said, the child had gone. Vincent realized the implications very quickly and had the child adopted, because he knew that English adoption laws at that time were so stringent there was very little chance I would ever be able to track it down. And he was right. Even with all the resources of Keltner Industries I was never able to discover with whom the child had been placed. Shortly afterward Vincent was killed, and I drew a line under the whole sorry affair.

"That really should have been the end of the story, but there was a postscript. Several years ago I was approached by someone who said he knew where my grandchild was." Louis Keltner crossed the floor and stood behind Jeff Williams's wheelchair. "Jeff here came to me with a proposition. Apparently he'd something of a relationship with the child's mother, and she'd told him everything about Vincent, everything about us. He wanted money and a senior position in the company, and in return he would keep what he knew about us to himself, and he'd also tell me where to find Vincent's child. By this time, of course, I'd realized my mistakes in handling the situation with Vincent. So I accepted his offer, but only on condition that he not only told me the location of the child, but also put me in touch with the child's mother.

"She was still living in England but in very reduced circumstances. She had a heavy alcohol addiction and was dabbling in drugs. I offered to look after her, but on condition she come and live with me in Switzerland. She didn't need much persuading. So shortly afterward I flew her out to Zurich and installed her at a private clinic. We cleaned her up and then I brought in a research team to run some tests. I needed to find out what made her so special."

"And did you?" Lars Petersen spoke up for the first time.

A shadow passed across Louis Keltner's face. "Unfortunately the years of alcohol and drug abuse had given her a very fragile constitution. The tests were fairly rigorous and her body just couldn't cope with them. It finally gave up. She's been in the wheelchair ever since."

"You mean . . ."

Louis Keltner nodded and moved toward the woman in the wheelchair. "This is Maria, my former daughter-in-law, now my new wife." He lifted the veil covering the woman's face and tossed it back over her head, revealing her face for the first time.

For a moment there was absolute silence in the room as the guests stared at the woman in the chair.

Emma sat forward in her seat, staring hard, unable to comprehend what she was seeing.

Maria Keltner had *her* face. Older, more lined; the hair was gray instead of blond, but the nose, the mouth, even the skin tone were Emma's own. Only the eyes were different. The shape was the same, but the eyes themselves were a washed-out, pale blue, and filled with so much suffering it was almost painful to look into them. The pale blue eyes stared back at her but there was no recognition in them. In fact there was very little in them at all, just a vacant, faraway look, as if they were looking inward at her own soul instead of out at the faces studying her.

"Do you mind a question?" Yamada said, breaking the silence.

"Of course, Keichi."

"This may be impertinent, but why did you marry her? Surely not for love."

Louis Keltner laughed. "Good God no! Sheer convenience. She'd picked up a number of convictions for drug offenses. I smuggled her into Switzerland, but I would never have been able to get her out again, and I needed her to be able to move freely. Marrying her made things a little easier. She travels now as my wife, and I can use my influence to arrange visas and suchlike."

Alex crossed to the wheelchair and crouched down, looking at Maria closely, then flicking his eyes back to Emma to compare what he was seeing. Even though his face was just inches away from Maria's the woman gave no sign that she was aware of his presence. She continued to stare blankly ahead.

Emma found her voice at last. "I don't understand," she said, rising to her feet.

"Sit down!" Louis snapped.

"No, I'm sorry. I can't stay here."

"You need to hear the rest of the story."

"I've heard enough," Emma said. "I'm going."

"If you try to leave, I'll have Erik restrain you," Louis said.

Emma glanced at Erik, who was sitting crossed-legged and relaxed in his seat, staring at her with an enigmatic smile on his lips.

Emma hesitated for a few seconds more, then bolted for the door, but stopped no more than a yard away from it. She was frozen, incapable of movement. She tried desperately to move her legs, but it was as if they were stuck in treacle. She glanced back at Erik, who was rising slowly from his seat, dark glasses removed, a look of furious concentration in his dead eyes. She turned, her legs moving now, but not of their own volition; she had no control over them. In jerky strides she walked back to the sofa and sat down next to Erik, sweat pouring down her face from the effort of trying and failing to control her movements.

Erik Keltner leaned in close to her and grabbed her by the wrist, his fingers crushing her bones. "Now sit here and shut up, or I'll do you like I did your girlfriend," he whispered in her ear.

The whispered words hit her like a physical blow, confirming what she had feared. Helen had died because of her. The realization numbed her completely, dissolving her impulse to escape. Whatever happened to her now she deserved. *Helen, my poor Helen, I'm so sorry.*

Alex was still crouching down in front of Maria. He looked back at Emma and shook his head. "The likeness is remarkable," he said to his father.

Louis Keltner looked at his son and smiled. "Yes, it is, isn't it?"

CHAPTER 35

"He's with me every minute of every day," Nathan said. "In my head, in my thoughts. He's sharing my body, and has been for the last five years."

"How?" Tony said.

Nathan took another mouthful of beer. "That I don't know . . . at least not for certain. I told you the relationship was symbiotic. I think that when he died his spirit, soul, call it what you will, was reluctant to move on. He came to me because he knew I'd take him in. And I did."

"But you said he died in seventy-two. What was his soul doing for thirty years? Floating about in the ether?" Jim said.

"I said he was reported dead in seventy-two, but fortunately his father's attempt to kill him failed. The plane he was flying was sabotaged and midway across the channel the engine cut out. The plane went down but Vincent survived. He was picked up by a Portuguese fishing boat and taken back to Portugal. He was pretty banged up but, as I said before, Vincent and his kind have remarkable recuperative powers. Within a year he was back to his old self. But he stayed in Europe. He couldn't risk coming back and giving his father another chance to kill him."

"But *why* was his father trying to kill him?" Tony said.

"For the same reason we're all here today. Emma."

Tony scratched his head in bemusement. "You've lost me. How does Emma figure in your story?"

"Because, Tony, Emma is Vincent Keltner's daughter."

"His daughter?" Tony said.

"Yes. As far as I know the only offspring of a coupling between a human and one of them. She was only a few weeks old when she was adopted and, to the best of my knowledge, was never told of her real parents. She was given up for adoption for her own protection. Because once Louis Keltner knew of her existence he was out to destroy her. It was the only way Vincent could keep her safe."

"But that's absurd. She can't be his daughter. I knew her parents. They died in a car crash a few years ago."

"Her *adoptive* parents died in that crash. And it was Louis Keltner who orchestrated the accident. He needed to get them out of the way. The same way he needed to remove your sister from Emma's life."

"I don't understand," Tony said. "Why did Helen have to die?"

"Because she was a barrier to Keltner's plans. Once he realized the significance of Emma's existence he tried to find her. It took him years, but eventually he tracked her down. I can only imagine his disappointment when he discovered she was gay."

"I'm sorry; I'm not following you. Why should Emma's sexuality matter so much to him?"

"He wanted her to reproduce. To have children, to see if there were any throwbacks to his own race, and to see if the congenital defect blighting him and his kind, which was absent in Emma, reoccurred in her offspring. The eyes, Tony: one of their few weaknesses; their Achilles' heel. Emma's eyes are perfect. Theirs are not. They can't tolerate bright light. Naked sunlight blinds them. Even electric light causes them pain. Attack the eyes and you can kill them. You remember in the photo I showed you they were all wearing dark glasses?"

Tony nodded.

"That picture was taken before Louis Keltner used the wealth he had accrued over the years to invest in a small Swiss company that specialized in creating lenses. He brought in some of the finest technicians in the world and set them the task of developing lenses he and his kind could wear to protect them from the damaging effects of light.

"They were successful. The contact lenses these creatures wear now filter out the harmful ultraviolet and infrared rays and also polarize the light, allowing them to function normally. Despite sharing her DNA with them, Emma doesn't have that defect. Light doesn't affect her. If Keltner can discover what it is that makes her immune, and if he can harness it, it would make his race powerful beyond belief. But there's something even more terrifying than that." He drained the remainder of the beer and reached out for another half-drunk glass on the table.

The others waited patiently for him to continue, realizing it would be counterproductive to rush him.

He put down the glass and wiped his mouth with the back of his hand. "Emma doesn't share their need, their hunger."

"Why's that so terrifying?" Jim said. "I would have thought that would be a blessing."

"Think it through, Jimmy." Nathan said. "If Keltner can identify the genetic strand that makes her immune to light, he may also be able to discover the reason why

Emma can live without resorting to sucking the life force from others. And if he can pinpoint that and make it work for him and his kind then the human race is in big trouble. At the moment they need humans to feed from. Without that they can't survive. What happens if they can find a way to survive and flourish without feeding?"

It was Tony who answered. "We become surplus to requirements. Obsolete."

Nathan slammed his hand on the table. "Exactly! Except for the weakness with their eyes and their dependence on the human life force to sustain them, they are more powerful in every way. Using Emma's DNA Louis Keltner has a chance to make *his* race totally invulnerable and self-sufficient. And once that happens, then mankind is doomed. They become the dominant species on Earth, and I've absolutely no doubt they wouldn't hesitate to wipe out humanity and take the planet for themselves. Keltner's plans can't be allowed to come to fruition. We have to find a way to stop him."

"That's easy," Billy said. "Kill the girl."

"Kill Emma?" Tony said, pushing himself angrily to his feet. "You're mad."

"You tell me why the hell we should we care about her?" Billy said, standing up to face him. "She's one of *them*." The sourness in his voice was mirrored by the sneer on his scarred lips.

Tony swung his fist and connected with the point of Billy's jaw. Billy shrugged off the blow and launched himself at Tony, hands reaching out for his throat. Jim Davies stuck out his foot and tripped him, sending him crashing to the floor.

"Bastard!" Billy sprung to his feet, hands balled into fists, ready to fight.

"Leave it, Billy, or I'll deck you again." Jim stood between the two of them, glaring at each of them in turn.

"You too, Tony. Don't make me hit you, 'cos if I do you won't get up again."

"Calm down, all of you!" Nathan held up his hands placatingly. "We can't afford to be fighting among ourselves. We need to focus on who's the enemy here," he said. "But you're right, Billy. Removing Emma from the frame is a solution, but it's only one of many, and it's the one I would only go to as a last resort. The poor girl is innocent in all this. She didn't choose her parents." He got to his feet. "We've wasted enough time," he said. "We'll take my car. I packed it this morning with everything we need."

"It's rather convenient that the girl happened to end up working for Keltner Industries," Theo Bronstein said.

"Convenient, but not a coincidence. Again we have Jeff here to thank for that. He headhunted her from another company and brought her to work for us so I could keep tabs on her. Started her at the bottom; that was the clever part. It gave her no reason to suspect anything."

Emma remembered what then appeared to be a chance meeting in a Soho wine bar with Jeff Williams. Him plying her with glass after glass of Chianti, her amused, thinking he was trying to bed her. He talking about the exciting, get-ahead company he worked for; she bemoaning her lowly position with an anonymous insurance company in Ryder Street where the highlight of the day was making tea for the directors. Two days later when he phoned and told her there was an opening at Keltner Industries if she wanted it, she was flattered beyond belief. She'd jumped at the offer. An offer that, like everything else in her life, she realized now, was nothing but smoke and mirrors.

She sat on the sofa, staring at the woman in the wheelchair. "It's not true," she said, almost to herself.

"None of it's true." But as the words had left her lips she knew from the evidence of her own eyes that she was wrong. And the thought was devastating. Everything she believed, everything she knew about herself and her life up until now had been shattered into a million pieces. She couldn't understand why her parents, or the people she'd believed were her parents, had said nothing of her adoption. She'd been kept in the dark; the truth hidden from her by the people she had loved so unquestioningly.

She was shaking uncontrollably, but whether through shock or anger she couldn't tell.

"Ah, but it *is* true," Louis Keltner said, smiling broadly. "This is a happy day for me, to be reunited with my granddaughter after all these years."

"I'm not your granddaughter," Emma said, glaring at him. "I'm nothing to do with you."

"Like it or not, Emma, my blood runs through your veins."

"And human blood," Alex said, standing upright. "And is it that which gives her the immunity?"

Louis Keltner smiled. "I suspect it's the unique combination of the both, but that's what I'm hoping to find out. I'm flying back to Switzerland tomorrow and taking Emma and Maria with me."

"Tomorrow, Louis?" Sylvia Bronstein said. "But you've only just got here. I hoped we would have the time to catch up."

"Time is of the essence, Sylvia," Louis said. "I have a team at the clinic waiting to run tests on Emma. We have to find out if she holds the key, not only to curing this defect, but to guaranteeing the survival of our race."

"You exaggerate, Louis," Theo Bronstein said. He was still angry, furious at being deceived.

"Do I, Theo? I think not. In fact I think I'm understating the case. At the moment our two weaknesses are

our eyes and our reliance on humans in order to replenish ourselves. But who knows what else will surface
several generations down the line. We are witnessing
the gradual deterioration of our race. Our gene pool is
muddied, decaying. I think Emma's genes could arrest
that decay. It's too late for us, I grant you, but think of
our grandchildren, our great-grandchildren. What we
do today could have a huge impact on them. Our race
could become strong again, invulnerable."

"It makes sense, Theo," Sylvia said. She turned to the
others, to the Steiners, Yamada and Petersen. "What do
you think?"

"I think we should trust Louis to know what is best for
us," Rolf Steiner said.

"I agree," Keichi Yamada said. "Louis, if there's anything I can do to help I would be most honored."

"Thank you, Keichi. I knew I could rely on you. In
fact that goes for all of you: Lars, Rolf, even you, Theo. I
wanted you to be the first to know about this because
you are the people I trust the most. I'm afraid there are
others who don't warrant that trust." He walked across
to Jeff Williams and stood behind his wheelchair, resting his hands on Jeff's shoulders. "Betrayal comes easily to some. But you, my friends, I'm inviting to share a
vision of the future where our race will be able to walk
in the sunlight without protection; a future where we
will no longer be at the mercy of specimens such as
this." He took Jeff's head between his hands and
wrenched it savagely to the right, snapping his neck,
killing him instantly.

As Jeff Williams's head lolled forward onto his chest
Emma began to cry. It was too much to bear, to know
that so many people had died, and would continue to
die, because of her.

"Well," Louis Keltner said. "I suspect I've given you all
lots to think about. No doubt you'll wish to talk about

this among yourselves. My boys and I will leave you to do this. But before we do . . ." He crossed to a wall of books, pressed a button concealed under a shelf. "Before we do I'd like to show you the entertainment I've organized for you all."

With a soft hiss a section of the wall detached and slid to one side, revealing a large plasma screen. The screen blossomed into vibrant life, showing a scene of the Bexton Hall dining room. There were a dozen people in the room, most sitting at the large rectangular dining table. One of them, the chef, Didier, was at the door, turning and pulling at the handle.

Keltner turned to the group and smiled. "My gift to you, my friends. Please feel free to pick any one of them you like, or two if you prefer. They are yours to do with what you will."

The Bronsteins and the Steiners rose from their seats and approached the screen. Sylvia Bronstein's eyes were glittering with excitement. "Louis, you're too kind."

Rolf and Marta Steiner were smiling broadly.

Louis beckoned to his sons. "Come; let's leave our friends to their pleasures. Erik, bring Emma. Alex, if you'll push Maria, I'll take care of Williams. Theo, the key's in the door of the dining room. Please feel free to use any of the rooms upstairs. Enjoy your meal. We may join you later." With a smile Louis Keltner pushed the dead body of Jeff Williams from the room and closed the door behind him.

CHAPTER 36

Nathan nosed his Toyota through the trees, crushing bracken and twigs under his wheels. They reached a clearing and he stopped the car. "We walk from here."

"But Bexton Hall's over a mile away," Billy Farrier said.

"So what do you want to do, drive up to the front door and knock?" Nathan said. "We walk the rest of the way." He got out of the car and opened the trunk, waiting for the others to join him.

Tony was the first. Nathan handed him a large spotlight. "Halogen bulb, about five million candlepower," he said. "Shine it directly into their eyes and you'll blind them temporarily, despite their contacts. It will give you a small advantage, and a chance to use this." He handed him a screwdriver. The blade was eight inches long and it had been sharpened to a fine point. "Aim for the eyes, and don't hesitate. You might not get a second chance." He handed a spotlight and screwdriver to the others. Billy tested the point with his thumb, satisfied when he drew a small bead of blood with very little pressure.

"Salt," Nathan said, passing them each a small metal container with a perforated lid. "Like the light it will blind them, but also cause them intense pain." He smiled grimly. "I'm banking on getting close enough to use it."

"And if we can't?" Jim said.

"Then we're fucked. We know what they can do; we know what mind tricks they can use. We have to strike quickly and decisively. And we also need the element of surprise working for us. We are also going to need a huge amount of luck to be able to pull this off."

"You're not painting a very optimistic picture," Jim said.

"I'm realistic. The odds are stacked against us. I wouldn't want anyone going into this thinking it's going to be a cakewalk. If we give them the chance they'll fry our brains, or worse still, turn us against each other. Come on. Let's go." He closed the lid of the boot and strode off into the trees.

Jim and Billy followed him quickly. Tony stood by the car, looking down at the weapons he'd been given. A spotlight, a gimmicked screwdriver, and a condiment. It would almost be laughable, if it weren't so damned frightening. He saw Jim's leather jacket disappear into the pitch black of the forest and hurried to catch up with him.

They reached the Lodge within seconds of each other. The place was in darkness, deserted.

"This isn't the Hall," Billy said.

"Full marks for observation," Nathan said, making the younger man nettle.

"I don't understand," Tony said.

"Nathan has a plan, I'm sure." Jim Davies switched on his spotlight and shone it over the front of the building.

"Well, do you?" Billy said, not even trying to disguise the aggression in his voice.

Nathan ignored him. "Jim, shine your light down there, by the side of the front door."

Jim did as he was instructed, swinging the spotlight down and illuminating a thick snake of cables, virtually hidden behind a large, lichen-covered flowerpot. "Is that what you're looking for?"

Nathan Wisecroft nodded his head and crouched down beside the pot. From the pocket of his coat he produced a large pair of wire cutters. Within seconds the snake was severed. "Right, now we can go inside without worrying about Keltner's hidden cameras and microphones capturing our every word and sound. I very much doubt there'll be anyone in the forest to-night, but one of us should keep watch here, just in case."

"I'll do it," Jim said.

"Okay," Nathan said. "You two come with me. Jim, I'll call you when we're ready."

'Ready for what?' Billy said.

"You'll see soon enough."

Nathan jimmied the front door and stepped inside. He pulled the smaller of the floor plans he'd been given from his pocket, opened it out and checked it. The kitchen was at the end of the hall. "This way."

Once in the kitchen he switched on the light above the worktop. The illumination was dim, but it would serve his purpose without advertising their presence. "We need to lift the floor covering."

Billy got down on his hands and knees and worked the point of his sharpened screwdriver under the edge of the vinyl. It lifted easily, and tore like paper. Beneath it were bare floorboards.

"It needs to be lifted to here." Nathan stood in the center of the room, pointing down at his feet.

Tony hovered in the doorway, half watching what was happening in the kitchen, half listening out for Jim should he raise the alarm. A thin line of perspiration trickled down his back, making him shiver.

"Enough?" Billy said as he peeled the vinyl back to where Nathan stood. Nathan stepped back, staring down at the wooden floorboards. "Another two feet should do it," he said and took another step backward.

With the floor covering lifted the trapdoor was plain to see. A small metal ring was set into one of the boards. Nathan got his fingers into it and tugged. The hinges had long rusted and they screamed as the door was opened. The opening was a yard square and gave onto a metal ladder that led down into the darkness below. Nathan switched on his spotlight and shone it down into the blackness, then swung himself down onto the ladder and descended.

Billy crouched by the rim of the opening and watched the light dance about below as Nathan moved around, finally appearing at the bottom of the ladder, smiling. He hauled himself back up the ladder. "It's all as it should be down there. Tony, fetch Jim. We're in business." He pulled his cell phone from his pocket and punched a number into the phone. Seconds later his call was answered. "It's Nathan. We're on our way. How long do you need?" He listened for a moment. "Good. We'll be there shortly." He switched off the phone.

"Who were you calling?" Jim said as he entered the kitchen.

"I told you I had a contact at the Hall. I was just letting him know that we're here."

"Fine, but who is he?"

"Someone who feels the same way about the Keltners as I do. Don't worry. He's a friend, and he's going to help us."

"I still don't see the point of coming here. Why didn't we go straight to the house?" Tony said.

"I'll show you," Nathan said. "Follow me." He dropped into the hatch again and climbed down.

The cellar was large, but clean and dry and completely empty. The only feature in the otherwise bare walls was a door.

"Okay," Jim said. "Why have you brought us down here?"

Nathan smiled and crossed to the door. "Because this will get us into Bexton Hall unnoticed."

"I don't understand," Tony said.

"Me neither. The Hall's still a mile away," Billy said.

"A little under a mile actually," Nathan said. "And behind this door is a tunnel that will take us all the way there."

"You're kidding," Jim said.

Nathan shook his head. "Bexton Hall was used by the army as a communication center during the war. The land around here is riddled with tunnels, dug out by army engineers. Brick built, ventilated, and safe. This one will take us to the cellars of the Hall."

"If it hasn't collapsed in the meantime," Tony said.

"Only one way to find out." Nathan pulled the steel jimmy from his pocket and inserted it into the crack between the door and its frame. One heave later the door swung open, sending a waft of fetid air swirling around the cellar.

"Nice," Billy said, slapping his hand over his nose and mouth. "And you want us to walk a mile in that stink?"

"You'll get used to it after a hundred yards or so." Nathan shone his spotlight through the doorway, revealing yellow brick walls, blackened by a sixty-year accumulation of dust and cobwebs. "The floor's dry. That's encouraging." He took a few paces into the tunnel, watching the beam of his light peter out in the distance. He looked back over his shoulder at the others. "Okay, coming?"

*   *   *

Marta Steiner and Sylvia Bronstein stood in front of the plasma screen, anticipation shining in their eyes as they made their choices.

"I like the blond waiter," Marta said. "Very Ayrian."

"I have my heart set on Didier," Sylvia said with a girlish giggle. "There's something about French men." She called to her husband. "Theo, come and choose. There's a beautiful Asian girl. Great bod, hon."

Theo Bronstein and Rolf Steiner were sitting on one of the sofas, deep in conversation. Bronstein ignored his wife. "I'm not happy about this, Rolf. Louis should have been up-front with us."

"But I agree with him that it could have far-reaching implications for us," Steiner said.

"I can see that," Bronstein said impatiently. "I can see that only too well. Okay, let's say Louis discovers the Holy Grail; let's say he finds the *cure* or whatever you want to call it. What happens then? You don't think for one moment he will just hand it over in some kind of grand magnanimous gesture. No, he'll market it, he'll control its dispersal."

"That would make Keltner Industries very rich."

"And in turn make Louis and Alex very rich, not to say powerful. They could hold us all to ransom. They would hold the future of our race in their hands. So much power in the hands of one family . . ." He ran a hand through his thinning gray hair. "I don't think I could stomach that. Lars, Keichi, what do you think?"

Petersen and Yamada were standing behind the women, staring at the screen. Yamada glanced back over his shoulder at the two men sitting on the sofa. "I meant what I said earlier to Louis. I would be honored to provide any help he needs to make this thing succeed. I trust Louis to do the right thing."

"Then you're a bloody fool," Bronstein said. "Lars?"

Petersen was about to reply when his cell phone rang. He pulled it from the pocket of his jacket. "Excuse me, I need to get this." He walked across to the far corner of the room and spoke into the phone in hushed tones. When he'd finished the conversation he joined the two men on the sofa. "Sorry about that. My secretary, just checking when I'll be returning home."

Steiner glanced at his watch. "At this time of night?"

"She's a very diligent girl."

"So, Lars," Bronstein said. "What's your take on this . . . this bombshell Louis just dropped?"

Petersen shrugged. "I need to give it more thought."

"Theo, are you going to sit there with your cronies all night?" Sylvia said impatiently. "Let's go along to the dining room."

Bronstein looked at the others and raised his eyes skyward. "Very well, my dear," he said, then turned to Steiner and Petersen. "We'll continue this conversation later." He went to join his wife by the screen. "Asian you say? Ah yes, I see her. Very nice," he said, but his mind was elsewhere.

They filed out of the library, all except Petersen, who had picked up a book and was leafing through it.

At the door Yamada paused and looked back at him. "Are you joining us, Lars?"

Petersen looked up from his book. "I'll be along presently."

"I can't guarantee there'll be any left."

"I'll take my chances," Petersen said and looked down at the page again.

"As you wish," Yamada said, giving Petersen a searching look. Then he went to join the others in the dining room.

Once he was alone Lars Petersen closed the book and laid it down on the sofa beside him. He'd been expecting Nathan's call, but now that it had come he was nervous. He leaned back in the deep cushions of the sofa and closed his eyes. He had come here knowing he was going to betray Louis Keltner. The betrayal had been planned for a long time. Having heard what Louis had to say tonight only strengthened his resolve. He had to stop Louis's research going ahead, and Nathan Wisecroft would be his weapon of choice. Why he was putting all his faith in a human Petersen couldn't say. It was just an instinct that told him he could trust Nathan to get the job done. And it was *his* job to oil the wheels and see that that everything went smoothly and according to plan. He pushed himself up from the sofa and left the library, taking the back stairs down to the kitchen.

Thanks to Keltner's surprise treat for his guests the kitchen was empty, which made the first part of his job easier. He walked past counters on which food was in the process of being prepared. Pans were positioned on a large industrial-scale cooker, but the rings had not yet been lit. The door he was looking for was almost hidden behind a huge Smeg refrigerator, and he had to edge the fridge to one side in order to open it.

A flight of wooden stairs led down to the cellar. At the bottom he stopped and tried to get his bearings. It was difficult; the cellar was crowded with boxes and crates containing the many treasures of the hall that were being stored here out of the way from the potentially clumsy builders. He threaded his way between them, stopping every so often to see he was headed in the right direction. By rights the door to the tunnel should be in the north wall, but when he reached it he was dismayed to find that several large wooden crates had been stacked against it.

He put his shoulder against one of the crates and heaved, but it only traveled an inch across the rough stone floor. Sweating and cursing he heaved again, but it was useless.

"Do you need a hand?"

He spun round and found himself face-to-face with Theo Bronstein.

"I'm a lot stronger than I look," Bronstein said.

"Yes, I'm sure you are." Petersen turned back to the crate. "I suppose you're wondering what I'm doing down here."

"It crossed my mind." Bronstein rested his back against the crate, braced his legs and pushed. "What are they storing in here? Lead weights?" The crate shifted another inch. "Are you just going to stand there?"

Petersen moved in next to him and threw his weight against the crate. Slowly it began to move across the floor.

"The question I'm asking myself is not so much why you're down here," Bronstein said, his voice straining with effort, "but why you're not up there enjoying the diversion Louis laid on for us. It's an almost irresistible smorgasbord."

"An interesting choice of word. *Diversion.*"

"Well, isn't that how you see it? Throwing fish to sea lions. A suitable reward for performing as we've been trained. Louis says jump, we jump. That's the way it's always been."

"I have the impression you're getting tired of jumping."

Bronstein stopped pushing. The crate had moved fifteen inches. The door in the wall was half-exposed.

"I got tired of jumping years ago, as I suspect you did. And we're not the only ones. You probably noticed Nicci and her brother's absence tonight. I like Nicci. She has spirit. She's part of a new breed; not content to settle for the way things have always been."

"Where did she and her brother go?"

Bronstein shrugged. "Who knows? I didn't ask, like I didn't ask Louis why we were the only ones who were invited here. But I suspect she fell out of favor in some way. Come on. One more effort should get this thing moved." He braced his legs again.

"He said something about trust."

The crate shifted another two inches.

"Don't be misled by that either. Louis doesn't trust *anyone*. He's frightened. Scared of losing control of us . . . which of course he is by degrees. Why do you think he's so desperate for this experiment in genetics to succeed? It will put him back on top, where he thinks he belongs, and fools like Yamada, Steiner and my wife will keep him there for another generation or so, because they believe the sun shines out of his ass. We can't allow that to happen. What's behind the door?"

"A friend."

'Really?'

"He's an enemy of the Keltners. He intends to destroy them."

"*'The enemy of my enemy is my friend,'*" Bronstein said thoughtfully, remembering a quote he'd heard a long time ago. "Has he the means?"

"I believe so." The crate was finally away from the door. Petersen turned the handle. It opened easily. "I thought you and Louis were close."

"We were . . . once, a long, long time ago. Before he started playing me for a fool. Before he started playing us all for fools. Louis Keltner wants to be God and wants us all to worship him." Bronstein gave a bitter laugh. "Never going to happen. Not in my lifetime anyway. What's the name of this friend of yours?

"Wisecroft. Nathan Wisecroft."

Theo Bronstein shrugged. "Never heard of him."

"There's no reason why you should have done. He's human."

Bronstein raised an eyebrow. "Really. And what's his gripe with Louis? Must be something bad if he intends to kill him because of it."

"Something that goes all the way back to Jamaica."

"Jesus! That was a long time ago. To hold a grudge

that long shows dedication and strength of character. That's good if it's something that works to our advantage. Of course, it's not only Louis he has to deal with. There's Alex and Erik as well, not to mention Yamada and Steiner. The odds are stacked against him."

"He's not alone."

"How many with him?"

"Another three."

"Still not enough, in my opinion," Bronstein said. "What do you hope to achieve if this Wisecroft succeeds?"

"Autonomy."

"As simple as that?"

Petersen nodded. "Keltner's been running things for too long. He treats us all like his lapdogs."

"So you're trying to shorten the odds, is that it? Give Wisecroft a helping hand, so you get what you want and at the same time you keep your hands clean."

"Something like that. Keltner has as many friends as he has enemies. I don't want to spend the rest of my days looking over my shoulder. It's easier all round if a third party does the dirty work."

"Very wise," Bronstein said.

"You've already said you want the same thing as I do. Why don't you help me?"

"Louis and I, we go back a long way. Could I live with my oldest friend's blood on my hands?"

"It's your decision," Petersen said. "But I should tell you now, that if you decide your loyalties lie with Keltner, you're not going to leave this cellar alive," He reached into his jacket and produced a 9mm automatic.

Bronstein's eyes widened in surprise. Then he smiled. "Let's go and shorten those odds," he said.

CHAPTER 37

Five hundred yards into the tunnel Nathan Wisecroft was hit by a seizure, the intensity of which he'd never experienced before. There had been no hint that it was coming; no dull throb at the temples to herald its onset; just a full-blown explosion of white-hot agony in his brain. He dropped his spotlight, clamped his hands to his head and reeled back against the cold brick wall. His cry echoed along the tunnel, an eerie, gut-wrenching sound that made the short hairs on the back of Tony's neck prickle.

Jim was at Nathan's side immediately, supporting the big man's body as it slid down the wall.

"What's happening?" Billy shouted, an edge of panic to his voice. He was hating this journey. Claustrophobia was starting to inhibit every step he took, not helped by what he saw when he swung the beam of his spotlight up to the ceiling. Small fibrous roots were pushing their way through the mortar between the bricks as the forest reclaimed the space that rightfully belonged to it.

"I don't know," Jim said, on his knees now beside

Nathan, whose body was slowly curling into a fetal position. Tony crouched down beside them, shining his light on Nathan's contorted face. Nathan's eyes were squeezed tightly shut and his mouth was open, stretched wide in a silent scream. His whole body trembled violently and Tony could see droplets of sweat popping out on his brow.

"Nathan! Nathan, can you hear me?" Jim said.

Nathan said nothing but continued to tremble. His mind had retreated from the tunnel, from the three men he was with, from the pain. It now occupied a small space inside his head where it was being battered by images of violence and death. Inside his mind he could hear quite clearly Vincent Keltner's voice repeating all the things it had told him before, quietly insistent. The images were changing, taking him now on a journey back in time, back to the dirt-poor existence of St. Xaviour. His mother, dancing with her friends under the blazing Jamaican sun; the small corrugated iron shack in which she met her death; his grandmother clutching her Bible, praying to a God that had long since abandoned them; Louis Keltner, staring at him and his mother across an open grave.

As suddenly as it had come the seizure passed. Nathan opened his eyes and stared up at the concerned faces of Tony, Jim and Billy. He let the air out of his lungs in one long sigh as his body gave a final shudder and relaxed.

"Get me to my feet," he said.

Jim and Tony took him underneath the shoulders and helped him stand.

"Are you okay?" Tony said.

"Jesus, you had me worried," Jim said, relief making him laugh nervously. "I thought you were going to peg it."

Nathan smiled grimly. "Not just yet," he said, pulling a handkerchief from his pocket and wiping the sweat away from his brow. "But I've no doubt it's going to kill me eventually. He doesn't realize what he's doing to my body . . . or maybe he does and he just doesn't care."

"Who?" Jim said.

Nathan leaned against the wall. "Vincent. That was him reminding me he's still around; still up here." He tapped the side of his head and closed his eyes. Then he took a deep breath and pushed himself away from the wall. He bent down, scooped up his spotlight and set off down the tunnel again.

"Is he all right?" Tony came up beside Jim and spoke softly.

Jim Davies watched Nathan make his way unsteadily along, the spotlight beam swinging drunkenly. He shook his head. "I don't know. I really don't know."

Just concentrate on putting one foot in front of the other. Block out the visions. He's been wrong before. Nathan felt a swell of nausea in the pit of his stomach. He was reaching the end; the end of something that started all those years ago in Jamaica. How could he justify putting these other lives in peril for something that was essentially *his* fight? The answer was that he couldn't. He stopped walking and turned round.

"Something wrong?" Jim said as he caught up with him.

Nathan waited for Tony and Billy to reach them before answering. "I'm going on alone," he said.

"What?" Jim said.

"I have no right to ask you to do this. This is my fight. Go back now."

"No way," Jim said.

"The Keltners have no quarrel with you, Jim. Go back and run your pub. Forget this ever happened."

Jim shook his head in bemusement. "I don't understand. What's changed?"

"What did Vincent tell you?" Tony said. "I take it that's what this sudden change of heart is about."

Nathan avoided his eyes, staring back down the tunnel into the impenetrable blackness. He nodded his head sharply. "It could be suicide for you to go any farther."

"Did he tell you that we're going to fail? That we're all going to die?" Tony said.

"Not exactly that."

"What then?" Billy said. He'd felt his resolve to face the Keltners crumbling the farther he'd gone into the tunnel. The claustrophobia he was experiencing was gnawing away at his bravado. Although he would never admit it to the others, he was more frightened than he'd ever been in his life.

"He reminded me just how powerful his father and his brothers were. He showed me things, horrible things they had done in the past." His whole body shuddered as he recalled the images that had swamped his mind. "I can't expose you to that kind of danger."

"I'm sorry, Nathan, but this is no longer just about you," Tony said, an edge of anger to his voice. "They killed my sister, for Christ's sake. They've got Emma, and fuck knows what they're going to do with her. I'm coming with you. We fight them together."

"I'm not going back," Jim said. "Not after what that bastard Erik did to Wayne. Besides, I don't think you stand a chance against them on your own."

"Billy? I'm giving you the same choice I gave the others," Nathan said. "We won't think any less of you if you turn round and go back."

Billy shifted uneasily from foot to foot. He looked at each of them then, without a word, he turned and started to walk back down the tunnel toward the Lodge.

"Just the three of us then," Nathan said.

"Let's press on," Jim said. "We must be nearly there."

"I'm sorry I had to deceive you, Alex," Louis Keltner said. "But I'm sure you appreciate why I did."

They were in the study. Louis was seated at the desk, Alex and Erik at opposite sides of the room. Maria's wheelchair was positioned at the side of the desk, while Emma was beside Erik where he could keep an eye on her. She was silent, her eyes half-closed, her mind still reeling, trying to assimilate what she had learned in the last hour.

"Of course I appreciate it. You had no choice. Still, it was something of a shock to learn I had a niece." He looked across at Emma. "Hard to credit really."

"What about me?" Erik said.

"What about you?" Louis Keltner's eyes narrowed as he looked at his other son. That was always how he thought of Erik; his *other* son. The one that didn't live up to expectations; the one that was always a potential embarrassment. Both Alex and Vincent were worth ten of him.

"Aren't you going to apologize for deceiving me?"

"You were told what you needed to be told," Louis said dismissively.

"Fine," Erik said, getting to his feet. He turned to his brother. "You can babysit your *niece*. I've got things to do." He left the study, slamming the door behind him.

"You're too hard on him," Alex said.

"You think? I don't. He's a liability. I sometimes wish it had been Erik and not Vincent who . . ." He shook his head. "Never mind. Theo surprised me. I thought he would have been much more enthusiastic."

"Theo's getting old. He's losing his grip. There are others better equipped to run things in the States. It might be an idea to pension him off and put a younger person in his place."

"I've been thinking along the same lines. What about the others? Yamada's very loyal."

"And very shrewd. Hardly likely to bite the hand that feeds him. The same goes for Steiner. They know they wouldn't be where they are today without you. Petersen I worry about."

"You don't trust him?" Louis said.

"No, I don't. He's very ambitious. He's got Scandinavia, but I don't think that's enough for him."

"Needs watching then."

"I think so."

Louis put his hand behind his head and leaned back in the chair. "And what about you?"

"What about me?"

"Are you still happy running Keltner Industries?"

Alex frowned. "Where's this leading?" he said.

"Don't worry. I have every confidence in you. In fact I think I'm underutilizing you. How do you feel about taking over my role?"

"I'm sorry, I'm not sure I understand."

"You said about Theo getting old. Would it surprise you to know he's actually younger than me?"

"Yes, it would."

"Well, it's a fact. And it's also a fact that I'm getting tired. The weight of responsibility for looking after our people is beginning to become a burden. I think the time is coming when I'd like to shift that burden onto younger, more capable shoulders. Yours, to be precise."

Alex laughed. "And what would you do? Retire? Find yourself a little cottage somewhere and take up watercolor painting? Come on, you'd go out of your mind within six months."

Louis smiled. "I didn't have anything that drastic—or that boring—in mind. But I'd like to have more time to devote to this research. I believe passionately in what I told them tonight. I'd like the opportunity to explore all the avenues that might open up. And I can't do that while I'm watching out for everything else. Give it some thought. Let me know in the morning what your decision is."

"I can tell you now. I'll take the job."

"And that's exactly why I offered it to you. You're very much like me. Decisive. I like that."

Outside the door to the study Erik listened to the conversation, his hands clenching and unclenching as anger threatened to overwhelm him. Always Alex! It was always fucking Alex! He wheeled away from the door and went up to his room.

He had one of the larger rooms on the second floor. Decked out like a bachelor pad with a low leather couch and glass-topped coffee table, the room also boasted a king-sized bed and a desk. On the wall across from the window was a bank of screens, each with a feed to the cameras in the rooms. He threw himself down into a chair in front of them and flicked a switch, bringing them all to life.

In the dining room the Steiners and Yamada were reveling in a lake of flesh, their appetites far from sated as they moved from one body to another. Sylvia Bronstein was sitting astride Didier, the chef, riding him like a pony, her fingers burrowing deep into the muscles of his shoulders. The expression on his face was one of ecstasy mingled with sheer terror. Erik had half a mind to go and join them, to forget what he had just heard by indulging himself in an orgiastic feast. But something held him back. There was something wrong with the scene he was witnessing. Theo Bronstein was nowhere to be seen; neither was Lars Petersen.

He checked the other screens carefully. They weren't in their rooms. Then where?

A movement on the screen in the bottom right-hand corner of the bank attracted his attention. Bronstein and Petersen were entering the kitchen from the cellar stairs, brushing dust from their clothes and talking animatedly. Erik reached out to a block of controls at the bottom of the screens and hit a button, zooming the camera in to get a better look at them. There was something grasped in Petersen's hand. A gun. What the hell were they up to? They had no right to be roaming about the house, and even less right to be carrying weapons. He reached for the intercom on the desk to summon his father, then withdrew his hand. No. This was something he would handle alone. He didn't need help from either his father or his brother. He checked the screen that showed the study. They were still there, drinking, talking, excluding him. *Well fuck them!* he thought. One way or another he'd force his father to recognize him; to realize that he, Erik Keltner, had something to offer that not even the precious Alex could compete with.

There was another movement on the bottom screen. Bronstein and Petersen were no longer in the kitchen, but the cellar door was opening again. He watched, then smiled as three men stepped through the doorway. He recognized Tony Carver immediately. The black man he'd never seen before, but the other one he realized was the landlord from the Three Crowns. He knew why they'd come to the Hall. This was even better than he'd anticipated.

He went across and flipped the light switch, turning off the overhead light so that the only illumination in the room was coming from the screens, then he took off his dark glasses. He kept his set of contact lenses in the drawer of his desk. He rarely wore them, finding they irritated his eyes, but now he took them out of their sealed container and slipped them in. They darkened his eyes, made them look more human. He blinked once or twice to lubricate them and stared at his reflection in the mirror. He could feel the metamorphosis coming. Quickly he stripped off his clothes and braced himself as his bones and skin stretched and contorted. The pain, as usual, was excruciating, but also exhilarating. The act of reverting to his natural form filled him, as it always did, with feelings of immense power and satisfaction.

When the transformation was complete he looked again at himself in the mirror, the thin, lizardlike lips twisting themselves into the semblance of a smile. He was ready. He flexed his long, sharp fingers and drew in a deep, steadying breath, then loped to the door.

CHAPTER 38

Petersen and Bronstein reached the entrance hall.

"Put the gun away," Bronstein said. "There's no point in showing our hand before we have to."

Lars Petersen slipped the automatic into his pocket and pulled out his phone. A few keystrokes later he said, "I'm ready. Let's do it."

They walked along the corridor to the study. Bronstein knocked, once.

"Come."

Louis and Alex were seated on the chesterfield, both relaxed, both sipping whiskey from cut-glass tumblers. "Theo, Lars, is the entertainment not up to scratch? I thought you would be indulging for the rest of the evening." Louis Keltner got to his feet. "Let me get you a drink," he said.

"That won't be necessary," Bronstein said.

"We have a few problems with your announcement tonight," Petersen said, his eyes flicking to Emma, who was sitting in an armchair, staring into the glowing coals of the fire, a lost, helpless look in her eyes.

"Really," Louis said. "I'm disappointed."

"You didn't really expect our support, did you, Louis?"

Louis Keltner smiled. "No, in my heart of hearts I don't suppose I did. At least not from you, Theo. I know you too well, old friend. But I'm surprised at you, Lars. I had you down as something of a progressive. Not an old stick-in-the-mud like Theo here." He turned to Alex, who was watching the two men carefully, his body tensed, ready to move quickly if the need arose. "What do you think, son?"

"I think our friends are being very shortsighted," Alex said.

While Bronstein and Petersen's attention was diverted by Alex, Louis went and sat down at the desk. The agate-handled paper knife lay where he'd dropped it earlier in the day. He laid his hand over it, careful not to let the two men see.

"Far from it," Bronstein countered. "We're not so shortsighted that we can't see where this is leading. This is all about wealth and power, Louis, and your craving for it. Well, I'm sorry, but we're not just going to sit back and let you get more control over us than you already have."

"So this is all about jealousy, Theo? You want that power for yourself."

Theo Bronstein flushed angrily. "We don't all think like you," he spat.

"Enough talking," Petersen said. "Let's do what we came here to do." He reached into his jacket pocket and pulled out the gun, but before he could even take aim Louis picked up the paper knife and threw it. The knife hit Petersen in the throat, just under his Adam's apple, splitting his windpipe. With a strangled cry Petersen dropped the gun, his hands flying to his throat. Slowly he sank to his knees as blood pumped out of the wound.

With panic flaring in his eyes Theo Bronstein spun on

his heel and ran for the door, but as his hand reached for the knob he was yanked backward.

Alex was on his feet, staring at Bronstein, a look of deep concentration on his face. Louis still sat at the desk, composed, a slight smile playing on his lips.

Bronstein tumbled to the floor, his legs useless, his whole body no longer under his control. He felt himself being dragged across the carpet. Out of the corner of his eye he could see the gun, lying on the floor where Petersen had dropped it. With a supreme effort of will he stretched out his arm but, as his fingers brushed the barrel of the gun, the weapon spun away from him.

"Don't fight it, Theo," Louis said. "Alex is far too strong for you."

"Damn you!" Theo said as he was rolled over onto his stomach. His breath was coming in short, hot gasps and his heart was thumping in his chest, sending the blood coursing through his veins and arteries, making him dizzy. "Let me up," he said. "You'll regret this."

Louis got to his feet and walked over to where Bronstein lay. "Enough, Alex."

Alex closed his eyes and turned away.

Immediately Theo Bronstein's heart rate slowed and the feeling started to come back to his body.

"Get up," Louis said.

Bronstein pushed himself up until he was kneeling in front of Louis Keltner.

"No," Louis said. "On second thought, stay there on your knees. It's where you belong."

Lars Petersen was lying on the floor a few yards away, hands still at his throat. He was making a horrible, wet, wheezing sound as he struggled to breathe.

"Well, what a pathetic pair you make," Louis said. He turned to Alex, who had sat back down on the chesterfield and was watching the scene play out with a look of wry amusement on his face. "What shall we do with them?"

"It's your call," Alex said. "But I think we should make an example of them."

"But Theo and I have been friends for years. That must count for something." He turned away from Bronstein and went across to where Lars Petersen lay. He reached down and gripped the agate handle of the knife, pulling it from the man's throat. "Lars, on the other hand, I've never liked." He plunged the knife into Petersen's eye, watching with satisfaction as his body convulsed.

Theo Bronstein started to shake, as if in sympathy. "Louis," he said. "Be reasonable."

"Shut up! Alex, do you think it's worth upsetting the Americans over this? Theo here has quite a following over there. We could be creating unnecessary problems."

"He would have happily stood by while Petersen killed you."

Louis swept his hand through his iron-gray hair. "That's true." He started to pace up and down in front of Bronstein. "You see what a dilemma you've put me in, Theo. My instincts say to kill you for your betrayal, and I usually trust my instincts. But then it was my instinct to trust Nicci Bellini, and look where that got me. But if I let you live, I'll always be watching my back; waiting for you to betray me again." He stopped pacing. "Oh fuck it!" He spun round and lunged with the knife.

Theo Bronstein gave a small gasp of surprise and pitched forward onto the carpet.

As the bodies of the two men went through their final contortions, Louis Keltner went across to Emma and crouched down beside her. "Sorry you had to witness that, my dear," he said, reaching out and stroking her hair. Emma continued to stare into the fire, not moving away from his touch. "I'm not really a violent man, as you'll discover, once you get to know me."

In the wheelchair Maria started rocking from side to side, a thin, keening sound issuing from her throat. There were tears trickling down her cheeks. Louis stood upright, looked across at her and sighed. "That's all we need," he said.

The cell phone vibrated in Nathan's pocket as a text message came through. He checked the screen. A message from Petersen. One word: STUDY.

Nathan turned to the others. "They're in the study." He took out the larger floor plan and spread it out on the kitchen counter. "Here," he said, jabbing at the outline of a room on the first floor with his finger.

"So we just walk in and get her?" Tony said.

"We'll hook up with Petersen first." He hit the speed dial on his phone.

"Petersen?"

"Lars Petersen. He's my contact here." He let the phone ring for a full minute. "He's not answering," he said and switched off the phone. "Something must be wrong."

"How do you know?" Jim said.

"Because Lars agreed to stay in contact. He would have answered my call if he'd been able to." He folded the floor plan and slipped it back into his pocket. "Okay, we'll have to do this without him. Let's go."

At that moment the kitchen was plunged into darkness. Nathan reached for his spotlight, but something whistled through the air, catching him on the point of his chin, lifting him off his feet and sending him flying backward over the counter.

"Nathan!" Jim shouted and flicked on his light, swinging the beam in a wide arc. He saw Nathan's crumpled and unconscious body lying in a heap by the wall, but before he could run to him steely fingers closed around his throat. He tried to call out again but no air would pass through his restricted windpipe. He dropped his light to the floor, clutching at the hand encircling his throat. As the light bounced on the cold tiles a beam of light illuminated his assailant. A creature from his worst nightmares had its face inches away from his. He got only an impression. Dark cold eyes set in a gray leathery face; a thin-lipped mouth grinning, showing a row of needle-sharp teeth. He kicked out but was lifted into the air, his feet flailing and failing to make contact with anything but empty space. Then his eyes widened as the creature plunged its other hand into his stomach, rending skin and muscle, fingers closing round coils of intestine and wrenching them out through the entry wound.

He was dropped to the floor, his head cracking on the tiles, a white-hot fire burning in the empty space where his guts should have been. He died with a scream of agony trapped in his crushed throat.

Only seconds had passed since the lights went out and Tony had spent those precious moments fumbling with the switch of his spotlight. It refused to work, no matter how many times he pressed it. When he was struck from behind the light went spinning from his grip, bounced off the cooker and smashed on the floor. He staggered under the blow but managed to keep his feet and turned to face his attacker.

The creature reached out with both hands and grabbed Tony's jacket, forcing him backward until he collided with the counter. He was pinned there, the small of his back pressed against the hard metal edge of the counter, unable to move. He could smell the rancid stink of the creature's breath as it opened its mouth. "You look like your sister," the creature hissed at him. "Nice."

"Keltner!" The realization hit him like an electric shock, galvanizing him. Weeks of grief, pain and loss washed through him, leaving in its place only anger and a cold, hard hatred. He threw his head back, then brought it crashing forward into Erik Keltner's face. Keltner cried out as his nose split. A fountain of blood gushed out, splattering Tony's shirt. Keltner staggered back, but lashed out with his hand, catching Tony on the side of the head, knocking him to the floor. And then Keltner was on him, hands choking, the weight of his monstrous body pinning him down.

Tony felt his thoughts clouding as the oxygen was cut off to his brain. He was going to die. He'd soon be joining his beloved Helen. He could almost welcome it. He forced his eyes to stay open, wanting to stare into the face of his killer, the murderer of his sister. A final defiant act. Keltner's mouth twisted into an obscene, feral grin. A long black tongue flicked across the lips.

He was still grinning when his right eye exploded as a needle-tipped screwdriver was rammed through the back of his skull. Then the grin turned into a rictus and he collapsed forward, trembling and convulsing. Seconds later he was dead.

Tony drew in a ragged breath and crawled out from beneath the already decomposing body. A hand reached down to him. He took it and was hauled to his feet, staring into the ruined face of Billy Farrier.

"Changed my mind," he said, prodding Keltner's lifeless form with the toe of his boot. "Glad I did now."

"Thanks," Tony said as a groan sounded from the corner of the room. "Nathan?" He turned to Billy. "See if Jim's okay. He's over by the door."

He could barely put one foot in front of the other. It felt as if his entire body had been drained of energy. He crouched down beside Nathan. "Are you all right?"

Nathan struggled to sit upright. "Yeah. Think so. What happened?"

"Erik Keltner happened."

"And you're still here. That's promising."

"I wouldn't be if it hadn't been for Billy."

"Help me to my feet."

Tony reached down and pulled the big man upright.

"Jim's dead," Billy said, coming toward them, swinging his spotlight. For a moment the beam danced across Nathan's face. "What's the matter with his eyes?" he said to Tony and brought the light up to shine on the two men. Nathan turned his head away quickly, but not quickly enough. Both Tony and Billy had seen it. One eye dark, almost black, the other pale and washed out.

"Fuck! He's one of them!" Billy said, the screwdriver clenched in his hand again, arm coming up, ready to strike.

"No, Billy! Hear him out first. Nathan?"

"Get that light away from my face and I will."

In the study Alex Keltner's glass slipped from his fingers and he clasped a hand to his head, crying out in pain. Louis looked around sharply at his son. "What is it?"

Alex pushed himself to his feet. "Erik," he said. "It's Erik. Something's happened to him. I felt it! My office, quickly."

Locking the door to the study and hurrying along the corridor to Alex's office, Louis said, "What's happened to him?"

"He's dead," Alex said, and rushed through to the anteroom. He flicked on the screen and navigated from room to room until he reached the kitchen. "There," he said, pointing to the three figures lit by a spotlight one of them was holding.

"Who are they?"

"The one holding the spotlight is Billy Farrier, the idiot Erik had a run-in with last year. The one next to him is Helen Carver's brother."

At that moment Nathan Wisecroft looked directly up at the camera.

"Him!" Louis Keltner said. "Vincent told me he was dead."

"Who is he?" Alex said. "And what's he doing here?"

"His name is Nathan. I remember him from Jamaica."

"The one Vincent made his pet."

"In name only. Vincent was grooming him for greater things. He asked my permission to turn him. I refused of course. The gene pool was—is—polluted enough. But he went ahead and did it anyway. When I found out I ordered Vincent to get rid of him. He told me he had."

"And you believed him?"

"Stupidly, yes. Now it looks like my stupidity has come back to bite me. Help me get the women to the car. I'm flying back to Switzerland tonight."

"Tonight? You're running away from this . . . this Nathan?"

"I think circumspection is the best policy for now. First the Bellinis, then Theo and Lars, now this. This visit hasn't turned out to be the triumph I envisaged. I can't take the risk of anything happening to Emma. I've invested too much time and money in her for things to go wrong now." He picked up the telephone and rang the airfield.

The conversation was brief.

"Right. I'm flying out at midnight. Now, are you going to help me get Maria and Emma into the car, or shall I do it myself?"

"Erik's dead. Doesn't that mean anything to you?" Alex said.

Louis held his gaze for a moment then looked away. "Frankly, no. It's one less thing I have to worry about."

Alex made a sound of disgust in his throat and walked back to the study.

CHAPTER 39

"I'm sorry I didn't tell you," Nathan said.

"You should have done." Tony was struggling to digest this latest shock.

Billy had turned away from them and was carving his initials in the counter with the screwdriver. He wanted to plunge it into Nathan's lying eyes, but if he tried anything he would have to get past Tony first, and he had no quarrel with him.

"So you're no better than they are," Tony said.

"That's not quite true." Nathan rubbed a hand over his face. "I don't kill. I try to abstain from sex as much as I can. I only feed when it's absolutely necessary, and then I take the bare minimum to keep me alive. I never wanted this, but Vincent insisted and I was too weak to resist him. But it haunts me every day."

"So your reasons for wanting the Keltners out of the way are . . ."

"Exactly as I said before. Nothing's changed."

"Jim Davies is dead. That's one change." Billy

wheeled round from the counter and hurled the screwdriver. It embedded itself in the wall inches to the right
of Nathan's head. "It wasn't even his fight, you son of a
bitch!"

"I know," Nathan said. "And believe me I'm going to
regret it until the day I die. But this is war, and sacrifices
sometimes have to be made."

"Bollocks!" Billy said. "I came back here to help rescue the girl. Are we going to do it or not?"

"We are," Nathan said.

"Right. Once we've got her safe, you're on your own.
Understood?"

"Understood."

"I'm with Billy on this," Tony said. "I just want to get
Emma out of here. I don't give a flying fuck about the
Keltners. As far as I'm concerned, from now on, that's
your battle."

"We'd best get moving then," Nathan said, and walked
from the kitchen.

Tony and Billy exchanged looks. "I knew there was
something about him I didn't trust," Billy said. "I'll watch
your back, you watch mine."

Tony glanced across at Jim Davies's body and shook
his head. "Poor sod. He didn't deserve to die like that.
Come on, let's do this," he said.

In the garage that stood alongside Bexton Hall, Louis
Keltner laid Maria down on the backseat of the Mercedes. She'd stopped crying and just lay there, immobile and silent. But something had shifted in her
expression. She looked up at Louis with something like
loathing in her watery eyes.

Alex was holding on to Emma's wrist tightly, but she
made no effort to pull away from him. There was little
fight in her now. The events of the past few days had left
her physically drained and mentally numb. It didn't

matter what they did to her now. Nothing she could do would bring Helen or the others back. Let them take her away; let them kill her. She really didn't care anymore. Why should she live when so many others had died because of her?

"Put her in the front," Louis said.

Alex opened the door to the passenger side and pushed her inside, then slammed it shut and started to walk away.

"Come with us," Louis called after him.

Alex stopped midpace and looked back at his father. "No. Not while Erik's killer still draws breath."

"As you wish. Strange. I never figured you as a sentimentalist." He climbed in beside Emma and started the car.

Alex didn't wait to watch his father depart. He turned and started to jog back to the house.

The study was empty.

"What now?" Billy said.

"Nathan?"

Nathan was standing, staring down at two piles of discarded clothes lying on the carpet. A few coins were scattered about, a pocketbook and a wristwatch, together with a cell phone. He reached down for the phone, but even before he picked it up he knew whose it was.

"Nathan?" Tony said again.

"Petersen's dead," Nathan said, wondering about the other clothes on the carpet. He tried to piece together in his mind what had happened here but drew a blank. Two deaths. The Keltners found out about Lars, but who else had they killed? The fact they'd uncovered Petersen's duplicity surprised him; he'd always been so careful.

"Nathan!"

"We'll have to search the house. We've got to find them."

At that moment the sound of a car's engine being turned over drifted up from the grounds below.

"I think we just have," Tony said, and ran from the room.

As Billy passed the clothes on the floor he noticed the wristwatch. A gold Rolex. He could sell it and buy himself another loft of pigeons. It would be some reward for all this. He bent down and scooped it up, slipping it into his pocket, then ran to catch up with Tony.

Keichi Yamada climbed the stairs, arm in arm with a young Filipino boy. Yamada's clothes were disheveled and his hair was awry, and there was a stupid grin on his face. He showed no surprise or alarm when Tony and the others appeared at the top of the stairs and started running down the stairs toward him. Tony took in the appearance of the young boy: half-dressed, a glazed look in his eyes; a series of puncture marks on his chest. Another victim. He brushed past Yamada, then heard him cry out, but didn't look back. His only thought was for Emma. He reached the bottom of the stairs and stopped to get his bearings. Billy Farrier came up beside him, blood dripping from the screwdriver still gripped in his hand. "Another one down," he said, jerking a thumb back over his shoulder. "Where's Nathan?"

"I thought he was right behind us."

Tony looked back up the stairs. The Filipino boy was rigid, staring in horror at the thing that had once been Yamada, writhing and decaying where he had fallen. Of Nathan there was no sign. He couldn't wait for him. "This way," he said, and ran for the front door.

He pulled it open and found himself face-to-face with Alex Keltner. Keltner grabbed him one-handed around the throat and, with very little effort, threw him the length of the hallway. At the same time his other arm came up and he punched Billy in the face, knocking him off his feet. And then, quite calmly, he closed the front door again and stood with his back to it. "Right," he said. "Which of you killed my brother?"

Nathan ran down the back stairs and out into the garden. He knew he'd never be able to stop the car if he went to the front, but this way there was a chance. The garage was at the side of the house toward the back. As he turned the corner past an old dilapidated greenhouse he saw the Mercedes pull out. Louis Keltner was at the wheel, a look of self-satisfaction on his face. As the car picked up speed Nathan sprinted forward, flicked on the spotlight and shone it directly into Keltner's eyes. The effect was instantaneous as the car lurched to a stop. The door was thrown open and with a cry of rage Louis Keltner launched himself at Nathan.

Both men went down hard, crunching on the gravel. Keltner's hands groped for Nathan's throat but Nathan dropped the spotlight and grabbed Keltner's wrists, forcing his arms wide. Their strength was equal. Nathan twisted his body and threw Keltner off, following through with a punch to his kidneys. For a moment Keltner paused, but within seconds he'd recovered. He sprung quickly to his feet and ran back to the car, throwing himself behind the wheel and ramming his foot down on the gas pedal. The car shot forward. Keltner spun the steering wheel and before Nathan had time to move, the wing of the car smashed into his thigh, numbing his leg and sending a sickening surge of pain flooding through the rest of his body.

Keltner reversed and aimed the Mercedes at him again. This time Nathan threw himself to one side, landing on the gravel on his hands and knees. He had only a moment before the engine roared again. He pushed himself to his feet, but realized he was much too slow.

The car hit him square on and he was hurled backward into the wall of the house by the impact. His back hit the three-hundred-year-old bricks and he felt something break. In agony and weak beyond belief he tried to get to his feet, using the wall as support, but his pelvis had fractured and it felt like white-hot spikes were being driven into the bone marrow of his legs. He collapsed back into a sitting position and waited for the Mercedes to plow into him again to finish the job.

Instead the engine was switched off and Louis Keltner got out of the car. He walked toward him. He was smiling.

Alex Keltner crouched down beside Billy Farrier and plucked the bloodied screwdriver from his grasp. He studied it for a moment, testing its sharpness with the ball of his thumb. "Is this what you used to kill Erik?" he said.

Billy spat at him.

Alex wiped away a trail of bloody saliva from his face and rammed the screwdriver up to its handle into Billy's thigh. Billy bucked in agony but clamped his teeth together. He wouldn't give Keltner the satisfaction of hearing him scream.

Alex gripped the handle of the screwdriver and wrenched it from right to left, opening the wound, watching with satisfaction as sweat poured down Billy's face. "I'll ask you again. Is this what you used to kill my brother?"

"Leave him alone." Tony had picked himself up from the floor and was leaning against the wall, trying to get his strength back.

Alex Keltner glanced around at him, blinked once and a searing pain exploded in Tony's head. Blood started to pour from his nose and ears and he staggered away from the wall, pitching forward, landing on his face on the cold marble tiles.

"I'll deal with you in a moment," Alex said, and turned his attention back to Billy. He pulled the screwdriver from his thigh, thought for a moment, then, with great deliberation, punctured Billy's neck with the point.

"Just kill me and get it over with, you bastard," Billy said, tears starting to dibble down his cheeks.

"Oh I will, believe me. But not until you tell me what I want to hear."

The dining room door opened and Sylvia Bronstein staggered out into the hallway, giggling to herself. "I'll say this for you, Alex, when you hold a party . . ." She looked at the scene before her with bleary, sated eyes. "Sorry, am I interrupting something? I'm looking for Theo. He said he had some business to attend to with Lars, but he never came back. He's missing all the fun."

"He's dead," Billy said, remembering the name he'd seen inscribed on the back of the Rolex. *Theo Bronstein.*

"Shut up!" Alex dug the screwdriver in farther.

"Dead? What do you mean?" She swayed on her feet, confusion clouding her face.

"They killed him. The Keltners killed him."

"Alex? What's he talking about? Who are these people anyway?"

"I'm sure you'll find him," Alex said. "Try upstairs."

Tony pushed himself up onto his hands and knees. His face was a mask of blood. "It's true. Your husband's dead," he said, following Billy's lead, then cried out as another lance of agony shot through his head.

"Alex, stop it," Sylvia said. "Let him speak."

"Leave it, Sylvia," Alex said. "Go up to your room and let me deal with this situation. I'll come up and speak with you shortly."

While Alex Keltner's attention was diverted Billy reached into his pocket and pulled out the Rolex. He slid it across the marble tiles where it stopped at Sylvia Bronstein's feet. She stared down at it blearily, then her arm swept down and she picked it up, turning it over and over in her hands. Theo's watch. She'd given it to him on their anniversary twenty years ago. Tears sprang to her eyes. "It *is* true," she said, her voice barely audible. "Why, Alex?" She looked across at him.

"Sylvia, I . . ."

And she could see it there, written on his face. The guilt, the lie. "Bastard!" she said. "You bastard! Theo thought the world of you, and this is how you repay him?"

Even as she spoke she was beginning to change. Her limbs were stretching, fingers becoming points, face contorting, lips stretching over a gradually widening mouth. Before the change was complete she launched herself at Alex, fingers clawing for his eyes.

Alex was knocked backward as Sylvia landed on him. They rolled across the tiles, bodies locked together, each trying to gain the advantage. Fueled by grief and rage Sylvia's strength was a match for him. She clawed, she bit, she shredded his cheek with razor-sharp fingernails.

Tony was on his feet, the pain in his head nothing more than a memory now that Alex Keltner's attention was diverted. He ran across the hall and helped Billy to his feet. "Let's get out of here."

Billy was hobbling on his wounded leg, but he still managed a well-aimed kick at Alex Keltner's head as he passed them.

Louis Keltner grabbed Nathan by the front of his coat and hauled him to his feet, ignoring the cry of pain that sprang involuntarily from Nathan's lips. "Why are you here?" he said.

Nathan said nothing. He felt faint. He could feel the broken bones of his pelvis grinding against each other. He prayed for unconsciousness; anything to stop the agony coursing through his lower body.

"Did you come for the girl? Well look, there she is, in the car. Go and rescue her." He let him go and laughed as Nathan slid slowly down the wall. "Pathetic," he said. "You and traitors like you make me sick to my stomach. I wish I had more time; I'd enjoy making you suffer. But I have a plane to catch. You lost, my friend. You lost everything." He hoisted Nathan up again, his index and middle finger extended. He raised his arm to strike, but hesitated. There was something wrong. His arm wouldn't move. He strained every muscle, but to no avail. He stared at Nathan in disbelief, but even as he stared, the black man's face began to change, the features shifting, remodeling, until it became a face Louis Keltner knew well.

"Vincent?" His arm dropped to his side. "No. I don't believe this."

"Believe it, Father." The voice seemed to come from Nathan, but his mouth wasn't moving. It was as if the voice were hanging in the air between them. "You can never win."

Louis Keltner let go of Nathan and backed away.

At that moment Tony Carver and Billy Farrier turned the corner. "Nathan!" Tony shouted.

With a cry of frustration Louis Keltner spun on his heel and raced for the car. He rammed his foot down on the gas pedal. The wheels spun on the gravel but finally found purchase and the car shot forward. Tony pushed Billy to one side as the Mercedes flew past them. It swerved onto the drive and out through the front gate. Within seconds there was nothing but the sound of the engine growing fainter in the cold night air.

Nathan Wisecroft leaned against the wall, head bowed. The pain was easing slightly, his broken pelvic bone already knitting back together.

Tony ran to him. "Are you all right?"

"I'll live."

"Was Emma in the car with him?"

"She was."

"He won then," Billy said in disgust.

Nathan shook his head. "He might have won this battle, but the war's only just begun. We'll get another chance."

"How can you be so sure?"

"Vincent told me . . . before he left."

"He's gone?"

Nathan nodded his head slowly. Somewhere from inside the house came a high-pitched scream. "Let's get the hell out of here," he said.

CHAPTER 40

They stepped into the elevator of the Hilton Hotel and pressed the button for the twelfth floor. They'd checked in under the nom-de-plume they frequently used when traveling incognito, Mr. and Mrs. Galina. It had served them well over the years, guaranteeing anonymity. Not even the Keltners knew of the name. Under this guise Nicci found it easy to relax, confident they could not be traced.

She leaned back against the elevator wall and closed her eyes. It had been a long day and all she really wanted to do now was to sink into a hot bath and to stay there as long as possible. Massimo paced backward and forward in the confined space, an anxious look on his face, glancing every other second at the floor indicator, willing the elevator to go faster.

"Oh, for God's sake, relax," Nicci snapped at him, irritated by his restlessness. "They're not going to find us here, and first thing tomorrow we go straight to Heathrow and get our flight home. Once we're there they'll never be able to touch us."

"You're so certain," Massimo said. "So sure of yourself. But Louis Keltner has a long reach. I don't believe we'll be safe wherever we go."

"Trust me," Nicci said.

"That's the trouble. I always have and look where it's got me."

The elevator stopped and with a whisper the doors slid open. Their suite was along the hall to the left. Massimo walked quickly to the door, eyes alert, and swiped the key card through the slot in the lock. Nicci followed him into the room, closing the door behind her. It locked automatically.

"Happy now?"

"I'll be happier when we touch down in Milan."

Nicci walked across to the bed and lay down, kicking off her shoes and closing her eyes. "Be a dear and run me a bath. I need to soak for an hour at least."

Massimo gave his sister a furious look, threw his bag onto the other bed and stalked across to the bathroom. He opened the door and stared into the implacable face of Mario Bernardi. Bernardi was holding a gun, small and silenced. It coughed twice and Massimo fell backward into the room as Mario shot him in both eyes, the bullets blowing the back of his head out.

Nicci jumped up from the bed, a cry on her lips, but the cry was silenced as Mario stepped out of the bathroom, the gun steady in his hand, pointing at her face.

"Mario," she said, her gaze flicking from the gun to the door, calculating her chances of escape. She'd been a fool. So confident had she been that the Keltners couldn't find her that she'd left Mario Bernardi out of the equation. He'd traveled with them many times and knew the Galina name. "I suppose you just phoned all our usual hotels until you found us," she said.

Mario inclined his head but his face showed no flicker of emotion. He took two paces toward her.

"Mario, please. I only did what was necessary."

His finger tightened on the trigger.

"Please."

He fired twice.

The bullets whistled past her ear, shattering the window behind her.

Nicci let out a breath. "I knew you couldn't kill me. Not after all we've been through together. Dear Mario, my loyal and faithful servant." She held out her arms to him. "Come," she said.

He dropped the gun on the floor and took another two paces toward her, letting her wrap him in her arms.

"That's better," she said, her fingers caressing the surgical dressing that covered one side of his face. "You poor thing. What did they do to you? Here, let me show you how much you mean to me." She reached up and found his lips with hers. They kissed; a hard passionate kiss, her tongue stretching, feeling its way hungrily down his throat, while her hands slipped under his shirt, stroking the hard taut flesh of his back, fingers lengthening, looking for a soft spot to burrow into.

And as they kissed his huge hands cupped her face, thumbs tracing the contours of her cheekbones. Finally he pulled away from her lips and stared hard into Nicci Bellini's face. "This is for Monica," he said softly, then plunged his thumbs into her eyes, the sharp nails puncturing the soft orbs.

Her scream was like music in his ears. Holding on to her head tightly, thumbs finding the bone at the back of her eye sockets, he lifted her into the air and sprinted across the room, diving through the shattered window.

"It ends here," he whispered in her ear a split second before their bodies smashed into the granite-paved piazza below.

* * *

The Lear jet arced across the azure sky, swallowing the miles between England and Switzerland effortlessly. Maria Keltner sat by the window, her hand clamped fiercely around her daughter's, eyes staring out at the few wisps of cirrus as they passed beneath the aircraft.

Emma's eyes were closed but she was awake. She was aware of the older woman's fingers gripping her hand but was reluctant to pull it away. So much had happened over the last few days. She felt as if she had been pulled apart, deconstructed by some mad sculptor, and pieced back together randomly. Nothing seemed to fit anymore. The image she had once held of herself no longer gelled with an unkind and unsettling truth she had been forced to accept.

Her thoughts turned to Helen, the woman she had shared her life with; the woman she had loved and in loving had destroyed. A sob broke in her throat, and the fingers tightened around her hand.

She opened her eyes and looked at Maria, but she continued to stare out through the window, as if frightened to acknowledge Emma. But although there was an impenetrable wall between them Emma drew comfort from their physical closeness. The woman was her birth mother and, despite the years of separation, the genetic link was powerful.

"Ah, you're awake. Good." Louis Keltner crouched down in the aisle next to her. "We should be landing soon."

Emma's instinct was to spit in his face, to scream and shout at him, to pummel his saturnine face with her fists. But she did none of these things. Instead she closed her eyes again and ignored him.

She heard him sigh as he pushed himself upright and went to join the pilot on the flight deck.

When she opened her eyes again she found Maria staring at her. The woman's mouth was working, but no sound issued from her lips. "What is it?" Emma said to her. Maria's fingers were digging painfully and insistently into her wrist. Emma watched the lips working, forming the unuttered words. Finally she recognized the shapes they were making.

"Kill him."

"You want me to kill him?" she said softly, glancing round to make sure her words were not being overheard. "How?"

The silent mouth worked frantically for a few moments, then snapped shut. Maria stiffened and her eyes rolled back in her head. And then she slumped back into her seat. When she looked at Emma again there was a new expression on her face; the eyes were glowing, alive with a fresh vitality and intelligence. "You know how." The voice when it came was deep and resonant; a man's voice. Maria sat forward suddenly in her seat, her hands reaching out and cradling Emma's face. "I've tried to protect you over the years," she said in the same bass, mellifluous voice, her face inches away from Emma's. "But this you must do yourself. You must destroy my father before he destroys humanity."

"Your father? What do you mean 'father'? I don't understand." Emma tried to pull away but the hands held firm. Fiercely passionate eyes burned into hers. And suddenly it all became clear. She was looking into the eyes of Vincent Keltner, her *own* father. His spirit was inhabiting Maria's broken body, imbuing it with speech, and with a fresh, vibrant life force. "Search within yourself. Discover what you really are. Only you can stop him now."

The light in Maria's eyes flickered and went out. The blank look returned. The hands fell away from her face and the woman slumped back into her seat, mouth lolling open, a thin line of spittle dribbling down her chin, eyes staring into space.

With a numbing shock Emma realized that Maria Keltner was dead.

She opened her mouth and let out a wail of despair. How many more people would die before this was over?

The door to the flight deck opened and Louis Keltner stepped out. He fixed Emma with a harsh glare, then his eyes flicked to Maria and he strode along the aisle toward them.

"What happened?" he snapped, and crouched down in front of his wife, grabbing her by the hair and pulling her head back, examining her dead face with all the passion of a person examining a squashed bug.

He turned to Emma, another question on his lips. But the question went unuttered as Emma's hand shot out. With a cry Keltner reeled back, a hand clasped to his eye, blood seeping from between his fingers. He fell to the floor, body writhing, changing, reverting to its natural form.

Emma watched Louis Keltner's body start to disintegrate in front of her. And then she stared down at her hand; the hand that inflicted the fatal damage to Keltner's eye. The fingers were long, attenuated, and tapering to thin and bloody stiletto points.

She stared at the hand for what seemed a lifetime, and then Emma Porter started to cry softly.

The door to the flight deck opened again, and Alex Keltner walked out into the cabin. He looked down at his father's decomposing body with mild indifference, and then sat down next to Emma. "I see I will have to watch you very carefully, dear girl," he said with a smile.

A STRANGER WALKS INTO A PLACE OF BUSINESS...AND STARTS SHOOTING.

Three of horror's most terrifying authors challenged each other to write a novella beginning with that simple idea. But where they each went from there would be limited only by their own powerful imaginations. The results are incredibly varied, totally individual, and relentlessly horrifying. Prepare yourself for three very different visions of fear, each written specifically for this anthology and available nowhere else.

JACK KETCHUM

RICHARD LAYMON

EDWARD LEE

TRIAGE

ISBN 13: 978-0-8439-5823-2

THE DELUGE

MARK MORRIS

It came from nowhere. The only warning was the endless rumbling of a growing earthquake. Then the water came—crashing, rushing water, covering everything. Destroying everything. When it stopped, all that was left was the gentle lapping of waves against the few remaining buildings rising above the surface of the sea.

Will the isolated survivors be able to rebuild their lives, their civilization, when nearly all they knew has been wiped out? It seems hopeless. But what lurks beneath the swirling water, waiting to emerge, is far worse. When the floodwaters finally recede, the true horror will be revealed.

ISBN 13: 978-0-8439-5893-5

SIMON CLARK

THIS RAGE
OF ECHOES

The future looked good for Mason until the night he was attacked…by someone who looked exactly like him. Soon he will understand that something monstrous is happening—something that transforms ordinary people into replicas of him, duplicates driven by irresistible bloodlust.

As the body count rises, Mason fights to keep one step ahead of the Echomen, the duplicates who hunt not only him but also his family and friends, and who perform gruesome experiments on their own kind. But the attacks are not as mindless as they seem. The killers have an unimaginable agenda, one straight from a fevered nightmare.

ISBN 10: 0-8439-5494-9
ISBN 13: 978-0-8439-5494-4